# GLENN PARRIS

# THE PAINKILLERS

MVmedia, LLC

FAYETTEVILLE, GEORGIA

*Glenn Parris*

MVmedia, LLC
PO Box 14352
Fayetteville, GA 30214
www.mvmediaatl.com

Publisher's Note: This is a work of fiction. Names, characters, places, and incidents are a product of the author's imagination. Locales and public names are sometimes used for atmospheric purposes. Any resemblance to actual people, living or dead, or to businesses, companies, events, institutions, or locales is completely coincidental.

Book Layout © 2017 BookDesignTemplates.com

The Painkillers/Glenn Parris. -- 1st ed.
ISBN 979-8-9905121-1-5

To Joan & James Parris

Thank you for the amazing wisdom and guidance you've provided through every twist and turn life's thrown in front of me. You taught me to transform obstacles into opportunities, so I learned to use words as art, not just tools, to express not just my thoughts, but also my dreams. So, I hailed each of your transitions with cheers, not tears. I know in my heart that you're both together again with no more speed bumps, hurdles, or walls to scale.

Peace,
Glenn

# CONTENTS

PART 1 ................................................................1

Chapter 2: Fame Days ........................................4

Chapter 3: Clean Up Detail................................9

Chapter 4: The MIT Boys ................................21

Chapter 5: The Norsemen ................................28

Chapter 6: Happy Hour....................................34

Chapter 7: Hunting Cavemen ..........................46

Chapter 8: Bang! ..............................................51

Chapter 9: Femme Fatale ................................62

Chapter 10: Lost................................................66

PART 2 ..............................................................72

Chapter 11: Atlanta Drift................................73

Chapter 12: The Pit..........................................80

Chapter 13: Ghosts of the Past........................93

Chapter 14: A Well Woven Web ....................105

Chapter 15: The Ramp ..................................116

Chapter 16: Cut..............................................122

Chapter 17: Dinner at Maynard's..................127

Chapter 18: Hell of a Night ..........................138

Chapter 19: Daybreak ....................................150

Chapter 20: A Stroll in the Park....................154

Chapter 21: Ghost Writer ..............................158

Chapter 22: Swimming with Sharks................165

Chapter 23: The Expert..................................175

Chapter 24: Evening at ........................................................ 189

the Lattimore ..................................................................... 189

Chapter 25: Behind the Curtain ........................................ 205

Chapter 26: A Dark and .................................................... 208

Stormi Night ...................................................................... 208

Chapter 27: On the Town .................................................. 217

Chapter 28: Shanghai ........................................................ 223

Chapter 29: Lucy's Way ................................................... 232

Chapter 30: Caipirinhas .................................................... 243

Chapter 31: House of Brasil ............................................. 253

PART 3 ............................................................................... 264

Chapter 32: On the Run .................................................... 265

Chapter 33: Librarian ....................................................... 275

Chapter 34: Styx ............................................................... 284

Chapter 35: Taking Khandi .............................................. 287

Chapter 36: Safe House .................................................... 300

Chapter 37: Eagle Eye ...................................................... 305

Chapter 38: Mommie and Poppie ..................................... 318

Chapter 39: Chill .............................................................. 334

Chapter 40: Mouse Trap ................................................... 343

Chapter 42: Shell Game .................................................... 361

Chapter 43: Pass the Bar .................................................. 366

Chapter 44: The Sharper Edge .......................................... 373

Chapter 45: Tech Support ................................................. 383

# PART 1

# Chapter 1: The Interview

The local anchorman waited for his producer to count him in. The production assistant gave Murphy the signal and the journalist dropped into character.

"This is Ron Murphy reporting for the Sharper Edge on last summer's Fame Days massacre. Tonight, we'll hear from someone who can bring clarity to the murder spree that terrorized Atlanta and claimed the lives of twenty-six people. At the center of it all, we have Dr. Jack Wheaton, the veritable eye of the storm. Thank you for agreeing to this interview, Dr. Wheaton. The story we're getting from the police is, well, unbelievable. I mean, really, all over a pain killer? Doesn't America have enough of those drugs?"

Jack shook his head deliberately. "NSAIDs? Muscle relaxants? Opiates? No, this is different. Fibromyalgia is different."

"But just what is it? No one seems to be able to answer that."

"Do you know what Fibro is? It's got to be the Devil's favorite mischief. It muddles thoughts, denies the minds the refuge of sleep and every inch of the body hurts like Hell, yet it doesn't leave a mark."

"Still, how could a drug for a disease that does no harm be worth enough to kill?"

"Let me answer your question with a question: If you suffered from eternal pain, what would you do for a cure? A cure that's worth billions. Then I ask you: What won't they do to own it?"

Ron Murphy shrugged his shoulders. "I honestly don't know."

Jack's brow furrowed. "They'd do anything."

Murphy ruffled through notes on a yellow legal pad and asked, "What about the identity thief, this mystery doctor?" His gaze grew intense. "Who is the real Anita Thomas?"

Jack arched an eyebrow in thoughtful reverie. "Well... now that's a story."

# Chapter 2: Fame Days

## *March 12, 2010 Boston, Massachusetts*
## *FaM DaS Study Phase II subject #328 statement: account of protocol deviation*

They made an unlikely pair that first day in the waiting room: a plump, middle-aged, southern divorcee and a skinny, 60-year-old African American hotel worker from Roxbury, Massachusetts. They huddled over a Sudoku booklet like two schoolgirls: Subjects 328 and 329, respectively. Going over the details of the process and recounting their late-autumn introduction to the clinical research project, they crafted their plan.

The induction chaos had settled down to an organized crowd of mostly women with something in common to talk about: pain and misery. That's when Helen and Annie had found one another and clicked right off the bat. Their attention refocused on a distinguished figure passing them in the aisle between chairs. One of the principle investigating physicians had made her way to the front of the room. The attractive woman looked serious and bore the smooth contoured face of one who didn't laugh enough.

"Alright, ladies. . ." Dr. Anita Thomas began her announcement, but cleared her throat when she noticed two men in the back row. "And gentlemen. Everyone's eager to get the last of his or her Christmas shopping done, so let's move expeditiously. I need you to stand and form two lines."

Dr. Thomas was young, younger than any of the other Principle Investigators, but her voice carried the same self-assured confidence. A commanding presence. "Those candidates assigned odd numbers to my left, those with even-numbered cards to my right."

When the randomization process was over, Helen and Annie found themselves headed toward different rooms and on different paths. Helen was in the active arm while Annie was in the control arm. Neither they nor the study investigators knew who got what as all participants were blinded to placebo versus active drug. That had been three months ago. But this time, before they split, the twosome sat side by side conspiring to beat the system.

"Now, you can't tell anyone that you'd already known how the real drug would work when you get it, okay, Annie?" Helen Holcomb looked furtively from side to side as she whispered to the woman seated beside her.

The drab, blue reception room in the Crawford Research Center, lit by fluorescent lights, was lined with molded plastic chairs filled by eager subjects, all hoping to qualify for the next phase of the clinical study. They were invitees to the Nordstrom Clinic, one of the most prestigious research institutions in Cambridge.

Both women were about the same age, give or take a couple of years. Helen was from the Georgia suburbs. Marietta, home to the Roberts family, famous for the actors Julia and Eric. Helen found herself lying about knowing the sister and brother celebrities. The only time she had actually seen them was at a homecoming celebration for the opening of *Mystic Pizza,* but when Helen craved attention, she occasionally claimed that as a teenager she nannied for preschool-aged Julia, the younger sibling.

Now, afflicted with fibromyalgia, Helen had lost her last three jobs and was living on her aged mother's savings. For more than ten years, whether due to sedative analgesics or "Fibro fog", Helen Holcomb could not concentrate long enough to remain gainfully employed for more than three or four months at a time. Helen had not only lost several jobs, but also a few husbands over the eccentricities of life with chronic pain, depression, and fatigue characteristic of fibromyalgia syndrome.

On his way out the door for the final time, Zack Holcomb, her last husband, had dealt the ultimate wound saying, "-and that waistline really doesn't work for you at five-two, honey. Either lose weight or grow a foot."

It landed like a punch to the gut. No snappy comeback. No turning the blame around on him. Helen's only response was silent tears. Zack Holcomb had had the last words and for the first time, they weren't "yes, dear".

Always chubby, Helen had gained an additional forty pounds in the last decade. She openly attributed the obesity to the muscle relaxers and anti-depressants. Her greatest fear was that she might gain even more weight on the experimental drug. She couldn't bear to change her name back to Britt. Appearing to be a spinster would only magnify her failure in life. She adopted the mantra; Mr. Holcomb is simply "no longer with us."

Yeah, sure, as if that spin worked.

She had affected the *southern belle* persona, claiming to run the family business. Often when referring to the Britt fortune, Helen would embellish the tale of how *Daddy* had made his money in the textile industry.

In truth, her family was just lucky. Herman Britt had the good fortune to own a marginally successful farm smack dab in the middle of the I-75 corridor. Daddy was stubborn enough to hold out for top dollar, ten million in fact, for the 120-acre farm, now home to some of the most exclusive mansions in the metro area. Subsequent investments in Dalton's carpet industry were only modestly profitable.

Annie Henderson was a housekeeping supervisor at the Waverly & Dunne, an old Boston hotel known for its four-star luxury. She had good benefits and over thirty years of service to the Dunnes, owners of the properties. They loved Annie like family and allowed her to stay in a rear-entry, ground-floor suite as a perk. That's where the rape took place, right on the premises.

The Dunne matriarch convinced Annie to stay on after she had been so obscenely violated. They never did catch those maniacs. Intervention brought Annie the best psychological care Boston had to offer, but nothing helped the deep muscular pain that had come to plague every day of her life. Then, she lucked into the Fame Days study.

The Ides of March had arrived. Now that the control portion of the study was complete, the subjects were moved into the crossover phase, where the code was broken, and those who were treated with the placebo were moved onto the real drug.

"Remember Annie, not a word," Helen warned. "Just play along with their *protocol*."

The word was part of neither woman's working vocabulary, and always made them laugh as they labored to pronounce it.

"Imagine, you'll feel good again. Just like before."

Annie smiled and rubbed her hands together. "I can't wait. I can get to know my children again, maybe even go back to work."

"Not before you come down to Atlanta and spend a month wreaking havoc at the malls with me, you don't!" Helen laughed.

"I wish we could bring that nice lady, Professor Thomas," Annie said. "Whatever happened to her? She seemed to just disappear."

"She was a real sweetie, wasn't she? And so smart!" Helen declared. "Better than all those old farts running the show these days, that's for sure."

"Hope this stuff works," Annie said. She scowled, then became quiet. "Relief from all this pain. Maybe I can begin to talk to men again, begin to trust them."

"They're opening the doors, Annie," Helen said, thankful for the interruption. "Let's go."

FMDS was filled out to FaM DaS and pronounced "fame days" by its authors. It was said that you couldn't have a clinical study without vowels in the acronym. Most investigators just added vowels until a name made sense, or at least pronounceable syllables. The logline for the clinician recruitment brochure was *Turning fibromyalgia same days to Fame Days!*

The intravenous infusion went as smoothly as ever for each woman. When it was done, the two best friends left Crawford, and walked across the street to the ice cream parlor for a little guilty pleasure before parting ways for the day. They laughed like best friends all the way back to the lot where Annie's Chevy Malibu was parked.

"Can I drop you anywhere, Helen?" Annie asked.

A stream of women hollered their hellos as they ran past. Five of the other subjects had begun to feel well enough now to start a running group and aerobics class. On average, the subjects reported losing fifteen pounds each in the first six months. The runners lost more. For patients suffering from fibromyalgia, an FMDS400 infusion was like getting a shot of liquid life.

"No, I'm going to catch one of my favorite soaps." Helen glanced down at her watch and pointed to her hotel across the street. "It's already 3:30." She waved. "See you next month."

Annie waved back, hopped into her solid American car and made for the parkway to Roxbury. She merged onto the I-90 and felt a funny little flush followed by a shiver. She shook it off.

Annie pressed the accelerator and matched speed with the traffic. The sensation of an army of ants crawling on her scalp began building and the image of the I-90 melted into a swirl of colors as she drove. That was the last thing Annie remembered. The traffic reporters described the accident as one of the most horrific in years.

# Chapter 3: Clean Up Detail

Dr. Jack Wheaton had been like a fish out of water in Boston. Originally from Louisiana, the second year medicine resident physician had never been outside of the southeast except for the few college interviews he attended along the Great Lakes rim ten years ago. He appreciated the unique accent, but found that the dialect extended from Buffalo to Chicago.

Boston, at least, bore some similarities to New Orleans where he was raised--seafood, old world architecture, even some aspects of the New England accent had qualities in common with his own.

Somehow, the liberal mind-set seemed at odds with the lack of open hospitality he was accustomed to in Atlanta where he trained. The hospital setting, more familiar to him than the town, if only because medicine was medicine everywhere in the world and hospitals differed little more than the practice of good medicine allowed.

Every doctor-in-training soon learned that the nurses he worked with could make or break his career. Work with them, and they will work with you. Demean them, and residency could be a living hell. Word got around.

There was that assortment of male nurses and average-looking women a young man might not look at twice on a busy day. His favorite nurse at Mass General was Harriett. She was a matronly woman of the portly variety. She entertained aspirations of wealth and notoriety. On quiet coffee breaks, Harriett sought the young doctor out and taught Jack about keeping his eyes peeled for investments early in his residency. Property, practice offers, medical inventions, anything.

Her own children had milked her dry of savings years ago. Hence, she still worked harder than Hades at her age. Surgical scrub nursing supervisor was a physically demanding job at any age: tougher yet, when suffering from fibromyalgia.

Somehow, Harriett never did manage to scrounge up enough money to do anything but pay most of her bills each month. Still, she and several others managed to "mother" Jack through the travails of a visiting rheumatology rotation at the world famous Massachusetts General Hospital. By the end of the rotation, he wondered whether he could have made it without them.

Then there was Bobbi, a brassy, 49-year-old Licensed Practical Nurse who refused to age gracefully. Sporting a Wonderbra and that Weight Watcher waistline, Bobbi bragged about how she was mistaken for a 29-year-old all the time. She stuffed herself into tight dresses that might have looked quite fetching on a woman 20 years her junior. She struck a provocative pose whenever Jack drifted by, making sure he saw her caring for the sick and injured.

All the same, she was a good woman who, Jack realized, just worked too many hours on too many double shifts on those hard floors for too little thanks and too little money. Evidently, it had taken its toll, and as the years had worn on, she had become a defeated soul.

"Hi Bobbi. What's shakin'?" he asked

"Just what you see, Dr. Jack," She quipped. "Plans tonight?"

"Gottta hit the books. Rheum's not something I can fake."

"I never fake, Doc," Bobbi said with a wink.

As far as Jack knew, Bobbi was single. He chalked her antics up to harmless flirtation. Still alone and past the *cougar* stage of standing a chance of attracting a twenty-something physician in training. Her overdone eyelashes were batting laboriously to draw attention away from laugh lines and crow's feet that had taken up residence in her once nubile face.

Bobbi ached daily from the time she arrived at work until she went home, maybe after that as well. She and Harriett sometimes commiserated about their common affliction as if fibromyalgia were an unwanted family member they shared.

Jack learned three things about fibro: 90% of sufferers were female, a quarter of them had a history of physical or emotional abuse, and few physicians looked forward to managing the disorder.

Jack had seen both Bobbi and Harriett cry many times at the end of their shift when anyone else would have been overjoyed to go home. A quote from his mother crossed his mind once as he watched them moping out of the building: *Sometimes "Home" is where the heart breaks.*

After his final presentation in two weeks to the head of rheumatology, Jack planned to head back to Atlanta, the city he now called home.

He checked his watch. *Five thirty. Man, that was a long clinic!* Then Jack's attention shifted to Harriett's intense expression as he saw on his shortcut through the ER. She spoke to a woman in a sharp, dark pantsuit. *Who is that?*

He wanted to check out the face that went with the figure but couldn't without going into the small room with them. Slowing at the door, he called a goodbye to Harriett. Neither woman turned to acknowledge the courtesy.

*Massachusetts General Hospital, 5:20 pm Friday, March 12, 2010.* The remains of Annie Henderson were wheeled into the morgue from trauma room 1 in the ER. The body, covered with a simple white sheet with the logo and *Massachusetts Hospital System* stenciled across the top, now lay in silent repose.

The orderly delivering the gruesome package whipped out the trauma surgeon's report with the brain CT scan and EMT /nursing staff records. The pathology resident scanned the papers to familiarize himself with it before his attending physician arrived. He knew what to expect from her. Standard operating procedure dictated a full autopsy, given the nature of the motor vehicle accident.

The pathologist entered with an air of annoyance. This was her day off. She had just begun making preparations for an intimate evening when she was called in for this post-mortem examination. Her request to postpone the examination until morning was denied. She could do the damn thing in forty-five minutes; an hour tops if there were no surprises. Still, the stench of blood and antiseptic couldn't be washed out of her pores before her date.

*Shit!* She gowned up and gloved for the post.

"Any time now, doctor," she said to the resident. She expected a second-year pathology resident to begin briefing her the moment she walked in the door.

"Yes, ma'am. This is the case of a 60-year-old African American woman with a history of depression and fibromyalgia syndrome. She was reportedly in her usual state of good health when she veered off the highway directly into a stone embankment. Estimated velocity at impact was 55 miles per hour."

The young resident bit his lip in anticipation of her majesty's assessment of the presentation. She all but ignored him.

"And this is what got me in here on my freakin' day off?" The pathologist huffed. "Wicked smart."

She reached for the overhead microphone as she prepared to dictate the post-mortem findings, and she chose the tools needed to take Annie Henderson's remains apart for analysis. The resident read the pertinent facts from support documents at hand.

"Ma'am, we're still awaiting the MRI/MRA brain study. It was done before they called the code, but the neuro-radiologist wasn't available to read it." He looked up. "It may be relevant, don't you think?"

"If it were relevant, they would have pulled a god-damn neuro-radiologist in to read it, wouldn't they?" She stared the resident down for a moment.

Her glare was met with silence.

"Let's get this over with, son," she added, "Please!" as if the task could not be completed fast enough for her plans.

He nodded and reached for the spreaders as his boss made the initial incision

Trauma 1 surgical suite was cleared and prepped for the next case. The head nurse lingered after the rest of her team left. She glanced at each camera in turn before crossing to the media panel. She reviewed the ER record-Henderson case. The MRI report came in after change of shift. She scratched her head. Before she could place the report on the ER chief resident's desk, Harriett felt a delicate hand grasp briefly at her shoulder. The woman behind her wore a navy blue pants suit and a simple white blouse. She had the look of a detective. No. More like a government agent failing at looking unofficial.

"Excuse me, nurse, were you involved with that motor vehicle accident case that came in this afternoon?" A surge of ginger hair swept up in a simple clip at the back of her head, a forelock of white escaped containment only to be tamed into a bang off to the right side of her forehead. The "suit" donned just enough make-up to show that she hadn't forgotten that she was out in public.

"Nurse Harriett?" the woman continued, reading the nametag on the uniform. "I'm Agent Stefano, DEA." She flipped an impressive-looking I.D. at Harriett and pressed on with her requests. "I'm investigating the death of the woman killed on the interstate this afternoon."

Harriett looked the woman up and down before answering her questions. "Ms. ...Stefano, you should really address questions to Sue, my supervisor, or the ER doc on duty—"

"I already have their statements as well as copies of the EMT and ER nursing staff reports." She brushed a wisp of hair back behind one ear with her fingertips. "I've been waiting all afternoon for that MRI brain scan." She smiled, pointing, "—which I believe you have there in your hand.

"I spoke to Dr. Jackson and the nursing supervisor, Ms. Critelli, earlier. She invited me to wait for the brain scan report to come in. I've been in the visitors' lounge waiting. I thought somebody would come get me when it arrived. Guess I was wrong."

"Do you need the whole file, Ms. Stefano?" Harriett asked. She watched Stefano's body language closely, as if sensing something was wrong.

"No, I already have copies of that. I just need the MRI." She stepped closer to Harriett. "May I have that?" She smiled a little wider, pointing to the sheaf of papers in the nurse's hand, "Please?"

"Sorry, Ms. Stefano, you'll have to go through channels to get a copy of this report." Harriett began to spindle the paper and curled it behind her back.

"Harriett—may I call you Harriett?" Stefano asked softly. "One of the parties involved in this accident may have serious mob affiliations. We've been following him for months. The longer this report is out here, the greater the chances his people will get wind of it. We know he has connections with the local authorities."

She watched for Harriett's response. "The government can make cooperation worth your while."

Harriett arched an eyebrow. "Come again?"

Stefano smiled a crooked smile. "The DEA has some discretionary funds to secure intelligence that leads to a conviction. Usually, it's used to procure information from underworld informants, but there is nothing in the law that says it can't be utilized to compensate an upstanding citizen who wants to help the government get that kind of scum off the streets."

Harriett pondered the possibility as Stefano gently patted her on the back, whispering sweet enticements in her ear.

Nurse Harriett. The residents at Mass General talked about her as if she had been there forever. She was 56 years old, but looked older and wore a jacket over a scrub dress instead of shirt and pants as everyone else did. She recorded the MRI study to a blank DVD and proceeded to erase the original on the imaging server.

She gained access using an administrative passcode revealed by a negligent IT engineer. He had navigated from one of the ER desktops a week earlier. Harriett peeked while he fixed a crashed server, a casualty of a late-night thunderstorm. Too lazy to walk up to the third floor in the dark, he broke security protocol. Back-up generators fed essential equipment only.

She slipped the disk into a jewel case and folded it into her skirt. She paced the nurses' locker room ten times and checked the time on her watch nine times within eight minutes of filching the disk. Finally, she retreated to the surgical lounge behind the locker room, where the communications equipment for research and dictation was state-of-the-art, and the furniture was plush. Surgeons brought in the money.

It was 7:35 p.m., half time, third shift. The nursing staff would be dropping to a skeleton crew. The hospital grew eerily quiet. Harriett returned to the locker room and resumed pacing the floors and wringing her hands. Another nurse joined her. The nurse appeared to be as chubby as she was, and similarly dressed except for an ostentatious pair of costume earrings.

Harriett nodded to the newcomer.

15

The nameless nurse wore a surgical mask. Presumably right out of a case. Oddly, the woman fiddled with her earrings as she greeted Harriett. She lingered by the mirror in obsessive efforts to adjust those baubles to suit her. As far as Harriett could see, their hair was the same mousy shade of brown as it spilled from their respective scrub caps.

"Stefano?" Harriett whispered.

The woman nodded.

They synchronously inspected the room to assure privacy, and Harriett asked, "Got my money, Agent Stefano?" She surreptitiously showed the unlabeled DVD jewel case and then waited for the newcomer's response.

"Depends." The other woman asked. "That the original copy?"

"The one and only," Harriett said. She scanned the room again. "I want cash."

"Let's go in there," Stefano said, pointing at the restroom while nudging Harriett in that direction.

Harriett was already nervous, but her emotions had begun to escalate.

"Ten thousand dollars? That's a lot of cash to carry around." Stefano said upon entry to the restroom. "We usually transfer the cash to a numbered account for our assets." She closed the door behind them after checking the outer room once more.

Harriett had heard those words in a hundred spy movies. The agent always tried to get the suspicious package without an outlay of money. Still, Harriett actually thought about it.

"No, I want cash or it's no deal." Harriett clutched the disk to her chest.

"Come on, Harriett. Let's have it. I can give you $500 in cash right now, and we'll transfer the rest to an account for you. I'll give you the bank's phone number and your account number so you can see-"

"Not a chance. I want my money now or you can come back and get your damn DVD later when you do have my money." Panting the words, Harriett danced back and forth in place as if she would soil herself any minute.

When Harriett realized that Stefano was between her and the only door out to the lounge, apprehension gave way to sheer panic. Then Stefano dropped her surgical mask from her face, took a deliberate step toward Harriett, and reached into her pocket. Harriett didn't even realize that her contact was wearing flesh-colored facial prostheses. The aged appearance bore a striking resemblance to the reflection Harriett saw each morning as she dressed. She didn't notice the latex gloves until Stefano reached for the disk.

Harriett's instinct was to hold the coveted prize in front of her like a shield until there chanced an interruption that might have spelled salvation.

"Excuse me," Bobbi whispered, coming out of a bathroom stall. Neither negotiator had seen the third woman enter the bathroom.

Harriett shot Bobbi a nervous but welcome look. Maybe she thought Bobbi could turn the tables here.

"Look, girls, I don't want to be in the middle of this so I'm just going to slip out and leave you two to whatever business you may have 'cause I don't know shit." Bobbi said.

Making for the door, Bobbi had only heard parts of the conversation and seen slivers of the altercation through the slit in the stall door. *Drug deal,* was her conclusion.

"Oh, shit," Stefano muttered. She was unmasked but padded to mimic Harriett. No reason for Bobbi to recognize her.

"This is a federal operation, miss, national security," Stefano said. "And you are ruining it."

Stefano took a step back, blocking Bobbi's as well as Harriett's exit. She reached a hand into her pocket

17

ominously and intoned, "I'm going to have to swear you to secrecy and get some info on you now. Please step over there with Harriett."

Harriett, now drenched in sweat, was getting dizzy. She knew that the agent was probably armed. Harriett dropped the disk and leaned down against her knees to catch her breath, gasping, "Oh, shit. Ooh, shit."

"You're a nurse," Stefano said to Bobbi. "She could have a heart attack if we don't slow her heart rate down."

The agent pulled a large plastic bag out of her pocket.

Confused, Bobbi asked, "Okay, but shouldn't we call for help?"

"Better to keep this between as few people as possible," Stefano said. "This is an ongoing investigation, and Harriett's our key asset."

"No," Harriett said. Somehow knowing that escalation of lies never led to anything good in legitimate dealings, she fell to her knees sucking for air.

"She's pooping out, girlfriend, her heart's weak." Stefano looked at Bobbi urgently. She read the name on Bobbi's I.D. badge, now close enough to smell liquor on her breath, and smiled. Stefano had read a police file on this one. "Are you going to help me with her or what?"

"Okay. I'll call the operator for help and--"

"No time. There's an oxygen tank in the operating room. I'll get it, but you see if you can get her to slow her breathing," Stefano said, dumping the miscellaneous contents of one pocket out in the sink. With a little sleight of hand, she produced a small, tan plastic grocery bag. Stefano tossed the crumpled sack to Bobbi.

As instructed, Bobbi slipped the bag up and over Harriett's mouth and nose. Bobbi understood that if Harriett was to slow down, she'd have to get her to rebreathe much of the carbon dioxide she was expiring. There was a puff of white dust in the translucent bag as Harriett took the first two breaths.

"What the hell?" Bobbi said. "What's in this bag anyway?"

Already on the move, Agent Stefano reached into both jacket pockets at once. She closed the distance between herself and Bobbi and cupped a large gauze pad over the screaming woman's face.

"Shush. I'm DEA," Stefano said. "You're both in danger, Bobbi. You have a record of misdemeanors as long as my arm. I've got to get you out of here alive, but it calls for drastic measures." Stefano spoke softly, reassuring Bobbi.

Bobbi's hand began to tremble. The gauze was still over her mouth and nose. Cocaine generously embedded in both the gauze and in the grocery sack was doing its work.

Bobbi coughed and flailed her arms wildly, now on her knees. Stefano reached into her inner pocket to retrieve a small Russian pistol. Dropping the gauze pad to the floor, the agent reached into her pocket one more time.

She screwed a sound suppressor onto the muzzle, a silencer, then said, "I've got to get you out of here. Head toward the door slowly and wait for me outside, Bobbi. I'll get Harriett together."

Stefano helped Bobbi to her feet then spun her around toward the exit and away from Harriett. She gave Bobbi a little shove of encouragement.

One step, two steps then... zip, zip. Two in the back. Stefano made sure at least one bullet was placed straight through the heart. Eyes open, Bobbi's pulse stopped instantly, then she dropped.

Prostrate on the floor, Harriett, with lips trembling, then turning blue, watched the death of her co-worker. Stefano put the gun in the dying nurse's limp hand, aimed in the general direction of the exit door above Bobbi's corpse, and pulled the trigger once with Harriett's index finger. Stefano then pinched Harriett's nostrils shut and held her mouth closed until she succumbed.

Without an emotional expression in her cold, dark eyes, Stefano checked that the pulse on each victim's neck had stopped before she left. Tossing a baggie with eight ounces of the same white powder on the floor in front of Bobbi, Stefano scattered $500 in cash across the floor.

The only conclusion to draw from the scene would be a drug deal gone bad. Collecting the spiked gauze pads and extra paraphernalia, Stefano realized she had lucked out with Bobbi. Head nurse, Sue Critelli, had told her that Bobbi was not a reliable witness to interview. Bobbi failed a drug screen earlier that month at another hospital and she was on probation at the General. Stefano had confirmed that history independently through her own sources. True or not, with her background, no one would believe Bobbi wasn't involved in illegal transactions.

Stefano smirked. She didn't have to figure out how to get rid of Harriett's body now. She gazed around the room, recording the confirmation of her task's completion. Stefano had built-in suspects for the crime. She left them both there as they lay. Stefano could keep the rest of the bribery cash. She paused at the clock on the wall and re-placed her surgical mask.

*Ah, 19:50. Just enough time to go shopping. Now, where did I see those cute boots?*

# Chapter 4: The MIT Boys

*Friday, February 26, 2010*

The shores of the Charles River have long borne institutions that forge some of the most brilliant minds in America: MIT, Nordstrom and nearby Harvard. Admission is very selective. The students say getting in is hard. The faculty says getting losers out is harder.

Gil Hargrove had bottom quartile standing in the class of 2010. He designed and submitted the graduate proposal for the group thesis: *Correlation of early hominid behavior with enzyme evolution for digesting various nutrient proteins, sugars, and lipids through the ages.* A good idea and he coerced his two partners Harry and Monty to sign on to it.

Harry Mehta was a neat freak. Every item in his lab had a place and was usually in it. That's why his partners, slobs all, liked him. Of course, it was not the only reason for his popularity. Harry was a genuinely nice guy. One you count on in the home stretch of a project. Harry never missed a deadline.

Lamont "Monty" Hill was a superb analyst. He could dissect any data set and find precedents for a solution. Access to the NIH databases was just added value, complements of Monty's father's position.

In spite of his shortcomings, Gil was brilliant in his own right, albeit a little lazy and a lot sloppy. Not good traits to carry in the precision research needed in DNA mapping. Not at the graduate level. Gil was banking on Harry's punctuality. That and Monty Hill's data resources.

With the guidance of Professor Levine, their faculty sponsor, Gil had refined the topic to the development of enzymatic digestion of lactose and myosin in early man. Budget cuts found the faculty sponsor picking up a heavier teaching burden in the spring semester. The professor dropped mentorship of Gil's project.

The default sponsor in the line of succession was the head of the Molecular Genetics Department. She had even less time than Professor Levine. Despite having Harry and Monty in his corner, Gil had little confidence in the completion of their thesis, much less an effective defense before the faculty panel at the end of the semester.

An introduction to Anita Thomas furnished Gil just one last ration of good luck before his fortune turned cataclysmic. Maybe even two more.

Dr. Anita Thomas had an addiction to caffeine. The line at the Starbucks extended through the door and to the corner of Memorial Drive. There was a thirty-minute wait just to place an order. Down the street, a few blocks northeast, the story wasn't any different.

The student unions of Nordstrom Institute, MIT, and Boston University pooled resources to lease the warehouse kitty-corner from the other Starbucks on Massachusetts Avenue and John F. Kennedy Street. They set up a student-run gourmet coffee shop that was turning out to give the old Seattle establishment a run for its money. Still, seating there too was limited.

Anita eventually got her mocha latte, but she was hard pressed to sit and enjoy it. Were it May or June, she'd have savored it leisurely on a park bench or while strolling between campuses. But it was nearly March, twenty degrees Fahrenheit and icy.

*Damn,* she thought, checking her watch. *Gotta move Heidi in a couple of hours.*

Gil saw her desperate gaze darting around the room, looking for a familiar face or some signs that a patron was about to vacate a table or stool. That glint of despair proved especially captivating when cast from large, piercing eyes nestled in a beautiful maple syrup complexion. Anita's look of disappointment inspired him to gallantry. He and Harry had a corner table.

Gil caught her attention and beckoned her to join them, then offered her his seat as he perched on the radiator against the wall. Anita unbundled herself from her winter layers and made herself comfortable.

Gil began to fidget as she made friendly small talk to break the ice. His restless adjustments in position were as much to avoid roasting his buttocks as consequent to distraction. He found it hard to take his eyes off her. As she settled in, he noticed her interest in the spreadsheets on 'Deadline Harry's' laptop screen.

"Are you acquainted with gel electrophoresis, Ms....?" Gil stretched his palm out as if to receive her name in it somehow.

"Anita. And, yes, I know a little about the subject." She sipped her coffee as she analyzed what she saw. "What are you guys working on?"

"We are tracking genes by evolutionary age, searching for the development of specific digestive enzymes." Harry paused to see if she could keep up. To him, it was most likely that she was just another pretty face in the coffee shop looking for a seat.

"Which enzymes?" she asked absently.

Still not convinced she was expert enough to understand the study parameters, Harry offered a little background.

"Humans are one of the only species that feeds off other species' milk," he stated. "We parasitize lactating cows, goats, reindeer, and llamas. Very unique. 'When and how did we develop the enzyme to digest the foreign protein?' is our central question."

"Interesting. What are you using as a yardstick?" she asked, as she searched his eyes for permission to scroll through the table on the screen. He nodded.

"We have indexed the soft tissue and bone marrow for genetic material from early humans mummified in ice," Gil said.

He made a notation on a napkin and tucked into his pants pocket, not taking his eyes off of Anita as he did so.

Harry picked up the explanation from there. "The specimens are few, but diverse enough to be statistically significant."

"Our hypothesis is that early man probably began drinking milk or blood from these gravid animals killed in the hunt," Gil said, moving closer. "Probably made some of them sick, maybe killed some of them. Anaphylactic reactions, you know."

She nodded. "Again, how do you correlate the enzymes' introduction?"

Harry blinked twice. "I'm sorry?"

"Timeline. How do you associate the progressive consumption of foreign milk with survival?"

"Damn, you do know what we're talking about!" Gil exclaimed.

Harry also moved his chair closer to the table and to Anita with the same light in his eyes that she sparked in Gil.

"We figure these early peoples started feeding off of the milk of other breasts about the same time or very soon after they started skinning them for clothing. We thought we'd start comparing genes at 5,000-year intervals." Gil grazed her hand with his, but she drew it back. "We figure we'll catch evolution in the act."

She smiled. "You know, you could get established genetic milestones already cataloged for reference. Check out the Stanford genomic database."

Harry and Gil first looked at each other, then at Anita, and asked, "Who are you?"

"I'm Anita Thomas, Nordstrom Institute Department of Molecular Engineering."

"What's your PhD in, doctor?" Gil asked, humbled by her knowledge.

"Well, actually, I have doctoral degrees in the disciplines of molecular engineering and genetic anthropology, as well as doctor of medicine specializing in internal medicine, subspecializing in allergy, immunology, and rheumatology."

Gil placed his palms together, looked at the ceiling, and said, "Please tell me you are on faculty or medical staff at MIT."

Anita chuckled at the foibles of the two would-be researchers. Her laughter resonated like the soft tinkle of wind chimes. She treated them both to a second, then a third cup of java. No better a foundation for friendship had ever been conceived than a good cup of coffee.

Gil's interest in the good doctor quickly ripened from academic salvation to a warm desire. Anita shared ideas with her new colleagues while scrolling through files and offered advice for over an hour before they finally exchanged e-mail addresses and cell numbers and then prepared to go their separate ways.

Anita's eyes caught sight of the opened newspaper on an adjacent table. A ring of spilled coffee circled an entry in the obituary section. She didn't blink for fifteen seconds. Gil waited for her to explain, but what she came out with was little more than babble.

"Darren Scott was one of our techs," she said, still focused on the paper. "We just wrapped up the biggest project of my career." She sniffed. "There's going to be a party tonight."

Gil craned around to look into her eyes, nearly floating in tears before allowing the overflow to drip to the pages below as she read. He found himself reaching for her hand reflexively. This time, she did not pull away.

She read into the half-page spread on the opposing side.

"He fell down three flights of stairs." She read, now lifting the abandoned pages. "Says he died instantly of extensive injuries, including broken bones and severe closed-head injury…" She stopped reading and crumpled the sheets.

The tears were streaming now. "He had his first baby at Christmas."

Harry moved behind her. "I'm sorry, Doctor Thomas. Did you know him well?"

"Not well enough." She sniffled, then tried to laugh.

"Is there anything we can do, Anita?" Gil asked.

"No. No, guys. Thanks, though." She wiped her eyes and nose with a napkin. "I think I need to call it a day. I'm not much in the mood for this party tonight."

She collected her belongings. "You have my number and e-mail address. Hit me back if you want to talk any of this stuff over, huh?" She shook their hands.

"You have some interesting ideas here," she said returning to her academic persona. "I'd love to help." She grabbed Gil's wrist and gently rotated it to expose the watch face. "I'm late. I gotta move my car before it gets towed. I hate this alternate side of the street parking."

They flanked her as she stood from the table to walk toward the door. Harry lagged to shut down and pack his laptop.

The conversation between the three did not go unnoticed. On their way out of the coffee shop, Harry bumped into a smallish man planted in the narrow egress, ostensibly engaged on his cell phone. More of a body check by the man than an accidental collision.

The patron was dressed in an overcoat, a woolen hat, a flannel shirt, and cargo pants. Harry turned to apologize to the man, who gave him a dirty look. Harry thought he heard a soft click, before following his friends.

After Harry made his way out of the shop, the small man pulled up the fresh image on his cell and appraised it for quality. Jason Brasil thought it was good enough to distribute to his associates.

He knew his cronies, Joey and Ralphie, weren't the sharpest tools in the shed, but then sometimes blunt instruments were the best for crude jobs. They'd need the picture of "Deadline Harry" to make sure the visit was as effective as Mr. Quirk would want it to be when the time came.

# Chapter 5: The Norsemen

## *Saturday, February 27, 2010*

The late winter morning was crisp as was so often the norm in Boston, not a cloud in the sky, blue and sunny. From a third-floor boardroom of the Crawford Center, Granite Street traffic seemed scant save for the dawn runners, bikers, and the visiting high school students at neighboring MIT hurrying to meet their Saturday morning tour guides.

The Nordstrom Institute spread over three acres northeast of its research hub at Crawford. Two and a half football fields of prime, riverside property represented the smallest member of the academic powerhouses on Cambridge's university row.

The party to close the Fame Days Study lasted until almost ten o'clock Friday night. The research team and support assistants celebrated the end of a landmark project. The fight against fibromyalgia syndrome had a new player. FMDS400 was the first biologic, targeted drug for mitochondrial stimulation, safely administered intravenously to the largest placebo-controlled cohort in medical history. The data were in, and everyone on the team would now take a well-deserved break while the statisticians crunched the numbers.

Leif Nordstrom was Chairman and CEO of The Nordstrom Clinic. From his third-floor window, Leif watched the janitorial staff cross the atrium with trash cans brimming from the party. Liquor and wine bottles lay drained on top of crushed Styrofoam cups, grease-stained paper plates, and bones of hastily scarfed-down chicken wings.

"The liquor probably did them good." He snorted. "Most of the geeks I had on this project needed some help cornering a little piece." The middle-aged man was clean-shaven with neat salt and pepper hair and wore a three-piece suit, German cut, charcoal gray. He loosened the red, silk tie about his neck under the collar of a monogrammed cotton shirt.

Leif's brother, Claus, sat at the table with another man seated at the far end. "The splash of pentothal in the punch got most of those prudes drunk enough to get lucky last night." Claus said. "We'll go over the recordings of the party later."

"I just want to know what they have to say and which ones are talkers when they're not… inhibited," Leif said. "We can't follow them all."

"Then my men will keep an eye on the watch list when you're done." said Claus in a heavier Swedish accent than his younger brother did.

In contrast to his sibling, Claus sported a black turtleneck, silver French sports jacket, and jeans. The fashion contrast highlighted the slim, swimmer's physique of the elder Nordstrom.

"The question is, do we have a preview of the data breakdown?" Claus drew the blinds shut.

His brother moved to switch on the overhead lights. Claus shook his head in warning and stroked a short beard of white mixed with the few red hairs that remained from his youth. "Let's keep it subdued in here for a while, shall we, Leif? At least until we hear more of what Mr. Quirk has to say."

The third man in the room had been silent. Even now, his first response to the question was to raise a bound report to eye level before placing it on the polished maple conference table and shoving it toward the two brothers. Seated just below the No Smoking sign, he continued to puff plumes of rich smoke from a fat Cuban cigar.

Claus Nordstrom stopped the document's slide with his fingers, then turned on a desk lamp to its lowest setting.

"Tyler," he began. "You know that Dekker, Nordstrom, and Andersen cannot see results of an American drug study before the data are analyzed and presented to the FDA, don't you?"

"This file doesn't exist, sir." Tyler Quirk smiled a tight-lipped smile as smoke spilled from his nostrils. "And as of Thursday, neither does the technician who delivered it to me."

He let the two brothers gather over the bound sheaf. Each approached two meters in height.

"Mitochondrial stimulant— hell of an investment. We better have more than 60% efficacy on this bugger, Tyler, or you get to explain the $700 million expenditure to the board."

Tyler puffed again in silent response and spun around in his chair.

The Nordstroms squinted and turned pages wildly back and forth as they summed up the data.

"Is this correct, Quirk? I mean, have the results been verified?" Leif Nordstrom ran fingers backward through his thick, silvery mane.

"Ninety-eight-point-five percent effective," Quirk whispered with a savory rasp.

"Are you kidding me?" Claus declared. "That's unheard of, Leif. Where's the P value?"

Leif turned to the last page as Tyler Quirk rocked in his chair.

Leif still could not believe what he read. "What was the N value again?"

"The P value is valid, well under five percent, and the number of subjects was 20,483 with 10,039 in the control arm. It's real." Quirk nodded. "One of your researchers is going to be a problem, though."

Leif clapped his brother on the back in congratulations. It took less than two seconds for the announcement of concern to set in on the Nordstrom brothers.

"What?" said Claus sobering from the giddy euphoria. "Trouble? What kind of trouble?"

Leif shook his head, throwing a cautionary glance at his brother.

Not the right question.

"Who, Quirk? Who?"

Quirk pulled out a photograph of a young African American woman from his briefcase.

"Pretty little thing," Quirk said. "Anita Thomas."

He tossed it on the table without sliding it to the Nordstrom's this time.

"Seems she's been digging where she doesn't belong." Quirk stood now. He was eye-to-eye with the two Viking scions. A beefy man with thinning white hair, but soft in the face and middle. He had deceptively well-worn smile lines around his eyes and mouth. There was no softness in his manner, though, and no mercy in his soul.

"What has she found?" Claus glanced at his brother.

Leif shrugged.

"She's a star on your team," Claus said. "Don't you know what she's up to?"

"Great research. Look, she's just a baby," Leif explained. "Twenty-six years old. Medical Doctorate at twenty, great basic scientific work. Assistant professorship by twenty-two. The primary investigators resent her talent and youth, but…"

"She's digging into the genetics, gentlemen," Quirk interrupted. "And it gets worse. She's playing with the children down the street." He nodded toward MIT's campus.

"And I take it they're taking her quite seriously," Claus finished, cold sober now.

"Who?" Leif asked.

"Two guys," Quirk replied. "Harry Mehta and Gil Hargrove."

"I know of them," Leif said. "They're young but very bright."

"They could learn more than we can afford for them to know at this stage," Quirk told them.

"Tyler," Claus looked Quirk up and down. "Are these results as clean as they appear?" He thumped the report now rolled up in his fist.

There was only a beat of hesitation.

"No."

"Leif, you must get rid of her." Claus now faced his brother. "Discredit her. Shut her down. She must have no future in research. Ruin her!"

Quirk walked up to his boss and placed a concerned hand on Claus Nordstrom's shoulder. "That won't be enough, sir," he whispered. "She once testified against her father."

Claus nodded. "Both of you take care of this. Do what you must, Leif." He turned back to Quirk. "Mr. Quirk, find out what they know. I mean all of it. Take your time but do see to the permanence of this... solution, please."

"As you wish, sir." Tyler Quirk stood and strode toward the door. "I'll be flying out this afternoon."

He left the two executives to their troubles as he descended the stairs and began his task as ordered. As he reached the last step, he pulled out his cell phone and pressed a speed dial number.

After two rings, the tenor male voice answered. "Yes, sir?"

"Jason, I have some work for you and the boys. Are Joey and Ralph in town?"

"Ralphie is."

"Good. That will be enough, I think." Quirk paused on the steps and nodded thoughtfully. "I'll leave you full instructions in the usual manner."

He hung up, pocketed his phone, and glanced up the stairs toward the boardroom, where the two brothers surely still dwelled on his words. Tyler Quirk shook his head, chuckled to himself, and made his way to the building's exit.

# Chapter 6: Happy Hour

"So… this is your –lab?" Anita smiled an incredulous, forced smile as she appraised the room. *Dungeon* would have been a more apt description— dingy lighting, low ceiling, dank, moldy stench. Had she not walked through the MIT campus, entered those long-hallowed halls, and descended the elevator to the basement floor herself, she would have accused her new friends of pulling a prank.

Gil smiled as she blenched. "Nice digs, huh" He reached the knob to a second door at the back of the chamber that threatened to confine them. Gil's smile widened to a grin when he opened the door that led from the oversized antechamber to the lab.

"We were the last team to get lab space assigned. We nearly balked at this one, too, until Harry here discovered the large room behind it. The whole suite is labeled B105. The rear section is not on the blueprint. Near as we can gather, when this building went up in the fifties, there was an architectural error. They ran the steam pipes through here and couldn't figure a way to reroute them to salvage the space. They used it as a junk room for decades. Took us two weeks to get it suitable for lab use. All the outlets worked, but we had to get them updated for three-pronged plugs. Since we found the extra space, the Institute was only too happy to oblige with a little funding. I think this will be slated for hand-picked grad students next year." He laughed.

The lab behind the door made Anita envious. Twenty-five by thirty feet of floor space with 10-foot ceilings. Big as a classroom. No windows, but fluorescent lighting from one end of the room to the other and adequate fresh air return from the vents to make the lab comfortable for extended use. "Now this is a surprise." Anita's smile became sincere.

"We don't have digital white boards down here but we have all the colored markers you can ask for," Harry said. He stood behind the workbench as if he owned it. His pride in the stone table and its sink beamed through the room.

There was a desktop computer in the corner with a laser printer on the cabinet beside it. Reams of paper were visible behind the partially closed cabinet door, neatly stacked next to ink cartridges. Anita folded her arms and nodded approval. She looked at Gil and gestured graciously.

"Not me, Doc," Gil said. "This is all Harry."

Harry glowed all the brighter for the acknowledgment.

"Well, guys, let's see what you've got." Anita redirected the attention from getting-to-know-you small talk to the meat of the project.

Gil hooked up the computer to an S-video cable and powered on a projector affixed to the ceiling. When the projector's lamp warmed up, it projected Gil and Harry's data onto a wide section of the room-length whiteboard.

"We may be low tech, but we know how to improvise." Gil grinned.

Anita tore into the data. With little guidance from Gil or Harry, she grasped the working hypothesis, reviewed the boys' premises and study design. In less than an hour, she was ready to begin work, fleshing out steps and data-gathering techniques.

"Okay, so… we're looking at a species of hominids who all evidence indicates were hunter-gatherers. The first 'meats' consumed were likely fish."

"I agree," Gil said. "As far as protein is concerned, that would have been low-hanging fruit… No pun intended."

Anita smiled while her fingers furiously typed at the keyboard as she craned her neck to follow what appeared on the whiteboard. "Let's see. The Belgian anthropology database may have profiles of paleolithic teeth from the various periods in question." She downloaded the results of several queries.

"Right. There should be less calcium in the teeth than after milk becomes popular," Gil said.

"We'll look at the results of scraping analyses. You know, there's a pattern to bio plaque that resides in decaying enamel, more so before the development of modern dental hygiene techniques."

Anita accessed the first query. Columns of colored blotches opened in several pages of spreadsheet graphs.

"These are patterns rich in iodine. Even today, this is consistent with a diet rich in fish consumption," she said.

"No milk there," Harry said.

"Here we see an increase in iron and albumin signatures," Gil said as he watched the electrophoretic patterns on each subsequent page of the spreadsheet. "This suggests an increase in mammal and egg consumption. They must have started the shift from just fishing to hunting about then."

"Dental fossil records still favor more than 80% nuts, fruits, and berries than fresh meat, though," Anita said, no disappointment in her voice.

She looked over her shoulder at her new protégés and smiled at their anxiety. She hit the combination of hot keys on the computer, displaying the tabs of pages in the spreadsheets, and said, "Have heart, boys, this is only the first three of 638 pages." She chuckled. "Just 635 left to study."

Gil groaned.

Two men stood in the darkening shadows just outside the skirt of light cast by the streetlamp. Much of the dusting of snow had begun to ice over beneath their feet.

"They were in there for hours, Mr. Quirk," Jason Brasil said. "I guess they were working on the kids' little project." He chuckled.

Brasil respectfully offered the pictures he took of Anita, Gil, and Harry going into the building, then coming out. The first photos shone in afternoon daylight, the second by streetlight. Quirk examined them with a small LED light.

Puffs of vapor accompanied each syllable as he spoke. "Not good enough, Jason." Quirk shook his head. "I need to know *exactly* what's going on in that lab."

He handed the man a sealed envelope. "Use whatever resources you need, but I need eyes in that room. Do you understand?" Quirk waited for the nod and the 'yes sir' before retreating back to the warmth of his Mercedes coupe idling quietly at the nearby curb. He eased it into gear for an inconspicuous cruise away from the meeting site, leaving Brasil alone in the dark to ponder his next move.

The next morning spawned an awful rush hour. The ice was either directly or indirectly responsible for 90-minute delays all over town. Harry arrived an hour before Gil. He had a pot of hot coffee brewing in the personal corner of the lab by the time Gil and Anita arrived.

"How the hell do you always get in here on time, Harry?" Gil asked.

"The usual way: I leave home early."

Anita chuckled and, from Gil's perspective, warmed the whole room. She poured herself a cup of coffee, then set two empty cups and the condiments out for the men to partake.

"We're making good progress, guys," Anita said. "You'll beat that deadline yet."

Harry smiled at her optimism. He had a reputation to maintain.

Gil just nodded, sipping hot coffee as he mentally planned the morning. "We're more than halfway through. I never would have believed we could have caught up this fast. Anita, I don't know what to say." He stepped toward her a couple of paces. "How does a mere mortal thank a guardian angel?"

"By doing her proud and finishing his project, loser." Harry tossed a dishrag at him.

"Look, I'm getting something out of this, too, guys," Anita said. "Learning a lot about cavemen." She eyed Gil with a wry smile. "I've had questions about early man and development of a number of modern quirks anyway."

"I'm amazed we survived at all," Gil said. "The more I look at the nutritional status of paleolithic man, the more I question how they fed the whole group. I mean, the baskets and storage caskets unearthed contain enough for about half the individuals accounted for by the fossil evidence. Did they send the women and children south or have some super-secret storage bins somewhere we haven't found yet?"

"True enough, the numbers certainly don't add up. If they split the food evenly to survive, surely the hunters wouldn't have been able to keep up the strength to stalk and bring down large game or fend off attacks from predators or marauding tribes."

"I guess it's a mystery we'll never solve," Gil said in resignation.

"No such thing," Anita said. "I've never met a mystery that couldn't be solved. Now let's get to work."

The three scientists began their work for the day in plain, clearly focused view of a new one-eyed electronic serpent stealthily peeking in through the dropped ceiling.

The gray van sat several hundred yards off campus on Fruit Street. Jason Brasil ran the operation with his usual, patient efficiency, recording the conversation and as many of the keystrokes as the spy device could capture. He personally reviewed the data for quality before storing it for Mr. Quirk. He'd never leave that kind of thing for the two bozos he used for the wet work.

Brasil made a point of packing it in about an hour before Anita and the grad students knocked off for the day. He knew it took them about half an hour to clean up for the day at best. Harry would see to that.

By Friday of that week, Anita had begun to spend more of her days at the grad lab than at the Crawford Center. The FMDS principal investigator noticed. Dr. Stevenson had time on his hands with the Fame Days study on hiatus while the statisticians analyzed the data, and recruitment for the next phase began. He quietly took his notes on Anita Thomas and assembled a disciplinary report. He planned to present them directly to Leif Nordstrom. Quirk was aware.

Brasil sat in his van at the control console. He eyed the monitors wearily. He didn't understand any of the mathematical jumble the eggheads thought was so important. Looking at the equations and notes was giving him a headache. He was more ill-tempered than usual.

"Hey, Jason, want to take a break?" Ralphie winked. "I wouldn't mind watchin' the hot chick for an hour or two while you get some shut eye, hey Joey?"

Brasil scowled, but said nothing.

"Hey Ralphie, maybe we should move that camera. Like under the desk or something. Get a new slant on things, huh." Joey laughed so hard at his own joke, he spilled some of his coffee on Brasil's lap.

Brasil jumped up and whisked the brown spillage off his slacks before it had time to seep in. He fingered the sidearm in his belt for a moment. Jason Brasil eyed both goons with a look that literally could kill.

Ralphie and Joey didn't dare to move until Brasil returned his attention to whisking his pants off.

"I'm going out for some air," Brasil said. He looked at Ralphie. "Watch the damn monitor." Then marched out the sliding door. He heaved a cleansing breath and took a short walk down the street to clear his head and cool his temper. Turning to head back to the van, he bumped into a man five inches taller and twenty pounds heavier than he was. He shouldered past the man without so much as an *excuse me.*

"Sorry, buddy, I guess you didn't see me standing here?" The man shouted, arms spreading in challenge. He watched Jason Brasil's back shrink down Fruit Street without response.

"Come on, Jack, don't worry about assholes like that." A young medical student tugged at Jack Wheaton's sleeve. "He's probably got more problems than you need to get into right now."

"Tough guy," Jack said, looking after the man who had already disappeared from sight. "Sorry, man," Jack said to the medical student. "I didn't get much sleep last night. Guess I'm a little cranky."

"Hey, didn't I read about you escaping from Middle Eastern hostiles or something in the papers a year or so ago?" Jack's guest asked. "Wasn't that you?"

"It wasn't all the media made it out to be," Jack said and hung his head. "It was a skirmish with some locals... over a girl. My brother taught me a few moves."

"Ah, army or marine?"

"Photojournalist," Jack answered. "Lebanon beat. He gets into more trouble than a drunk sailor, though."

The student nodded in understanding. "So, are you going to be my resident this month?" he asked with hope.

"Sorry to say I'm finished up as of next week, but we'll have a little overlap. Let me show you the hospital, though. Ever been to Mass General?"

A shake of the head was the student's only response.

"You have to check in with the chief within the hour before starting the rotation, you know?" Sensing the newbie's apprehension, Jack said, "I hear you're from Emory. You'll do well here. I'm from Hamilton, downtown from y'all. How was your flight from Atlanta anyway?"

Upon his return, Jason Brasil was no calmer than he was when he left for the walk. He looked around at his men. "Ah, hell with it. Let's knock off early today, fellas. There's nothing we're gonna see today that we haven't seen all week. See ya Monday."

Brasil transmitted the digital recordings to his boss, then lit a cigarette after transmission confirmation. He climbed behind the wheel when his two henchmen got out of the vehicle, started the van and drove to the south side before afternoon rush hour began.

"It's 3 o'clock, Anita, and it's Friday," Gil said. She didn't move from the computer screen. "Happy Hour. Anita, we got drinkin' to do! Come on. You gotta meet Monty."

Still, she didn't respond. Harry tapped her on the shoulder, and she recoiled. "Dr. Thomas, you alright?"

"Yeah, Harry, I'm fine. There is something here that's almost coming together for me, but it's eluding conscious analysis. I don't quite have a handle on it, but it's right here in front of me." She scribbled symbols used in Boolean logic on the whiteboard.

"What is it, Anita?" Gil asked.

"It's something to do with the calorie economy of these people. There's something we haven't seen," she turned to Gil, then to Harry in frustration, "but *they* solved it. I know they did."

"I understand your angst, Doc," Gil said. "Hard to admit you can't get something so easy even a caveman could do it, huh?"

She shoved him playfully, grabbed her jacket and scarf, then followed her friends to the door.

It was a short walk, in Boston distance, to the Yellow Mushroom, and happy hour was already in full swing. Jack Wheaton and his new posse gathered round a pitcher of beer and a large pepperoni pizza. His supervising fellow bought the first round. Jack and his two medical students had met the in-patients and were getting psyched for rheumatology clinic Monday morning.

After pouring the first cup, the senior fellow began dispensing wisdom on his recommended approach to rheumatology, interrupting his monologue to greet someone coming in with her own party of three. He tipped his cup. Jack wheeled around to see who drew his friend's attention, only to see the swell of libation-seeking academics overwhelm the hostess at the door.

"Late comers?" Jack asked.

"Yeah, and one I wouldn't mind sharing a table with. Dr. Thomas gave the best grand rounds I've ever seen last year. Maybe you'll get to meet her, Jack."

Across the bar, Gil found the last table in the place and staked his claim. He gallantly seated Anita and waved Harry and Lamonte Hill, Gil's database guru, into a pair of chairs before some other party tried to abduct them. As they all settled in, Anita whipped out her phone, which was vibrating a notification that an e-mail was coming in.

She opened the e-mail. It was from her sponsors, the Nordstrom Clinic and DNA Laboratories. A priority e-mail at 4:30 on a Friday afternoon couldn't possibly be good news. She opened the attachment and read it silently, then became solemn.

"What's up, doc?" Gil asked, seeing her glum facade.

"I've been dismissed from the project." Anita's next words were lost in the myriad conversations of the crowd she herself could no longer hear.

Gil came close to ask her to repeat what she had just said, only to hear her shout, "Son of a *bitch!* Bunch of insecure good-old boys. Too damn much testosterone to let a female into their private men's club."

As she got that declaration out of her system, she caught the sound of an enthusiastic woman at another table scream, "I need a designated driver, boys, 'cause I'm gonna drink myself into a coma tonight!"

The expression on Anita's face went blank.

Gil called her name twice, then shook her gently. "What's wrong? You okay, Anita?"

She grabbed him by the collar and shook him emphatically. "Get me back to the lab," she demanded, slinging her scarf around her neck. "We've got to go *right now*. Can't afford to drown this one in beer."

"What's up with Anita?" Harry wondered.

"I think I just solved a 50,000-year-old mystery."

Anita led the three young men back to the lab like a mother hen running for a worm. And hungry chicks they were, too. If she didn't know it by maternal instinct, Anita knew it by the grumbling of word and stomachs. Gil's team followed for the promise of knowledge; a weak incentive on a Friday night.

"Okay, Harry, open her up," she said.

Harry Mehta was right behind her. He exhibited the most self-discipline and voiced the least exasperation of the three grad students in Anita's wake. Of course, he alone had the presence of mind to down his beer when Anita proclaimed her "eureka" moment. He unlocked the door and disabled the security system. Anita found the lights and flicked them on.

She went straight to the whiteboard while talking. "Okay, so check this out. We've been trying to figure out how early man was able to make it on the meager nutrition available during the harsh central European winters, year after year."

She drew a group of X's and O's on the board. Suppose the X's are men able to hunt and the "O's" represent women, children and the elderly as well as crippled individuals who earned their keep making tools and weapons needed for the hunt." She nodded to Harry, who was firing up the old desktop. "Digging through the refuse, we begin to see patterns."

The projector glowed to life. Harry yielded the keyboard to Lamonte Hill. Monty accessed the NIH database.

"This is our summer marker—*Campanula barbata*, the bearded bellflower." She smiled. "It only grows in the Swiss Alps and only in the summer. Ergo, when we see these petals in great numbers, we can be reasonably certain we're seeing summer settlement sites. Let's see how nuts and berries stack up on these periods.

"I went hiking in the Alps once with Gil, Amber, and- err, with some people, and we saw this indigo flower called…the snow gentian," Monty said. "What's the scientific name for that again?"

Everyone looked to Harry.

"I don't know. I'm not a botanist," Harry complained. "And you guys didn't invite me to go on that trip with you."

"Yes, we did," Gil said. "You couldn't go because you had to go to your cousin's weddin–"

*"Gentiana nivalis,"* Anita supplied, thumbing through her phone's browser and drawing everyone's attention back to her subject. "During the Pleistocene period, seeds, nuts, and berries represented a major portion of the hominid diet. Edible vegetation becomes scarce at the same time, game reserves dry up each year, late fall/early winter. Sooner during heavy or extended glaciation."

"Okay, so what?" Monty asked.

"So," Anita said with satisfaction at the segue. "The volume of refuse and content of animal and fish bones drops off in the winters. There is less poop." She looked around the room as she elbowed Monty out of the way to query the solution to her hypothesis. "Why is there less poop?"

"'Cause they were as full of shit as you are." Gil was losing patience.

"No." She sneered. "Because they were in low metabolic states."

"Like in suspended animation?" Harry asked. "How?"

Gil said, "Hibernation. That's the secret."

"Exactly, my young apprentice." Anita intoned in her best Emperor Palpatine. "In this state, more than half the population burned almost no additional fuel. The hunter class could protect the rest and pile up meager food stores for the time when the rest would come back to life."

"Oh my god. Adding this to our thesis will take another six months," Gil complained.

"Don't worry, guys, this is personal curiosity." Anita mused. "It leads me into another puzzle, though." She seemed to zone out and scribbled ponderously at the whiteboard until the guys dragged her away and back to the Yellow Mushroom.

# Chapter 7: Hunting Cavemen

"She's spending a lot of hours with the MIT boys," Brasil said.

He stood as the burly man sat and made himself comfortable. Quirk lit a cigarette.

"What's she working on that takes more time than she spends on the FMDS project?" He sat at Brasil's computer desk and exhaled the smoke as he rolled the question around in his mind. "Jason, pull up the summary recording of the lab chronicle."

Quirk tilted his glasses down and read as the images streamed by. "I don't like it. Not one bit, I don't." He swiveled in the chair to face Jason Brasil. "It's going to be harder now, Jason. Nordstrom fired her today."

"The cutie pie?" Brasil said. "Why? You told him you had an eye on her."

"Not Claus, that idiot brother of his, Leif." Quirk smacked the arm of the chair. "Now she'll be mobile, looking for a new job. Probably outside of New England. Harder to track."

Brasil smirked. "Just a little harder, sir."

Jason Brasil's walk-up office was on the upper floor above a solo attorney's practice. Situated just off Essex Street, on the edge of Chinatown, the private investigator outfit drew little attention. Tyler Quirk liked that. So much so that he kept Brasil and his two associates on a generous retainer.

Quirk stroked his chin thoughtfully. "The lab, trash it." He locked Brasil's gaze and added, "Make it look like townies. I don't want too many questions asked. We'll have to get rid of the four of them—discretely. Capiche?"

## *March 13, 2010*

Anita woke up Saturday morning at 8:06. Late for her. During the week, she would have already been in the parking lot at the Crawford Center, on a good day, settled into her desk by now. She kept her sleep schedule even on weekends and holidays. Up for a run the days she didn't have to go in. Today, she'd overslept: Why?

Then it hit her. The momentum of her revelation last night must have given her amnesia. That gone, the realization that she was fired finally set in. Looking around her room, everything seemed to be in the usual order. Maybe the whole thing was just a bad dream. She slipped on her robe, slid into her house shoes, went to her laptop, and opened her e-mail.

It wasn't a dream. The notification was still there:

```
Dr. Thomas,

    We are deeply disappointed in your
lack of decorum and failure of loyalty
to the Crawford Center. Your signed
oath of confidentiality obviously has
very little meaning to you.
    It has come to our attention that
you are engaged in a competing project
for our neighboring institution, MIT.
    Effective immediately, your par-
ticipation in the FaMDaS project is
terminated. Your access keys and
passcodes have already been deac-
tivated. Please turn them in to
security at the gate. All of your per-
sonal belongings have been carefully
gathered and placed in packing boxes.
Please examine and confirm that all of
your property has been returned to you
and sign the receipt. The guards have
instructions to escort you off campus
immediately.
```

Unfortunately, we cannot offer a recommendation on your behalf. Any prospective employer will be told of your tenure here strictly in terms of time and attendance. Notification of separation and cause will be forwarded to the independent review boards and the ethics committees of all Massachusetts higher education facilities. The State Board of Medical Examiners has also been notified. We deeply regret the choices you have made. We thought of you as a promising young researcher.

Respectfully,

Leif Nordstrom, M.D.
CEO Nordstrom Clinic and Director of the Crawford Center for Advanced Bioengineering Research

There were no other new emails. Usually, the FMDS project sent a flurry of SUSAR messages— Suspected, Unanticipated Serious Adverse Reaction reports. Today, there were none.

She logged out. Tapping her foot and staring at the blank screen, Anita didn't know what to do next. She had no family in the Boston area, and all of her professional network was wound up in the Nordstrom Institute either directly or indirectly. Half knowingly, she reached for her phone and called Gil Hargrove.

After a few moments of listening, he said, "I know somewhere with research potential, but no alternate side of the street parking to clear snowy streets." He chuckled. "I know how much you hate that."

Harry woke at his usual time, 8:30, Saturday morning. His bladder full, he trucked across the one-room apartment to the bathroom, relieved himself, grabbed his toothbrush, and shoved the business end into his mouth. Cranking the "H" knob, he jumped in the shower before the water warmed up. The shock always helped shake out the cobwebs of sleep as he brushed his teeth in the bracing spray.

He had no reason to go in today. The research was ahead of schedule thanks to Anita. The revelations were important to her, though. He thought about her furious scribbling on the whiteboard. He thought it best to record her notes in the cloud files for future reference. Completing the 3-minute shower with his typical efficiency, Harry toweled off his hair, then slung on an MIT sweatshirt and jeans while the rest of his body was still wet.

He biked down to the lab and executed the usual security ritual to gain entry. He had wrestled his bicycle through the inner door to the main lab before he realized that he didn't hear the outer door close with the obligatory thud.

An uninvited guest stood in the inner doorway, suddenly assisting him with his bicycle. The lean intruder looked stern in spite of the smile on his face. The smile faded in seconds as two brutes appeared at the smaller man's flanks.

As if realizing that he had dropped his smile, a leer replaced the forced grin, and Jason Brasil asked, "Harry Mehta, I presume?"

Harry would have said *yes* had he had the chance, but after the third punch to the head, Harry went down. Vision in his left eye went blurry, then black. He became vaguely aware of the movement of other men in the lab. There was also the sound of breaking glass and the hiss of a spray paint can in action.

His last fuzzy thought, *He really didn't want an answer to that question.*

Soon, Harry just didn't feel the gut kicks anymore.

# Chapter 8: Bang!

### *March 27, 2010*

By dawn, Gil was up. He felt restless yet somehow comfortable in the company of Dr. Anita Thomas, his savior, once again. She had offered him shelter from the storm that finally brought them together last night. A night ending a month of his fruitless pursuit in her own time of need. The trek down to his home in Atlanta was awkward. Not at all what he had planned when she came to him for refuge after being fired from her position.

*Come on down, my dad will save you.* He thought, *He's building a big research department. He could use a brilliant scientist like you in his team,* Gil remembered. *Wait til you meet him. 'What a great guy,' I told her.*

Instead of the sage mentor, his father had behaved like an adolescent in heat. *And in front of mom, no less.*

The trip ended prematurely. Anita was silent on the flight home. No small talk. No shop talk. Certainly, no couple talk. The last flight out of Atlanta set them down in the middle of a Boston blizzard. He indulged a lingering look down at his sleeping angel, stretched and dropped to his feet, taking care to leave her undisturbed and cozy in the bed.

Gil lingered in the kitchen long enough to put on a pot of coffee and left her a sticky note: *Went down to move your car before you get a ticket.* Inspired by the tenderness of the night, he trudged down to move her car.

Anita awakened moments later to a cooling bed and the aroma of fresh brew. She followed it to the kitchen. She had just picked up the note to read it, when a bone-rattling boom rocked the building. Dropping the note, she ducked reflexively to her knees. The concussion shook plaster dust loose from half-century-old beams around her.

In another moment, all was still. Anita sprang from her crouch and raced to the window. Her Hyundai Sonata was on fire. A charred arm dangled from the driver's window of the vehicle. The car's roof, partially in place, mercifully hid the rest of the grisly scene from her eyes.

She had not taken a breath for twenty seconds. Anita aimed herself at the phone, but rather than walk on command, her body began to shudder incessantly. Eventually, she did reach the phone and on the third attempt, she successfully dialed 9-1-1.

The police arrived in less than three minutes. Likely, they were on patrol close enough to respond to the explosion before even getting the dispatch summons. Soon, what seemed like a battalion of policemen filled the street. After an initial investigation, the uniforms gave way to the forensic team, which swarmed the site.

For over an hour, Anita watched strangers in blue invade her very personal space as if through the lens of a camera. It was documentary of the unthinkable. They went through every item in Gil's bag and each room in her place. The air in the apartment grew stifling. Anita ambled down the stairs to the foyer escaping the crush of law enforcement personnel. Propping the door open, she beckoned relief from the bracing breeze already busy scattering stray snowflakes from surrounding rooftops.

The bomb squad complemented the crime scene investigators' efforts with chemical analyzers and specially trained dogs. No traces of explosives except the obvious gasoline in the tank.

After caffeine-fueled forums between the various officers, Anita overheard a lieutenant conclude, "So it was just an accident?"

Several hand-waving cops tried to explain to the ranking officer. "It was a freaky malfunction," they said, "The fuel line must have frozen closed with ice from condensation."

"The Hyundai was 12 years old, lieutenant." The officer shook his head. "Our theory: after a dozen years of salt and corrosion, the fuel line burst in the subzero temps, and the starter arced. The explosion would have caught anyone. No one could have anticipated or prevented it."

That was their explanation. For the time being, Anita 'bought' it, but found no comfort in the words. Two EMTs rolled a black body bag away on a gurney to the back door of a waiting ambulance. The four men turned and looked at Anita with absolute sympathy, a rare sentiment for hardened Boston cops.

More tragic news: The Massachusetts State Bureau of Investigation arrived. They briefed the local police on an independent case their database linked to this accident. It seemed that their Dr. Anita Thomas and Gil Hargrove were connected to one Harry Mehta by a cooperative research. The duty fell to a stocky female detective who stepped in and comforted Anita as a person of mutual interest.

Sergeant Wade made formal introductions. Maybe they thought Anita would identify with a fellow African-American woman and relax a bit, open up.

The officer was good. Sensitive, compassionate. Wade found Anita at the foot of the steps and handed her salvation in the form of steaming coffee in her favorite mug, hot out of her own Cuisinart, where Gil had brewed it.

The cop had good instincts. The mug, although clean, had deep brown stains from frequent use. Impressed but not fooled, Anita recognized the cup selection for what it was; the detective had had unfortunate experiences in ugly matters. Wade took her statement.

"His name was Gil, Gil Hargrove. I spent the ten days in Atlanta," Anita began. "A week of that at the Hargrove family home. I needed to explore new avenues of research. My continued academic future anywhere in the Boston metro area was looking dim."

"Why was that, doctor?" Wade asked.

"Because, Sergeant, as of the beginning of the month, I was unceremoniously out of a job!" Anita said. "After a miserable February in Cambridge, Gil Hargrove had invited me down to his Georgia home for the break to forget that I had been fired," Anita snorted, "with the most derogatory letter of dismissal I have ever seen."

"Who did you work for? MIT?"

Anita shook her head. "The Nordstrom Clinic, Crawford Research Center. We had just wrapped up a land-mark research project when I was let go. I was the youngest member of the primary investigative team." She laughed harshly. "My *ethics* were in question, and I didn't have 'a clear understanding of research protocol'."

"Do you have family in Georgia?" Wade asked.

"No," Anita answered flatly.

"Okay, so why Atlanta?" Wade eyed her intensely. Something about the story apparently didn't set well with the detective.

"Gil's father, Dr. Wesley Hargrove, is an important man in Georgia." She smiled a humorless smile. "Old money. Dean of the Hamilton School of Medicine and Chairman of the Department of Internal Medicine. Dr. Hargrove was very interested in my work."

"What do you do exactly, Dr. Thomas?" Wade asked.

"Primarily, micro molecular research and genomic engineering," Anita answered.

"So is your title PhD or M.D., doctor?" Wade asked, as if it made a difference.

"Both, actually. Dr. Hargrove and I talked about gene activation and cataloguing mostly. He was fascinated by the concept, but only superficially versed in the actual science of the Genome Project and its ramifications," She stopped.

*This detective neither knows nor cares what the Human Genome Project is about.* Anita realized. *All she wants to know is why this young, white man is dead and what this 'pretty black girl' has to do with it.*

Anita sighed, then stepped outside and sat on the stoop overlooking the clean-up process. Wade followed suit. Didn't matter that she was black too. Detective Wade was a cop.

"Didn't you find it unusual for this family of such repute to open its doors to a stranger from the north?" Wade asked. "People like that tend to be..., well, let's just say very selective about their house guests."

"I'm very well published, detective. My research is on the crest of a new wave of biomedical engineering with a unique perspective that has not been duplicated in this hemisphere. Hamilton Medical hadn't seen research like mine in years."

"So, it was purely professional, then, was it, Dr. Thomas?" Wade fixed her gaze on Anita's eyes.

"Dr. Hargrove liked me." Anita glanced at the tire tracks from the ambulance that had carried Gil's body away and dropped her head again, fighting to hold back tears. "He liked me for his son, Gil. The speculation wasn't subtle that Wesley Hargrove liked me a little too much for himself, though. An old man's whimsy, I think. I've seen it before. Nothing serious."

"Maybe the start of a midlife crisis, though?" Wade asked. "Did Hargrove's wife notice, too?"

Anita snapped her gaze to meet that of the detective. "Their son, Gil, was bright, but in his father's view, he was a slacker. Dr. Hargrove credited me with saving an expensive, Ivy League career. Both Dr. and Mrs. Hargrove knew it as basically true, and they were grateful." Anita looked down at her slippered feet, wondering why they didn't feel cold in the Boston snow. "Still, I found sitting across from her at the dinner table awkward."

"So did you put the moves on this young guy to get a new position, or did you just 'not get out of the way' when he chased you into bed?" Wade asked coolly. As Anita inhaled to speak, the detective cut her off. "Not that I'm mad at you. A woman has to use whatever resources necessary to stay on top in this game."

"What game?" Anita tried to keep the defensive edge out of her voice.

"Research," Wade said. "From what I hear, it's very competitive."

"Not for me." Anita could no longer hold it in.

"Still, you were fired," Detective Wade finished.

She waited a moment or two to allow Anita to recover. She still needed information from the good doctor. "So you went for the kid, huh?"

"In spite of the great disparity in our respective career achievements, Detective, Gil was only two months younger than me."

"Okay, but still, why did you go all the way down to Atlanta, Georgia, to meet Gil's parents anyway? That's generally considered a big step in any relationship."

Anita was as alluring as any entertainer ever to grace the covers of Essence or Ebony magazines, but romantically, she was as adept at flirtation as a nun in a bordello. Socially awkward, she hid behind her academic persona under stress. Anita couldn't relate to most blue-collar types either. Except cops. Cops she understood well.

"We shared a love of black and white movies. Both 1940s stuff and foreign films. Otherwise, our relationship was kind of dry, stilted, you know. We hadn't been intimate. Not until last night. Given my professional aspirations, I didn't feel right staying with him and his parents, so I moved out to a mid-level hotel. There sure are bunches of them down there. Gil helped me select one from the yellow pages. I passed the final few days there until spring break was over."

"So again, how'd he end up in your bed, Dr. Thomas?"

"We returned from Atlanta together last night. The red-eye flight arrived in Boston just ahead of the storm. I don't like driving through the snow." Anita pointed to her eyes. "Snow blindness. I don't care so much when it's already on the ground, but not when it's coming down. Especially blizzards like this one. Well, Gil didn't mind. He drove us here in my car from the airport. My apartment was closest." She smiled at the memory. "Down-shifting and counter-steering like a pro, he made his way through the snow and ice-covered roads. He sure could drive. He pulled her right up to the curb."

"Who's 'her'?" Wade interrupted.

"Heidi, that's what I called my car." Anita glanced up at the remains of the vehicle on the tow truck. The off-white sedan, now totaled, was caked with a layer of charcoal gray soot.

"I was certain I couldn't have made the trek by myself. Gil carried my luggage up from the car. The snow was really coming down by then." Anita smiled in Wade's direction. "Well, you know, more than fifteen-inch accumulation." She said and kicked at the moist, fluffy white stuff piled on the edge of the steps at her feet. "The rails weren't running at that hour, and I certainly wasn't going to take him to his place last night, not even a short hop of only six or seven blocks away."

"So…?" Wade prompted.

"Gil was very sweet. I was really starting to like him, and he knew it. I couldn't make him walk, not in that mess. I asked him to stay."

Anita finally began to bawl uncontrollably. "He knew by the way I asked- I wasn't offering that he just 'sleep' on the couch. I'm not good at this. Attracting men isn't something I really work at, I guess."

A uniform turned an appraising eye to her sitting there on the steps. It certainly wasn't her grey flannel *lingerie* that caught his eye.

Noticing the gesture, Wade said, "Looks like reeling men in is nearly automatic for you, isn't it?"

"I spent most of my younger life running from romance. When I finally wanted it to happen, I felt clumsy." Anita gathered her blanket around her like a shawl, more out of embarrassment for the loose fit of her pajamas than from the cold. "Clumsy, very vulnerable, and guilty."

"Guilty?"

"I've never been uncertain of my future before, detective," Anita admitted.

Detective Wade mocked her haughty tone. "So, you decided to let him stay over last night, and added 'sullied' to that list by morning."

"Wade." A tenor voice interrupted with the rasp of years of cigarettes smoked by the carton. "That's out of line! Dr. Thomas has had a hell of a morning."

Anita looked up absently, not focusing on her rescuer. Instead, she remembered twelve hours earlier placing imploring fingertips on Gil's. He looked wearily around her living room for a comfortable sofa to sleep on, red-nosed with a sniffle from braving the icy air outside. She was glad she conveyed her needs clearly as he stood at her open door, her luggage in tow. She could have lent him her car last night, but she did not. She closed her ungloved hand around his, resting on the handle of her suitcase, and led him to the only bedroom in the apartment.

The detective continued to question Anita as she reminisced about her last moments with Gil Hargrove. Wade reported the details of Harry Mehta's demise, which occurred while Anita and Gil had been away in Georgia. A break-in at the lab, it seemed. Vandals. Nothing taken, but graffiti on the walls, broken specimen tubes, an unplugged freezer left open, files deleted electronically, or documents burned to unrecognizable ash.

She showed Anita a photo of the graffiti on her cell phone. Wade indicated a peculiar flourish in the last word sprayed on the whiteboard. Anita wrinkled her nose and scratched at it with her fingertip at the unusual squiggle, almost a signature curlicue. It emphasized a misogynous reference apparently directed toward Dr. Anita Thomas.

Wade pointed out how the racist epithet on the next wall added insult to injury. That and repeated blunt trauma to poor Harry's head. "Internal and external hemorrhage was the cause of death, they said."

As Anita listened, she rested her chin in her hand and then moved her fingers absently up to her mouth to stifle a cry. A moment later, she hung her head and rocked it by her temples from side to side with her cupped hands.

"There was a third guy in all this," The detective said. "His name was credited in the title of the science project."

Anita found her voice. "Graduate thesis, detective."

The detective nodded. "It couldn't be a coincidence. Lamont. Lamont Hill. Know anything about him?"

"Not on campus," Anita said. "He's in Maryland. Been there since the beginning of the month."

"Okay. I guess that wraps it up for now, doctor."

Anita sighed.

Wade handed her a business card. "If you think of anything else that might be helpful, call me anytime, huh?"

Anita nodded without looking up. The police picked up their paraphernalia and evacuated the building and street. It was as if they were never there except for where the burn cleared the melted snow at the curb and all the footprints in the slush.

Anita had held back on one thing. She still had Gil's cell phone. She didn't know Lamont's number, but Gil must have. She knew she had to talk to him— to warn him. He and Gil had been friends since before prep school.

Lamont spent some time at the NIH, shoring up some of Gil's data and suppositions during the winter break while visiting his folks in Maryland.

Anita found Lamont on Gil's cell phone and dialed him from the contacts list. The speed dial entry showed as Monty. She called him by his nickname when he picked up.

"It's Anita. I don't know how to tell you this. Gil and Harry are both dead."

She waited for his response. It seemed like an eternity. Monty and Gil had been friends for fifteen years. When Monty finally spoke, he was dead calm.

"I knew about the lab," he said. "Dad's been pushing the local authorities to investigate behind the scenes. Homeland has not had a clear reason to delve into this incident."

Monty's father was a high-ranking staffer in the Department of Homeland Security, Anita recalled. *A Major General or something, two stars? Worked at the Pentagon.*

"He's already looking into what happened to Harry," Lamont said. "I got the word yesterday afternoon. Dad's people got a break last night. They were able to investigate the vandalism at the lab under the auspices of Homeland Security because of the genetic engineering angle and the murder. Sounds like we can't tie Gil's death to this incident, though. Not directly."

"You know, you and I are the only surviving members of this project." Anita stood, climbed the final step to the front door, and entered the vestibule of her brownstone, finally retreating from the cold.

"Get out, Anita," he said. "Get out of your apartment and out of Boston. Get out this weekend."

She clutched the phone close to her cheek as a child clung to a parent in a thunderstorm. She sought sanctuary in his words.

"Don't tell Nordstrom where you're going. And don't trust the local authorities. My dad can investigate this whole mess without their input now. He says he smells a rat. Whenever he says that, he's usually on to something really bad.

"You have your degrees. You're licensed in medicine and surgery, aren't you?"

"Yeah, but they can be tracked." She wasn't following Monty's train of thought.

"Get here and we'll secure your credentials, get you
professional reciprocity somewhere. We need to get you to
a safe haven until we can sort this all out. I'll talk to Dad. I
have an idea."

"Why is this happening?" Anita asked him.

There was no response from her friend. She half
hoped for an answer to the rhetorical question. Friends and
colleagues dropping all around her. Not to mention her research career had just dissolved like a snowflake on a warm
parking space.

Anita climbed the thirteen stairs to the second floor
and found her door ajar. With so many cops in and out that
morning, she entered with no trepidation. She crossed the
living room to look out the window again. The smoke had
ebbed to faint plumes lingering in the air in front of her
apartment. All of the official vehicles were gone now.
Their tires left black, serpentine tattoos in the snow, already
filling in with drifting flakes from trees and rooftops.

*It was my car that Gil died in.* She thought. *If it had
been deliberate, the explosion might have been meant to
finish both of us.*

General Hill would find out. In the meantime, she
wasn't safe on Beacon Street. She couldn't go home to
Long Island, but she knew she had to get the hell out of
Boston.

## Chapter 9: Femme Fatale

***March 25, 2010 1:00 pm.***

The offices of Eyes of Brasil Investigations occupied the second-floor walk-up above Finklestein's Deli. The seedy community at the edge of Boston's Chinatown nearly qualified as a Raymond Chandler movie set. Jason Brasil stood at the door, formal as a butler, as he admitted the woman. Tyler Quirk sat in the desk chair while he beckoned the new arrival to his side. A stripe of white contrasted the rest of her wind-tossed auburn hair. She moved sensuously with the deliberate, dangerous gait of a tigress on the prowl.

Carelessly shedding her topcoat, she revealed a fitted black mini dress, its hem extending just past the elastic bands of nylon stockings. Snow-caked black leather boots wept melted slush and salt down four-inch heels to the hardwood floor.

She came to a stop at Quirk's side, a little too close to be casual, and handed him a CD jewel case with a mini SD card taped to it. Accepting them, Quirk reached an arm around her without looking up, fondling her buttocks. Closed lips curled upward silently at the corners of her mouth in response.

"Look at this, will you?" he asked her, a little too loud for her proximity. "Everything broken to shreds, just as I asked. Great, right?"

The woman said nothing, moving receptively to the invading fingers caressing hips to the cheeks of her butt. To be certain, she knew every word Quirk uttered to inform her, also served to chastise Brasil.

"The problem is that they never checked the quality of the recordings taken from the lab before they wrecked the fucking place. The data that the brilliant Anita Thomas just declared a 50,000-year breakthrough. Based on her final comments on the previous evening, she had some sense that this discovery had a bearing on the fibromyalgia genetics she had already begun snooping into.

"Do you see this white board?" he asked. "Original thoughts. Scribbled insights like the notes of Leonardo Da Vinci."

"I can't make it out. Looks like it's covered with… is that, that street graffiti?" the woman asked.

"Exactly, my dear. Some morons sprayed permanent paint all over irreplaceable handwritten notations. Possibly Nobel Prize winning notes," Quirk added. "Data now in the hands of Homeland Security." Again, he glanced side long back toward the door. "Where we can't get at it."

"Is the source intact?" The new arrival's voice was husky, aroused, and anticipatory, as if she already knew the author of that composition was her new assignment. Supremely confident; that was why she was summoned. She was like a beast with the scent of raw meat in her nostrils.

"Yes, thanks to the fortunate incompetence of this idiot." Quirk hiked a thumb over his shoulder at Brasil. "Dr. Thomas survived the explosion. Might as well have used napalm."

"I need a scalpel instead of a battle-ax, my dear. I need finesse." His hand glided upward from her hip to her waist and reeled her in tightly to his side. "I need you, Lucy."

### 4:30 pm March 25, 2010

The black sedan idled in front of Anita Thomas' Beacon Street brownstone. Lucy occupied the passenger seat while Jason Brasil sat behind the wheel, drumming his fingertips on it. Dressed in a grey jacket and black button-down shirt reminiscent of 1940s gangster attire, he felt overdressed for surveillance work.

"I haven't seen any movement in the last twenty minutes, have you?" Brasil nervously stripped his white tie from his collar and stuffed it in a jacket pocket as they waited.

Lucy said nothing. She was busy looking in the right-side mirror. She bit her lips and grabbed the neck tie, from Brasil's pocket. She hurriedly wrapped it around her right ankle like a bandage.

No sooner did she complete the task than a boy came into view on the sidewalk from behind them.

"Excuse me?" Lucy said. "Can you help me?"

The boy stood back as she opened the car door. He couldn't have been older than twelve.

"I desperately have to get a message to my cousin. She lives on the second floor right over there." She pointed across the street.

"I don't know, lady. I'm not tryin' to deliver no 'packages' for anybody." the boy said, backed away another step then returned to his course.

"Oh, it's nothing like that." She smiled weakly, then groaned. "I've been trying to call her all day. There's been a tragedy in our family.: My auntie." Lucy grasped her ankle. "I sprained my ankle yesterday. See?" She displayed the wrapped limb. "I was hoping that with my husband's help I could climb the stairs myself and see her, but I'm just hurt too badly." She grabbed a handful of snow and massaged it into her ankle.

"Please. Just a note. Nothing you can get into any trouble for." She smiled, offering a simple note. "You can even read it if you like."

Tentatively, the boy reached for the folded paper. "Well…" He half opened the note, then folded it back at the reassuring smile from the pretty lady with the *broken leg*. "Okay. Where does she live exactly?"

Lucy pointed. "Right up there." Her face conveyed the sincerest gratitude.

Halfway across the street, the boy turned back. "Hey, why can't he go?" he said, pointing to Brasil.

"Bad asthma. The cold makes it worse. He's already wheezing." She frowned. "No way could he make it up those stairs. He's worse off than I am." She looked in his eyes. "I'll give you five dollars. It's really important." Her hand trembled as she offered up the bill.

The boy nodded and headed for the brownstone again as asked. When he disappeared through the door, she relaxed, glanced at her watch, and waited patiently. Less than ten minutes later, the boy reappeared at the door.

"Sorry, miss," he said, rounding to the passenger side of the vehicle. "No one's there. I knocked on the door and waited a long time. A neighbor lady says she saw your cousin, Anita, leave with bags packed." He had the five-dollar bill still in hand. "Do you want me to shove it under the door or something?"

"No. Maybe she spoke to one of our other cousins, and she's already on her way to see our auntie." She took his hand in hers and said, "But thank you so very much for helping." She grunted in mock pain.

"Hope your leg gets better, lady. That must really hurt."

"I'll be okay" She said, closed the door,, and nodded to Brasil to start the car and drive, waving to the young Samaritan as they left.

"She's skipped already." She smirked as he drove off. "Orson's not going to be happy with you."

# Chapter 10: Lost

*March 26, 2010 2:23 am*
The day's last Path train arrived in Newark from
Penn Station, New York City, depositing a solitary passenger. Anita wore a knit hat pulled down low around her
head, and her scarf wrapped twice around her neck. She
traveled light—a tote bag, her purse, and a small rolling suitcase. Discarding an issue of a popular magazine, The
Sharper Edge, she had read on the ride, she surveyed the
station. The platform was nearly deserted, as the hour was
late. The only person in sight was a ticket clerk ending his
shift. He helped Anita carry her bags up the stairs.

"You all squared away, miss?" he asked.

Anita nodded. "Thanks."

"You know, a woman alone shouldn't be traveling
this late at night. Don't you have anyone you can call for
help?" he asked.

"I'll be okay," she lied. "A friend's on the way to
pick me up."

He appraised her for a moment, then said, "Suit
yourself." He shook his head. "Just hope I don't read 'bout
you in the papers tomorrow." Fatherly concern compelled
that scrutiny to linger a bit longer, then he checked his keys
and disappeared into the late-night fog.

Anita was alone. Still inside the station, but no gates
or fences remained to separate patrons from the general
public.

A shuffle followed by barely audible footsteps startled her. It might be a distorted echo of her own steps. She
thought. *Maybe my imagination. This setting's right out of
a horror tale.*

Anita listened for a few more seconds and heard
nothing. She collected her belongings and sought out a

bench when she heard the footsteps again, this time too distinct to ignore. She retreated to an alcove where the overhead light had burned out, and she became still, then waited.

The footsteps stopped. *There 's that grind again,* she now recognized it as the pivot of a booted foot against concrete. Silence again.

*He's not just passing by. Shit.*

She pulled back away from the corner. Her tote bag rustled when she did.

The grinding sound was shorter and faster this time, followed by urgent footfalls. They sounded heavy. *Whoever's coming this way is big.*

A soft wolf whistle sounded as her escape routes were closed off. She would have to face this stalker. Anita reached for her keys. Why had she kept the keys to a car that was surely ruins in some junkyard? Habit. She was grateful for them now, but wondered if they'd provide enough protection.

A shush sound came from the direction of the whistle. She tightened her grip on the keys and braced herself.

Light temporarily blinded her.

"You Anita?" a young tenor voice asked. The tone seemed non-threatening. He lowered the LED flashlight, but when she regained her sight, the first thing that came into focus was the barrel of a pistol. She dropped her keys and raised her hands slowly. Her heart beat triple time.

"Are you Dr. Anita Thomas?" The man wore a black leather jacket, collar turned up over a dark tee and jeans.

He waved the tip of the gun up and down. "The question was not rhetorical."

"You already know who I am if you're out here at this time of night lurking with a damn gun." Anita found her voice, but it was no more than a husk in the dampness.

"I guess if you wanted to kill me, I'd already be dead, with or without that gun." Her head didn't reach his chin.

He looked furtively from side to side. As he did, it occurred to her that the jacket was tight on him, and he was too big to see past to the platform beyond.

"Well, it looks like you're a valuable commodity, doc," he said and lowered the gun, but did not tuck it away.

"Who the hell are you?" Anita asked and took in his whole image.

"I'm Tony."

He was big, but lean. Lots of dark curls covered his head past his ears, and a five o'clock shadow hugged his face. Heavy army boots explained the grinding sounds. She was surprised that he was able to move as stealthily as he did with them on.

"So where are we going?" she asked.

"For a ride, doc." He holstered his gun and grasped her arm. "You're goin' away on a ship that don't sail."

## *June 27, 2010 Philadelphia shipyard*

The William Jefferson Clinton was under construction. The latest heavy cruiser had its progress stalled due to defense budget cuts. The bow was solid, a few hundred feet from the ocean it would someday call its home, but the engines and propellers were still crated up on the dock. The administrative headquarters were housed in trailers while Navy workers and engineers soldiered on with what they could to bring the vessel to seaworthiness.

Any ship, once commissioned required an assigned chief medical officer. A lieutenant would do. Not many sailors in his charge. The officer needn't have a specialty yet, just an M.D or D.O. degree.

Three sharp raps at the door roused Anita from her bunk. Disoriented, she poured cool water from a glass at her bedside into the palm of her hand and splashed it on her face. She patted it dry with her bed sheet before the next arpeggio at the door summoned her once again. She crossed the compact quarters and opened the door to a now-familiar face.

"Morning, doc. Sleep well?"

She looked up at a clean-shaven Tony Fusco dressed in a white tee and white running pants. She couldn't decide whether she liked the short, military haircut or the wild ringlets he wore when they first met.

Peering out onto the deck, Anita asked, "What day is this?"

"Wednesday, June 27th." He suppressed a grin as she sneered at his sarcasm. She knew the month, but keeping track of the days of the week had become difficult for her. Her routine had grown monotonous.

"Ready for our run?" he asked, checking his timepiece. "We only have an hour before the satellite crosses overhead again."

She looked up and shrugged. "I guess so. Let me get into some shorts and running shoes, and I'll be right with you."

While she spoke at the door, an ensign caught up with Tony and presented a sealed envelope. "New orders, sir." The young man stood at attention and fired off a sharp salute. Lieutenant Antony Fusco, M.D., opened the envelope and read the half-page of text.

"Lieutenant Commander Compton is in the office. Says he wants to see you immediately, lieutenant." Having completed his assigned task, the young man was dismissed with a nod from Tony.

"So, what is it?" Anita asked.

"It's what we've been waiting for," Tony said. "I have my new assignment."

"And?" she asked impatiently.

"It's Atlanta." He folded the orders into his shorts. "Pack ASAP and meet me down at my bike. As soon as I transfer command of sick bay, we're out of here."

Twenty minutes later, Anita waited by Antony Fusco's motorcycle with a tightly packed duffle bag. "Problem?"

"Not for me." He looked at her with a wry smile. "Commander Compton was pissed about relieving a lieutenant JG, without explanation."

"Why didn't you tell him?" she asked.

"Couldn't." He showed her the order sheet. Stenciled across in transparent red ink were the words: `recipient's eyes only`.

Tony laughed. "It was above his pay grade."

"So, I'm top secret now?" Anita asked.

"You have been for over three months," Tony said. "Not just covert, but strange. Orders came from a Major General. Superior rank, but not in this branch of the service. That means I'm now on detached duty from the Navy."

A perplexed look on her face begged further explanation.

"These orders..." He smacked the letter against his open palm. "...took precedence over previous orders issued by the Rear Admiral. They came from the Department of Homeland Security, and they were cosigned by the Undersecretary of the department."

"So, this is a good thing?" she asked.

"Kind of. I guess I'm in the intelligence community now."

Anita took the sheet in his hand again. The orders read:

```
Effective immediately, you are re-
lieved of duty aboard the U.S.S.
Clinton.
    New assignment: orthopedic intern-
ship Atlanta, GA. Hamilton Medical
Center. Secure the safety of one Dr.
Anita Thomas. To this end, deadly force
is authorized, and you are directed to
carry a concealed sidearm. Report di-
rectly to Dr. Wesley Hargrove until
further notice."
```

# PART 2

# Chapter 11: Atlanta Drift

*Narrative of John Wheaton, M.D. R3 Resident Internal Medicine and supervisor to Anita Thomas, M.D. PhD*
*Public Record (DOJ Petition to redact denied) See Interview by Mark Wheaton September issue of The Sharper Edge, and the expose, The Painkillers.*

July 2010 was a rainy month in Georgia. Thirteen days in all. Not a record, and the showers failed to cool the days down much. It was "Hotlanta" after all.

Jack Wheaton was the third-year resident physician on the team. Monday, July 2, 2010, was his first day on service. He felt great that morning. Every house officer got a three-day weekend once a month. Jack Wheaton had just finished his. Worked out, he got Sunday off as part of his last 'golden' weekend as a second year. He walked into Hamilton Medical Center whistling that Bony James tune he liked so much.

For an urban hospital, the campus wasn't bad. Manicured lawn, old world stucco front with stacked stone accents and slate framed entry. It wasn't Emory, the premier, elite private institution ranked in the top twenty U.S. medical centers, but it wasn't the county hospital, Grady Memorial, either.

Hamilton was a private, multi-campus, inner-city hospital system, which exclusively accepted only top medical students and interns. Well-endowed by federal, state and private donors, it had more than adequate funding for training faculty and basic research. Its reputation for research rivaled some of the best the South had to offer, top 25 or 30 nationally, so it was able to justify that kind of demand for excellence.

Of course, Atlanta was one of the most popular cities in the South, a draw unto itself. Even the poor side of town looked good. The landscapers had recently freshened up the flowerbeds by the main entrance, and the rainbow of colors there was picture perfect.

Jack had a spring in his step, no rhythm as he was often told, but he bounced to the tune in his head all the same. Security might have thought him a fool, but the nurses smiled at his cheerful mood, so to Jack, it was all good.

His stride turned to a jog as he rounded the corner, out of sight of the guards, and he ran up the stairs to the fifth floor. He was tall, a shade under six feet, with a runner's physique. Down the hall he went, checking for familiar faces among the nursing staff.

Most of them were that terrific, matronly type. Like his Boston favorite, Harriett. He truly missed her, but then there was the *Christie*-type; smart, sharp, young, and pretty. Newly promoted to head nurse, Christie had a bright, shiny master's degree, diligently earned at night school while working the units of Hamilton Medical Center by day. She waved a salute Jack's way, whistling, *Hail to the Chief* as he danced by her station toward the 5A resident's office.

Jack settled in to his new digs filled with the well-worn, 1980s, commercial-grade furniture, tapping his feet to the rhythm in his head on the newly tiled flooring installed over the weekend. The administration always took advantage of the changing of the guard to spruce up the hospital: Best face on for the new recruits.

Jack's assignment was to run the A-wing of the fifth-floor medical service. Blue team. He started by reviewing the list of patients left by the outgoing resident.

The flush of a toilet heralded Alvin Williams' exit from the bathroom. He was one of the team interns. Jack hadn't realized he had been beaten to the office.

Al greeted him, still fastening his white slacks around sinewy hips.

"Morning, Boss." He beamed.

Jack was a little embarrassed, and it showed in the sarcasm of his answer. "Yeah, right." He grinned.

He liked Al. They had worked together on call a time or two and clicked. Jack was uneasy with Al's deferential disposition toward him that morning, though. Al looked up to him as senior resident.

Al came right in and went over the patients on the list for whom he had been responsible, and gave Jack a bullet presentation as best he could on the rest. Jack happily whistled "*Here She Comes*" as he reviewed lab results and developed a mental picture of each patient from the combined data.

That's when she came in. Laden with a purse and a green, canvas Whole Foods bag filled with stuff for a night on call, was the most beautiful girl Jack had seen in months.

"Morning," she said, putting her bags down. "I'm Anita Thomas. Is this Blue team?"

"Yep. I'm Jack Weston... I mean, Wheaton." *Smooth move, Jack,* he thought to himself. Then he tried to do that little tic that he did, twirling naturally, curly blonde hair as he stared. Always his secret weapon with girls. *Damn that summer haircut!*

He resorted to the authority tactic. "I'll be your senior resident this month." Recovering from his first of many faux pas, Jack asked, "Where are you from, Anita?"

"Boston, but I've had enough of the cold. I'm looking forward to some nice warm Georgia weather and hospitality."

"I know what you mean." He agreed. "I spent a couple of months there myself this winter. Brrr."

She put her bags in the office's only closet then joined him at the desk. The institutional air conditioning put a 68-degree chill on the room. The temperature would rise as the human traffic in the halls picked up through the day. Anita snuggled right up to him to see the list better. He let her read as he took in her profile.

*Absolutely gorgeous.* Not that "made-up" gorgeous. Anita, he decided, had that "beauty without trying" look working for her. He shifted his eyes back to the list each time she turned to him in conversation, then zoomed back to where he left off when her eyes returned to the list or computer screen.

Her inventory included the most serene pair of doe-like eyes dominating a flawless face and full lips around a slight overbite. Her complexion was an even milk chocolate glaze. Jack liked what he saw. The hairdo fit that face well, too. She wore it at shoulder length, and it had a light, sweet scent. He couldn't exactly identify the aroma, but it was a welcome contrast to the antiseptic odor of the hospital floors.

They accidentally touched the mouse together. Anita's hands were smooth, and her fingers seemed to flow like cocoa syrup. Even with his weekend tan peeling already, he was shades lighter than her deep Hershey tone. As he was sizing up her figure, Blue team was interrupted.

Christie, the ICU charge nurse, dipped through the door. "Heads up Jack, cardiology is already rounding in the unit."

He hadn't slept with Christie, but she was working on it. Jack was too distracted by the new muse in his charge. Christie lingered long enough to begin a sneer before moving on her way.

The blue team started rounds after Jack assigned cell phones to each intern. Dr. Dan Feinberg was attending that morning, followed by his entourage of obsequious cardiology fellows hanging on his every word. Feinberg was pontificating on some obscure observation from when he was a fellow, slowing the progress to a crawl. The cardiology team hadn't gotten to Blue Team patients yet, so they had a few minutes.

Anita followed her chief around the fifth-floor Cardiac Care Unit. She was on top of her cardiac physiology. She thoroughly impressed Dr. Feinberg. In fact, she did not miss a single pertinent physical finding or diagnosis all morning. Jack even threw some rheumatology cases into the mix to challenge her.

*Never saw an intern so much on her game.*

Jack didn't think she knew the hospital, the medical records system, or the city of Atlanta very well, but she sure knew her medicine. Rounds were finished by 11:30 am.

"Let's get some lunch and we'll go over a few things before attending rounds this afternoon," Jack suggested.

*Doctor Patel will likely want to show off her new long coat when she arrives,* Jack guessed. "I know it's a little early, but I want you to make a good impression. It makes me look good if you look good." He smiled his most charming smile.

"Do I look good yet?" she asked.

She exaggerated her posture and raised her shoulders, humoring his condescending comment while unintentionally accentuating her remarkable figure.

"Eh, you're getting there, you're getting there." Knowing how the nursing staff loved gossip, Jack tried to keep the innuendos to a minimum, but Anita was intoxicating to him. He engaged her using his big green-eyed gaze, which usually went over well with women he wooed.

He kept ushering her in front of him all the way to the cafeteria. A loose strap on her shoe caused her to reach down and fasten it repeatedly. Jack imagined that shoe is heaven-sent.

As it was, he feared everyone in the hall could see his salutation to her in the front of his pants. He needed a distraction from Anita, or he was going to say something stupid.

"Where's your phone, Anita?" he asked. He pulled a chair out for her at the lunch table he selected.

"Oh, shoot! I forgot it in the office, Jack. I'm sorry. Do I have time to go get it?"

He shook his head, using his most disappointed look. The dour expression on her face nearly made him regret that ploy.

Then he came up with something he thought was really clever.

"Sit, finish your lunch." Jack said, "I'll just call the operator and ask her to page you overhead if you're needed. It's a bit old-fashioned, but it still works."

He went over to the wall phone, dialed "0," and instructed the operator to page Dr. Thomas over the public address system if needed. He wrote down the extension on the palm of his hand while talking to the operator.

Anita and Al returned to the table with plates of Southern fare off the menu. After a few bites and medical mumbo jumbo discussion, Jack punched the number into the text frame on his cell phone with a message that read: "Dr. Thomas needed to call extension #4623."

"Whoops, ICU," he said when the operator paged her on the public address system. "You better find out what's wrong, stat, Anita."

He'd have failed the straight face test with anyone who knew him. Anita didn't. Not yet.

She popped right up and trotted over to the wall phone, dialed the number, and calmly replaced the receiver on the hook without saying a word into it. In a few seconds, she dialed again. Each time she called it, she got a busy signal. It took her a while to get frustrated. By the third time, Jack began a chuckle that bubbled into full laughter, and she was on to him.

*What Kind of sophomoric asshole did they stick me with?* She returned to the table, her eyes fixed on him, an inscrutable expression on her face. Without saying a thing, she fished around in her bag for her personal cell phone, her breasts brushing his leg as she did so.

Anita dialed the extension after the hospital area code and exchange prefix. The phone on the wall began to ring. She turned her head leisurely, looked at the phone on the wall, stood, and walked over to the phone. She lifted the receiver slowly to check the number on the cafeteria phone.

*Same one.* She cut her eyes back to Jack. She mouthed, "Son of a bitch."

Jack knew he was caught. He smiled a Cheshire cat grin. This was it. He was going to see if 'Miss Intense' had a sense of humor or not. His palms became clammy as she walked back to the table.

Anita walked deliberately, almost in slow motion, like a supermodel on a runway. He knew she meant to be threatening, but to him, it was just sexy as hell. She knelt on the chair next to him and grasped his chin gently between her thumb and forefinger. The feel of her warm breath on his face made his legs restless.

Her voice came across as sensuous as great phone sex. She caressed his face, then pinched it between her thumb and forefinger.

"I know it's cliché, but payback really is a bitch." Then Anita threw his face away from her and returned to her own seat.

Jack laughed nervously as she glared at him. Anita was a siren, and he could not resist her.

The rest of the lunch break was hard to get through on a professional level. His cell began the peculiar 'Whup, whup' noise of a police siren as programmed to indicate a page from the ER. His team was on short call. Admissions started at 1:00 PM. Jack hated being on call the first day.

# Chapter 12: The Pit

Blue team went down to the *Pit* together. That's what the staff called the Emergency Department when they were on call. Jack's team squeezed into the first available elevator like a bunch of grapes. Another medical team and several medical students pressed in behind them, shoving Jack against Anita and her against Al.

Fortunately, Jack learned that Dr. Thomas was a forgiving soul. She didn't seem to mind the crush and apparently forgot his lunchroom prank. She was very mature for her age or for that matter, even for his. All professional. By contrast, Al was comically facing the corner as he often did in crowded elevators.

Herd behavior. Sometime during psychiatric training, Al heard that it was very disconcerting to people to see someone facing the back of the elevator while everyone else faced the door. Jack had to suppress a laugh every time he watched Al do his little antics.

The elevator let them off on the basement floor. Blue team lost most of the crowd to the snack bar on the way to the Emergency Department.

*Poor bastards had to make do with junk food before getting to the ER because they didn't have time between rounds for a real lunch.*

Upon entering through the heavy swinging doors, Jack took the measure of the triage area. The line-up carried the usual traffic of status asthmaticus, diabetic noncompliance, alcoholics with ketoacidosis, or electrolyte disturbances, as well as the assortment of myocardial infarctions and weak and woozy dumps. The ER doctors couldn't get through it all in one shift. Jack got a total of seven. Al took four and Anita took three. As chief of the service, Jack was responsible for them all.

Their admissions weren't bad. All legitimate teaching cases. Jack wished he had a student to help Al. He had a lot of running around to do that really didn't require a doctor's skill set. One of Anita's admissions deteriorated and had to go to the ICU, so Jack spent most of the early evening working with her and her unit patient. He didn't mind that much.

Jack got a late text from the Attending. It seemed that Dr. Meena Patel couldn't make attending rounds the first day of service. The "Pretending" physician had been just a senior resident three days earlier. Supposedly, she had a meeting at Hamilton Medical Associates. It came out the next day that she had a four-star lunch with a regional pharmaceutical representative named Velasquez.

Attending's privilege. Faculty members don't have to explain themselves to mere peons. Just as well. Bringing Meena up to speed would have taken another two hours that Jack really didn't have to spare.

Jack thought he knew most of the Pharma represent-atives. He had never heard of this, Velasquez, before. Strange. Just one novice attending for lunch? Why? She couldn't have enough clout to merit that kind of one-on-one attention and expense at this stage of her career.

Jack had little interest in guidance from Dr. Patel. Her strength was infectious disease. She planned on start-ing an I.D. fellowship after she delivered her first child. She and her husband had been trying fruitlessly for six months already. Meena was brilliant, but not very helpful in acute care situations. She was knowledgeable and metic-ulous with differential diagnoses, though. A good Monday morning quarterback, as it were.

Meanwhile, Jack and Anita were still in the ER dealing with Polly Harker, another patient destined to end up in the ICU at this rate, trying to restart an intravenous line. She had no useful veins left. Anita finally got a chance to sit down and complete her admission note after Al helped an ER nurse start an intravenous line. Before she could finish the note, Anita looked up to see the head nurse confer with Jack for a moment as they huddled over Mrs. Harker.

He beckoned to Anita. "Al was able to get a 23-gauge angiocath into a vein he seemed to have conjured up in the crook of her arm. The nurses poured enough fluid through that little I.V. to reanimate her. Just enough vitality for her to find her intravenous line and pull it out. And that just after Al and his magic fingers left the building."

Jack had served in Central America, Sub-Saharan Africa, and Southeast Asia, working in third-world medical clinics and disaster relief for over a year. He figured he could replace the damn thing himself and look like a star in front of Anita. He thought himself proficient at starting difficult IVs. So, he tried. Lord knew he tried. Medicine can be a humbling profession. Polly Harker was proving to be a venous access nightmare. She had a network of blue lines in her skin that could have been blue crayon marks.

"That old woman is dry as a prune. She has nothing. She received nearly a liter of saline, and I still can't find a single vein," Jack said. "She's on Coumadin for atrial fibrillation, so I don't want to try for a central line. Not for something as trivial as hydration in someone who isn't obtunded with a reasonable blood pressure."

Jack found himself slinking up to the residents' desk in the ER with his proverbial tail between his legs. Defeated, he looked up the anesthesia resident on call.

*Dasher Clay.*

The last name Jack wanted to see at the top of that damn list. He checked to see if there was another resident or chief resident he could wrangle a favor out of, but no such luck.

Anita sidled up to him and asked, "Anything wrong, Jack?"

He chewed his bottom lip and thought for a moment. It was pointless, but he decided, "No." he hesitated, "Let me call Al."

"He went home already," Anita told him.

"I have his personal cell number. *Maybe he has another miracle in his pocket.*

On the second ring, Jack got him, but the reception was thready. Al was in the subway.

"What's up, boss?" Al asked. "I forget something?"

There were few legitimate reasons for calling a resident who had already signed out. The most common being that the off-duty resident made a major mistake, and the caller was trying to cover the former's ass for him.

"You on the train already, or are you still in the station?" Jack asked, turning away from Anita.

"Yeah, I'm on the train, but I'm only three stations away from the hospital," he said. "What didn't I do?" Then there was static, followed by a dropped call tone.

Before Jack could call him back and tell him to never mind, Al was already calling Jack's personal cell phone.

"Jack, what did I do?" Al sounded worried. "Was it serious?"

"It's nothing, Al. I was hoping you had dilly-dallied in the building or something before going home. I just wanted you to do me a favor. No sweat."

"Are you sure? I'm really only four stops away. I can make it back in 35-40 minutes," Al offered.

He was such a sincere guy. Most residents would have chewed Jack out or hung up after they knew that they weren't at fault for anything.

"I got it, Al," Jack said. "See ya tomorrow," He hung up and looked at the list again with disdain. *Damn.* His muscles ached everywhere.

Jack dialed the anesthesia on-call resident's phone number and waited while it rang. He didn't expect the soft, sultry voice that answered the call.

"Anesthesia resident, please hold."

The voice sounded familiar, but it was replaced by the expected radio announcer vocals of Dasher Clay.

"This is Dr. Dasher Clay speaking…"

Jack actually looked at the receiver in his hand in disbelief, imagining the budding anesthesiologist's butt-shaped chin as he did.

"Hey, Dasher. This is Jack Wheaton, Medicine. We have a nice little lady down here who is dehydrated and on Coumadin. We need a line," Jack said, cutting to the chase.

"So, start one," Dasher said with a yawn.

Jack covered the receiver and turned to no one in particular and muttered, "I really hate this guy." Then into the phone, "If I could start the I.V., I wouldn't be calling you, now would I?"

Before Dasher could say another thing, Jack said, "The consult request will be in your box in the ER." He hung up the phone and muttered "prick" under his breath.

"Jack?" Anita asked.

He had nearly forgotten that she was even there, he was so angry.

"I called anesthesia to get venous access."

Anita looked at Jack as if she were looking into his soul, and he added, "He's up there getting laid while we're down here working our butts off, that's all."

She was still staring at Jack sympathetically. She wanted to offer her help, but she knew she had to hold back. After all, she was supposed to be just an intern. A novice. The Anita Thomas of record was an average graduate of Boston Medical School, aspiring to become an internist, not a full professor of medicine capable of placing any peripheral line, central line, or even a venous cut down if necessary. She had to let him flounder while she watched.

"I don't know, Anita, but that guy just rubs me the wrong way." He added. "And he looks like Dudley Do-right to boot!" He laughed at the intensity of his emotional investment in the situation.

"You mean the cartoon character?" she asked, chuckling.

Just the sound of her laughter, even in the cacophony of the ER, made him feel better. "He's on his way. I'll let you be the judge."

The two decided to use the interlude wisely while waiting for the illustrious Dr. Clay. They re-examined the old woman's heart and lungs, checked the computer for any lab updates, and then sat down to write an interval note.

It was about twenty minutes later when Dasher made his arrival in the ER. All the chaos of the room with drunks shouting, gang members bleeding, and old women crying over their loved ones looked out of place in contrast to Dasher's gallant entrance. It reminded Jack of a slow-motion close-up in a romantic comedy movie.

Jack folded his arms and looked at Anita, then back to Dasher as he made his way through the ER. She followed the focus of his gaze through the crowd to the star performer and began to laugh. Not the restrained melodic laughter that Jack had heard throughout the day, but a real, genuine, raucous howl.

Dasher Clay had been having sex with some woman earlier, but still took the time to shave, lotion his face, and style his hair before coming down. His scrubs looked like they had been pressed. None of this was lost on Anita.

She whispered before Dasher was within earshot, "Dudley Do-right, indeed." She said in Jack's ear. "Butt-chin and all." She glanced down at his watch, which she had gently turned upward to read. Jack found his heart racing every time she touched him.

"As a woman, I can tell you, getting that look together in just fifteen or twenty minutes isn't easy. All things considered, he deserves applause for speed." She chuckled.

"Okay, Wheaton, what's the emergency?" Dasher said in that golden tenor voice full of undertones. He smiled when he saw Anita at Jack's side. Dasher actually spread his legs, put his fists on his hips, crinkled his forehead, and looked side to side for the patient.

Jack pointed to the gurney bearing their patient, and Dasher marched over to her side.

Jack bent down and whispered to Anita, "All he needs is a red cape and a letter on his chest."

She nodded agreement. Jack never got tired of the sound of that laugh.

"I'll need a 22-gauge 1 inch angiocath, betadine and a two by two gauze pad," he said to Anita with one eyebrow cocked while twirling a half used roll of paper tape around his index finger as he spoke.

"You can find it on that cart right there, little lady." He pointed to the supply cart in the hall.

Anita turned and retrieved the requested supplies without objection.

Dasher accepted them, picked and prepped his entry site, and got right to work starting the I.V. He placed the angiocath in a vein in Mrs. Harker's left forearm. Dasher made a point of commenting that Jack had already blown most of the veins in her right arm.

Dasher looked over his shoulder at Anita and smiled a sideways smile. Hooking the tubing attached to the bag of saline to the catheter, he turned and said like a movie hero, "Now tape that down before we lose this one too."

Anita put on the sincerest expression of sympathy she could muster as she pointed twice at the I.V. site. Dasher turned to see his handiwork expand into a big purple bruise as he opened the stopcock on the tubing.

"Shit!" he said. "She has veins like wet tissue paper."

"So, what do we do now?" Anita asked.

"Now, you and I get started putting in an EJ to IJ."
He said without losing an ounce of confidence.

"External jugular to internal jugular?" she exclaimed. "Cool!"

"We'll run a Swan-Gantz catheter through it when
we're done to monitor her volume status. " Go get me a kit
from Central Supply, will you?"

Anita took off like a shot to get the central line tray.

"Nice girl, Wheaton," he said, watching Anita
bounce down the hall. "She new?"

"She's new and very smart, Clay. Not your type,"
Jack said. "I don't need her distracted."

"I do smart girls, too," Dasher said with a snicker.

"She's off limits." Jack planted himself at 12
o'clock in Dasher's personal space. "Am I being clear?"

Dasher stood a good four inches taller than Jack, but
he had a lot invested in that face of his, and he knew Jack
had the potential to do it some damage. His brother Mark,
working with some of his black ops buddies, taught Jack a
few survival moves, Special Forces style, and it came in
handy. That little adventure the brothers shared in Lebanon
led to a fine mess. It was really no more than a skirmish
with some locals over the honor of a belly dancer. He and
his friends got out of that one with a few bloody lips, but no
one died on either side. All the same, it had become the
stuff of urban legend around Hamilton.

Dasher stared down at Jack and backed off a foot or
two. "Fine, fine. I'm only playing, Wheaton." Then he tried
to laugh it off. "I don't want your little girlfriend."

"Yeah, Dasher, that's the problem. You're always
just playing. You better take some of these women more
seriously before you get hurt. They're not all pushovers."

"I don't have time for the ones who aren't," Dasher
said with a salute. He backed his way between the gurneys,
turned, and disappeared through the double doors to exit
the ER. "Call me when your little girl gets back, huh?"

Anita couldn't have missed him by more than 30 or 40 seconds as she returned with the central line kit.

Jack thought of how many different movie endings in which he would have liked to see Dasher Clay meet his demise. Shaking his head, he pulled at Anita's free arm to get her out of the traffic of the paramedics removing some of the empty gurneys.

"Let's get her into one of these rooms and set up the central line material." He directed Anita to a room labeled #2. "I'll wheel her in, you set down the kit before someone else claims that room. Call up to the unit and order a Swann-Gantz catheter to the bedside for when we get there."

It was already past 9:00 p.m., and Anita still seemed to have plenty of energy.

"Long first day, huh?" Jack said. It was just short of an apology. He should have been able to start the I.V. himself.

Jack broke protocol and paged Dasher overhead. He wanted to draw attention to the son-of-a-bitch, wherever he was and whatever he was up to. He called Jack back on his cell phone, which Jack allowed to ring four or five times before deciding to answer it.

"Clay," he answered without asking for the caller's identity. "We're in room 2 in the ER. Everything's here." Jack waited for his acknowledgement of their preparedness before hanging up.

Dasher opened the door to room #2 eight minutes later. Jack said nothing to him. Dasher spoke directly to Anita.

"Okay, so, Anita isn't it?" he asked, "Have you ever started a central line before?"

"No," she lied. "But that I did assist on a couple as a student."

"Let's select our site. Now, usually we'd choose a subclavian approach, but as your chief has explained, she's full of rat poison." He alluded to the Coumadin used to thin her blood. "So, we'll have to pick an insertion point that allows us to maintain hemostasis in case of any bleeding complications." He glanced silently at Jack. "Of course, there's little chance of that with an experienced physician performing the procedure."

He returned his attention to Anita, smiling and prattled on in teaching mode. "Still, caution is the better part of valor, isn't it? Besides, you need to learn as many helpful techniques as you can. Even if you never get a chance to use them, you'll always know where to go for expertise."

Anita accepted the advice graciously, but Jack thought he detected signs that her patience was wearing thin with this jackass, too.

"So, we find the external jugular in the anterolateral root of the neck and tilt her into a little reverse Trendelenberg position to get the EJ to engorge with blood, you see?"

Dasher was a good showman. He pressed the stretcher's pedal to tip the head of the table down as he spoke.

"We insert with gentle, even pressure and follow the external jugular to the bifurcation with the internal jugular, then give the catheter a little torque to make the detour into the Internal Jugular vein. Always make sure your angiocath is long enough, at least two inches. There's nothing more disappointing than getting on top of one of these babies and not having enough length to get the job done." He cracked one of his annoying, sarcastic smiles at Jack, then turned it towards Anita.

She responded with a noise that sounded more as if she was clearing her throat. Jack was glad she hadn't shared her musical laugh with Dasher.

When he was done, Dasher said, "Once you get blood return, you can technically use the catheter for whatever you need." He smiled a cautioning smile. "Technically. You want to confirm placement by X-ray first. Why don't you two roll her over to radiology and let me know how she looks? Call me when you're done, but not overhead. It's bad form around here. You shouldn't pick up bad habits so early in your career."

As Dasher was leaving, Anita deliberately let him get out into the main hall of the ER then said, "Thanks for showing me how impressive two inches can be, Dr. Clay." She waved. He scowled as the innuendo sank in. He ducked out of the ER without another word or smile.

Jack found himself grinning at Anita's sense of humor again.

They got Miss Polly cleaned up and covered her with a clean sheet. Jack steered and Anita pushed the gurney to radiology. There was no one else ahead of them, so they were able to get their patient right in for her films. Ten minutes later, they were in the viewing room searching for her films.

Hamilton used the old-fashioned portable machine and processors for the ER instead of the new digital equipment used in the main hospital. The board of directors didn't believe in wasting a thing. The lights were kept low for the comfort of the radiologist, who read images in the dark for hours at a time.

He set the X-rays on the light box and went through the anatomy with Anita. She quickly suppressed a yawn and apologized for it.

"You should be sorry," Jack said. "Those things are contagious, you know?"

She giggled, then turned back to the film.

"What have we here, central line placement?" Without turning, Jack recognized the same sultry voice that answered for Dasher Clay earlier that evening.

Stormi Seales was the radiology resident on call. Her claim to fame was that she had been a one-time swimsuit model while in med school. Most of the male house-staff had Googled her pictures at least once.

She was impressive. Her breasts were natural and shapely, but just a little too big to secure a successful modeling career, it had been said. Most of the male residents would disagree.

She rubbed her index finger at the catheter insertion in confusion. "There's a funny kink in the catheter. You should consider replacing it." She frowned.

It seemed to Jack that radiologists had little regard for the effort or risk involved in performing invasive procedures.

"It's an EJ to IJ insertion. Our patient is on Coumadin." Anita told her, pride billowing up in her voice. "Neat procedure, actually."

Just for fun, Jack added, "Dasher Clay showed her how. He's an excellent hands-on teacher, you know?"

Stormi's frown deepened, and she looked at Anita. "Be careful about emulating bad techniques. They tend to stick with you for a long time, doctor."

"Huh, that's funny. Dr. Clay warned me in not-so-many words of the same exact thing half an hour ago."

Anita knew just why she got the cold shoulder from a fellow female resident and enjoyed a private little smirk. Jack knew, too, and he loved it.

Jack and Anita got through the rest of the night with few problems. Anita floated the Swann-Gantz catheter to the right half of Mrs. Harker's heart like she had done it a hundred times before. They wrote the ICU admission note together, and Jack dictated it. She waited for him and they paged the long call residents.

Jack Wheaton's Blue team signed out to Yellow team run by Jody Mazur. It had to be at least 11:30 pm when they finally got outside. Warm July night. Word was it was blistering hot earlier that day, but they had both been trapped in the air-conditioned prison called Hamilton Medical Center.

The Nor'easter had blown in and nipped about fifteen degrees off the day's high. Then there were those stars and a new moon. Off duty, and time to go home for the first time since they met, Jack escorted Anita to the front door of the hospital. He asked her how she was getting home, intending to get her to come out for a late bite, when she dropped the bomb on him.

"My boyfriend is on his way to meet me at the front doors, Jack," she said. "But thanks anyway."

Jack felt like kicking himself. He didn't know why he thought a woman as amazing as that was alone. Maybe it was that she was new to the city. Maybe he thought it was his irresistibly scintillating personality, but what it obviously was, was just wistful thinking.

Jack nodded in deference, "If you like, I'll just wait with you until her boyfriend arrives."

She nodded toward the security guard five feet from where they were standing. Jack understood. He bowed out, made his way to the MARTA station up the street, and headed home.

# Chapter 13: Ghosts of the Past

The next morning Al arrived three minutes before Anita.

"So how did the night go, Jack?" he asked, spinning a chair under him to sit.

"Oh, not too bad, all things considered," Jack told him. His muscles were still aching all over. "The only wrinkle we had was that dried up prune, Polly Harker. Pulled out her I.V. after you left."

"So that's why you called me back, huh?" Al said nodding.

"We had to call in Dasher Clay to get access."

He let Al connect the dots. He knew how Jack felt about Dasher.

Al just whistled. "That sucks. How was he?"

"He was Dasher Clay." Jack shrugged. "He's banging Stormi Seales. Or at least he was before we interrupted them to start the central line."

"Stormi Seales? Seriously?" Al asked. "Lucky bastard. She's like a centerfold, isn't she?"

"You mean you haven't seen her photo shoots?"

"I heard the rumors. Everyone talks about it but no one ever tells me where to look."

"I'll have to send you the link," Jack promised.

"Wait, did you say central line?" Al asked, the medical aspects of last night's drama catching up to him. "Why did Dasher drop a central line? Did she crump on you?"

"He blew her last peripheral site." Jack snickered.

"That must have messed with his ego a bit."

"It doesn't show when he has an audience to teach."

"Anita?" Al asked.

"Anita."

"Well, how did our star intern handle him?" Al was eager to hear this one.

Unfortunately, they heard their Dr. Thomas making her way down the hall to the office, greeting the nurses at the station around the corner.

"I'll tell you later, Al, but it was beautiful, man."

They cut their guy talk short and planned rounds. They couldn't actually start them because they had Morning Report. Jack reviewed their write-ups on the new admissions. He was peeved because his dictated admission note on Polly Harker had not been transcribed yet.

He hated it when the transcriptionists ran behind. The attendings got restless and asked a bunch of unnecessary and useless questions when they couldn't follow the case easily. They started teaching ad nauseum. So Jack called down to the third floor and asked the supervisor for a draft copy which he manually corrected, hole-punched, and placed on the chart himself.

He coached Al and Anita on their patients in the 5A office and then they trotted off to Morning Report. It was just on the second floor and the chief resident was presiding.

In the department of medicine, the chief resident was more like an attending physician. Fred Albright was their chief that year and he was good. Not just in cardiology, he was one of the brightest medical residents they'd had in years. As a senior resident, Fred was Jack's hero when he had been an intern.

They all respected Fred even though they called him by his first name, unlike the other full-time faculty. If you did an honest job with your work, he wouldn't beat you up too much. He knew what you'd been through.

On the other hand, if you were a slacker, look out. When he finished with you, you went back to your floor feeling like you'd been ridden hard and put away wet.

Morning Report was usually held in classrooms just like the one they were in this morning. It had an old wooden desk with years of useless junk piled in its drawers that no one ever looked at or bothered to remove.

The attending usually stole a secretarial chair from the nearest nursing station for comfort and moved the old wooden chair back into a corner somewhere. Rank had its privileges.

The call services sat in a semi-circle around Albright's desk. A worn metal chart rack sat beside it with nineteen charts. Seven were from Blue team but the bulk was from the two long call teams. They went first.

When it was Jack's team's turn to present that day, Fred seemed to focus exclusively on Anita. She seemed to be everybody's focus, but Jack thought there was something strange about his interaction with her. At first, Jack thought the motive might have been racism, but that would have been out of character for Fred.

Fred probed her a lot for an intern, though. Anita handled herself well and confidently. Again, she didn't miss a trick, and it wasn't Jack's coaching that got her through either.

*I'd have missed some of the questions he threw at her.* Jack thought.

After Morning Report, Fred pulled Anita to a corner and spoke discreetly to her before blue team reconvened for rounds. Dr. Wesley Hargrove, chairman of the department of medicine, joined the quiet little conversation.

Hargrove spoke with a level of respect usually reserved for professor level colleagues, while Fred nodded deferentially to Anita. The two faculty members left Anita's side before Jack could get close enough to hear. He didn't like anyone picking on his interns, not even faculty.

He asked, "Everything all right, Anita?"

"Yes, of course, you prepared me well," she said.

"I didn't prepare you *that* well, Anita. You hit it out of the park with those presentations to Dr. Albright."

"I did a little research online when I got home last night. You inspired me, Jack."

For the first time, Jack felt like she was playing him. No, not for any obsequious, academic reasons, but she was hiding something somehow. And it seemed everyone knew she was brilliant, but she seemed to downplay her smarts too much, as if she were somehow ashamed of her intellect. Jack hadn't figured her out yet, but it was at that moment that he decided, *Come hell or high water, I will.*

They finally started rounds. Jack started them with Al's patients. They were watering down one of his two alcoholics from the night before. Al had pulled his labs for review. Most of them were back, but a few were still pending.

"He's looking better," Jack said to Al at the bedside.

The patient was nursing a nasty hangover. Al had started the alcohol withdrawal prevention protocol: betablockers, Diazepam, and lots of fluids.

Jack spoke in a loud voice to make sure the patient was paying attention. The loud noises made the patient wince, which was okay. Jack didn't want him to get too comfortable anyway.

"You're doing much better, Mr. Di MariniDi Marini. How's the nausea this morning?" he asked.

They had pumped him full of Phenergan and omeprazole. As long as he hadn't developed pancreatitis, he'd be improving by leaps and bounds.

"Get me some food, will ya? I'm starving ova' here!" Di MariniDi Marini held his head in misery, not pain.

Di Marini didn't make eye contact when he spoke. Jack raised his head a little gently, nudging his chin upward. He shook the hand free of his face. Al knew the drill. He turned on the lights.

Di Marini shunned away. "Turn off that damn light."

Jack gently took his head and rolled it from side to side shadowing his eyes from the fluorescent light.

"Al, did we scan his head last night?" Jack worried about an intracranial bleed.

"Sure did. Tapped him too, just to be sure." Al said indicating that he performed the lumbar puncture.

"Any blood?" Jack asked still eying his patient suspiciously.

"Boss," Al responded in a wounded tone. "Is there ever any blood on my LPs?"

"Sorry, Al. I had to ask."

Al smiled triumphantly.

"Mr. Di Marini, are you hungry?" Jack shouted.

"Hell yeah, I'm hungry. What have I been sayin' all night? You're killin' me here," Di Marini complained.

Jack nodded to Al and he disappeared into the hall.

"Where are you from, Mr. Di Marini?" Anita had moved up to the bedside and into Di Marini's view for the first time. His manner softened.

"I was born and raised in Brooklyn, but I lived in Boston for the past ten years before endin' up here. You know Boston, babe?" he asked her.

That was more information than any of the staff had ever gotten out of him in months of frequent flying through the ER

"Yes, I lived there for a while. You know Beacon Street?" she asked.

"Do I know Beacon Street? What're you, kidding me? That's a pretty swanky part of town there." He beamed. "Your folks musta' had some dough to live there!"

"It was a loaner while I was... doing some work up there," she said.

Jack noticed that self-deprecating tone that had bothered him earlier.

"I'm originally from Long island, New York. You know Centerville?" She tried to change the subject.

"As I said, you must come from money. That berg ain't bad either. You sound like you already made it." He smiled at Jack and Al, who had just walked in with a lunch bag for him. He reached for it around Jack and Anita. A tattoo showed from under his sleeve that looked familiar to Jack.

"So why you wearin' the short coat like these losers?"

By convention, anyone from medical student to resident wore a short, white coat. Subspecialty fellows and attendings wore long coats. Most of the regulars noticed the ranking after a while. Even the drunks knew Anita was something special.

Di Marini ate voraciously. This was their opening to listen to his lungs, heart, and abdomen between bites. Al and Jack tag teamed him examining different organ systems. They finished their exam before Di Marini finished his breakfast.

They backed out of his room, but it was Anita that he invited back. Down the hall, Jack tossed the team a few words of wisdom as they walked briskly to the next patient.

"When you have an alcoholic admitted to your service, it's usually for one of four reasons: Keto-acidosis with electrolyte imbalance; Infection, usually aspiration pneumonia; Acute coronary syndrome, or closed head injury with altered mental status. On the latter, you tune them up and turf them to neurosurgery," he said.

Jack sounded very officious when he was teaching. They all did.

"Why do we do what we do here, Anita?" he asked. Jack pointed back up the hall toward Di Marini's room without turning to face her.

"Well, the yellow bag is full of water soluble vitamins, electrolytes and sugar in the form of dextrose," she answered. "Al described your withdrawal protocol with beta blockers and benzos. At Mass General, we used Librium. It works quicker and is shorter acting if the patient's sensorium is in question. We didn't feed them in-house either. We gave them a voucher through Social Services and sent them to a soup kitchen near a shelter. The hospital saved a lot of money that way too," she finished.

"That has some merit, it has some merit," Jack conceded, half turning now to acknowledge her opinion. "We use Valium so that our guys don't go into Rum Fits in the middle of the night if the nursing staff is too busy to pass the medications on time.

"They're overworked as it is and it really gets crazy around here. You'll see. Valium lasts longer and is less sedating. We feed them because protein will keep an alcoholic out of alcoholic ketoacidosis for longer than sugar will. It's also a diagnostic test. Sometimes amylase and lipase levels don't come back by the time the patient is stable. If he can eat and keep down food, he doesn't have pancreatitis. He is alert enough to swallow without choking and he can go home, or wherever his wobbly legs can carry him."

"As long as it's not here," Al added.

Jack smiled at Al's comment without verbally acknowledging it. Most residents felt that way about drunks, but they didn't want to come off as insensitive.

Jack didn't see it as hypocritical. Battlefield humor. Gets you through the days and nights—and the deaths, which were inevitable.

"A goody-bag with a sandwich and bag of potato chips is cheaper than a swallowing study, an additional day in the hospital, or changing an I.V. site and hanging another bag of fluids even at full wide open rate," Jack said.

"What you don't do is what they do over at St. Frances Hospital. Don't make the food too good. We give one slice of bologna on dry bread, one slice of American

cheese, no mayonnaise, no mustard, no ketchup. Plain potato chips and bottled water is better than a second bag of
normalized saline rich fluids. We give them a generic 8 oz.
bottle of water, room temperature unless the patient has a
fever. The cool water allows us to get a lower body temperature reading if we think it's a minor matter and we've
checked them out for the major causes of infection. No des-
sert. They get their sugar I.V. so they can't enjoy it. Then
we send the social worker to them. Always drop that consult in their box in the ER so it's there waiting for them in
the morning. Social services usually start their rounds about
10:00 am and arrive at the bedsides after we've seen the patients and tuned them up a bit. They'll put the nix on a
discharge if the patient has a fever. Make sure the nursing
support team gives him a good shower, gets him to brush
his teeth—or tooth, and comb his hair. They're really good
at coaxing these guys to do the right thing, at least as far as
personal hygiene's concerned. Always keep your floor's
social worker's pager number on you. If a stable patient is
not on the launching pad by 1:30 pm, you need to be on the
phone finding out why."

"Where's Polly Harker, Anita?" Jack asked, looking
at his list.

"Five-A ICU, Jack. I think she can step down to te-
lemetry though. She looked pretty good this morning."

They rounded the corner toward the elevator when
someone called out of a room, "Professor Thomas?"

Anita stopped short. Her face went pale and she
turned to deal with the developing situation.

"Hold on a minute, guys," she said.

She held up her hands indicating that she wanted to
handle this encounter alone. Privately.

Jack felt the hairs stand up on the nape of his neck.
He sure as hell was not going to let her off the hook. He
turned right around and followed her into the patient's
room.

"Mrs. Holcomb? What are you doing here?" she asked, grimacing as Jack and Al followed her.

Helen Holcomb was a late middle-aged woman, moderately obese, "a little more than pleasantly plump," as Jack's mother might have said.

"Dr. Thomas! It's so good to see you. I told you and your residents I was from Atlanta when I entered the study," Mrs. Holcomb reminded her.

She spoke with a native Georgia accent, well-educated and cultured. Southern society, privileged.

Anita said nothing to Jack or Al, but addressed the patient directly. "I thought you were all better."

"I was. I was." She beamed. "For six months after the treatment, I was completely and utterly pain free! That experimental treatment was the best thing I've ever had. I had energy, focus, stamina back to normal. I was great, I tell you."

Anita looked back at Jack and Al sheepishly, and then asked the obvious question. "Then, what happened?"

"I don't know, Dr. Thomas; about three months ago, I started having seizures. They called them partial seizures, but they were random. The neurologists say partial seizures usually have a focus, but mine seem to… migrate." Mrs. Holcomb rubbed her head. "Odd."

She adjusted her hospital gown when she saw Jack and Al appear from behind Anita. Al obviously made her uncomfortable. Although he was lighter than Anita, Al was clearly black and Mrs. Holcomb didn't know what to make of Jack with his blonde hair and deep summer tan.

"The seizures don't respond to gabapentin either." She looked at Al and Jack. "That's an anti-seizure medication, you know." She whispered.

"Yes ma'am, we know what gabapentin is," Jack said calmly. "What treatment did you get? I mean, what was it for and all?"

"For fibromyalgia syndrome of course. I was one of the ten thousand Fibro patients that were randomized to that FMDS drug." She looked at Anita. "They finished the Fame Days study after you left and I found out that I was in the active arm all along," she said proudly. "Of course, I already knew I was because I felt so good all year."

She saddened for a moment. "Poor Annie. You remember Ann, don't you? We often rode in together."

"Yes, ma'am. I remember her. How is she doing?" Anita asked, now oblivious to her teammates, in pure clinician mode, getting a compassionate history from the patient.

Helen Holcomb appeared grief stricken at the question.

"Well, poor Ann. She was in the pesio, plesio…?"

"The placebo arm?" Jack suggested.

"Yes. That. She had the sugar pill or sugar water as it were. Well, at eight months, they revealed who had been on what and allowed a crossover? Yes, a crossover to the active agent. I was so happy for her. She was going to get the relief that I had been getting."

"Mrs. Holcomb, there was no guarantee that she would respond to FMDS400 as you did. It was experimental. Nothing works in Fibromyalgia Syndrome more than 60% of the time anyway," Anita advised her, but Jack thought it more for his benefit than Mrs. Holcomb's.

"Oh, dear. I guess you didn't hear. After you left, they told us the good news. Every one of us who took the active drug achieved 100% remission of symptoms. We were all getting the drug every month for free at the Crawford Research Center. That's at Nordstrom Clinic in Boston. It's world famous you know," she said, again for the benefit of Jack and Al. Mrs. Holcomb was beginning to annoy them with that condescending tone of hers.

"Yes, ma'am. We all know where the Nordstrom Clinic is. Highly respected Ivy League institution, right up there on University Row with Harvard and MIT," Jack told her.

"I'm sure Professor Thomas has taught you well. You are so lucky to have her as your instructor," she said.

Anita interrupted. "That was a long time ago and a different circumstance, Mrs. Holcomb. Here, I'm an intern in medicine and this is my resident, my supervisor."

"Oh, well, that is different. I didn't know you could go backward in medicine," she said, puzzled.

"Whose service are you on here, Mrs. Holcomb?" Jack asked.

"Neurology, doctor...?"

"Wheaton, Jack Wheaton, Mrs. Holcomb. I'm the senior resident on the service. The Medicine service." Jack nodded to her and began to lead his team out of the room. He realized they were clearly intruding on another team's patient.

"Al," he said. "Check and see if there is a Medicine consultation request on the chart here for Mrs. Holcomb. If she is having a drug reaction, it needs to be reported and managed."

"Jack," Anita pleaded. "I'm sure the Neuro guys can handle..."

"Dr. Thomas, as you are obviously involved, you may have a conflict here. I don't want you directly involved if we're asked for assistance, do you understand?"

It was the most formal he had been since he took over the blue team. It didn't feel good to take that tone with either Anita or Al. Instinct told him that he had to somehow.

Before leaving the room, Jack added, "By the way Mrs. Holcomb, how did you 'know' that your friend would respond to the experimental drug?"

"Oh, dear." She peered over at Anita again, now averting her eyes to the sheet covering her lap. "Once, Ann and I switched bags as we passed at the bathroom. The nurses didn't notice. We switched back again after the fluids were all out to avoid getting caught when they did the final check out and accounted for the bags by number. I'm sorry Dr. Thomas, I just wanted Ann to get better like I did."

"Why do you keep referring to Ann in the past tense, Mrs. Holcomb?" Al asked.

Helen Holcomb became tearful. "Annie died, Doctor. She had a seizure while driving on the I-95. Hit a solid stone wall at 55 miles an hour they estimate. Nothing in her way, no one else hurt. Another motorist claimed she was shaking with her tongue hanging out of her mouth looking sidelong right at him when she failed to follow the curve of the highway as he did."

"Thank you, Mrs. Holcomb." Jack said, as he glared at Anita. She was looking down at her feet by then, not at him, Al, or Mrs. Holcomb.

They left Mrs. Holcomb's room in single file, Anita bringing up the rear.

"Polly Harker, guys." Jack turned toward the ICU without another word to either intern.

# Chapter 14: A Well Woven Web

She laid an unmarked folder on the desk before the vice chief of rheumatology and smiled knowingly at him. Dr. Robert Lee picked it up and glanced at the red head before leafing through it for a moment.

"This Anita Thomas isn't just a young trainee straight out of medical school, that much is clear." Lucy said watching Dr. Lee flip through the file.

His guest stood at ease two steps into the room, as she had still not been invited to sit. She wore a fitted, frost gray two-piece suit, jacket open.

"Somehow, Dr. Thomas had built a career before Hamilton," she said. "The notion that so young a woman could have gotten to professorial rank to begin with is highly improbable, but to do all of that and then start all over again as a lowly intern without losing her mind? Unbelievable."

Dr. Lee looked up at her. "So is she an imposter?" he asked. "But usually, candidates for internships are trying to play *up* their accomplishments not trying to deny them."

He eyed the woman carefully now.

"Why are you bringing this to me Ms. Velasquez?" He asked. "Credentialing fraud should go to the chairman."

"My boss came by this information indirectly. Accidentally. He wasn't sure of what to do with it." She moved closer to him. Lucy placed her hands on the desk near the folder, looking at Dr. Lee as he studied the dossier. He noticed the shear eggplant blouse, as he inhaled her cologne. They were less than two feet apart.

"He didn't want to jeopardize Glazer Corp's relationship with Hamilton Medical's administration." She shrugged. "Fraud's a serious matter."

She sat on the edge of his desk and crossed her legs. Dr. Lee's eyes followed the fluid motion of flawless, stockinged legs up to the mid-thigh hem of her skirt.

"Pharma should never be involved in that kind of whistle blower thing." Bracing her arms against the surface beneath her, she relaxed her lean torso. "At least that's what's my boss, Orson, says."

"Orson?"

"Orson Quirk, regional director for Glazer Corp's field reps." She said. "He says this mess just fell into his lap."

She fondled a decorative pen extending obliquely from its desktop cradle. "I just thought you might be far enough out of the loop to be clear of these… escapades?" She caressed an antique Korean letter opener from the same set and turned the black porcelain handle in her long fingers tipped in plum colored polish. Lucy appraised the Korean artwork adorning the walls behind Lee.

"Nice," she said with a nod. "*Daisho*." The word purred as a sexy husk in her throat as her gaze settled on the paired long and short swords behind him.

"Do you speak Japanese, Ms. Velasquez?" he asked surprised.

"Not much. Orson is almost an authority on feudal Japanese culture, though." She continued in the same tone, "But I've always found the long blade profoundly appealing."

"This dagger is the matching *tonto* of the set." He said as he tapped its place on the desk.

"Snow Tigers." Lucy said examining the handles, "Those characters are Korean, though. I wasn't aware that there were Korean Samurai?"

"Family heirloom. A token of appreciation for my ancestors' cooperation with the Shogun one hundred years ago." He smiled. "One of a kind."

"Can I meet this *Orson*, Ms. Velasquez?" Dr. Lee asked. He absently twisted the gold band on his ring finger, then gestured to retrieve the antique blade.

Lucy dragged her fingers gently across his as he took the item, her face affecting a look of woe. Lee seemed to consider her touch before replacing the letter opener.

"I'll arrange it," she said with a nod that unfettered fronds of hair loose from behind her ears. Leaning forward, Lucy extended a hand inviting Dr. Lee to help her off the desk. He inclined his head slightly to inhale her essence as the tresses brushed his face. She held his gaze as he did so and bade him goodbye.

Lucy strode out of the room with the confidence of a woman who knew she held a man's attention when she made an exit. She didn't have to look back to know it.

By 11:45am, Jack decided it was time for lunch. Looking at the schedule on the medicine department office door, he patted his wallet. *Looks like I can save a few bucks today.* The next meal was on the house: *Drug lunch.*

A 'drug lunch' allowed pharmaceutical representatives to provide lunch and get a chance to tout their products to the house staff. This one was a combination anti-hypertensive and lipid lowering agent of some sort. The second floor conference room was in the old south wing of the hospital. Large with a dropped ceiling and off white walls that should have just been left unpainted for all the contrast with the bare sheet rock of the walls. Scuffmarks and fingerprints gave the chamber the look of a warehouse or loading dock.

"Who's the host?" Jack asked. He entered the room still empty except for the caterers unpacking thermal bags and the familiar house officer, which Jack now addressed.

Sam Reardon arrived far enough ahead of Jack and his team to wolf down half a slice of pizza already. Sam was an emergency medicine resident. He wore a dirty blonde ponytail down to his shoulders and neatly cut beard that he kept at a length thirty-six hours longer than 5 o'clock shadow.

"Glazer Corp." Sam mumbled, mouth full. "Don't know which rep, she's not here yet."

Jack nodded. "Get it while it's hot, huh?" He sized up the food supply and estimated there was enough for twenty residents if everyone had two slices and two bottles of water.

"What are they selling?"

Sam cleared his mouth before speaking this time. "Nothing we use down in the ER."

"Cost of doing business, bud. We get federal and state funds, a break on malpractice insurance and subsidized salaries." Jack laughed, "If you can call them salaries." He piled a slice on a Styrofoam plate. "In exchange, we show restraint in spending charitable dollars on poor folk."

"And we get to show our high ethical standards and resist great bribes to boot." Sam raised his plate in salute, a second slice still steaming there, "Don't forget the perks, Jack."

"The generics are pretty good, though, you have to admit." Jack said. "In spite of—"

The verbal traffic stopped dead upon the arrival of their hostess. The two men were riveted by the woman casting the polite, Mona Lisa smile their way. She set her tablet computer up for her references to the young attendants. Many of the newer drugs were restricted to senior residents, fellows, and faculty. These sessions were used to teach the interns and medical students about different drug classes. The residents and fellows showed off their medical knowledge a bit.

The lunch cuisine was never very interesting. There was a concern that too indulgent a menu might sway young impressionable doctors' decisions. The reps brought in pizza or sandwiches or something. They didn't even bring cold sodas anymore, just bottled water.

The real attraction was the drug reps themselves. Most of those sent to Hamilton were what Jack would describe as *hotties*. Inexperienced, though. It's where new reps came to cut their teeth. Much like the residents they came to engage, hospital pharmaceutical reps were sharp, talented, and right out of training. Uniformly great looking women almost exclusively under the age of twenty-eight. The other constant was the reality that each was in perfect shape, some of which was surgically enhanced as if it were a pre-requisite.

A little older than most, thirty-two or more, stood a legendary best of the best. Her name: Luciana Velasquez. Jack had not seen her before. He nudged Sam Reardon. "What-the-Hell?"

Eyes synchronized with Jack's, Sam whispered, "Lucy Velasquez. Third generation Cuban American. Sweet cinnamon complexion you could almost smell." Sam sipped his water between words to hide his lips. "Incredibly toned, must have been a dancer sometime."

"Huh, no ring on her finger." Jack said. "Does she talk to residents?"

"That hot body doesn't even slow down for attendings." Sam shook his head. "Lucy is cold as ice.

"She never flirts, and she's strictly business. Asks appropriate questions, smiles just enough, and always knows her stuff."

"She any good at her job?" Jack asked.

"Always delivers medical literature references as requested, usually highlighted." Sam raised an eyebrow, "Great source for references on toxicology cases."

Still watching her every maneuver, Jack asked, "How long has she been coming here and how the hell did I miss her?"

Lucy was dressed to the nines, in a form fitting designer skirt suit. Pale gray with a jewel colored purple blouse. Make up and jewelry, just right. Jack's attention was at last drawn to that peculiar white forelock.

Noticing Jack's focus, Sam said, "It's natural. She never colored it. It's as much a signature feature to Lucy's appearance as Marilyn Monroe's beauty mark was to her own iconic image."

The stark flash of white was brushed down to one side and curled in contrast to her deep, red hair. When Jack's eyes drifted back to her dark eyes from the distracting stripe, they were met by a penetrating gaze, potent enough to sell him stale air.

"Hello, Dr. Wheaton." She said, extending her hand while reading his ID badge. "Luciana Velasquez. Call me Lucy."

Jack shook her hand and tried not to look as eager as he felt. Had she worn an ancient, Egyptian headdress, he could have as easily been looking through time at the smiling face of Queen Nefertiti as any modern beauty.

"So what have you to show us today, Lucy?"

"Glazenol," she said. "Our flagship drug. More than 11 billion pills sold worldwide in the past five years alone and we haven't reached our peak yet!"

"Yes, I've used your drug just this morning. We had an asthmatic with malignant hypertension. Frequent flyer. Breathing shuts down even with selective beta blockers."

"Ah, you're an R3, Dr. Wheaton, wonderful. I'm glad you can write for our drug now. I hope you put in a good word for us when it comes before the Pharmacy and Therapeutics committee this year. It could save a lot more lives.

Anita arrived before Jack could respond and greeted him before foraging for her share of the pie.

"This is one of my team members, Dr. Anita Thomas."

Jack, with a flourish of his hands, introduced the rep, "Our hostess, Lucy Velasquez, Glazer Corp."

"Doctor." Lucy shook her hand cheerily as Anita offered a hello and sincere thanks for the lunch.

Another dozen house officers filed into the room and filled it with a rising murmur before Dr. Fred Albright entered to greet the Glazer rep on behalf of the faculty.

Most of the men found some way to work a personal angle on the drug's erectile dysfunction issue into the conversation. Somehow, each one of them seemed to think he came up with such original lines related to his own sexual endurance. Lucy never flinched or blushed. She just told it like it statistically was, and moved on to the next topic.

The chief resident, Fred Albright, always made time to speak with her about the hospital's needs. He recognized her for her real strength, industrial influence, and resourcefulness.

Anita noticed the professionalism and dedication of the chief resident. She folded her arms, *Now that is how a gentleman conducts himself.* Lest she allow the male of the species redeem too much respect, the voice from the door behind her heralded the contrasting mores of Dr. Dasher Clay

Dasher edged up to Lucy. "Ms. Velasquez. Where have you been?" His hands moved independently of his conversation to score a free slice of pizza while he hit on the Rep. "I haven't seen you for months."

"Hello, Dr. Clay." Lucy responded without looking at him. "I'm so happy you could make it to a department of medicine meeting."

"Wouldn't miss it for the world. Ours are so boring." Dasher said mouth full of pizza. He shrugged, "So?"

She smiled politely and sighed. "I spent three weeks in Fiji."

Dasher stopped chewing and stared. Jack was in earshot of the comment and stopped his chewing, too.

Lucy recognized the intensity of the attention trained on her. "It was on the company; all expenses paid." Lucy spread her hands wide before the table. "We moved a lot of Glazenol last year. I wish I could provide more than just a few pizza pies in appreciation."

Somehow, many of the residents' faces grimaced as if the pizza had just turned sour in their mouths.

Glancing at the naked left third finger, Anita asked, "Your boyfriend must enjoy those long vacations."

"Who has time for a boyfriend?" Lucy asked. "I'm in meeting after meeting, week after week. Granted, in some of the nicest hotels in the world, but still it's no picnic." She drifted through the stream of young doctors now crowding the lunch table to close in on Anita. "No matter how the cage is gilded, it's definitely *work,* you know?"

Lucy stood in front of Anita as she ate. She had finished her single slice after plucking the pepperoni off and discarding the little meat discs onto the plate beside her. Lucy had her cornered between a wall and one of the cardboard boxes many of the residents used as make-shift tables.

Swooping in between them, Dasher Clay continued his lusty pursuit. "I can't believe that you're alone, Lucy." Dasher grinned that killer grin, hooked an arm under hers and led her reluctantly to a neutral corner. "So some guy hasn't snatched you up yet?"

"No. Not yet," she said politely. "I'm sure my time will come."

Jack had been engaged in medical small talk with Fred Albright, who having satisfied his social obligation to the pharmaceutical sponsor, made his exit. Lucy sat back in the chair vacated by Fred. Showing nearly too much smooth skin, she crossed her legs. The motion caught Jack's attention again. Sam Reardon returned just in time to catch Jack's indiscretion. The two residents walked off to a safe distance as Dasher pursued his quarry.

"That's just all kinds of wrong." Jack murmured. "Stormi and this chick, too?" he said shaking his head.

"The ER nurses call her 'the Countess'." Sam told him. "Had the house staff thinking she was some kind of European royalty. Looks like she was cut right out of a 1950s Hollywood casting call." Sam laughed, "All the guys were disappointed when she had just a touch of a southern drawl when she parted her lips, not a hint of an accent."

He nudged Jack, "In any case, she's way out of Dasher's class as a potential plaything. Word is that she has a condo in Buckhead.

"Damn. Fiji, Buckhead?" Jack whispered, "How much does she make? She must sell a shit load of Glazerol."

"She admitted that she had also lived in Boston, D.C., 'Frisco, and London." Sam droned on, "Maybe Chi Town too, no one at Hamilton knows for sure."

"Not *My-jami*?" Lucy turned to look at Jack as he spoke the name with the fake Spanish accent as if she heard him. Jack looked embarrassed that he found it strange she might never have lived in Miami.

"Maybe a little stereotypical," Sam answered. "But a Cubana who didn't know Miami? For all of her globe-trotting, she never mentions Florida at all."

She watched as the doctors ate their slices and sipped their chilled water while they chatted among themselves. Lucy never did eat what she brought in for them.

Residents were perched around the conference table, which never had enough room for all of them at the same time. Some house staff, usually the interns, were relegated to the floor or unpacked cardboard boxes. It was quiet except for hushed conversations related to medical plans for the rest of the day.

It took a few minutes to slip away from Dasher's pursuit, but Lucy wound her way around to Anita again. She never showed much interest in any of the other female

113

residents or attendings. Most of the employees of Hamilton Medical suspected that Lucy had a boyfriend or secret husband somewhere, but now at least Jack was beginning to think maybe Lucy went the other way. She just looked overly interested in Anita for his tastes.

Jack wondered if Lucy heard about Anita's research background. Maybe Anita did research for Glazer Pharmaceuticals, he didn't know. To his knowledge, Lucy didn't have a Fibro drug in her company pipeline. Anti-hypertensives, lipid-lowering drugs, prescription strength antioxidants, some lab assays, innocuous stuff from the **DNA** corporate standpoint.

Jack spied Al in the hall through the open door. He waved to beckon him in, but realized that all the pizza was gone. Al was engrossed in a conversation with someone Jack could only see glints of through bodies mulling around between him and the hallway. He made his way out to Al just in time to see his departing companion disappear through the door to the west wing of the hospital.

"Who was that?" Jack asked craning his head to see over the passers-by in the hall.

"Khandi." Al said crossing toward the conference room.

"Girl friend?" Jack asked.

Al answered with a single nod. "She had a doctor's appointment, so we met for lunch."

"She looks hot." Jack said. "Why the down-low bit?"

"It's private, Jack," Al said. "Let's drop it, okay?" He peered side to side on the lookout for prying eyes.

Al turned to look at Jack to emphasize the end of discussion then found Anita to catch up on the afternoon's plan.

Sam Reardon appeared next to Jack and whispered, "Sensitive subject. You know where they met don't you?"

Jack shook his head.

"Urology clinic." Sam raised his eyebrows. "Thursday, urology clinic four months ago."

"Thurs—oh. Transgender and Gender reassignment clinic." Jack nodded knowingly. "I didn't know Al was gay."

"Didn't used to be." Sam gestured toward the door. "Fred gave him hell about fraternizing with patients."

"I must have missed all that." Jack turned to look Sam in the eyes. "I was in Boston for my rheumatology rotation."

"Names Khandi Barr, believe it or not. Well someone in the surgery department pressured the anesthesia chief and nearly got Al kicked out when they got wind of the situation."

After comparing a few notes, Al and Anita fled up the stairs to begin afternoon rounds.

"Well, old Al stood his ground." Sam continued to elaborate as he and Jack moved into the hall. "Fred got him accepted into the medicine program, but it cost Al a year. It's why he avoids these sorts of things." Pointing back into the room.

"This Khandi must be something else," Jack said.

The residents were drifting into the hall leaving the room like locust from a barren field. The table was strewn with pizza crusts, greasy plates and empty water bottles. Most of the residents deposited the refuse in the trash. Lucy was cleaning up the pizza boxes and tying off trash bags. She didn't seem to mind the chore. When Jack, Sam and the last of the stragglers dispersed, Lucy whipped out her cell phone and pressed a single button.

"You better come on down, sir. It's confirmed—She's here."

# Chapter 15: The Ramp

The next two weeks went by quickly. Blue team's service was running smoothly. Having two really good interns was great for a supervising resident. Jack just got his reports from Al and Anita and kept the attending faculty up to date the status of the patients and the interns.

Life was paradise for the moment. The medical census was down to five or six patients so everyone on his team got to go home by 4:30 every day they were not on call. Tuck the patients in by 8 pm when on short call, do a little reading, a little chatting on social media, a little BS-ing with the team or other residents. A medical paradise it was until that four-letter word, *call*, entered the conversation.

Sam Reardon was the Emergency resident in charge of admissions this shift. He called Jack when the ambulance was still five minutes out. "Mind if we get one of your interns to take this one, Jack? My team's tied up and we'd like to get this place cleaned out by 06:30, maybe grab a quick breakfast before the next shift comes in for a change."

Any resident knew the value of staying in the good graces of the admitting resident.

"What do you have, Sam?"

"Seems this night warrior took delivery on a stat dose of lead therapy for heartburn."

"Shot in the chest," Jack summarized. Sam read the text message from the incoming ambulance.

Jack read for himself over Sam's shoulder. "Blew a hole clear through his chest, huh." Jack whistled in awe. "The crew chief says they stopped CPR when the kid stopped bleeding. Looks like they're cleaning him up a little en route. I'll give this one to Anita. Thanks, Sam."

Jack summoned Anita to the ER and summarized the case for her.

"Okay." She crinkled her lip and simply said, "So where will he arrive?"

Jack advised her, "Meet the ambulance on the ER entry ramp, take report from the lead EMT, examine the body, and pronounce the kid there. Come back inside to fill out the paperwork and write a brief report for the hospital record."

The ambulance arrived almost as Jack finished his briefing. Anita stood, hung her stethoscope around her neck, and made her way to the Emergency Department ramp. Training at Boston General Hospital, she had assessed her share of gunshot wounds. This one sounded like a single shot, through and through.

"I'm Dr. Thomas. Where's the body, guys?" she addressed the man who appeared to be the EMT crew chief.

"Alleged body, doc. He's not dead until you say he's dead." The man smiled a joyless smile meant to take some of the sadness out of the death of such a young man. Gallows humor was often all that got you through the nights sometimes.

Anita lifted the white sheet covering the motionless form. Her eyes immediately went to the gaping hole mid-chest crusted with blood, rapidly darkening into a circumferential scab, then to the graying of the flesh, cold and dry now. The victim was a good-looking African American kid. No tattoos or scars. Between seventeen and twenty years old, clean cut and handsome. A Tsunami of horror ravaged Anita's expression as she turned the head and met the face of the victim.

Jack observed her reaction through the emergency department window. One of the techs grabbed her arm as she recoiled, lost her balance, then recovered. She was visibly shaking when she re-entered the ER.

Part of the job of a senior resident was to assess the performance of the interns and students in action. Jack watched her grasp for the wall then the back of a chair as she guided herself to the seat.

Anita handled the job, but she didn't do it well. Jack placed his hand on her shoulder when he saw her hand shaking as she wrote up the death certificate.

Her body stiffened as he asked her, "What's wrong?"

At the sound of Jack's voice, she dropped her pen, turned around, and hugged him for a full minute. Tears seemed to gush from her eyes accompanied by a low rumbling moan in her throat. The tears soaked his sleeve by the time she released him. When she collected herself, she stepped back, waved off his inquiries, and finished her task.

"I'm okay." She said, then she collected herself. "I'm just tired, I guess."

He watched her dispense with her paperwork, then wipe a lingering tear from her cheek.

*More secrets.* Jack thought, *No more about her research, though.*

Anita settled back into a steady groove, finishing work needed to care for the living. Jack drummed his fingers a few times, then migrated to a hospital desktop and pulled up an FDA website where he researched recent FDA adverse reaction reports. Nothing ever came out of Mrs. Holcomb's seizure disorder.

*Strange.* "An experimental drug associated with two case reports of seizure?" he muttered to himself. "Should hear something about it." *At least in the medical and neurology journals, if not in the national news.*

Nothing. Anita clammed up. Not a peep. In fact, there was no mention at all of this remarkable new Fibromyalgia drug treatment in the literature anywhere. Jack scanned the medical search engines. Remembering Quirk's discussion with Dr. Garcia, Jack crossed the main hall to the surgical side of the ER and checked the O.R. schedule for the next day. Helen Holcomb was slated for 10:00 am the next morning. He slapped the wall beside the roster. "I'm going to get some damn answers one way or another."

According to the nursing staff, they wouldn't see Lucy for a two-month's stretch after she brought a lunch. Jack was naturally surprised when he heard she was scheduled to sponsor brunch the next morning for Grand Rounds. This time she brought her boss, the regional director, Orson Quirk. According to Fred Albright, he only showed up in Atlanta twice a year.

Jack had seen him only once before, couple of days ago, talking to the faculty or a department chair, but never to lowly residents unless they physically blocked his way out of the room. Here he was hobnobbing with the common residents, as it were.

Introduction to Autoimmune Diseases: An Update on the State of the Art by Adele Garcia, Professor of Medicine and Chief of Rheumatology.

Usually, the department sprang for doughnuts and coffee from the cafeteria. This Friday, there was a pancake and omelet buffet with gourmet coffee in fancy brass urns.

House staff started to arrive early and in force for Grand Rounds instead of the usual reluctant trickle. Hungry, under-paid doctors loved pancakes.

Jack saw Orson Quirk talking to Dr. Garcia at the breakfast table. Orson was an older fellow. He was husky, nearly portly, but his six foot three inches of height distributed his weight well enough to deter the impression of obesity. His grey-blonde hair was thinning. He had a convincingly pleasant face and charming personality. He was cajoling Dr. Garcia.

*Blah, blah, blah.* Jack grinned to himself. *The stuff has gotta be torture.*

Professor Garcia's vice-chief was there too.

*Bullshit and small talk,* Jack imagined, *nothing of substance. They must be trying to give away some grant money before the end of the year.* Then Jack found his attention drift to Dr. Lee. *Why is Dr. Lee hanging on every word? Glazer Pharmaceuticals has no anti-rheumatic drugs to promote.*

As he inched closer, Jack caught just the tip of the conversation. "- brain surgery." The rest was lost in the murmur building as the medical attendees arrived. Jack made out only one name as Quirk finished his conversation– *Holcomb.* That piqued Jack's curiosity.

Orson seemed to hush upon Jack's approach. "Hi there." He said as he thrust his hand enthusiastically in Jack's direction. "Orson Quirk."

*Typical Pharma "glad-handing" mode.* Jack shook it absently. Dr. Garcia excused herself to prepare for her talk.

The lecture was phenomenal. Dr. Garcia seemed to be able to make sense of the most arcane connections of the immune system from embryonic development to adaptive immunity to auto immunity. Then there was the new horizon that made rheumatology so fascinating in this time of biologic agents for every disease process from Rheumatoid Arthritis to Systemic Lupus Erythematosus. She touched on all the biologics on the market and most of those in the pipeline. Most, but not all.

*Still no mention of Research on Fibromyalgia.* Jack kept those observations in the back of his mind. He scratched some notes on a little notebook he kept in his pocket as his peripheral brain. Things were starting to click.

Many doctors had photographic minds to varying degrees. Cramming rapidly changing information into their brains in short bursts under constant academic scrutiny. Like walking video recorders. Jack thought that he actually had a good chunk of the information he was looking for but couldn't seem to process it right, somehow.

As everyone began to file out of the auditorium, Jack caught little more than a shadow of a figure.

*Janitor?* Jack thought whipping his head to follow the man exiting the room. He somehow knew it must have been a hospital employee. Familiar, same one over and over, but Jack always seemed too catch him leaving of late. The back of his head in a crowd, sometimes just his heel as he whisked out the door. It was as if the man were invisible until he left the room.

Jack closed his eyes and tried to picture the room before the man left to recall an impression of him.

*Nothing.* He hammered the back of a seat with his fist. Just vague impression; *male, non-descript, small framed, probably white.* No more. That bothered Jack; it bothered him a lot.

# Chapter 16: Cut

Rounds were over by 10 am for Jack. Anita was attending to an insulin drip on an unstable diabetic patient. Jack estimated she'd be there for at least another hour with the endocrinology fellow. He checked on her progress before paging Al.

"What's up, Jack?"

"Remember that seizure patient we saw a couple of weeks ago?" Jack asked, pulling Al by the arm as he spoke.

"The one Anita knew from Boston?"

"That's the one." Jack said, "They're cutting into her head today." He raised an eyebrow at Al. "What do you think they'll find?"

"I don't know; what?"

"Well, bud, we're about to find out."

Jack and Al made their way to the surgical observation balcony to join three other faculty members. Oddly poor attendance for such a sophisticated hi-tech surgery.

Jack whispered to Al as they settled into the metal chairs in the deck. "The brain surgery is an exploratory procedure to map Mrs. Holcomb's seizure foci." he nodded toward the O.R. as the surgical team moved into assigned positions. "Elective ablation should be uncomplicated if necessary."

"Who's that?" Al pointed to a fat, elderly man already falling asleep in a chair too small for him.

"The chief neuropathologist. He's working with the interdepartmental residents involved in the case to assess the tissue and activity of the biopsy specimens in tissue culture." Jack said. "Who are the big guys down there, Al?"

"Department heads," Al answered. "Anesthesia and Radiology. Who's the tall guy? Looks regal, but he's not the neurosurg honcho"

Jack read from a schedule he copied. "Nathan Hughley. He's from down from up north: Credentials from Hopkins and Yale."

"So the Neurosurgery head's not interested in this one?" Al asked.

Jack cracked a wry smile, *"There can be only one!"* he squinted at two new entries. "Oh, come on." He scowled. "That's Dasher, and Stormi."

"Well, department heads need sycophants, you know?" Al said. "Stormi has some background in use of dynamic MR equipment. Good pick to help navigating the new equip brought in for the procedure, I guess."

"--and Dasher?" Jack asked.

Al shrugged, "Call schedule."

The Chief neurosurgery resident and his senior resident assisted 'his majesty', Dr. Nathan Hughley. Not witness, but assisting in a once-in-a-lifetime demonstration of surgical skill. Rumor on the deck had it that only robot arms could match him. Against Hughley's wishes, but per Mrs. Holcomb's request, they recorded the whole thing for posterity. There was a little maneuver he did after identifying each seizure focus before moving on to the next that no one seemed to understand. Apparently, Dr. Hughley had developed a technique for minimizing trauma to ablated gray matter that reduced irritability. He also discovered findings that the rest of the team was not aware of at the time.

"That's the whole map now." Dr. Zizzi said. The head of neuropathology woke up from his Pickwickian slumber and made notes on his tablet.

Jack took the cue, stood and departed the observation deck. He rounded the corner toward the staircase. As if synchronized with the exit, Orson Quirk made his entrance.

Jack and Al jogged down the stairs and made themselves comfortable in the surgeons lounge. Al felt at home there, Jack knew. Or did. Al sauntered up to the frig and clawed two cokes; tossed one to Jack seated at the computer.

He had already logged onto one of the terminals and reviewed Blue team's patient list. Jack was itching with curiosity to investigate Helen Holcomb's records. He resisted, but came across the name, Khandi Barr as he navigated to a patient with a similar name in the database.

"Al, I don't want to pry, but this Khandi Barr thing is getting under my skin. I can't handle three mysteries at once. What's her story?" Jack looked sheepish, "I just gotta know."

Al didn't discuss details about his relationship since it solidified. But this was Jack Wheaton.

"I met her on my rotation through urology: Chandekar Barr was the child of David Barr and a coffee colored Sri Lankan mail order bride." Al began, "Her first name even Khandi can't pronounce right.

Khandi had been born a baby boy with undescended testicles and severe hypospadia." He shook his head, "They named him Chandekar, after his mother's family. By age 11, he stood five feet tall and weighed a scrawny eighty-five pounds with big dark eyes and smooth caramel skin.

The pediatricians told them their son would never sire children. The undescended testes ran a major risk of malignant degeneration over time. The doctor advised resecting them and surgically modifying the external genitalia in stages. Both parents agreed."

Al hesitated before saying, "Now Jack, this is all very personal to Khandi. She's very private. These details can't get out."

Jack nodded solemnly for Al to continue.

"Chandekar officially became Khandi when they made the decision to start estrogen therapy. No more surgery. She grew only three inches taller but developed like an hour glass with slender lithe arms and a hell of a pair of legs." Al grinned. "She never measured up for her father, whom she idolized though. Khandi caught hell and shame from her extended family through her high school years. Only her mother seemed to understand her. When you're raised in a very vocal Jewish family, that's not enough." Al saw the look in Jack's eyes. "New York is not always as liberal as you'd think. Khandi ran away from home three months before graduation. She arrived in Atlanta four years ago at the age of seventeen.

Already in the running for a role as *The Girl Next Door* with a sultry voluptuous voice like an anime vixen, she spent a year lending her talents to an elite escort service." He clasped his hands thoughtfully, "Niche gig for lots of money. Did really well at it. Got pretty popular until it became clear that if preferred clients wanted more than mere company, she was expected to put out, too.

"She promptly quit and took a job as a waitress. That was when she found her way to the urology clinic for follow up of transgender care and monthly estrogen treatments. There, with arms and legs that looked almost too long for her smokin' frame, she met a humorous and sympathetic transitional intern." He pointed to his chest, "After a very professional and respectful visit, she asked him to lunch, and one thing led to another…" He slapped his thighs and stood. "That's the whole thing. Curiosity satisfied?"

"Nearly," Jack said. "When do I get to meet her?"

Orson Quirk strode in to the air-conditioned observation deck as if he owned the hospital. He rested his hands on the rail overlooking the operating room, his breath fogging the window as he looked in.

Hughley seemed to recognize the phenomena as a signal. He looked up, nodded to Quirk, and patted his breast pocket. From behind him, Quirk heard Dr. Zizzi speak and he turned to acknowledge the expert.

"Now they'll close and bring us some specimens." Dr. Zizzi smiled and stretched as if he, himself had performed the surgery.

Quirk returned his gaze to the operating suite and nodded back to Dr. Hughley. "I'm sorry I missed the procedure. I've heard Dr. Hughley is a marvel to behold." He laughed, "Good luck with your studies, doctor."

Shifting focus, Quirk eyed each member of the team and swept his hand across the rail before leaving the observation deck. An auburn haired Glazer tech, masked and scrubbed, but absent from the procedural process also watched Quirk's gesture. With a single nod, she turned and left the OR before the team.

# Chapter 17: Dinner at Maynard's

In an effort to mend fences, Jack and his team invited Dasher and Stormi out to Maynard's Bistro in the Virginia Highlands area. Surrounded by a nest of other casual restaurants, Maynard's somehow had become a favorite after hours haunt of the Hamilton residents.

There was Anita and her guy; Al was alone as his Khandi Barr had yet to arrive. Dasher brought Stormi, still trying to make up with her and get back into her good graces and warm bed.

Stormi had gotten wind of Dasher's antics with Lucy a couple of weeks ago. She wore a blue and white sundress. Lots of cleavage, lots of leg, lots of determination that Dasher Clay was going to be reminded what he put at risk if he decided to flirt with another girl.

Anita's date had to leave early. By the time Jack arrived, he was gone. The second pitcher of beer had just gotten to the table, still ice cold, the container was just beginning to sweat. A basket of fresh hot wings was served not three steps ahead of him. He had great timing.

It was good to see everyone in street clothes, too. Dasher was already talking about his exploits in the operating room by the time Jack sat down.

"Sorry I'm late, guys." Jack sat in the vacant seat next to Anita. She wore a simple, peach-colored cotton tunic cinched high above the waist with form-fitting jeans and tennis shoes. Two-inch hoop earrings were the only jewelry she wore and a hint of lipstick to contrast her cocoa skin. Elbows on the table, he asked, "What'd I miss?"

"Helen Holcomb." Dasher announced. "We mapped her seizure foci today. She was wide-awake and talking us through it. It was so cool. We went through each unstable focus and zapped it with the gamma knife. That Dr. Nathan Hughley, radiation neurosurgeon, he was something. The post op EEG was normal."

"So was the pre op EEG, Clay." Stormi's air was still brisk, but no longer frigid since Anita arrived with a date. "But it was cool to see the correlation between the readings of that new intra-operative MRI and the brain activity on the EEG under the gamma knife."

"Intra operative MRI? You mean like, a mini scanner that allows you to work within the magnetic field?" Jack scratched his head. "We actually have one of those?"

"We don't have one, Jack. It's on loan, courtesy of the Glazer Corporation," Stormi said. "And Dr. Nathan Hughley, one of two radiation neurosurgeons in the United States. Hopkins wanted him, but Glazer had the money, so…"

The longing for that operative MRI machine was evident in her voice. "I did some work in med school on low Gauss MRI scanning in the setting of a dynamic target like the heart or lungs. They've taken it one big step further. Amazing stuff."

"At MIT, they…" Anita stopped herself, but covered deftly. "…have been looking at rapid sequence MR Imaging in rat circulation."

"That's not news, honey. MIT had better get on the stick if that's all they've got." Stormi was still condescending to Anita.

No retort from Dr. Thomas. She would have bit her tongue until it bled to avoid blurting out what she knew beyond Stormi's science project level knowledge.

"Yeah, Anita, it's always better on the stick than off." Dasher Clay never missed an opportunity to make a "stick" innuendo.

Jack found it funny too, but none of the women did, and Al was quiet. Jack stared for a moment at the proud face of Dasher Clay. *I'm not that bad am I?* He thought about the joke and felt a little guilty. *Do I always describe women in terms of their looks?* Jack shook off his doubt.

Dasher's nudge to Stormi's hip under the table compelled her to slide toward Al, seat and all.

"Hey, folks. What's this stuff about sticks?" A Dravidian beauty appeared out of the crowd and joined the conversation. Khandi Barr had arrived. She had a medium pitched voice, wore simple black shoes, skinny jeans, and an oversized tank top.

As Jack mused about what his friend's first date must have been like, a distracted waiter dropped a tray near the door when Khandi brushed past him to borrow a ketchup bottle from a neighboring table. His body turned, but his head didn't. *Wham!* Shattered glass everywhere.

Jack thought, *If they had used her for that role in* **The Crying Game**, *every man in the audience would have been in tears at the end of the movie.* The little band of colleagues continued the medical conversation for a few more moments, then switched to general entertainment topics. Khandi ran down the artists playing at the outdoor amphitheater venues around town. Mostly smooth jazz, but she sometimes talked Al into going to see spoken word or symphonic guests also.

She wore her thick, black hair parted and wound into a single, long braid down her back. Al liked to tug at it from time to time to distract her. She smiled at his teasing and wrapped it around her neck like a scarf to get it out of the way.

A snapshot could slip into the pages of any upscale magazine—actors in a luxury car commercial. Not one of them, but Dasher could afford as much as a used economy car, though.

They laughed and talked for another hour or so while they finished another pitcher of beer and another basket of wings. Eventually, Stormi got tired of watching Dasher ogle Khandi and Anita all night. She waved him back to his chair when he offered to walk her to her car. She threw in her $20 for her share of the meal and beer.

Khandi yawned and stretched her bare arms up and over her head. The curves she threw around in that clingy blouse got every man's attention within a two-table radius. She stood and announced that she had to bow out too.

"My shift begins at 10 pm and there's no way I can make it on time now," she said. "Fats, my boss, doesn't like it when I'm late."

"What's he going to do to you if you're late, flog you?" Dasher asked.

"He seems to tolerate my tardiness better than he does from the other girls," she said. "He appreciates my brains."

"That's nice to hear for a change," Anita said, although she wasn't sure she believed that it was just brains Khandi's boss respected.

Lifting a menu from the nearby bar, Khandi reviewed the food and beverages consumed during the meal. "This is all going to come to right about $87 so 15% gratuity will be $13, give the guy an extra ten bucks." Khandi figured the bill in her head. "I'm sure they're gonna nail him for the broken dishes." Tossing the menu back on the bar. "Anita don't let these guys scrimp on the tip."

Anita rose with the others to go to the ladies' room, which was on the way to the exit. Dasher was summoned by *natures' call* about then so he tagged along behind Anita and company toward the rest rooms.

Actually, Khandi was not too different from the rest of the guys that night. She had seen Stormi's YouTube clip, too, so Khandi was doing some ogling of her own. Khandi had a sexy way of swaying her hips, with sort of a grinding action, when she was around pretty women. Her voice took on a raspy purr, kind of breathy. Jack decided he liked it.

As discretely as possible, he asked Al about that when they were alone.

"I don't mind dating a beautiful woman who appreciates the attributes of other beautiful women without getting weird about it," Al said. "Doesn't hurt that she enjoys being on exhibit." He stretched out proudly and laced his hands behind his head.

"So where does she work anyway?"

Al laughed. "Magic Pony."

Jack's eyes went wide. "Seriously?"

"Calm down, partner; she does the books and occasionally serves drinks there when they're short-handed. No table dances, no stage shows."

He wasn't offended. Al was always so good-natured.

"I never did get you that URL for Stormi's lingerie pictures," Jack said.

"Man, if I had to wait for you, I'd never get a peek at anything good." Al said.

"You found the site?" Jack asked.

"Khandi found it after I told her the story,"hHe said. "She actually jumped out of bed, skipped to the computer, then navigated to the pictures in no time. She went through Stormi's photo gallery one lingering image at a time. After five minutes of moaning, I had to remind her that I was still in the room."

He thrust his chin in the direction of the restrooms and rubbed his baldhead as he chuckled. "Why do you think she's walking three steps behind Stormi and Anita on her way to the parking lot?"

As the two men laughed, it occurred to Jack that Al's head looked like a giant Milk Dud sitting on the shoulders of a gymnast. *Al must shave that thing every day then polished it.*

"Probably didn't mind switching her tail back and forth in Dasher's face either. If he only knew," Al finished.

"So the two of you Googled Stormi, huh?"

"Googled her in cyberspace, ogled her at the table, fantasized about her other times. Khandi really wanted to see Stormi and Anita in the flesh, up close and personal. She agrees with you by the way, Jack. Says Anita's hot, too." He smiled. "She can't wait to see Lucy Velasquez."

Al stood. "Hey, chief, I'm going to have to get my knees in the breeze. See you tomorrow?"

"Eight sharp, bud," Jack said.

Al looked uncomfortable for a moment, his hands in his pockets.

"What's on your mind, Al?" Jack asked

"Look, any chance I can come in a little late tomorrow? Khandi gets off at 4:00 am."

He shot Jack a wry smile. "I'd like to get her off a few more times before I come in for rounds. I never see her for any quality time anymore, Jack. I get home, we walk Lollipop together and have a little dinner…"

Jack interrupted him with an exaggeratedly firm hand on Al's forearm. "'Lollipop'?" he asked, holding Al's gaze.

"Khandi's dog. A rescue Labradoodle, she says." Al told him. "More poodle than Labrador. Maybe part schnauzer. Runt of the litter is my guess. Had her teeth kicked out by her previous owner. Completely toothless. Licks or gums everything she gets hold of nowadays." He smiled. "Khandi says Lollipop's got licking down to an art form, so I have some competition."

Jack looked at him first with disdain then Al's smile spread into a grin and he said, "You do know where the term 'lap dog' came from don't you?"

Thinking of Khandi and her special needs, Jack realized it must be complicated and a little different between her and Al. So he smiled politely and said, "Sure, but be there no later than 9:00 am and ready to work, too."

Al fired off a formal "Ay, ay," accompanied by a vigorous salute and headed for the door after tossing forty dollars in for himself and Khandi as he left.

Anita returned to the table a bit confused by the absence of their companions.

"Did I do that?" she said, smiling and pointing to the empty chairs in aggregate.

Dasher Clay snuck up behind her and clapped his hands around her upper arms. Anita startled as intended, satisfying Clay's high school prank.

"I gotta go too, guys." He waved. "This was great, gotta do this again soon."

He blew Anita a kiss, which she playfully swatted out of midair.

The table grew quiet after Jack and Anita shared an uncomfortable laugh as Dasher disappeared through the exit. Anita had worked increasingly harder to avoid Jack's unanswered questions each passing day on this rotation.

Apparently, "Professor" Thomas had made quite an impression on one Helen Holcomb. Jack didn't know how to feel about the developing mystery. He didn't like secrets.

He tried the subtle approach to weasel the information out of her. He suspected she was too smart to fall for any of those tricks even with a few beers in her. They talked about Boston, then Long Island for a while, but Anita just wouldn't hold up her end of the conversation.

A chair at the bar swiveled back and forth. It was empty now but Jack knew it was occupied when the ladies went to the restroom. He couldn't clearly picture the occupant, yet he could not shake the sense of familiarity. *A little guy maybe?* Was it a college kid or a wiry woman?

Pondering the absent patron for another moment, Jack touched the chair in passing as if he could divine the answer by the deed. He gave up and offered to walk Anita to her car. He settled the final bill and let Anita tip the waitperson. They made their way through the lobby to the parking lot.

He took the side of the walkway next to the bushes rather than the street as was customary when a gentleman escorted a lady to her ride. Jack had the uneasy feeling that they were being watched, but he couldn't put his finger on why. The darkness beyond the bushes disturbed him somehow. His apprehension was decidedly for Anita's safety, not his own.

That empty stool at the end of the bar haunted him. The person he nearly caught leaving the auditorium earlier came to mind.


The next morning began as usual. The whole evening before had started to fade from Jack's mind. Blue Team was two weeks into its internal medicine rotation together. All was going well until Anita came to her chief with an unusual request.

"Jack, I'm going to need to take a trip up north. Just three days. I'll be back by Sunday noon at the latest." She stood behind him as they finished rounds for the day.

"Are you okay, Anita?" Jack turned to give her his full attention. "Is it a family member or something?"

Usually requests of this nature involved a deceased family member or a death vigil for one. Anita hesitated and averted her eyes.

"No, but it's business I can't put off."

"Business you can't handle by phone or e-mail?" Jack asked. "What the hell, Anita, it's not our Golden Weekend. You can't just drop everything and traipse off to see friends on a whim!"

Jack started to say something to her about her request being denied, but she sheepishly presented a signed letter on Hamilton stationary. Her leave was officially sanctioned by the department of medicine.

Jack seethed. The formal letter, signed by the chair, was almost waved in his face when he complained to the chief resident. Jack wondered if that might be why his service was down to three patients. No long call nights were scheduled for his team before Sunday.

The chief of service pulled Jack aside and said, "You have as many doctors as patients on your service. You can't tell me that a resident as capable as you can't spare an intern for a couple of days, now can you?"

What could he do? Jack just smiled and waved as he backed out of the office. He and Al had no trouble covering the service, so Jack supposed the chief was right. Anita was back by Sunday. Jack and Al had discharged one of Al's patients so they were down to two by the time Anita checked back in for duty 12:30 Sunday afternoon. Antony Fusco brought her in from the airport.

It was the first time Jack had seen him. Tall, swarthy, overly developed. Jack thought that Tony was probably on steroids or something.

The way Jack saw it, if this guy had time to work out that much, he had time to get to a barber. *Besides, if he really had that much testosterone, his hairline should be more manly, receding a bit.*

All that and he was a doctor, too. Kind of… an Orthopedic resident. Jack often said behind their backs, "Strong as an ox, dumb as a yoke."

Not all of them, of course. Jack just hated the fact that Anita could be swayed by a pile of muscle.

"Jack, Al, this is my friend, Antony Fusco," she said as she slipped her arm as far around his torso as she could then slid it down to his waist. He draped his arm around her shoulders as he reached to shake hands.

"Great to meet you guys, Anita told me you had a great time last week at Maynard's. Sorry I couldn't stay, Jack." Antony had a solid grip, but he didn't try to overpower with it.

"Yeah. Same here, eh, Anthony."

"Antony. Like Antony and Cleopatra, you know?" his laugh faded when Jack failed to join in and Antony smiled at Anita. "It's a little different. You can call me Tony, most of my friends do."

"Well, thanks for seeing Anita back from the airport, Tony." Jack said. "She's got some work to catch up on. So if you were hoping to do something recreational when she came back…"

"Oh, I wouldn't let her out of my sight. I went with her. Nice weekend. We had a view of the Chesapeake Bay. Cooler than Atlanta this time of year."

Anita's wince was reflex.

Jack looked at one then the other.

Al intervened with a summary of the discharge details for her patient. Jack nodded, clench-jawed, as Al's brought Anita up to speed.

Jack checked out to the long call resident after rounds. He had swapped a favor to have the night off.

Anita whispered, "Jack, we need to talk."

"Now? Can't it wait 'til tomorrow?" Jack nodded at Antony. "You look like you're going to be busy for the night."

That hurt her. She took two steps away from him, shaking her head.

Christie, the ICU nurse Jack introduced Anita to the first day, poked her head in the door.

"Jack," she drawled. "Are you done? The movie starts at 1:30 and I love the coming attractions."

Christie had changed out of her usual crisp, tight nursing uniform that she wore so well and into a pink tee that rose up past her navel, melon green short shorts and leather open toed sandals with just enough heel to be provocative. At the site of Anita in the room, she bounced in to grab Jack's arm and hauled him away.

Before the door swallowed Jack and his date, he noticed Anita's face. It wasn't jealousy. It was different. He wouldn't forget that look. Her expression implied, *I need to tell you something that I really shouldn't.*

Jack went off to the movie with Christie, but he didn't remember what they saw. He barely remembered sleeping with her that night. Nothing makes a girl move faster sexually than the threat of another woman in the hunt, even if it is too soon. Jack's head was still with Anita.

As much as he wanted to, Jack didn't hear any more about the need to talk from Anita for the next week. Then the shit hit the fan.

# Chapter 18: Hell of a Night

Blue team was on long call. They'd had a busy night. Five admissions to each intern by midnight. Ten hits in all to the team. Four of those ten were critically ill. Jack had been bouncing back and forth like a maniac helping each of the interns stabilize his and her patients. Usually that closed a service down for the night.

"Damn, Jack." Anita said. She had just finished stabilizing her last admission and look harried. "We're under water already and the night's not half over. Are we going to get hit again?"

Al yawned. "The Bell Commission conclusions of the 1980s limited the number of hours that a resident could work without a break."

Anita nodded remembering the precedent. "Oh yeah, the death in that New York hospital. An exhausted resident on call really blew it. The young doc's lawyer claimed that the burden was excessive for any reasonable human being, especially when lives were at stake. The Commission found that young doctors began making mistakes after too many consecutive hours without a break."

"Looking back, faculty and private practitioners have always considered *call* a rite of passage for residents and interns." Jack finished the summary, "Of course, during our training years, *call* is just a FOUR LETTER word." He scowled, "Never complain about the hours or the load. At least not to the faculty—"

"Or the ER resident." Al said.

Still, patients had to be taken care of by someone. Teaching hospitals, in spite of their great reputations, were usually located in inner city communities and underserved by the private sector. They saw heavier traffic than most private community hospitals.

Hamilton Medical Center dealt with the problem the way most hospitals in that setting did: It allowed fellows and senior residents to *moonlight* for an hourly fee as long as they weren't on ward duty that month-*Nocturnists*. This arrangement augmented the complement of four medical teams composed of two interns and a senior resident, two of which were on short call and two on long call.

This particular night the ER resident had burned through the two teams on call, the House resident who was to take the overflow in such situations, the three moonlighters and even the three attending physicians on call. The cycle came back around to Jack's team for an eleventh, twelfth and thirteenth admission.

Triskaidekaphobia; the irrational fear of the number thirteen. Jack never believed in it before, always thought it was silly. But July 23 changed all of that.

Helen Holcomb showed up in the ER at 2:00 am, the thirteenth admission. The admitting resident assigned her to Blue team directly without first assessing her. She was seizing when she rolled into the main hall by Emergency Medical Services.

"Sam, come on? Give us a break, will you? We've already taken twelve hits. Now this train wreck as number 13? Are you serious? Where's the work-up? Where's the prep and assessment? Scan her, tap her, stabilize her, contact the family, hell, hold her over 'til morning for God's sake," Jack pleaded.

Sam Reardon was a good guy; two days growth of beard made him look shabby but he had been hammered as hard as Jack had that night. His eyes were as red as Jack's too.

"Look, Jack, we're three gurneys deep here." He pointed to the rows of stretchers, with sick patients triple parked, end to end against each wall of the ER. "We have had a record 162 ER visits today. Nearly fifty admissions to medicine and thirty-five to surgery and GYN. We have either treated or bounced people out of here that any sane doc on the planet would have admitted. We're running a damn clinic in here."

The braid of his ponytail was the only part of his appearance still neat and tight.

"There is no way we can handle another case through the night. Now if you insist, we'll do the work up, but it will be crappy and fast. We'll scan her, tap her and pan-culture her for bacteria, fungi, viruses and whatever the hell else you want but we won't wait on the results. I don't need them to determine that she needs to come in.

Alternately, you can get started on her now and have all your tests done in the next hour, put her to bed and write a crappy note yourself and call it a night. No attending worth his salt will call you on it. Probably won't even get to her in Morning Report today. Now, you choose."

Sam was right. The workup wouldn't take more than an hour. Jack and his team would be awakened by 3:30, 4 am at the latest. Any way you sliced it, it was going to take an hour on his part. At this time of the morning, tired interns were apt to make stupid mistakes anyway.

Jack decided to do it himself and assign it to Al when the sun came up. Jack talked one of the EMTs, Karen Gleason, into helping him start an I.V.

Mrs. Holcomb's right arm thrashed around. She was conscious, but not responding to verbal cues. Jack selected her left arm to start the I.V. He restrained her right arm against his body while the EMT got the IV in and had a good blood return. She taped it down and helped Jack secure the right arm with foam rubber and canvas restraints.

He had Holcomb nearly trussed up when her left arm began to thrash back and forth. Karen and Jack went after the floppy needle set up at the same time. Karen got to it first and held her as best she could, but the older woman was big and stocky. She bucked and Karen went with her,

needle still in hand. It pierced Jack's hand deeply, still full
to the hub with Helen Holcomb's blood.

"Fuck!"

It hurt no more than getting a splinter. The exple-
tive that escaped Jack's lips was loud, but related to the
contaminated blood with which he had just gotten inocu-
lated, not to the pain.

The details of the experiment, the seizure events,
and the lack of reporting associated with this damn study
agent all came rushing back to him. Jack's profanity strung
into a 12 word repeating litany. He was fit to be tied.

He was bleeding freely, which meant that it wasn't
just a subcutaneous inoculation, but an intravenous one. It
was already circulating. Too late for a tourniquet to limit
the exposure.

Karen was apologizing profusely but Jack almost
couldn't hear her. Then her training kicked in; Karen compressed his forearm at the puncture site and pulled the
needle out before he could stop her. The problem was when
a needle or angiocath is pulled out, healthcare professionals
are taught to compress the vein to minimize bleeding
through the wound. When that's done, there is a slight suc-
tion created: A blood flash in reverse.

Jack calmed down and started contamination control protocols. He applied the tourniquet anyway and
cleaned the wound first with an iodine solution, then hydro-
gen peroxide followed by direct pressure gauze. He
wondered what just got into his blood stream. He gave the
convulsing patient a ten milligram shot of Diazepam in the
meatiest part of her upper arm and almost dared her to stop
breathing on him. He sent five tubes of the patient's blood
off for every organism and toxin he could think of, then
completed the incident report begun by the EMT who stuck
him. Jack submitted it to the administrator on duty.

He called up Anita stat and told her to "bring her
ass down to the ER now!". Anita came down in complete

disarray. Hair pulled back, glasses had replaced contact lenses and her shoulders were slumped. She looked a wreck.

Jack was pissed. "This is your patient, Anita. I already did the work-up. Help me get her to x-ray for a chest film and a CT scan of the head."

For the first time in nearly a month, Jack couldn't see Anita as anything but an outlet for his wrath.

"Jack, what's wrong?" she asked.

"Let's roll her," he said, nodding his chin toward the x-ray department without elaborating on his own injury.

They got the patient to radiology and the techs took over.

Jack pulled Anita into an unoccupied room and laid into her. "Enough pussy footing around, Anita. Tell me about this goddamn experiment of yours!"

"W-What?" she stammered.

He felt like Samuel L. Jackson ready to recite Psalm 23:15 in a *Pulp Fiction*-esque rant.

"Damn it, whatever you put in her six months ago is now in me." He pointed first in the general direction of Mrs. Holcomb, then he showed Anita his puncture wound. It was only then that Jack realized that Anita didn't know the patient they had just hauled over to radiology was Helen Holcomb.

"Jack, I swear. I don't know anything about that. I left the project halfway through it," she said.

Jack was only just beginning to see past his own anger. He spoke several languages. Part of the way you pick up a foreign tongue is to read body language. Anita wasn't lying, but she wasn't telling him the whole truth either. She knew more than she was saying that was for sure.

"You were trying to tell me something Sunday. What was it?"

"Jack, not here. Not now. Please," she begged.

Her sincerity would have eased his nerves any other time, but not this night.

"Yes, right now, Anita." He pushed her, physically pushed her. Technically, she had a case for assault.

She fell silent. It wasn't an ordinary quiet, but that infectious quiet that starts with one person, but soon envelopes a whole room and consumes everything else including the murmurs from the hall and traffic on the stairway above.

Inanimate objects became eerily silent--the clock on the wall, the leaky tap in the corner sink, the hum of the radiology equipment in the next rooms. Jack could not even hear her footsteps as she walked slowly across the room to lock the door.

"Jack. I know I haven't been honest with you."

"No shit, Sherlock."

"What I'm trying to tell you is that I'm in danger. Real danger. I didn't want to get you or Al into this." Anita squeezed her eyelids shut.

*She is bone tired.* Jack could tell now that he really looked at her. *Not just tonight either.*

Thinking back, he realized she had been weary for nearly two weeks. *Troubled,* he thought. *More than sleep deprived, like someone with a price on her head, always looking over her shoulder might be.*

"You know I was involved in research at The Nordstrom Clinic up north." She licked her lips before saying more.

"Go on," he said.

"Well, we discovered the gene that led to down regulation of Mitochondria. The information garnered from the Human Genome project saved us years, maybe decades, in our research. Using that finding as a starting point, some of the Stanford techniques to develop the model of a small RNA molecule that could suppress activation of the code. Prevent expression of the gene. Do you understand, Jack?"

"This was a designer molecule then?" he was slower than Anita. Much slower. Jack did catch the allusion to recombinant RNA technology.

*Viruses?* He was still trying to put it together.

"That's not new, Anita. How can that put you in any kind of danger? Everyone's looking for a new biologic infusible or injectable. So what?"

She leveled her gaze at him as if he could read her thoughts had she concentrated hard enough. "Jack, do you know how many Rheumatoid Arthritis patients there are in the United States?"

"Probably a few hundred thousand. It is a common disease. What's your damn point?" He was still befuddled by her line of questions.

"Try two million. Forty percent of insured Rheumatoid Arthritis patients are on biologic agents. Tumor necrosis factor antagonists, T or B lymphocyte inhibitors, anti-cytokine Antibodies. They all average between $1500.00 and $2,000.00 a month per patient. Therapy is chronic. No end in sight. The cost of production to the companies is perhaps a couple of hundred per dose, but they'll never admit it. *Cost* goes down with the economy of scale, but not *price*."

She saw his confusion and squinted at him as she spoke the next sentences slowly and deliberately. "There are four or five times as many Fibromyalgia patients alone as Rheumatoid Arthritis, not to mention those treated for Chronic fatigue, non-cardiac chest pain, Irritable Bowel Syndrome, and some forms of non-migraine headaches or depression.

Imagine the revenues generated by monthly infusions of FMDS400. There is no drug more than 60% successful against the symptoms of Fibromyalgia Syndrome. This demonstrates a 100% efficacy rate. One hundred percent, Jack. Do you understand that that's unheard of?"

He looked at her now comprehending the significance of what she was saying. "And it causes seizures. I don't think the FDA will pull it from the market. More commonly used drugs have worse side effects than that."

"You're right about that, Jack. The FDA will have a black box warning slapped on it, but it will still get approved."

Jack was tired of feeling stupid. "If they already have the formula, the patent, the resources, and the clinical data, what kind of threat could you possibly pose to them? Seriously. This is pure paranoia, Anita."

"Jack, I was kicked off of the study for unethical activity. That's why I have such limited knowledge of the final results."

"Unethical behavior? What did you do? Fudge results? Spike the stuff with steroids or something? What?" He rubbed at the back of his left hand as he grew tired of the cloak and dagger routine.

"My 'transgression' was advising a team of grad students at MIT on primate gene sequencing and identification. Basic technique and transcription."

"That's got nothing to do with what you described at Nordstrom. Wait a minute, is the Nordstrom Clinic in any way related to Decker, Nordstrom, Andersen Laboratories?" Jack asked.

That revelation was a quantum leap for him.

She stared back at him quizzically. "Yeah. Good, Jack."

*She didn't expect me to figure that out yet.* He guessed that it didn't occur to her when she started putting it all together in Boston.

She nodded. "They're brothers. The CEOs of the Clinic and DNA are brothers and they talk. Leif Nordstrom, Chairman of the Board of The Nordstrom Clinic, shared the transcripts on FAME DAYS with Claus Nordstrom, CEO of Decker, Nordstrom, Andersen Laboratories. Because

Nordstrom is a privately owned institution and DNA is a Swedish based multinational, the FDA has limited jurisdiction. The real threat was private sector competition." She laughed, "Last thing they wanted was MIT or the NIH getting wind of their research."

Her shoulders slumped. "I was so arrogant, Jack. Smartest kid in the room. Always trying to prove myself to my older colleagues who took my participation in their research as a joke. 'Pretty Little Thing' they kept calling me, then tried to shut me out from brainstorming sessions and protocol design meetings. I didn't realize why I was fired until after Gil died." She slapped her head as she spoke. "Stupid!"

"What do you mean, Anita?" Jack asked.

"I asked, 'Where did this gene come from in the first place? There must have been an evolutionary advantage to it at some point.' Well, I was totally ignored. Or so I thought. The boys at MIT biomedical didn't ignore me. They took me seriously, when they stopped ogling me. Even that I didn't mind much. I sort of dated one of them for a couple of weeks. Gil Hargrove."

"As in Dr. Hargrove, chairman of the department?" Jack asked.

"Yeah. I didn't know that connection either until I got down here to Atlanta for spring break. Gil invited me home to meet his family. The Nordstroms knew who Wesley Hargrove was. Knew his research ambitions for Hamilton University Medical Center. They must have panicked. They raided Gil's lab. Killed Harry Mehta. He was just there early one weekend…"

"Wrong place, wrong time, huh?" Jack finished.

She nodded. "Gil was so sweet. I really started to like him." Again, she paused. "I got them both killed."

By then, Anita and Jack were sitting facing each other on rolling consultation stools used in exam rooms. He moved in closer to lay a comforting hand on her knee. She

placed her fingertips on his in response. Jack was glad she
didn't misread the gesture as a sexual advance.

"He left me in bed and went down to move my car."
Her eyes welled up. "Even in the movies, you never expect
a car bomb, not even when it's a thriller." She shuddered.
"In real life…"

Jack wanted to reach around and comfort her, but he
knew it would be too much.

Anita sniffled a bit, then continued with the story.

"The police said it was a freak accident."

"What about the third guy, Anita? What became of
him?" he asked mercifully moving her along.

"Monty? Lamonte Hill. He was in Maryland. He
logged some time at the NIH shoring up some of our data
and suppositions. When the police left, his dad pulled a few
strings. He's a two star general at the Pentagon. He and Dr.
Hargrove were longtime friends, like their boys.

'Get out of Boston this weekend,' Monty said.
'Don't tell Nordstrom where you're going.' We had my
records and credentials switched with another Anita
Thomas, a graduate of the Boston University med school.

She ranked in the middle of her class. Wanted to be
a cardiologist. I saw her picture once, honey colored complexion. About my size. Wore her hair blonde." Anita
gestured an assessment with her head, "Pretty if you like
the Beyoncé look. She'd fit in at Stanford. Especially with
my records.

"Dr. Hargrove cleared my admission to Hamilton
under her grades. Got me reciprocity and safe haven for a
discrete residency until we could sort this all out."

She continued. "General Hill did a stint in the intelligence community."

"So why can't this General Hill protect you now?"
Jack asked. He didn't think there was any skepticism in his
voice, but his own emotions were running to high now for
him to be sure of that. It was a lot to swallow all at once

and Jack was still from Missouri. "I still don't see how this involves you anymore, Anita?"

Jack's cell phone rang. They had been talking for half an hour. Helen Holcomb's bed was ready and the radiology technicians were looking for him.

He asked them if they could transport the patient to the sixth floor neurology unit. Jack promised to call the neurology resident on call to see the patient stat. He had already done all the work and written a holding admission note on the chart.

Upon arrival, a slender brunette nurse took the chart from the orderly transporting Helen Holcomb and reviewed it. She wore a surgical mask and coughed from time to time while she took report. She ordered the transporter to place the patient in the hospital bed then took the chart to the desk and leafed through to the administrative section. She read the incident report and vigilant for watchers on the nearly empty ward, removed the chart copy. After stuffing it into her pocket, she picked up a hospital phone and dialed security.

"May I speak to Joey, please?" she waited for her party to pick-up.

"Joey--Lucy. There's an incident report on one Helen Holcomb from about 04:00. Remove it--discretely, Joey." She hung up, rose from the desk, crossed the room and checked on the unconscious patient that the orderly left in the bed. A phlebotomy basket left conveniently at the table between ward beds contained everything the needed to fill a serum separator tube with Helen Holcomb's blood. Placing two full tubes in one pocket, she didn't remove the mask until she reached the ground floor.

Exiting the elevator, she looked both ways, then stared at the lone security guard at the desk. A nod from him assured the disposal of the only other copy of Jack

Wheaton's incident report. She dropped her cap, wig, and mask into the trash can and left the building.

# Chapter 19: Daybreak

"Anita, we have to get out of here." Jack looked down at his watch. "It's already 4:30 am. We'll check her chest x-ray and write her ICU note. Not much time to get some shut eye before rounds. Everyone will be scrambling to get ready for Morning Report."

Anita just nodded absently, the exhaustion clearly overwhelming her now. She followed Jack like a zombie to the viewing room. He passed his badge over the door scanner to gain restricted entry, found his way around in the darkness, and led Anita through the maze of rooms to the reading room.

Hamilton had gone digital a couple of years ago and replaced most of the old style fluorescent light boards with 32-inch computer screens. Jack punched his resident ID code into the computer to access the files, then entered Holcomb's Medical record number. There were three levels of security needed to access medical records at modern hospitals.

The images of Helen Holcomb's chest x-ray appeared on the screen. Jack and Anita exhaled together. It was normal.

"Now all we need do is track down her head CT scan before turning her over to neurology or at least getting a consultation," Jack said.

They waited what seemed like forever for an elevator. There was more than heavy traffic in the halls that morning due to the night of hell. The two decided to take the stairs up to the fifth floor. Jack thought a six-floor jog might wake them up a little.

They arrived on the fifth floor near the ICU end of the hall. Jack's mind cleared with the endorphin rush. He wasn't so sure about how well Anita was doing. As she leaned against the wall, she began to slump and rubbed her eyes again.

*Definitely running on empty.* He thought.

They pushed through the heavy, glass doors to the ICU and found their patient. Helen Holcomb was tubed, but responsive. The endotracheal intubation procedure was performed mostly for airway protection, not for respiratory assistance. Helen Holcomb was sitting up reading a magazine. She waved at them cheerfully from the bed.

A chorus of chirps filled the ICU. Tired residents frantically frisked dingy white coats for cell phones. Jack retrieved his blast text from Fred Albright, as did all the other residents: "Due to extenuating circumstances, Morning Report will be delayed and abbreviated. Senior residents will present selected cases only."

What that really meant was that the attending faculty had been up all night with the House staff instead of in their comfy beds. They were exhausted too. Jack sent Anita off to her call room.

He examined Holcomb himself and ignored her request to communicate by writing notes on the yellow legal pad in her lap. Jack bowed out of the room, explaining that he had twelve other patients to see before 9:30. What he truly needed was at least a two-hour snooze. Most of the residents dismissed the interns at noon after they had their naps and completed the minimum work necessary to stabilize the patients. They cut out of there quickly.

Jack ended up leaving the hospital at 2 pm. Early by most standards, but a freakishly long day even for a senior resident. As a consolation, he didn't have to report in until 9:00 am the next day. Hell Night threw everything off. The last thing Jack did before leaving the premises was check the CT scan of Mrs. Holcomb's head.

Stormi Seales was still on duty. She started at midnight and stayed past her usual shift of 8:00 am to pull a double. She looked a little tired, but nothing like what the medicine and surgical staff had been through. Radiology had a much more civilized rotation schedule. Still, Stormi had read and dictated nearly 200 films.

The room was darkened to read fine details in the images and Jack was bathed in the halo of fluorescent light from the hall when he opened the door. Her eyes were red and she had to blink several times to recognize him when he came in to her office.

"What the hell, Jack?" She shielded her eyes from the blinding light.

"Sorry, Stormi. I need to know what you saw on Mrs. Helen Holcomb's CT scan before I leave. I am beat."

"CT of the head?" She turned back to her computer screen as much to soothe her eye pain as to search out the file.

"MR number?" she asked in that offhand way bus drivers ask for a passenger's ticket. Jack pulled an index card out of his pocket stamped with Mrs. Holcomb's Medical Record number and demographic information and then read it to her.

Stormi punched it into the imaging database and retrieved the appropriate file. Jack still couldn't get over how fast even an exhausted second year radiology resident could read those studies in detail.

*That's why they eventually get paid the big bucks.*

"She's got several UBO's in the cerebral hemispheres diffusely. Essentially normal for age," she concluded.

"Whoa, whoa, whoa. Back up. What are UBO's, Stormi?" Jack asked.

She stood and stretched, giving a big yawn before answering his question. Usually, that indicated that a short question had a long answer. Jack prepared himself for the diatribe to follow.

"Before you get all worked up, Jack. Unidentified Bright Objects; UBO's, are 'nothings', artifacts seen mostly in middle aged brains. These tiny lesions are usually physiologic or degenerative in nature, not acute. They are not the source of her seizures. It's probably metabolic."

Jack didn't feel like giving her the lecture about generalizing medical differential diagnostic lists to a budding internist. He just waved his thanks, turned, and exited the reading room then headed for the hospital lobby.

When he stepped outside, he welcomed the fresh breeze. When he reached the front steps, Jack cast his gaze over the row of taxis lined up there then at the MARTA train station down the block. Nice a day as it was, he began to search his pockets for change. He scraped together five dollars for a cab ride home.

# Chapter 20: A Stroll in the Park

Caught up on his sleep, Jack decided to go for a run before work. His fast was broken with half a cup of re-heated coffee and a two-day-old bagel with cream cheese. He had to steam the bagel to make it chewable again.

The pre-dawn run did him good, cleared his head. Beneath the glow of street lights, he got his second wind at the entry to the park, a good six-block jog. Jack hit the track and enjoyed the dark solitude. It seemed no one was out there but him at first, then joggers began to trickle in as the sun appeared over the Atlanta skyline.

He ran absently until he heard foot falls in the shadows in front of him. Anita and Antony paced each other in the opposite direction on the track. While Anita suffered the call from Hell on the medical end of the ER, Antony had been in surgery through two shifts. They both still looked whipped from the day before, but plodded along just the same.

Jack just kept his eyes on the track ahead of him like a horse with blinders on. A warning from behind startled him. "On your left!"

His feet reacted to *what* he heard before his brain understood *whom* he heard. The wind from Lucy Velasquez's bike billowed his jersey for a second as she passed. She wore a half tee with a gray sports bra under it, biking shorts, and sneakers. Her hair was pulled back into a shoulder-length ponytail sticking out above the adjustable strap on the back of her golf cap.

Only a glimpse. A lot to take in from just a streak, but Lucy made for a hell of a glimpse.

He kept running. Anita and her company passed him one more time before retreating to Antony Fusco's car at the Edgewood Avenue exit. Jack watched their departure until he spotted another observer.

The man had deep-set eyes below a bony brow, gaunt cheeks, deep nasal folds and thin lips. The image of a ghoul came to mind as Jack saw him emerge from the bushes munching from a bag of pistachios as the couple passed. He pulled out a small note pad from his pocket and a pencil from behind his ear. He jotted something into it as Antony Fusco's Jetta pulled away.

Jack hollered sharply to get the man's attention and started walking toward him to find out what business he had with Anita. He didn't, for one minute, consider that the stranger might have been looking for trouble with Fusco.

The man only half turned in response to Jack's bark as if it were a mere distraction, not a credible threat. Jack hesitated for a moment then strode right at him when he felt a tug on the back of his shirt.

"So you're the one."

Jack spun around to see Lucy straddling her bike right behind him.

"What? Lucy?" he said, confused for a moment.

She was incredibly stealthy on that gravel track. Preoccupied with Anita's safety, he didn't hear her bike grind to a halt there.

"Easy there, Tiger, I'm a fan too." She held up a restraining hand, but didn't appear any more frightened than the mystery man in the bushes.

Jack turned back to find him, but he had vanished. "What?" he said again, now more calmly, still looking into the bushes where the stranger had stood seconds ago. Somehow, Jack was sure that this was the phantom that had eluded him for the past two weeks.

"Hawks fan," she said. "I know they're not doing so hot right now, but they could use all the support they can get."

For the third time, Jack said, "What? Lucy, what are you talking about?"

She pointed at the Atlanta Hawks jersey that he was wearing.

"Oh," he said.

"You're not much of a morning person, huh, Jack?" She grinned one of those "gotcha" grins.

"Did you see—" he stammered, still peering into the bushes that spawned the stalker.

"Jack, you have got to move on. She's taken. Give it up." She pulled her cap off, shook her hair out and fluffed it in the morning sun. She was cooling off and still breathing hard.

"There are lots of fish in the sea."

She pulled the top off of her water bottle and turned it up drinking deeply.

*Nice image.* Jack took a mental picture. *Tight... and sweaty.*

"Do you run here every day?" she asked.

"Whenever I can. Two or three times a week, I guess."

"Do you have a bike, Jack?"

"Yeah, but the back brake is messed up. Dangerous to ride with only front brakes." Jack tried to keep his eyes from wandering too much.

"Humph," she said, then put away her water bottle and pulled a scrap of paper from her fanny pack. She wrote something on it.

"Bring it by sometime. I'm pretty handy with bikes. I'll get you in gear in no time." She smiled and again assumed that posture, infamous for emphasizing that perfect balance of physical assets.

"Give me a call, huh?" She mounted her bike again and started to pull off.

"Wait a minute." Jack held her handlebar to stop her take off. "Did you see that creepy guy in the bushes?"

Still grimacing from the restraint, she said, "The 'Birdwatcher'? He's here all the time. Supposedly watching

156

rare Georgia birds. Right." She wiped sweat from her brow. "He can probably tell you how many dimples I have on my butt."

"You have dimples on your butt?" Jack asked flirtatiously without thinking.

Lucy gave him a wry smile and rode off unimpeded, waggling that magnificent derriere side-to-side as she did.

# Chapter 21: Ghost Writer

Jack arrived at a quarter to nine. Al and Anita beat him into work rounds that morning. Both interns looked rested, and the usual bustle of the hospital was returning to normal. Since Jack did so much of the Hell Day work-ups, the team was able to make *lightning* rounds and mass discharge of its service. Jack cut out the work for each of them and began dictating discharge summaries for fifteen patients.

The hospital was on diversion, sending all emergency cases to other area hospitals until Hamilton could get its act together and open up some beds. No other area hospital could have absorbed that many medical and surgical admissions in a single night with as few casualties as Hamilton Medical sustained.

Blue team drew cheers from the medical teams that weren't on call that night as they rounded. Because of the diversion status, the other teams had gone through long call and short call with no admissions. A night that uneventful happened less than once in an entire three-year residency career. The relief teams didn't even mind babysitting the Hell Call teams' services for the couple of days of recovery.

"The covering resident had successfully *turfed* Helen Holcomb to neurology while we were out." Jack said.

"From the Samuel Shemm Novel, *House of God?*" Anita asked.

"To *Turf* a patient is to get them transferred to another specialty's service" Al elaborated. "or 'Turf', noun."

"Yes, I know the reference Al." She barely kept the indignity out of her voice. "It's been a classic for decades."

"Not an easy thing to do in Medicine: Bottom of the totem." Jody Mazur bragged.

Jody had managed Jack's service during his absence. "We got Mrs. Holcomb off the ventilator. We kept her a little dry with diuretic therapy and asked Neuro to take her. She was still lethargic, but she was at least breathing on her own." Jody said, "I talked to the neurology resident about reducing the diuretic administration as she became more alert and her breathing stabilized."

Jody turned over thirteen patients back to Jack. He discharged three already.

"Strong work," Jack said, taking the Sign out list from Jody.

Blue Team had discharged seven patients by 3 pm and they were planning to get three more on the launching pad by morning. They were packing up to go home for the day when Anita gave Jack that forlorn look, again. She was worried about Helen Holcomb.

*Considering the work she had put in on the FAME DAYS project, I guess she naturally feels responsible in some way.* Jack rubbed at the scabbed over the puncture wound on his left hand. *Poor kid.*

"Sure. Go ahead and visit." Then he warned, "She's not on our service anymore, Anita. Don't go nosing around through her record without permission from Neuro."

She went off down the hall mouthing, "Thank you." as she walked backwards before turning an about face in to a power stride to the Neurology wing.

Anita hadn't disappeared from sight five minutes before the code 99 was called overhead with the familiar location to follow.

Jack and Al looked at each other.

"Neuro unit," they said together and broke into a sprint in that direction.

They arrived to see Anita on top of Helen Holcomb performing chest compressions, giving orders to the nursing staff for stat labs and emergency drug administration per Advanced Cardiac Life Support protocols.

159

Two medical students arrived and Jack ordered them to relieve Dr. Thomas on CPR. Al guided one of them on the use of the Ambu bag for ventilating the old lady's lungs.

Anita was still giving orders to the students and nursing staff while Jack sidled up to her.

"What happened?" he asked softly, arms folded across his chest as he watched her run her code. Jack had no reason to take over from her. He suspected that she was better at running the process than he was.

"I don't know," she said. "I came in, sat on her bed and we began to talk. I asked her about the days leading up to the admission on Hell Night. She told me that she was still trying to lose weight and how she had stashed away some furosemide to wring out the water weight.

Says she always stopped the diuresis when she started to experience cramps and started on bananas. I told her that bananas weren't enough when you are really depleted of potassium and there might even be other electrolytes out of balance. She nodded at my reprimand." Anita watched the code proceed as she explained.

Jack realized that five-dollar words came naturally to her when she was stressed.

"You didn't yell at her, did you?" he asked.

"No, of course not. I just watched her for a moment. She began to hyperventilate and told me she felt a seizure coming on. She told me it always happened now when she got nervous or frightened."

"Sounds more like an anxiety attack to me." Jack said.

"Me too." Anita said. "Also she said that they became more frequent when she ate tomato sauce, or a lot of citrus fruits. She started to tell me something about sodas when the real seizure began.

"I lowered her back down to the bed, and turned her on her side to prevent aspiration but she arrested almost immediately. She stopped breathing. No pulse either. Too quickly for it to be due to the seizure itself, Jack." She summarized the history between resuscitation orders to the nurses. Cool as a cucumber. Anita was good at this.

"Where the hell is neuro?" Jack said turning to get to a hall phone and page the neurology resident. He just about knocked the neurology resident over at the door as he entered.

"What's going on, Jack?" Dr. Raja Kadam asked.

"We're not sure, Raj. My intern, Anita, found her in distress and she spontaneously seized up on her." Jack lied just a little.

It was apparent that there was much to hide here so Jack didn't think Raj needed to know about the FAME DAYS history, at least not immediately.

"Nice work here, Jack," Raja Kadam said.

Al had just slid the plastic endotracheal tube into place down Helen Holcomb's windpipe.

Raj leaned in to whisper in Jack's ear. "Let's talk outside."

They stepped out and Raj led him to a stairwell. Jack followed him through the door. Raj spoke only after the door closed behind them.

"Jack, this lady has been on some kind of experimental drug for Fibromyalgia Syndrome. The last resident told me so verbally. He signed out to me and referred me to the records for details, sketchy as he thought they were. I couldn't find any mention of the experimental drug in the record. In fact, when I confronted him about his poor record keeping, he insisted that he had spent at least a paragraph on the topic. We looked at the discharge summary together. Not only was the study and experimental drug not mentioned, but Marty said it wasn't even his dictation." Raj swallowed, then continued.

"I looked at him as if he were crazy. He showed me several examples of his discharge summaries to compare. Definitely a different writing style."

"Sometimes we write a little differently if we're tired or fresh off a rotation with an impressive attending–" Jack offered.

Raj shook his head before Jack finished. "What was in the record was a perfect generic summary commonly seen in throw away medical journals: Perfect grammar, punctuation, even spelling. Active voice."

*Ghostwriter*, Jack thought.

Physicians were trained to write and present cases in passive voice. Most throw away medical journals were written by professional medical writers, usually non-physicians or medical doctorates who had never practiced medicine. They often worked in the pharmaceutical industry preparing papers for presentation to the powers that be.

*People with that skill set have no business with direct access to personal data in the medical informatics system.* Jack thought.

Raj looked at him over reading glasses at the end of his nose. "Not even the chief resident has the security clearance to purge and replace a file, Jack. What the hell?"

"Damn, Raj." Jack shrugged. "I don't know."

"Word 'round the hospital is that your superstar intern knows something about this. And she's from Boston." Raj raised his eyebrows, awaiting a response.

"Why don't you go straight to the source, Raj?" Jack asked evasively.

"I did," he said. "I called the Rheumatology research division at the Nordstrom Clinic's Crawford Research Center. They reluctantly acknowledged that such a study existed, but that they were still crunching numbers and parts of the study were still blinded to the researchers, so they could be of little help to me. They further asked that I not inquire further because it could invalidate the study.

After I hung up, I got the bright idea to ask your intern directly."

"Without asking me first?" Jack protested. "You know better than that."

"I'd apologize for the breach in protocol if it had ever taken place. Thing is, Adela Garcia herself stepped in front of me as I approached Anita this morning and told me to back off." Raj locked gaze with him.

"Chief of Allergy, Immunology and Rheumatology, Adela Garcia?" Jack said incredulously.

"Physically restrained me, she did." He crossed his arms. "What is going on around here, Jack? Who is this woman?" Raj nodded his head toward Anita down the hall.

Without realizing he was speaking aloud, Jack murmured, "I don't know, Raj."

Jack shrugged and shook his head at the same time as he pulled the door open and made his way back to the room. Holcomb's bed was empty. The head nurse told him that she had been resuscitated and was on her way to radiology for an MRI of the head.

Jack nodded as he watched Raj read a text on his smart phone and walk absently down the hall as he did so.

This whole Anita situation was getting complicated too quickly for him to keep up. Jack didn't know if he could protect Anita much longer. He didn't know if he should. Moreover, he didn't know if he needed to. With allies like the Chairman of medicine, Chief of the A.I.R. division, chief resident and that 250-pound gorilla, Antony Fusco, what did Jack add to her defensive line anyway? He knew he was in over his head until he got much more information on her background, the experimental mystery drug, and a line on Anita's pursuers.

Jack found Anita sitting in the hall with her back against the wall, head between her knees, near radiology. She looked despondent, but she wasn't crying. He leaned against the wall and slid down the cool surface to sit beside her.

"How are you holding up, Anita?" he asked.

She brushed her hair back out of her eyes and gave him a weak smile. "As well as can be expected I guess." The subdued lights in the radiology department hall mirrored her mood. "She didn't look good. I'll stick around in case they need me again." She crossed her arms around her knees and wearily rested her head there again.

Jack watched her, wondering what he was looking at. As he said to Raja Kadam, Jack didn't know himself.

"Go home, Anita. There's nothing that either of us can do from here on." *Unless you are holding back more critical information.* Jack thought. "Hey, it's our golden weekend tomorrow after rounds. Live it up a little."

He patted her gently on the shoulder and climbed to his feet. He had his backpack with him and made for the front doors again and MARTA. The summer breeze wasn't cool but the morning rain had somehow freshened the air of underlying rancor so characteristic of downtown Atlanta. Jack took a deep breath of the afternoon air and thought, *Great day for a bike ride.*

# Chapter 22: Swimming with Sharks

Jack showered as soon as he got into his apartment. Two messages blinked on his machine. He still used a micro cassette answering machine. It was a gift from his mother the year he went away for college--a relic from when she attended Tulane. Somehow, it still kept him connected to her.

*I probably need to get rid of it,* he thought. Callers could hear him talking in his apartment if they were actively leaving a message because the line was opened. He learned that the hard way when he was filtering calls from an ex-girlfriend.

Anyway, at a glance, he could see how many calls he'd received on it during the day. He didn't even check messages until after the shower. One was from his father, the other was from Orson Quirk. An invitation to happy hour the next night. Jack knew who he was, but he just didn't understand why Quirk bothered to call him personally.

He threw on a clean Hawks jersey, some biking shorts, a new pair of tennis shoes, and raked a comb through his hair. He grabbed his bike and slung it behind his back. With his free hand, he grabbed a couple of condoms from his night table drawer and stuffed them in his pocket. He might get lucky.

Hope safely in his pocket, Jack took the elevator to the lobby and called Lucy on his cell to ask directions. "Hi Lucy, I'm headed out riding. Only problem is, my brakes are still stuck. Any thoughts?"

"Huh, I'll get my tools out for you."

He liked the sound of that. He memorized the directions to her apartment.

Lucy lived two blocks closer to the hospital than Jack. Very nice building. About fifteen years newer than his. In downtown Atlanta, that meant expensive. Her building was a quadrangle with a courtyard in the middle. One side of the building, the Tower, was three stories taller than the other three. Lucy had a three-bedroom deal on the top floor of the Tower overlooking Grant Park as well as the pool and health center that spanned the three other sections of the roof.

Jack came in the front door and immediately felt underdressed. It was not just because the flat was fifteen degrees cooler than the hall. The place was professionally decorated and expensively appointed. Stark contrast to most residents' and interns' lodgings: Persian carpet separated the hardwood from most of the heavy furnishings. Lucy spent some real money on the place.

"Come on in, Jack. Make yourself at home." Lucy was wearing a wet, white string bikini with a thong bottom. In the air-conditioned room absolutely nothing was left to the imagination and she was not shy.

*She is really working that swimsuit,* Jack thought.

He relaxed a little as she disappeared into the depths of the apartment and perused his surroundings. He decided the apartment fit her. European décor, framed original oils hung on the walls. There were several sculptures of bronze and marble set around the room. One drew his attention more intensely than the rest.

"That's my favorite piece." Lucy caught him admiring the small statue. "I didn't think you'd stumble onto it so soon. Do you appreciate fine art, Jack?"

"I really don't know much, but I recognize the Venus de Milo." He said.

"It's a replica of course." She laughed. "The original is white marble and taller than you. Quality has always been more important than size to me. She's carved of Etowah marble. Local to Georgia, but the pink and white serpentine bands make it prized worldwide. *Blood and Milk* it's been called." Lucy caressed the armless figure then folded her arms high behind her back mimicked its pose. "Polishes to an exquisite shine. It's why she's set off in this corner alone, wouldn't want her accidently knocked off while horsing around, you know?"

She took his hand and led him a step back from the piece. In spite of his shower and change of clothes, Jack didn't feel clean enough to sit on any of that furniture. Nothing in sight was ever "as advertised on TV", that was for sure.

"Sorry, Jack." Lucy seemed to become suddenly aware of her scanty coverage. "I was at the pool," she said as she sashayed toward her bedroom.

Jack wasn't complaining. Her damp skin, covered in goosebumps, steamed in the chill as expected after a swim. He imagined the texture of that glistening flesh against his fingers. Jack did notice her hair was perfectly styled, her makeup and nails freshly done, though. She came out of her bedroom empty-handed.

"Now where did I put that toolkit?" she asked herself aloud. She crinkled her nose and hung her little finger thoughtfully against her lower teeth. Her other hand came to rest on a curvaceous hip as she half faced him presenting all optimal aspects of her figure at once. She wore a ruby belly button ring. Jack's attention continued to drift as his nature compelled until she snapped her fingers.

"I know!" she turned and sauntered into another bedroom that she used as an office. It was different, but just as nice as the rest of the place. She had several seven-foot mahogany bookcases filled with an assortment of books ranging from recent best sellers, all hard covers, as well as classic literature and scientific works. Somehow, Jack didn't think they were for show either. Conversations overheard in the weeks that he had known her referenced many of the titles represented.

She opened the very bottom drawer in an antique file cabinet and fished around. Seemed like a ballet position; legs taut and crossed at the ankles, gracefully bending over at the hips. Progressing down from her blossoming cheeks, he noticed that she rocked sandals with five-inch heels, the kind with straps that wrapped around the ankles.

Jack knew very well what foot wear like that was often called, but he'd never say it aloud, especially not to her. At least not before he got a notch or two on the scoreboard.

He knew why he was there, and broken brakes had nothing to do with it.

Lucy squeaked a trill "Ah!" when she found her tool kit. She straightened one vertebra at a time like a cat and tapped a little victory dance with her feet. She came out of the office and right into Jack's waiting arms.

He landed a wet one on her lips as he intercepted her at the doorway into the living room. She draped her arms around his neck and leaned her head down for a few seconds, hiding her eyes behind loops of wine colored hair accented by that lock of white. Lucy breathed three long, cleansing breaths before stepping back from him still hanging her head down.

"Why, Dr. Wheaton, is that a bicycle lock in your pocket or are you just happy to see me?" She asked and pushed him playfully away.

She cleared her throat. "Let's have a look at your brakes, Speedy." Escaping his encircling arms, she crossed the room as if modeling the bathing suit she wore, sat down on an ottoman and got to work on his brakes.

"Oh, easy," she declared looking the parts over. She hung her tongue out the side of her mouth as she tightened the problematic brake bolt into place with a couple of exaggerated cranks of her wrench.

"Let me get into my riding gear and I'll be right with you. Can I get you anything to drink, Jack?" she asked as she triumphantly marched into her bedroom with a bouncing stroll.

"What have you got?" he asked.

"Check behind the bar. See if there's anything you like."

She left the door to her bedroom opened and from the bar, Jack had a perfect line of sight to where she was standing, working her way out of her swimsuit. An arpeggio of deep, rich chimes issued from somewhere in her room.

Jack double-checked to make sure he didn't accidently forget his condoms.

Back to him, Lucy seemed to be struggling with something. Soon he heard her call out, "Jack?"

He walked almost to the bedroom door before answering her. She seemed surprised to find him so close.

"I think I accidentally tied this thing in knots back here. Now that the strings are all wet, I can't get them loose with these fingernails. Can you help me?

Chains and bear traps couldn't have stopped him then, but all he said was, "Let's see what I can do here."

She really did have the thing in knots, one at the neck and one mid back. The bright white suit clung in contrast against steaming, cinnamon skin. The goose flesh had all but receded leaving only twin protrusions peeking through the wet top's cups. Over her shoulder, he inhaled her warmth like fresh apple pie on a stove. It took him a couple of minutes to loosen the strings. By the time he got the last knot out, he was ready to tear the damn thing off with his teeth.

"Thanks Jack," she said as she turned to face him. "I was afraid I'd have to cut it off. This is a hundred and thirty dollar bikini." She looked up into his eyes and said nothing.

Speechless, Jack lifted the swim top up and over her head and saw all he had hoped for and more.

Jack rotated through plastic surgery as an intern. He had been able to clinically detach himself from any cosmetic or reconstructive case without arousal. He found himself unable to demonstrate the same restraint here. This was one of the best augmentation jobs he had ever seen.

"You had better keep your hands where I can see them," she said pushing his hands away from her topless body with a single, half-hearted effort. She cocked her head to the side letting her hair fall into her face again. She drew her shoulders back and dropped her arms to her sides.

"Didn't you want anything to drink, Jack?" she asked, in the sultriest voice imaginable. "Open bar."

He scooped her up in his arms and felt her body temperature rise with his touch.

"What about our ride?" she asked.

The ratta-tat-tat of raindrops pecked against her window, and she sighed in resignation allowing her arms to go limp.

Sealing her lips with his, Jack ended the small talk for the evening. He swept her to the bed and spilled her there brushing the wind chimes into notion again with her toes. The rest was fluid. Neither his nor her motions ruled, just the rhythm of human nature.

The night was an erotic storm. Lucy performed the finale on his lap. When she was done, she stripped him of his protection without using her hands or her mouth. The Kegel exercise, taught to women after childbirth to strengthen their pelvic muscles, had other uses.

*This woman has skills.* Jack thought. *She could teach graduate studies in the Karma Sutra.*

Luciana Velasquez was a master of the *Kegel Arts*. She wasn't squeamish about disposing of the condom either. She took it into the bathroom and Jack heard the toilet flush.

He stood and stretched as he inspected her boudoir. Unlike the living room, her bedroom had an Asian theme.

"Ruby red, beautiful!"

"It's Dragon Red," she corrected him.

With a gentle thump to the chimes, she flopped on her back, hanging one leg off the side of the bed she now had all to herself. "It's a custom color they only make in China."

"Bullshit!" Jack said. "With today's technology, they can match any color there is, Lucy."

"Yeah, you'd think so, but I am telling you the truth, they can't quite duplicate this color. They come close, but when it dries, it is always a little off." She took a deep breath and arched her back then relaxed again.

"Jack, I'm exhausted, can you help me again?"

"I think I already removed just about everything God didn't give you."

"Very funny. I mean my tummy ring. I can do it myself, but it takes me a while. I just about have to hold a crunch position for two minutes or more to undo the clasp. I'm just too tired." She chirped, "You wore me out!"

By this time, Jack could refuse her nothing. It was almost 6:00 am and he thought, *One more torpedo in the tube, so why not ingratiate her one more time?*

Lucy laid spread eagle, turned her face away and relaxed as Jack dug his fingers into her navel to unfasten the jewel. From his position beside her, he couldn't see her smile at his efforts or how that smile widened when she felt the flinch as he pricked his finger good undoing it.

"I'm sorry, Jack." She said in response to his ouch. "I've been meaning to get that stupid catch fixed for the past week. I got it caught on a towel and broke it. Let me see that finger."

She popped up and dashed to the bathroom to retrieve a first aid kit with an alacrity that belied the bumbling around involved in finding her tool kit the night before or any signs of fatigue she just described.

Lucy moved like a thoroughbred on her second wind. She dabbed at the wound with several strangely absorbent gauze pads, placed them into a zip lock bag, then applied a thin bandage.

"Good as new. Now you had better scat. You have rounds to do, don't you?" she asked him, absent the passion she had shown for the past several hours.

"Yeah, I guess you're right," he admitted, "Can you give me a ride in?"

"Why? You have your bicycle and I've fixed it for you. Besides, I don't have a rack." She yawned and executed a feline stretch of her shapely nude body against the satin sheets.

Jack said nothing, but just scanned her body in the dim light.

She opened her eyes in the absence of a verbal response, saw his smirk, and realized the implication.

"A bike rack on my car, smart ass." She laughed.

When she turned to answer, Jack noticed something peculiar about Lucy. There was a light patch where her make-up had smeared on the left side of her face. He turned on the overhead light and gently rolled her face toward him to get a better look. She might have expected a kiss.

"So you have vitiligo, don't you?" Jack asked.

She indignantly turned her face away, slapped at his hand and closed her eyes tightly. "What of it? I never said I was perfect. You guys. Always want the Barbie doll, don't you?" She covered her face and eyes with her hands. "Well, real women aren't perfect. Those who are won't be forever."

"Lucy–"

"Go home, Jack."

He felt bad for her. He had gone "clinical" on her without realizing it. For young doctors, it was an occupational hazard.

Ashamed, Jack found himself toying with the now silent wind chimes. The tubes ranged two to four feet in length and performed a concert driven by the rocking motion of Lucy's bed last night. Now that serenade just reminded him of Anita's laughter. Absently he peered out the window taking in the view of downtown from the fifth floor window. Past the Atlanta skyline, he could see Stone Mountain from there and the hospital and… Anita.

She was in the apartment across the courtyard one floor down staring up at Lucy's window from her own as she sipped her coffee until she recognized him. Jack saw her turn around, spilling the mug's content on her night shirt when she realized that she was looking at her senior resident naked.

Jack stumbled over something heavy on the floor next to Lucy's bed as he tried to get away from the window. He realized that there was some kind of metal spike projecting up through the pile of newspapers on the floor there.

"What the hell, Lucy? Someone could hurt themselves on this thing," he said,"-or worse."

She shrugged causally, "*I* know where it is."

Jack couldn't believe she was so careless about such a dangerous item in her bedroom.

"Lucy, did you know that Anita lived just two floors down on the other side of the building?"

"Of course, Jack. We girls have to watch out for each other." She unfolded her arms from over her face. "*We* don't judge each other either."

She looked at him with cold determination. Glistening with sweat, she stretched slender arms out to full length across the bed, kicked the top sheet off and hung her right leg off the edge, swinging it gently.

173

"Lucy, I'm sorry. I didn't mean…"

She interrupted his apology, mid-sentence. "Jack, bring in the morning newspaper, please." She wasn't looking at him. "I like to read it over my morning coffee. Get a jump on the day, you know?" She lay lazily on the bed, face and eyes averted from him.

Vitiligo is an autoimmune mediated, localized loss of pigment. Jack knew that for fair-skinned people it's barely noticeable, but in people of color, it could be psychologically devastating.

As he left, Jack said, "Will I see you at happy hour tonight?"

"Oh, yeah. I'll be there," she said, half falling asleep. "The boss insists…"

"He called me up personally to invite me, you know?" he said in a last effort to impress her before he left.

"That's nice, Jack," was all she said and dozed off where she sprawled on her back, delicate fingers palms up with red tipped nails relaxed against off white sheets, eyes closed peacefully, with that dangling right foot now still.

The only movement, that of her chest rising and falling with slowing breaths as she relaxed. Auburn hair with its wispy white streak stirred by the gently whirling ceiling fan cooling the steam off her hot body. Her face no longer looked angry. It didn't look anything at all. Just beautiful, as if she had not a care in the world.

Jack closed the door and carried his bike to the elevator.

# Chapter 23: The Expert

It was Friday morning and Jack found himself look-ing forward to happy hour less and less all day. Last night with Lucy started out like a slice of heaven but ended up with him feeling like a piece of crap. He had woken with-out pain, but now ached across his shoulders and down his back.

He rode home, showered again, changed and made his way back to the hospital by MARTA. He dropped his backpack off at the office and checked his service's census.

*Back up to four.* Polly Harker had bounced back to them. She had become dehydrated. They had discharged her less than forty-eight hours earlier so again, she was theirs. Anita got her tucked into a floor bed without having to resort to any extraordinary intravenous measures.

Jack led Al and Anita to selected rooms to care for the three remaining patients. Before they finished rounds, Fred Albright stopped him in the hall.

"Jack, Dr. Garcia says she really needs help in Rheumatology clinic today. Would you mind?"

"What about my clinic, Fred?" he said. Jack thought he knew what was coming: *Work the Rheumatology clinic, then come back and all my own patients will still be waiting for me.*

"Oh, you want to cover too?" Fred said, confused. "I was asking you about Anita as a courtesy."

Recognizing the protest in Jack's tone, Fred asked, "You haven't done a rotation in Rheumatology yet, have you?"

Now Jack was confused. *What does he want with Anita?* "Sorry?"

"Rheumatology. Did you ever do a rotation?" Fred asked him.

"Yes. In Boston, as a junior resident, just a few months ago at Mass General," Jack said. "One of the best rotations I ever did."

"Great. You're in then. Clinic starts at 1:00 pm." Fred Albright turned and headed down the hall toward the stairwell. "I'll let Dr. Garcia know to expect both of you."

"Fred, what about...?"

Fred called over his shoulder without breaking stride. "Don't worry, the transitional interns will cover your general medicine clinic and Anita's too."


Fred Albright's edict got Jack out of rounds a little early. He checked his watch. *Time for lunch.*

As it was 15 minutes before noon, Jack leisurely meandered his way to the cafeteria. Upon entering the eatery he headed towards the doctors lounge when he caught sight of Al and Khandi. They were both laughing and seemingly having such a good time Jack decided to join them instead. As he approached the table, he realized that it was mostly a private conversation. As he began to turn Khandi grabbed his sleeve.

"It's all right Jack, you can join us." Khandi said. "We missed you last night."

"You sure?" Jack asked. "I hope I'm not intruding."

"Nah, man." Al said. "We just talking. But you really missed a great concert last night."

"Concert? Who?" asked Jack.

"New guy Khandi found, Valerie Rutkowski. Amazing guy, plays jazz cello of all things." Al laughed.

"Yeah, I found him online. He's got a YouTube video that is phenomenal. He does a few standards and has great renditions of some new stuff." Khandi said. "You should have been there."

"I was into something I couldn't get out of last night." Jack said.

"You must have been in pretty deep, Jack." Khandi said with a smirk. "You didn't answer your phone and Al must've called you five times."

"Yeah, I was in pretty deep," Jack agreed.

"Tight too I guess." Khandi said and then burst into laughter.

"What's she so bubbly about?" Jack asked.

"Lucy." Khandi blurted out.

"Don't mind her, Jack. She had a doctor's visit today." Al said with resignation. "Talked them into giving her a hit of Versed. The stuff's still wearing off. Never did knock her out though." Al wrapped an arm around her and shook her a bit.

"Why on earth would they have to use Versed?" Jack asked.

"They called me back in to go over some tests. I told them I felt fine, but they insisted that I come in," Khandi replied.

"You mind if I ask what the tests were?" asked Jack.

"A little blood in the urine," said Khandi.

Al gestured that the conclusion was obvious, but Khandi went on. "And since I don't get periods, they decided they needed to check my prostate." She threw her hands above her head in disbelief. She wore a halter top and three quarter length jeans. Jack noted a toned, slender belly with admiration as she pushed back in her chair. Al touched her arm to get her to lower her voice. She raised one thigh to her chest and hoisted her heel to the seat of the chair. A cuff rolled up nearly to her knee revealed a shapely calf.

"Oops," Khandi said quietly.

"It's okay, Khandi." Jack reassured.

"Does the whole staff know?" She said to Al, shooting him a cross look.

"Only the ones that heard you announce that you have a prostate."

"Okay, okay. Mia culpa." Khandi conceded.

"Jack heard that I lost standing over a relationship with a patient." Al explained.

"So?" she said.

"In urology clinic?" Al said slowly. "Didn't take a genius to figure the rest out. I just figured I'd take the weirdness out of the situation."

"Alright." She threw her hands up again this time just to the table top. "Nice to have one more person in my 'inner circle' anyway." She paused and reached across the table for Jack's hand. "So, Lucy, huh? I hear she's really hot."

"How the hell does she know about Lucy?" Jack accused as Al shrugged.

"Wasn't Al--" Khandi explained. "Anita. She had a few too many glasses of wine last night and I guess it loosened her tongue a bit. She said that you had been crushing on her pretty heavy, but when Lucy flashed you a little tail, you turned both heads that way.

"I saw her this morning coming into the building and asked about last night." Then to Al, "Hey, she knows my friend Helen, too." Then back to Jack, "She said she still had a headache, but got in to work sooner than you."

"'Helen who had a headache?" Jack asked confused.

"Not Helen--Anita." She smackied Jack on the arm. "Keep up, Jack. Said you were 'finishing up some business from last night.' When I asked what kind of business kept you from the concert, Anita told me 'Lucy business'. Said she must make better music than Rutkowski." Khandi finished still slightly dazed he thought. "So? What's up, Jack?"

*She's still under the influence of the Versed, I bet.* Jack realized. *Still, she knows too much.*

"So again, why the Versed, Al?" Jack asked.

"Well, it's like this, the resident who was scheduled to see me was this cute Dominican intern. She was out so another resident was covering. He was tall. Really tall. Had these long, skinny fingers, too." Khandi grinned. "Great fingers. Anyway, I told him I was really sensitive there so he needed to knock me out if he was going to probe my nether regions. He said they couldn't use twilight sleep for a simple rectal, but if he used conscious sedation, I'd be so relaxed I wouldn't care. So I said okay and he broke out the Versed. Great stuff. And he has such really long, skinny fingers."

"You said that already." Al reminded her.

As she began to describe how she positioned on the table for her exam, Al interrupted again with a clearing of his throat.

"Okay, but I'm gonna get some of that stuff for home use," Khandi said, nodding toward Al.

"Al?" Jack said cautiously.

"I don't need Al to get it for me," Khandi said. "I have other sources. Fats can get almost anything." She thought for a moment. "You know how to give that stuff don't you? I don't want to end up like *Michael*."

"That was propofol. And yes I know how to give it." Al said quietly.

"And Helen was here to get some IV stuff. From that tall Chinese doc and the big guy was there." Khandi turned to Al, "You know, the one that looked like the fat guy in that Bogart movie... *The Maltese Falcon*?"

Fred Albright appeared behind Al and the conversation came to an abrupt end.

"Jack, you're due in clinic in fifteen minutes. Don't be late. Dr. Garcia will eat you alive if you are." Albright shot an accusatory look at Al then at Khandi.

"On my way, Fred." Jack said rising from the table as Fred did an awkward about face and strode to the nearest exit.

Khandi laughed when Albright was out of earshot. "You have great taste in women, Jack. Kudos. I can't wait to see this chick, Lucy, tonight."

As he left, Jack frowned at Khandi as Al cuddled her, laughed at them both when their fingers intertwined, then he followed Fred Albright out of the cafeteria.

Jack showed up on the subspecialty clinical floor to find Anita sharing a sandwich and a coke with the Chief of Rheumatology. Anita drained her cup of cola and stood almost at attention when she saw Jack. He averted her eyes and addressed Dr. Garcia.

"Afternoon, Dr. Garcia. Jack Wheaton reporting for clinic." The only formality missing from his greeting was the salute.

This was Adele Garcia. Nine hundred peer reviewed publications as primary investigator. Editor in Chief of Rheumatology and Arthritis. The only Rheumatology Master to turn down the position of President of the Modern Arthritis and Rheumatism Society at the age of 47. Now chief of the division of Allergy, Immunology, and Rheumatology at Hamilton Medical Center. Jack thought she was absolutely awesome.

"Good to meet you, Jack." Dr. Garcia stood with alacrity. "The list is on my desk in the clinic. Here's your highlighter." She handed him a blue one. Anita held a green one in her hand. "Let's see some patients."

He nearly shouted, "Yes, Ma'am!"

Leading the way, Dr. Garcia stopped short, and turned on her heel to face him.

"Jack, this is not the army. You don't have to address me so formally." She half turned at the door. Glaring back at him, she said, "But if you ever call me by my first name, I'll have you assigned to morgue duty all summer, got it?"

He was on the verge of blurting out a denial of any desire to address Dr. Garcia in such a familiar fashion when Anita laughed out loud before he could make a total idiot of himself.

*Plenty of chances for that later.* He thought.

Dr. Garcia walked over to the patient schedule on the whiteboard and looked it up and down from top to bottom.

"Good teaching cases," she said. Dr. Garcia silently counted them off and nodded to herself. "Jot these names down people."

She assigned five to Jack and five to Anita. The remaining eleven Dr. Garcia and the nurse practitioner would see. The highlighters were to identify which clinician saw which patient. When they were done, all cases would be presented to Dr. Garcia for discussion and treatment planning.

Jack found himself managing a handful of interesting cases. A rheumatoid patient who had suffered significant deformity before starting monthly infusions with a T-lymphocyte co-stimulator antagonist. The woman was now in remission and had returned to work in the local custom clock factory.

Jack checked her lab tests for signs of potential toxicity. When he confirmed her tests were normal, he told her that they would see to it that she had adequate refills of her Methotrexate, the micro-dose chemotherapy that enhanced the effects of the intravenous biologic agent doing the heavy lifting for management of her Rheumatoid Arthritis. Then he scheduled her next infusion and follow-up appointment.

Jack waited for Dr. Garcia to see the second patient on her own list before preparing to present his case to her. She took notes as he presented then coached him on pertinent aspects of the history and physical examination to record electronically in her chart file. Dr. Garcia was amazingly patient for a guru of medicine. Even more so with the midlevel physician extender. The nurse practitioners were usually assigned Fibromyalgia Syndrome and Osteoarthritis since both diagnoses benefitted from modern medical advances.

Anita had a great case of acute Gout with Podagra of the right great toe. *Most patients with acute Gouty arthritis don't want the sheets to touch the swollen area.* He knew, *Even a breeze blowing across the affected joint is agony.*

He watched over Dr. Garcia's shoulder while Anita prepared to aspirate the first metatarsal joint under ultrasound guidance. He'd seen it performed several times, but he had only done three. Two of them badly. The usage of ultrasound imaging to guide the needle added a different dimension. *Smooth procedure for such a painful condition.*

As Anita performed the arthrocentesis, Jack noted the large nodular masses on the man's elbows and the smaller nodules on his upper ears. The patient was Asian Pacific by his appearance. He carried a black brimmed hat in his hands and wore a dark suit. Odd for 93-degree summer heat in Atlanta, until Jack realized he also wore a white collar.

The Reverend Manuel Concepcion was moderately overweight at 180 pounds and five foot six. He was also very pleasant in spite of the exquisite pain, which had required him to borrow a wheel chair at the clinic entry.

His daughter propelled him in the chair and guided him to the examination room where the procedure was set up. The resemblance was obvious except for the weight. None would label the daughter thin, but she was obviously fit despite her wide waist. Her empathy for her father's situation was evident by her close doting, furrowed brow and gaze locked on the chair bound man with frequent winces tossed toward the instrument tray set up on the Mayo stand.

Most relatives imagined their loved ones in much more pain than they were actually in during an arthrocentesis. In the hands of an expert, there is virtually no pain at all when the appropriate precautions are taken. Topical refrigerant, subcutaneous anesthetic, and careful guidance to the joint space without too much adjusting or manipulation of the needle or surrounding tissue en route makes for a very comfortable injection.

Jack obtained the history from Ms. Concepcion while Anita concentrated on her task at hand. There was no history of significant alcohol consumption, but he had passed several kidney stones. He took colchicine until the price went up forty fold last year. He had a bona fide Allopurinol allergy.

"Has anyone discussed a medication called Febuxostat with your dad?" Jack asked the daughter.

Dr. Garcia shot him a cross look, which stopped Jack mid-sentence. He said no more until Anita was done with the joint aspiration. The yield of white, pasty fluid was plenty for such a small space. She deftly changed syringes on the needle without disturbing its position in the inflamed joint space.

After the injection of an anesthetic/glucocorticoid cocktail, Anita withdrew the needle in one deliberate, clean stroke with its attached and then bandaged the toe with loving care.

There was a measure of instant relief to the foot, which Anita promised him would improve even more over the next twelve to twenty four hours with rest. His daughter promised he would comply.

Anita told the good reverend that the secretary would schedule an appointment for him to return in six weeks to begin a course of Febuxostat at 40 mg daily once this flare resolved.

"Starting treatment now might actually perpetuate the arthritic activity. Here's an order for blood work that you'll need to have drawn before you leave the clinic today," she said.

Jack felt foolish. He knew the right medications, but he was less familiar with their proper use than was Anita. He expected more repudiation from Dr. Garcia than he received as she simply told him to avoid discussing treatment with patients until they had a chance to discuss it as a group or advised differently by Dr. Garcia.

The fact that Anita had just handled the case like an attending professor was not lost on him. Obviously, Dr. Garcia knew more about Anita's background than Jack did and had the utmost confidence in her.

Jack didn't know her research background when she first came in. He had been briefed on a "different" Anita Thomas. One with an average academic background. Not the superstar before him who graduated college at eighteen, earned her PhD by age twenty and by the time she was twenty-three, had already made assistant professor at The Nordstrom Clinic, a national ranking, with several publications to her credit. She placed out of the first two years of medical school by virtue of her postgrad bioengineering and molecular genetics background.

He hadn't known she was a member of MENSA. And all of this two years before she started as his intern. Jack didn't know why they assigned her to him, but his life might have been a lot less complicated if they hadn't. The tension in his neck and upper back was building and he executed a cat stretched with his arms over his head. He crossed off his second patient and went on to his third.

Jack saw a case of Systemic Lupus Erythematosus with severe dermatitis, deforming arthritis, and resolving inflammation of the heart and lung linings. She was a young black girl of nineteen years old. She was short and slight for her age, giving her a deceptively juvenile appearance. She had a high-pitched, child-like voice, which added to the youthful effect.

She had been diagnosed four years ago and treated with hydroxychloroquine, Methylprednisolone, and ibuprofen. Azathioprine had been started, but stopped due to development of a low white blood cell count that resolved when the drug was withdrawn.

Dr. Garcia and Anita were already discussing the pros and cons of the new anti B lymphocyte antibody therapy. They reviewed the chart together and sighed. Her insurance did not cover the drug.

The young woman splinted with pain as she inhaled for Jack's examination of her lungs. He regarded her sympathetically. He knew what they were saying now was different from what she had been told for the previous three years. That story had been, 'Ms. Jones, there is no other treatment available for your condition. We're very sorry, but you'll have to learn to live with it.' Now they were telling her, 'Ms. Jones, there is a very effective treatment for your condition but you can't have it. You'll just have to learn to live with it.'

"Ms. Jones, we'll go up by fifty percent on your steroids for now. That will help with your symptoms. In the meantime, we'll see if we can get treatment approved on a compassionate basis and infuse it here at the clinic's expense," Dr. Garcia told her.

She held the patient's hand as she spoke. What she didn't say was that she would get the hospital to write off the infusion expense.

Aisha Jones was grateful and thanked them all before heading to the laboratory for the appropriate tests needed to monitor her condition and then off to the pharmacy to receive the medications per the new regimen prescribed.

Dr. Garcia and Anita watched her walk down the hall. They both shook their heads.

"It's a travesty that we can have all of these pharmaceutical miracles, but can't find a way to make them generally available where needed," Dr. Garcia lamented.

Anita hung her head. "It's not how the world works."

"It's not about need, it's about opportunity. If need is served in the process then so be it. If not, then it's just tough luck," Jack said in one of his rare moments of insight into Anita's psyche. He connected with both of them for a time.

"Okay, now we'll have to deal with the Fibromyalgia contingent," the Nurse Practitioner said.

The physician extender was a mature, tall woman with icy, blue eyes and white hair. Janice Walker had worked the subspecialty clinics since before even Dr. Garcia took over the department. She had maintained her fitness with a daily regimen of running and a healthy diet well into her fifties. Jack estimated her body fat content at no more than ten percent.

"We have three that seem to need more than a refill on their Pregabalin and Fluoxetine prescriptions, doctor," Janice Walker announced respectfully.

"Okay, so who do we have?" Dr. Garcia's demeanor visibly changed when they shifted from the more interesting rheumatology cases to fibromyalgia syndrome.

Ms. Walker was less visibly displeased with managing Fibromyalgia Syndrome than Dr. Garcia. "Campbell Brookes. A 32-year-old white female with a 6-year history of fibromyalgia syndrome treated with pregabalin, fluoxetine and cyclobenzaprine at the hour of sleep. She says she is not getting enough pain relief and that she has not slept in four days."

Jack interrupted almost involuntarily. "Everybody hurts. If she hadn't slept in four days, she should just stop long enough to pass out from exhaustion."

All three women looked at him with disappointment.

"Jack, these patients have a hard enough time dealing with public perception, their families and this disorder,"
Anita chided.

Walker went on. "She's asking for narcotics." She
held Dr. Garcia's gaze meaningfully for a moment. "What
do you want to do?"

"Has she been to physical therapy yet?" Dr. Garcia
asked.

"Yup. Make's her hurt more, she says," Walker answered before the question was completed.

"Well, what about massage therapy?" Jack said.
"That should relieve some of her musculoskeletal pain,
shouldn't it?"

Walker informed him. "Non-covered service, and
she can't afford it out of pocket."

Dr. Garcia crossed her arms, bracing for presentation of the history that she already anticipated, and that she
had heard over years in practice a few hundred times before.

"When you gave her the spiel about avoiding narcotic analgesics, how did the dialogue go?" Dr. Garcia
asked glumly.

"Circular, as always. The tangent always came back
to 'eleven' on a 1 to 10 scale of pain intensity with no relief
night or day and what were we going to do about it?"
Walker shrugged. "You know."

Anita, chewed her lip, silently frustrated. "Have we
tried a milnacipran titration yet?" Anita asked half-heart-
edly.

"Nausea," Was the one word answer from Walker.

"Let's give her some propoxyphene... oops. That's
right, that was pulled from the market last year." Dr. Garcia
missed a single beat then said, "Okay, she can have a thirty

count of tramadol 50 mg to be taken as directed for break-through pain. No refills, Walker."

Anita snapped a pencil between her fingers that she had been absently fidgeting with for most of the Fibro discussion.

"Done deal." Then she wrote into her chart note to be dictated by Dr. Garcia for transcription later.

Anita remained agitated through the next two presentations about dissatisfied Fibromyalgia patients. After her revelations two nights ago, Jack empathized with her. He realized his own prejudice toward these patients—these people.

After Campbell Brooke, there was a middle-aged woman, maybe fifty-five, Olivia Tyler. Same story. Anita knew how to help them but couldn't. Couldn't even talk about it.

"That's all for today guys," Dr. Garcia said. "Good work."

She and Ms. Walker finished up the charting and saw to closing down the rheumatology clinic. Jack watched the two pros gearing down. Whatever Dr. Garcia said to the three Fibro patients they had just discussed, they seemed to be surprisingly pleased with it. He wondered how she had phrased the "no help" verdict to get it to go over so well.

Jack heard Dr. Garcia call to Ms. Walker, "Monday is Allergy clinic, Walker. Get the charts together. Just put the list of Fellows, residents and med students for Monday on my desk."

Dr. Garcia checked her watch. "Have a good week end, Walker."

"You too, Ma'am." Walker replied.

# Chapter 24: Evening at the Lattimore

Jack and Anita got out of Rheumatology Clinic sooner than they would have finished General Medicine clinic. He learned a lot, but he felt totally inadequate after seeing Anita's performance that day.

*I'll never call this stuff "Rheuma-Holiday" again.* He thought, *It's no picnic. Not if done right.*

He had time for a haircut and shower before happy hour. He hopped a MARTA train down to Little Five Points to find an open chair at his favorite barber. Keith greeted him with a handshake, sat him in the chair, pumping it up to a comfortable height.

While Keith snapped the drape then checked his clippers and scissors, Jack got a text from Al.

Dnt 4get ☺ Hr @ Latmr HtL 6:30. C U thr.

*Good old Al. Making sure I had all the data. Lattimore Hotel lobby Happy Hour 6:30 pm. Business casual.*

With a flick, clippers hummed to life and the barber went to work. He knew what style Jack wanted and why. It had been the topic of many a Saturday afternoon discussion at the barbershop: *Girls.*

If nurses were invited, young nurses, all the male residents would be dressed to impress. The female house officers had slightly different motives to dress up. Mostly for a change of pace, but sometimes a woman wanted a different kind of attention from the male counterparts she worked with that didn't relate to her mastery of the medical arts.

Jack closed his eyes and tried to picture what was in his closet. He couldn't remember what was there. *If I don't have something clean in there, there won't be time to wash, dry and press anything.*

189

There was no Wal-Mart within half an hour of the barbershop so it was the local thrift store for underwear, a clean white shirt, some slacks, and a pair of dark socks, which would get him through the night with dignity and maybe ten new digits if he were lucky.

He stuffed the cheap new digs into his backpack and hoped he had some fresh glad rags in his closet at home. It was a fifteen-minute walk back home and he wanted a shower before heading out to the Lattimore.

It was 5:30 already. Jack wasn't going to be early but he was pretty sure he wouldn't be late. He found some clean party smart clothes in his closet and said, "Thank you Jesus!" He ran his shower and splashed on some cologne. He had to wear a pair of the socks he had just bought, but that was okay as they were actually the nicest things the thrift store had to offer. Matched his black slacks with flair, too. He decided to splurge for a cab ride to the hotel and raided his coffee can of odd single dollars and change.

Jack arrived at the Lattimore Hotel in Buckhead at 6:05 pm. The Doorman escorted him to the front door and ushered him through. Orson Quirk was there like a southern politician, smiling, shaking hands, hugging the ladies.

*Bet if there were any babies allowed, he'd be kissing them, too.* Jack thought.

He found his way over to Jack. "Dr. Wheaton. How are you sir? Glad you could make it."

"Thank you for inviting me, sir." Jack said. "This is some affair!" He gestured to the red carpet and uniformed staff.

Just then, Lucy Velasquez cascaded off of the elevator and strode directly toward them.

Jack caught his breath first, then swallowed hard. Lucy wore an amazing little red dress that fit as if it were painted on. The dress was backless with a plunging neckline and thin straps slipped over toned, bare shoulders.

Lucy walked up to them half a foot taller than when he last saw her and casually wrapped her arms around Quirk's forearm.

"Evening, sir." Lucy smiled as she greeted her boss. "Hello Dr. Wheaton. Don't you look dashing there?"

"Isn't she lovely, Dr. Wheaton? I don't know if I can keep my hands to myself if this young creature is par for the night!" Orson said.

"Sorry I'm a little late, but I'm sure Orson kept you entertained." She smiled a professional smile again and looked around the room at the parade of arriving guests. "We wanted to show the house staff how much we appreciate you all."

The new arrivals could not compare with Lucy's attire. Her hair was pinned up to showing off a beautifully made-up face, matching diamond earrings and a choker encrusted with pinhead-sized sapphires with a black pearl in the center the size of a concord grape. Based on what he had overheard nurses prattling about pictures in *Vogue*, Jack estimated Lucy's collection to be worth about $8,000. *With those long legs on those stilettos, who cares about the rest of the outfit.*

"Lucy, that dress is ravishing!" Taking her hand in his, Quirk asked. "What do you call that color?"

"Alizarin Crimson I believe, sir." Lucy answered obediently.

Something old and sexy by David Sanborn began to play over the sound system. Lucy started to sway her hips back and forth to the rhythm of *The Dream,* but refused to meet Jack's staring eyes.

He made small talk with Orson. At least he was open to conversation. "So how long have you been with Glazer, Mr. Quirk?"

"Orson. Call me Orson, Dr. Wheaton." He put one hand on Jack's back.

"Only if you call me Jack, sir."

"Deal." Orson Quirk sipped from his glass. "I've been with the company for ten years. I started out as a field rep, just like Lucy and the others."

He swirled his drink. Johnnie Walker with three generous rocks floating in the glass.

"I really loved that life. Sitting with enthusiastic young Turks ready to take over the world. Each one had his own direction. 'In MY Practice...' they would say, then describe how they would change the paradigms of traditional medical practice and make their fortunes.

Over the years, I had the pleasure of helping many of their ships come in." Orson stared down into his drink with a reminiscent half smile.

"So are you married, Orson?" Jack stole furtive glances at Lucy between sentences. She had turned her back to the men and was smiling at new arrivals and drifting toward the center of the room.

"I was once." He took a cleansing breath. "A long time ago in a small town so far away." He laughed.

"Hum." Jack said, letting Quirk carry the conversation.

"Two sons. Tall, handsome specimens of manhood they were, too."

"Were?" Jack asked before he caught himself. He had a habit of perpetuating conversations he found uncomfortable or boring. Still he kept Orson talking. Lucy wandered out of sight about then greeting other guests.

"They were both killed in the Gulf War. The first one, not this marathon we're dragging out now. They were awarded the Medals of Honor, each one of them. I was proud. So proud.

"Mary, my wife, was just mad. In fact, she was mad as hell. She was mad at the military. She was mad at our state senator who encouraged them to enlist, but most of all, she was mad at me." He smiled a closed mouthed, humorless smile.

"She must have been pissed with you on the road so much for work," Jack said, with genuine sympathy for the poor fellow.

"Oh, I wasn't always in pharmaceutical sales," he said, smiling again as he looked up from his glass now empty. "I had regular hours then."

"What did you do back then?"

"I used to be a mortician. I prepared both my boys when they came back. Mary insisted. Then she hated me for it for the months left in our marriage." Orson grinned. "So I like pharmaceutical sales better. It's much more gratifying to deal with clients who spend more time in the vertical position." He looked up and over Jack's shoulder and said, "Of course, horizontal has its advantages too." With a wink, he shook his glass, now empty of all but the bits of ice that rattled with a little clink.

"Hi, Jack!" Anita said as she strode up to them. Quirk acknowledged the newest guest to the conversation as he lowered the glass from his lips.

"I'm going to say hello to Dr. Hargrove over there," Orson said, making his polite exit.

Anita rendered a simple purple dress of some form fitting knit material as elegant as any ensemble in the room.

"Enjoy." Orson tipped his glass to the vision appearing before them.

"How do I look?" she said, smiling as she turned around to show off her dress. "Feel free to lie."

Peacock feather earrings tethered her earlobes with the lightness of a summer breeze. A wrap of some kind of gray print shawl finished the look. The perfect accent without a single gemstone on her body. She was the opposite of Lucy, but every bit as gorgeous.

A slim, silver chain strung around her neck. She wore two-inch heeled sandals laced halfway up perfect calves.

*Comfortably beautiful.* Jack thought, but searched for the right words to say if he could find his voice.

Jack didn't realize he was gliding toward her until Antony Fusco stepped between them. Anita's escort shook out a full-length black umbrella. The music had masked out the sound of the rain that had built to a torrent since Jack had arrived.

"Hi, Jack," he chuckled, sticking his hand out. "Tony. Remember?"

Jack eyes slowly drifted from Anita to Fusco's hand and he thought, *As if I want to shake it or something.* After leaving the opened hand hanging too long to be cordial, he took it and shook only once. "Yes, I remember you. Ortho intern, right?"

"Anita talks about you all the time, thinks you hung the moon!" Tony went on.

One of the male servers came to fetch his umbrella, showing more than a hint of irritation at the water dripping on the teal green carpet around the edge of the dance floor.

Jack inhaled deeply and drew his shoulders back thinking, *I could take him if I had to,* when a soft hand grabbed his and tugged him toward the dance floor.

Jack turned to see Khandi bouncing enthusiastically to an instrumental version of Tom Brown's *Funkin' for Jamaica.*

After a few measures of the tune, Jack eventually smiled a little. *Man, she can dance.*

They were in the lobby of the hotel. The wait staff had moved the central table to clear a dance area under the grand chandelier.

*Why is it that women seem to know how to dance no matter where they are from?* Jack asked himself.

Khandi Barr swayed her hips back and forth and swirled effortlessly to that beat.

It became confusing to think of how Khandi was born and how she turned out. *To the whole world, she was*

*just an incredibly great looking woman.* She wore white
slacks, a black sequined jacket over a bustier that pushed
her breasts up and in while fitting snuggly around that im-
possibly slim mid-section then flared past the waist.

Her shoes followed the evening's trend with five-
inch heels that accentuated perfectly round hips as she
danced.

As she spun, her extended arm over her head, her
hand in his to end the dance, all Jack could think was,
*Khandi Rocks!*

Jack finished the dance, thanked her for breaking
the tension and nodded for Al to cut in for the next song. Al
was as cool as ever. He wore a thin tan linen jacket over a
jet black, collarless jersey. He wore woven chocolate satin
pants. He spun her into his arms and picked up the beat in
one smooth move.

Al was built like a swimmer, naturally fit, *not all
that ridiculous bulk Tony carried.*

Al went to college on a baseball scholarship. Hell of
an arm, too. Outfielder. He didn't have enough talent to get
into the minor league but he was an unfair asset on any
weekend pick up softball team.

The D.J. played a mix of old school R&B, smooth
Jazz and appropriately redacted hip hop. The play list had
something for everyone at the party. Jack watched them for
a while. He envied Al his ease with Khandi. Another instrumental. Something originally by the Terror Squad with a
killer beat. Jack had forgotten that Khandi was from New
York City.

Al caressed her neck and turned her face up toward
his. Khandi had her hair pinned up away from her face,
which was made-up artistically with jade green eye shadow
a hint of blush and ruby red lip-gloss. *Now that's what love
looks like.* Jack concluded then, realizing he was staring a
little too closely at *Al's* girl, shifted his gaze elsewhere,
then frowned.

Tony was dancing with Anita. *Apparently, the ogre learned how to dance under whatever bridge he crawled from under, too. Doing pretty well for a bouncer.* He had to give it to him, *Tony could hang.*

Jack watched them dance, watching and secretly waiting for him to split his jacket in two, flexing those shoulders. His eyes found Lucy chatting with Dr. Lee. She seemed to be coaxing him to dance with her but he put his free hand up in protest while he clung to hers in spite of himself. It was as if he was asking her for something. Jack came around an intervening couple for a better look in time to see Lucy mouth the word "business" as she disappeared into the crowd. A nudge from the fourth goddess of the evening disrupted his voyeurism.

Stormi Seales stood there as if she had been there all night. She was the only blonde in the group. Jack thought, *Huh, and her hair's the same color as mine. Always hoped for a chance to match it up close.*

Now she looked like one of her photo shoots. Glamour make-up, black cocktail dress cinched at the waist and stilettos.

"Hi Jack." She looked him up and down. "You look good tonight." She crinkled her lower lip and chin in approval. "Clean up pretty good."

"Thanks, I think." Jack found himself talking to a super model. *Now she looked like one of her photo shoots.* Glamour makeup, black cocktail dress cinched at the waist and more stilettos.

"Nice soiree," he said, hoping she'd be impressed by his French.

*"Oui, monsieur,"* she whispered with sudden serious attention to Jack.

Something slow by Luther started about then and Stormi gently took his hand. She wore black, fingerless lace gloves rising past her elbows. *The ladies of Hamilton seemed to have a taste for old school. I need a copy of this play list for my own collection.*

He wrapped his arm around her waist, looked up and whispered again, *Thank you God.*

The Lattimore lobby made a great ballroom with its baroque mirrored walls framed in English walnut, marble floors, and wrought iron banisters topped in matching marble leading up to a mezzanine. Jack was fantasizing where this dance could lead.

He had just begun to snuggle up to the local legend when the radio voice of Dasher Clay interrupted, "May I cut in?"

Jack wanted to tell him where he could cut into but he knew Dasher and Stormi ran hot and cold so he let her take the lead on the response.

She released the grip on Jack's hand slightly and he knew where he stood. Jack was getting very good at bowing out gracefully.

He took a walk to the bar and got a drink. He downed it quickly then ordered another. He couldn't remember what he had the bartender mix.

Jack looked up at the bartender and realized he was the same man as the stalker from the park, the guy on the stool at Maynard's, the janitor at the hospital.

He asked, "Will there be anything else, sir?" as he slipped a cocktail napkin under Jack's glass.

Jack wasn't sure he answered him verbally, just shook his head. He opened his mouth to interrogate the man when another request overpowered the moment.

"Cognac, neat." Lucy pointed to the top shelf before the bartender could tell her that he didn't stock cognac for the party. "The Napoleon will do."

The server reluctantly complied.

"Thanks," she said as she took the half-full brandy glass and turned away from the bar. She just stood there as if waiting.

Jack thought he saw an opening, so he took it. "How's it going, Lucy?"

She turned to him slowly. "Fine, Dr. Wheaton. How are you?" she said, showing as much interest in Jack as a week old tuna sandwich.

"Look, I know I have foot-in-mouth disease sometimes, but can't we start over again?" he said. "Let's take a walk."

Staring off into the near distance, Lucy shook her head slowly. A tall man walked purposefully their way through the growing crowd, stopped right in front of Lucy, lifted her chin and planted a kiss softly on her lips.

He was dressed in a dark gray Italian suit, custommade shoes and an expensive watch. He wore his hair shorter than Tony Fusco did. Combed back and parted on one side, but he had the same over developed pile of sinew stuffed into those sleeves.

"David, this is Dr. Jack Wheaton," she said politely. "Dr. Wheaton, David Rivers."

"Nice to meet you, Dr. Wheaton. Work at Hamilton?" David asked.

The dim lighting probably made him look darker than he was. *Probably hid a few blemishes too.* Jack thought.

"Yup. Internal Medicine," Jack said.

"I have so much admiration for you guys," David said sincerely. "I don't know how you do it."

Jack shrugged. "We do what we have to do, I guess."

Jack caught Lucy puff out her cheeks at David then cock her head apparently in query. The new arrival turned to Lucy, shook his head once and his strong voice became gentle, "I put my bags upstairs already," he said, pointing to his outfit. "Just an over-nighter and the garment bag for these duds."

*Son of a bitch even has dimples when he smiles.*
Jack hadn't seen this much competition squeezed into such close quarters since the state football champions dominated the high school prom.

"I see Orson over there. Let me say hello to him." He nodded to Jack.

He pulled a silver object out of his breast pocket. Jack assumed it was a whisky flask. Lucy shook her head clearly referring to the item he withdrew from his pocket.

*Poor taste at a fancy affair like this one. No class.* Jack thought gloating. *Lucky he has Lucy to coach him through the proper etiquette.*

"Honey, I'm going to get myself a drink too. You want anything else?" he asked Lucy, shoving the container back into his suit.

She just looked him in the eye and raised her glass, still more than half-full, to indicate she had what she needed.

He left without another word. Jack hadn't realized that they had drifted away from the bar where he had been begging for her attention.

"Who's that, Lucy?" Jack's query was automatic.

"That's David. I just told you," she said into her glass as she sipped.

"Work for Glazer?" he asked.

"Yup," she said curtly.

"You guys staying here for the night? How did you know it was going to rain?" Jack asked. "The forecast was for clear weather." More curiosity than small talk.

"I live here, Jack," she said, and turned to face him. "The apartment downtown is for the convenience of getting back and forth to Hamilton and the airport quickly." She sucked her teeth over her glass. "Just for fun, you know?" Then she turned back toward the crowd, ostensibly looking for something or someone.

"So you can afford two apartments like these?" he asked incredulously.

*Together they must be $5,000-6,000 a month easy.* Jack looked at Lucy as if she were some kind of alien from another world. A world he sure couldn't afford to roll in.

She turned toward him slowly, tipped her head slightly to the side, smiled a tight-lipped smile and said softly, "You can lead a horse to water, but you can't make him think!"

She flicked his forehead between the eyes with just enough force to make him blink. "Good night, Jack."

She walked a slow victory walk away from him and towards the dance area. Jack took no pleasure watching her ass move that time.

"This is really nice, Jack." Stormi's voice snapped him out of dismal reverie. Dasher and Stormi were arm and arm.

"Um, hum," he said. "Excuse me. I'd like to get something to eat. I can't drink well on an empty stomach." Then he walked off with Stormi staring, puzzled, at his back.

Jack found Anita standing next to a bussing tray table. She had hors d'oeuvre and a half-finished glass of white wine. He leaned back against the wall and sighed.

"You guys go all out for house staff down here," she said. "We never got treatment like this in Boston. Not even faculty."

Jack said nothing, but smiled politely.

"Now that's interesting," Anita said craning her head around to look him in the face.

Jack's eyes were drawn to hers. Pain did not blunt his soppy attraction to her.

"What is?" he said reluctantly.

"Fred Albright has been dancing with Dr. Garcia all night. They only took a short break for a drink together." She grinned.

"Old news, Dr. Thomas." Jack said with a bit of one-ups-manship. "They've been an item for over a year." He nodded in their direction. "That is the real deal."

He ate his calamari and crackers and swigged his chardonnay. "What about you and your little boyfriend?"

"Jack, I have to tell you, Antony is not exactly a boyfriend. When I made the big retreat from Boston, I spoke with General Hill. He worked out an arrangement for this seal trained medical officer to watch over me in the guise of a live in boyfriend.

Remember I mentioned General Hill? He could not allocate resources for personal security for a civilian based on what we found. He had to circumvent regulations some- how so, he and Dr. Hargrove arranged for a young naval surgeon to get an orthopedic residency at Hamilton Medical Center. He could protect me and report discretely back to General Hill on anything we found. Since the hospital was paying his salary, there was no money trail back to Home- land or the Pentagon."

Jack felt as if he could have been knocked over with a feather at the revelation.

"Fusco?" he perked up. *Bodyguard!*

"Exactly." She nodded. "Navy Lieutenant Antony Fusco, working for Army General Douglas Hill and com- plicit with Dr. Wesley Hargrove in the investigation into the death of his son. No one in the government would make the connection."

"Smart." Jack said, but he still thought the good lieutenant was boinking Anita. Somehow that issue became secondary for the moment.

"You two seem a little intimate, Anita," he said, not sure if she heard the hope in his voice.

"It didn't start out that way, but he's really sweet." She said. "He takes my safety so seriously. I worked hard to get him to lighten up. Took me a week and a half to get him to laugh. Used three of my best jokes to do it, too."

Jack heard the rain outside then and nothing else. He just munched on more cheese and crackers. Chased it down with a fresh glass of wine. Merlot this time.

He looked away. Any way but hers.

There was Lucy getting to know Stormi and Dasher. Her boyfriend, David, was chatting it up with Al and Khandi. Actually, more with Khandi. From her body language, they were talking basketball.

She was laughing. Khandi had a really warm personality.

Jack looked back to Stormi and Dasher. Lucy was ordering drinks for them both. *She's got some kind of pull with that weird bartender.*

Jack decided he wasn't going to be kicked in the nuts all night long. He went right over to the three of them determined to join that party.

Just as he walked up to them, he heard Lucy say to Stormi, "No! You just have to go for it, girl. Bottoms up." Lucy clapped her hands together after pushing the glass into Stormi's hands, who gulped, nearly choking on it.

David, Al, and Khandi joined the little band out of pure curiosity. The upper register in Khandi's voice struck a tone Jack interpreted as horny, based on his few times socializing with her. She was alternately staring down at both Stormi's and Lucy's cleavage. An almost lesbian act but sly, like a guy would do.

Khandi declared. "I need the Paparazzi!"

Anita, Khandi, Stormi, and Lucy all posed for the camera phones at Dasher's behest. Jack snapped one or two for himself. Al got one with Jack's phone of all four beauties. Lucy evaded the pose, turned in left profile with her eyes closed.

Jack took a few minutes to e-mailed it to his brother Mark—Trophy picture.

Khandi seized Stormi's glass and said in too loud a voice, "I've got to taste what she's got!" then drained the remaining drink.

Khandi wildly grabbed both Stormi and Lucy by the hands and pulled them onto the dance floor. She wrapped her arms around each of them at the waist and began to dance to the music.

She dipped Lucy, tango style and with a little effort raised her back upright. Lucy was 3 inches taller and 15 pounds heavier. Laughing, Khandi turned around and cradled Stormi just below the breasts from behind like a Heimlich maneuver.

*Is Khandi Barr drunk or high?* Jack wondered, *Stormi too. Sensuous, like wild gypsies.*

He laughed but looked at the others for intoxication. *Dasher's grinning from ear to ear. Don't have to guess how he's going to exploit Stormi's impaired state.*

Stormi smiled and shouted to Lucy, "I need one of those wipes, Lucy."

Dasher looked at Lucy. "Wipes?"

Lucy looked up at him and shrugged coyly. She spoke over the music, "Certain parts of a girl's body are too delicate to leave to ordinary toilet tissue."

"Amen, sister! Delicate."

Al reached for Khandi to pull her off the dance floor. He was still nursing his beer in the other hand. He curled a calming arm around Khandi's waist and took a swallow of his beer while suspended so, Khandi let her arms go flaccid and announced at the top of her lungs, "Oh God, I think I'm pregnant."

Al coughed up his beer at that notion. It took Jack a second to absorb what he had heard, but then he collapsed holding his knees, howling out of control. He took as long to recover from that as Al did. Both men were crying with laughter.

*I needed tha,.* Jack thought.

203

Anita appeared at his side to rebuke him. "That's not funny. If she's really pregnant your friend, Al, should be more sensitive to her needs, don't you think Jack?"

He turned to look at her and broke out into the deepest belly laugh he had had in months.

While bent over, somehow he caught a glimpse of Orson Quirk. He was near. Watching. Not smiling. Nodding oddly to the wait staff.

Jack would have missed the gesture if that creepy bartender hadn't been the first to get the "hi" sign. Then Jack scanned faces of the other waiters that acknowledged the little signal.

*Big. Muscular.* Jack assessed them collectively, *Too muscular. Too hard looking for waiters in midtown.*

They turned almost as a unit toward the exits.

Jack stopped laughing.

He looked around at his friends. *Everyone's eyes are red except Anita's, Tony's, David's and Lucy's-and Orson's.* Jack thought, *Orson has been drinking since before we arrived.*

Jack watched as Orson Quirk began walking toward their group. The lights went out. Pitch black.

# Chapter 25: Behind the Curtain

There was a rising murmur of panic in the dark room.

Orson Quirk's voice rang out. "Don't fret friends. Stay calm."

Somehow he had an LED flashlight handy. "I'm sure the lights will be on in a moment. The night's young."

He panned the beam around the room. The faces were universally fear stricken, even the drunk ones.

The room soon illuminated with the eerie light of several dozen cell phones coming to life. Everyone was whipping out a cell phone, mostly to check for news updates. Panic-stricken patrons were dialing friends or family to let them know what was going on more so than for help.

A voice shrieked in the darkness, "There's no signal. Can anyone get a signal?" Jack didn't recognize the man.

*Why is Orson Quirk so damn calm?* Jack wondered.

"Glazer has six limousines outside. We'll ferry everyone safely home. Just stay calm."

Guided by his lamp, Orson made his way to the front doors and peered out. "I can see lights in the distance. Just a few blocks probably. It's not the whole city in darkness."

Jack could see his reassuring smile reflected on the glass door as they all crowded around the light like moths.

Orson opened the door shouting commands to his Glazer employees. "David, you have a rental, take these two wherever they need to go." He herded Al and Khandi to the front of the line.

"Lucy, you can't get upstairs anyway so you'll have to find accommodations elsewhere. It's on the company. Take one of the limos and escort these four." He selected Dasher, Stormi and another couple.

It was Raja Kadam and his girlfriend, one of the psychiatry residents, Rekha Reddy. They hurried toward the exit.

Jack saw Dr. Hargrove whispering to Tony near the door. They both looked around the crowd for someone they couldn't find.

*Anita no doubt.* Jack thought.

Tony dove back into the throng against the current and disappeared.

No sooner had Fusco disappeared than Anita found Jack. She rested her hand on his shoulder.

"Have you seen Tony?"

Jack hesitated. "He went that way," he said truthfully, pointing into the darkness engulfing the hotel lobby.

She turned her head in that direction and Jack grabbed for her arm. "You can't go there Anita, it's dark and dangerous. He'll be back. Just wait here, please?"

Before long, David came out of the shadows shaking his left hand vigorously. Jack could see that it was bloody.

"What happened, David?" Anita said, concerned but obviously more worried about the missing Tony Fusco.

"Damn marble floors," he said. "I slipped in a wet spot. Someone must have spilled a drink or something. I caught myself on my hand." He shook it out again.

"Let me see it," Anita demanded gently.

"I don't think it's broken, just bruised," David said, extending the hand for her examination.

After a brief exam, Anita agreed. The three were near a serving table stacked with silverware rolled up in sets of three utensils. She dumped the knife, spoon, and fork set out on the table and then wrapped the satin dinner napkin around David's hand and pressed softly.

David nodded a quick "thanks" then went off toward the door to rendezvous with Al and Khandi at the curb outside.

Hargrove appeared behind Anita and whispered something in her ear. Then he reached for Jack.

"I want you to watch out for Anita." He insisted, "Don't let her out of your sight, do you understand?"

He clasped Jack on the shoulders and turned his body towards Anita. Jack thought Hargrove's request was more grim than the situation called for.

Orson overheard and chimed in. "Don't worry, Dr. Hargrove, I'll personally see to it that they both get home safely."

Orson shoed them into the second limo. "Where do you two live?" he asked once they were settled in.

Anita looked over her shoulder, through the rear window and hiked her thumb in that direction. "Back thataway."

Jack nodded the same.

"Well don't worry. We're headed for bright lights and good music. There's power on the other side of Piedmont road. I know a nightclub where we can get comfortable until they fix the lights downtown." He grinned. "Or until daybreak, whichever comes first." Orson looked at his watch. "It's already 11:35, you know?" He must have seen the doubt in their eyes.

"Cheer up. This is an adventure." Orson said. "Oh, you'll be the talk of the hospital come Monday." He smiled. "Anyone for a drink?"

207

# Chapter 26: A Dark and Stormi Night

Anita crossed her legs in a vain attempt to stop them from fidgeting. *What the hell is going on tonight?* She was glad Jack was by her side, but Dr. Hargrove's urgency for him to stick by her was unsettling. *This black out is no coincidence. It's them again.* Until now, she felt safe. Felt that she was ahead of her pursuers. *And where is Tony?*

She knew Dasher and Stormi were in the limo just ahead of them. It peeled off at Piedmont Road and went right down Peachtree.

"Aren't we all going to the same place, Mr. Quirk?" She asked following their taillights as they disappeared in the other direction.

Jack placed a gentle hand on hers. "Don't worry. They're probably headed to Dasher's place in Buckhead. His family has a condo there and I'm sure he wants to show it off while Stormi's so rattled."

"Yeah, Dasher always seems to have an agenda doesn't he?" Anita said, but began to drum her fingers under Jack's reassuring hand. When he shifted his gaze to her restless digits, she tittered. Not the sound he had come to adore, but instead a sound that filled him with dread.

"Oh, Dr. Thomas, don't worry." Orson Quirk chimed in. "We're going to have some fun tonight. I'm not going to let a little rain and darkness ruin my plans for you two." He chuckled, a slow guttural sound.

"We'll catch up to the rest of them in an hour or so, right Mr.- Orson."

The same rasping snicker preceded his answer. "Sure we will, Jack. Sure we will."

He was wrong.

The first limo ended up at the Ritz Carlton Hotel, on the Glazer expense account of course. Raj and his date got connecting, but separate rooms closest to the elevator.

Dasher and Stormi were another matter. Stormi still hadn't come down from her high by the time they reached the hotel. She was laughing hysterically in the halls. Raja and his date were embarrassed for them both and the reputation of the institution.

Lucy and Dasher nearly carried Stormi, each taking an arm around their shoulders as they walked her, wobbly legged, to a suite several doors down the corridor.

Lucy had switched earrings. She was in action mode again as they made it to the room where Stormi and Dasher would spend the night. Dasher opened the door and scooped Stormi up in his arms, freeing Lucy to walk into the room and find the light switch.

"Let me get Stormi fixed up a bit before I go, huh, Dasher?" She said. "She looks a little green around the gills to me."

With a nod and a smile, he set Stormi on her feet, and Lucy guided her into the bathroom. The Mickey she slipped in her last drink at the Lattimore had taken effect. A cocktail of Methamphetamine with a heavy chaser of barbiturate.

Dasher Clay almost got his perfectly chiseled nose smashed by the door.

Lucy bent Stormi over the commode and whispered, "Go ahead and let it all out, sweetie."

Stormi's eyes were glazed and unfocused. Lucy unwrapped a complimentary toothbrush and eased the handle to the back of Stormi's throat. The normal gag reflex induced the expected sounds, which resonated into the outer room.

"Yeah she's puking her guts out in here, Dasher," Lucy shouted from the bathroom.

Lucy emerged from the bathroom with a spot or two of vomit on her little red dress, making a show of cleaning it with a wet hand towel.

"How is she?" Dasher asked.

"Oh, she'll be praying to the Shrine of the Porcelain Goddess for a while yet. She'll come out when she's done."

Lucy looked up from her chore and winked at him. "Then you can have your way with her. I suggest you give her a swig of that mouthwash first though." She laughed then pranced out through the outer door that way she did when she knew she was being watched.

Outside, she left the door ajar, walked down to Raja Kadam's room, and called back, "Night, Dr. Clay, Dr. Seales."

She stopped, turned to face back down the hall right in front of Raja's room as Dasher responded.

"Hey, Lucy, where's the icemaker?" Dasher's voice called in the distance.

Lucy rose up on tiptoes in her stilettos and stretched to yawn. "End of the hall, Doc." She smiled and turned slowly, briefly facing the peephole of Raja's door, then headed in the opposite direction toward the elevators.

Lucy's earrings recorded herself each time she passed a mirror. When the elevator doors opened, she got on, went down one floor and got back off. Taking her shoes off, she sprinted, quietly down to the staircase at the far end of the hall and ascended to the exit one floor up, just outside Dasher's suite.

She waited at the door for a second, and then gently knocked five times on the door. Listening for the sound of ice clinking in the bucket, she wanted to make sure Dasher had been recorded going back and forth from the icemaker on the hall security cameras. Lucy had pre-arranged to have the lower floor and stair cameras time off for a minute or two based on her pace.

Her chest heaved more with seduction than exhaustion as Dasher answered the door for her. She looked up into his eyes for two long breaths before she asked to come in. Lucy was like a puppeteer when it came to men.

"I can't go home this way." She said, looking down at her chest then up slowly. "This dress reeks!" then she strolled in as if she knew he couldn't resist. Turning her back to him, "Well," she said, "can you help?"

Like a drone, Dasher tugged her zipper down her back to her butt. To him, she was like catnip. Lucy peeled off one side of her dress and coyly posed before disappearing into the bathroom.

Stormi was still there, pulling herself together. Dasher had yet to go in to see how she was doing.

Lucy closed the door and said, just loud enough to be heard through the door, "How ya' doin', Stormi?"

The question elicited a little groan from Stormi followed by something barely intelligible.

She talked Stormi out of her dress. Then there was some laughter from both of them.

"Better prop me up, Lucy. Can't stand on my own–" Stormi snorted then slipped down to the floor, giggling in front of the commode. "Don't know which way is up."

Lucy sat on the toilet seat, rocked Stormi up right on the floor and steadied her between her knees. As Stormi wobbled there on her buttocks, Lucy dug into her purse again and  pulled out a moist wipe from her purse.

Lucy had developed a process of drying them a little then dousing them with a mixture of Chloroform and grain alcohol. The Softpack was perfect for this purpose with its re-sealable lid to keep contents moist. Lucy popped the lid, whipped out a single wipe and cupped it over Stormi's mouth and nose. She went limp in seconds, and Lucy loosened her clutch.

Unhindered, she unsnapped Stormi's bra and flushed the wipe before calling Dasher for help. The two women were in just panties, topless when he opened the door. After a moment of gratuitous gawking, Dasher helped Lucy carry the half-naked Stormi to the bed and dumped her there.

"Well, Dr. Clay, it seems you have a choice." She whispered. "Me, the quite willing and most able 'drug wench', or the lovely and unconscious Dr. Stormi Seales."

Right about then, as if on cue, Stormi drooled out the side of her mouth all over the pillow.

No contest.

"Maybe a threesome when she wakes up, you think? Maybe even while she's still out, huh?" Lucy smiled, pulled the ice bucket close. Unseen as lascivious eyes wandered to Stormi then back, she deftly dropped a decorative dagger in the bucket, stirred the melting contents using the thin blade as an ice pick. She reached in and fished out a cube. While Dasher stood there enjoying the show and anticipating a marathon of debauchery, she dragged the cube between her breasts then drizzled a few drops from the wet cube onto one of Stormi's nipples. No reaction. She rolled the young radiologist across to the other side of the bed and sat Dasher down in the vacated space with a domineering thrust.

Lucy Velasquez could make a living at such performances for a camera, a legendary living.

Lucy worked her legs between Dasher's knees and stood there. She pressed him down flat on the bed, and maneuvered herself astride his lap. He reached for her hips only to be intercepted by a smart slap on the wrist, "Ah, ah, ah, Dr. Clay. No touchie! Not yet."

She put one of his arms under the sheets and tucked the edge under him. She tried to do the same with the other, but the good doctor protested too much.

"I don't like bondage scenarios." Dasher said with that silky voice. "Sorry, babe."

"Yeah me too, Dasher." Lucy reached over and grabbed the ice pick. She drew the point up under his chin.

"Having fun yet?" She said staring down into his scared blue eyes.

"What?" She bounced up and down on his lap once or twice. "Where did 'Mister Willie' go? Losing your concentration, Clay?"

He reached up with his free arm, but she countered him by adjusting the dagger for lethal leverage against his throat.

"Put your fucking hand down." she said.

Dasher complied.

"Now under the sheet, I said!"

He hesitated.

"Maybe you want me to cut up little Barbie here. I like puzzles. Ever see them make an old-fashioned jigsaw puzzle, Clay? I did, in Amsterdam. It's fascinating. They actually take a jigsaw to a single, smooth piece of wood and carve it up into at least twenty-five separate pieces.

You see, if the saw doesn't cut cleanly, the puzzle won't fit together neatly. No one likes a sloppy piece. You don't want a sloppy piece, do you, Asshole?" She caressed Stormi's face with the point.

Just a little scratch on her cheek. She pressed hard enough to raise a weal. Just enough to show a little red in the dim lighting of the hotel room. Stormi didn't move. She was still out cold.

"I'll carve this bitch up and leave you here to take the wrap for it. Now put that damn arm under the sheet." Then she said softly. "I just want to talk to you."

Dasher slid his free arm under the sheets and Lucy pinned both edges down with her knees as she straddled him. Earrings dangling, she turned to find a mirror for video documentation of every rapacious step.

"Now that's more like it. So, tell me, what did you guys find after the surgery on old lady Holcomb? I know you found out something else in Path lab. I'd love to question that old fart himself, but your chief of pathology decided to go out of town this weekend. Pretty fucking inconsiderate of him wouldn't you say, Dr. Clay?" She bounced on him again. "I asked, what did you find?"

Dasher must have known on some level that he and Stormi were going to die this night. He told the truth hoping that it would somehow set them both free.

"We all gathered round as Professor Zizzi demonstrated something all of us who were actually in the OR missed." He swallowed hard.

"After each ablation, the tissue goes dark as it should when zapped. He noticed that the surrounding healthy tissue glowed briefly. None of us noticed. He seemed to think this had a poor prognosis for future seizures. We didn't get any biopsies. He reviewed the history. Zizzi believed it was why anti-convulsants didn't work. Stabilizing the excitable grey matter compromised the healthy tissue surrounding it. He theorized that people with no null lesions wouldn't have seizures in the first place. No one cared. It got us out of rounds."

He looked over at Stormi sleeping so soundly by their side. "Leave Stormi out of this, Lucy or whoever you are, she has no part in this."

That was the one and only noble act Dasher Clay ever performed. Caught on tape. Maybe he'd end up in heaven anyway.

"Okay, say I believe you. Who else knows?" Lucy asked.

Again, Dasher hesitated. "No one. Stormi was in the OR but didn't come to Morbidity and Mortality with me."

"Eh!" Lucy mimicked a buzzer. "Epic fail. I happen to know you're lying because I had my man, Jason Brasil, watching you seven at the restaurant the other night."

She wriggled up over his body a bit more.

"So you see, now I can't believe anything you say. How can I ever trust you again, Dasher?"

There were twelve thrusts, full arc with that sturdy blade. Both sides of the chest. Lucy made certain the thuds were clearly audible on the recording. There was a gurgling sound in the background when she finished. Dr. Dasher Clay lay drowning in his own blood.

That's a sound no conscious witness could ever forget. It might have been enough to stir Stormi from her chloroform slumber.

"Hey, who said you could wake up, Sleeping Beauty?" Lucy said, then reached for her purse, pulled out a fresh wipe and insufflated Stormi with another whiff of Chloroform. After a few coughs and some pointless arm movement, Stormi settled down again.

Lucy wiped the ornate blade clean of fingerprints and curled the handle into Stormi's palm several times. Overlapping prints. It's what forensics would expect if someone stabbed a person that many times with a handled instrument.

Lucy calmly climbed off Dasher, showered, got dressed and snagged a wet washcloth from the bathroom. She emptied a shampoo bottle from the bathroom sink, rinsed it and then filled it with a few ounces of Chloroform liquid she carried in her purse to recharge the wipes supply.

She poured a bit on a cloth and a drop or two into Dasher's open mouth between agonal breaths. Wiping the bottle, she wrapped Stormi's hand around it before resting it on the other bedside table near the still sleeping radiologist. A forlorn expression crossed Lucy's face as she

looked at the antique letter opener in Stormi's hand. She
turned her cameras off, walked to the desk and went
through the drawers. A simple stainless steel letter opener
lay there. Not the hotel's. Probably legacy of a previous
guest. She retrieved the treasured weapon, replaced it with
the cheap cast off and repeated the gripping ritual with
Stormi's limp hand. She compare the two blades. Thin-
ner than her precious antique, but not as sharp and made
of softer metal, she briefly wondered about the wisdom of
making the substitution. Forensics might notice the mis-
match if the investigators were on their toes.

Lucy cleaned her little trophy, admired it's sturdi-
ness for a moment and replaced it in her purse. She made
a quick survey of the suite to make sure she hadn't missed
anything, and then touched her earring. She performed a
cursory review of the recording on her smart phone,
wiped every surface she touched, then left in reverse
course down the same stairs she came up.

Stormi slept another hour or so, but when she finally did wake up that night, she was screaming.

# Chapter 27: On the Town

Anita and Jack cruised out of the darkness of the Buckhead blackout in Orson's limo. The bright lights of downtown Atlanta shone like the Land of Oz. The driver switched from brights to regular headlights. He navigated Baker Street at the speed limit and turned left down Peachtree Center then slowed.

At a chime from his breast pocket, Orson fished out his cell phone. "Ah, we have service." He checked e-mail and frowned.

"Something wrong, Mr. Quirk?" Anita asked.

"Just a bad real estate investment."

"I hope you didn't lose too much in the deal." Jack said.

Orson inhaled, then sighed it out again. "No. I guess the property ran its course. I've wrung all the value out of it I can. I'll just have to dispose of it as expeditiously as I can."

"Looks like it meant a lot to you." Anita said.

"Oh, it's just a small commercial property, but it had added recreational value I'll miss. No emotional attachment."

He let the phone drop to his lap for just a second exposing a glamour head shot of Lucy before closing it. He cast his gaze through his window into darkness for a moment and murmured. "What a thing of beauty, though."

Anita nudged Jack urgently and he dipped his ear toward her, "I think he likes Lucy." She whispered with an expression of sympathy for their host.

Jack nodded grimly, but said nothing.

The driver pulled to a stop at a pair of turn-of-the-last-century brick buildings, obviously town houses converted into a nightclub.

There was an old warehouse from the same architectural period where the club continued. A line formed outside at the warehouse livery doors.

A doorman seemed to recognize the car because he stepped up to the back passenger door before the vehicle stopped. He offered Anita a gallant helping hand and addressed Orson Quirk by name.

"I welcome you to *Crescent Point*, one of the most exclusive night spots in the ATL." Orson stated.

They climbed four rough-hewn stone steps to the threshold of twelve-foot double oak doors.

"Tonight, we have *carte blanche,* courtesy of the Glazer Corporation." Quirk opened the door himself and ushered Anita and Jack into the foyer.

Hardwood floors, rich fuchsia and gold foil wallpaper, and a crystal chandelier opened the foyer to a hall full of well-dressed partygoers streaming back to a kitchen and dining area. They followed the wait staff and Quirk back along the scent of Thai food. Until now, Anita and Jack had only heavy *hors d'oeuvres.*

The kitchen was top notch and it was buzzing. Situated behind a counter where orders were taken patrons received tokens, sort of a Monopoly theme, on a stem that they put on their tables. The Glazer party had an account and Orson invited his guests to select whatever they liked.

Jack ordered a glass of red wine to go with steak grilled medium rare, rice, and steamed vegetables, while Anita ordered a chilled bottle of mineral water to go with her mahi-mahi. She passed on the red meat. Even in the air conditioned building the oppressive heat invaded where people gathered. The dining room was sparsely occupied and six degrees cooler but the gradient was obvious.

Orson ordered a meal with roast pork and rice with plum wine sauce. A thoughtful order under the circumstances. He never intended to eat it.

After their host placed his order, he disappeared.

Anita and Jack finished their meals, chatting about the turns of events.

"Interesting times, huh." Anita said nervously. "The storm, the blackout, the limousine ride, the club."

"Yeah." Jack said, then lowered his voice, "And I agree, I think Quirk has a real thing for Lucy." He chewed a piece of steak that could have almost melted in his mouth. "I just hope she's not leading that poor old guy on."

"Funny, she strikes me that way too." Anita said. "He seems so vulnerable. He thinks a blackout is an adventure." Then, she chuckled. "He should spend a night in my world."

Orson reappeared in the foyer as if on cue with a girl on each arm. The Asian woman on his left could have been a Victoria's Secret model and wore a silver mini dress. The other was blonde and just as shapely as the first. Vacuous, bookend party girls smiling and giggling for their Sugar Daddy.

Jack and Anita hadn't finished their meals, but stopped chewing abruptly at the sight. They gulped their half chewed oral content, and while wiping the corners of their mouths exchanged quizzical looks.

Clearing his throat, Jack asked, "How about a dance?"

"'Bout damn time, Jack!" Anita said, tossing her napkin onto her plate. "I was beginning to think I had cooties or something."

She stood and followed Orson Quirk and company into the main dance floor in the warehouse section. Jack noticed that creepy bartender from the Lattimore skulking toward the kitchen counter as they crossed over into the industrial side of the establishment.

"That guy seems to have more jobs than a *Headley*."

*"In Living Color?"* Anita asked, "My dad used to love that show." She searched the direction Jack was looking in, but saw no one. Anita could only describe the club in one word, "Nice."

The main floor was sunken to street level in the center with a fifteen foot lounging deck and a matching second floor veranda bound by railing all around. The designer struck just the right cord with the lighting. Not so dark that one had to reach out to find his partner with his fingertips, but it still furnished that sense of discretion needed when getting to know someone new.

It was working that way for Jack at least. He and Anita danced to a couple of up-tempo sounds, then there was the inevitable slow grind.

Jack thought, *Maxwell, yeah.*

"Crazy night, huh, Jack?" Anita whispered. "But not yet 'an adventure'.."

She leaned her head against his chest and Jack, for once that night, felt just fine.

"Yeah, crazy, alright." he agreed, just floating along to the music. "Anita," he said, but it came out with that hoarse, upper register rasp that doesn't mean much in the din of a crowd.

"I sure do appreciate all the help you've given me, Jack. It's great to have a real friend when you're in a strange place and don't know anybody."

*Damn, the "Friend" speech.* Jack languished.

"Yeah, well, it was the least I could do." he rubbed at the scab on the back of his left hand.

He opened his mouth to say something genuine and candid, but he just didn't know what. The effort was interrupted by the ring of his cell phone. Jack frowned before accepting the call.

"Go ahead and take that, Jack. I have to use the ladies' room anyway. I'll be right back." Anita said, backing away gently, then disappearing into the crowd.

"Jack Wheaton," he said into the receiver.

"Jack, Sam Reardon. I thought I'd give you a call about this guy…"

"Whoa, whoa, whoa, Sam. I'm not on call tonight. It's my Golden weekend and I'm…"

"I know you're not on call, ass-wipe. I'm calling you as a courtesy. I know how protective you are of your interns."

"Al? What's up with Al, Sam?" he interrupted.

"Not Al, Jack, Antony Fusco. He's in here on the surgical side. Busted nose."

"You mean, *Lou Ferrigno*?" Jack laughed. "How'd that happen?" Jack peered back towards the re-strooms to be sure that Anita didn't see his glee at the news.

"Says he was assaulted, Jack." Reardon told him.

With that, Jack got serious. "Assaulted?" he re-peated.

"Yes. He says he was at the party down at the Lat-timore tonight. There was a blackout and he went to look for Anita." Reardon recounted the history including por-tions Jack didn't know.

"You sure he didn't just slip and fall, Sam? An-other bruiser of a guy slipped on a wet spot and scrapped up his hand pretty good." he said, then thought to himself, *David*.

"Nope." Sam said. "He says, this scumbag came up to him all nicely dressed, asked him his name, and when Tony confirmed he was right, the thug cold-cocked him with a good left.

Looking at Tony, it must have been a damn good left. He was out cold. Just got back from CT. Minor con-cussion, no bleed."

Jack resisted the impulse to say, *No brain either.*

"Is Anita with you, Jack, is she safe? This guy begged me to call her. I thought this was better," Sam finished.

"She's with me, Sam. She's fine." Jack didn't think of the double entendre at the time. "I'll let her know what's going on. Keep me posted, okay, Sam?"

Jack closed his phone and stood there thinking for a minute. Anita surprised him with a tap on the shoulder. "I'm back." She said with a sing-songy lilt.

"Yeah. Anita, I just..." She was looking over his shoulder.

"Wow, big guys." She gestured toward two men dressed in black tee shirts and black slacks walking their way. "Scary big."

*They were big.* he acknowledged. Jack swung his attention back to Anita, but was distracted by a trend of commotion building up behind her.

*Smoke.*

Plumes came up from the back of the club. Jack had barely recognized the danger when he heard someone yell, "Fire!"

Like dominoes, people started cascading toward the building's front exit. It was a stampede. Frightened people flowed all around them like ordered chaos. The doctors started moving with the flow until the two bruisers began shoving them against the current towards the smoky end of the room.

Anita and Jack both protested, but the chaos in the club was too much with all the panic erupting. After they cleared the crowd, the thugs manhandled the pair out the back door. They passed the door to the kitchen where there were two unconscious Asian men, one lying on the floor and the other slumped over a desk. Jason Brasil was standing calmly in the doorway, watching them.

# Chapter 28: Shanghai

They emerged in the alley behind the club to fresh air. Anita and Jack were both coughing the smoke out of their lungs. Their escorts were not. They must have held their breath through the thickest smoke. Of course, they had known what to expect. Jason Brasil, who Jack recognized as the bartender, appeared at the exit and closed the door behind him.

A black suburban idled in the alley. Jack suspected that Anita realized the motor was running before he did. Still coughing, Jack looked around taking in all the details of the surroundings.

It was dark except for a street lamp's cone of light a couple of dozen feet down the alley. The ground was damp from the rain earlier. The summer heat made the ground steamy. Jack braced against his knees gasping for air. He glanced sidelong to check on Anita.

Also still coughing, she had stopped trying to straighten for a moment, her eyes searching. Jack didn't know what she had in mind at first, but she seemed to settle on a wire hanger in the trash accumulated near the dumpster between them and the vehicle. She scooped it up and into her shawl.

Jack saw, but said nothing.

They were ushered into the vehicle and flanked by the goons. Joey and Ralphie confiscated cell phones. The Bartender got behind the wheel and took off. Jack noted one of the big guys used a name when asking instructions-*Sergeant Brasil.*

The digital compass in the rearview mirror indicated "E."

*Geography of Atlanta east of the club, what was there?* Jack began to calculate. *Depends on what they want with us.*

The suburban turned left when they hit Auburn Avenue and headed south. Jack knew this area. They were near the big Hamilton Outreach clinics at the corner of Auburn and Bell.

Last year, Jack had run an indigent clinic there as a project funded under the Access to Care program. There was a confusing fork in the road. *These guys obviously are not from around there.* Jack bided his time.

Brasil came to a stop trying to get his bearings when Jack made his move. Not a great one, but a move nonetheless.

Elbow to the ribs followed by a back handed fist to the nose with all his might and then crossed a spear hand to the trachea. Jack reached across to unlock the door when the guy's hand grabbed his wrist.

"Son of a bitch!" He growled. He tilted and stretched his neck then looked back at Jack, more insulted than angry. "Can you believe this guy, Sarge?"

He squeezed Jack's wrist until it hurt then continued until it went numb. *This guy could snap my arm like a dry twig.*

"I got to figure out where we are anyways, Ralphie." Brasil looked around. "Why don't you teach Blondie a little lesson?"

It was dark, no streetlights, no prying eyes. "Remember, just a little lesson, we still need him. We don't want another accident like we had with the Indian. Take the chick for a walk while we're at it Joe."

Ralphie dragged Jack out of the vehicle by his hair.

Less painful than humiliating. The mercenary grabbed him by the lapels and slung him against the nearest wall. Jack bounced off the brick wall back toward him to be greeted by a gut punch that nearly made him hurl. Jack doubled over, vision blurred.

The thug called *Ralphie* let the misery from the first punch sink in before he laid in to him again. Confused by the ground level vantage, shoes appeared on the ground in front of Jack. Jack felt the ground fall away from him fast while he focused on the hands gripping his lapels and those shoes. Big shoes, now toe to toe with his own. Jack had a feeling reminiscent of a kid facing his father when caught in the act of mischief.

Jack hadn't felt that feeling for a long time. When people get into accidents, they often describe the sensation of an immovable object racing at them. That was what Jack felt like when he was struck as hard as Ralphie hit. He was magically on the ground again.

Only his forearms kept him from munching dirt and grass as he fell. Jack rolled over on his side, disoriented. The only way he knew he was on his side was that he saw the side of the building again and not a close up of dirt.

He spotted Anita, now outside near the back of the car, safe but guarded by the other thug. Beyond them, he thought he made out a familiar name on the wall. As he sucked enough air back into his lungs to make his brain read again, he saw that they were at the Hamilton satellite clinic near Ebenezer Baptist Church. The building had been closed for six months.

There was a figure prowling around in the darkness, trying not to get noticed. Jack heard voices off in the distance. New voices. He couldn't sort out the sequence at the moment. He drew it out as best he could.

There was a new ache. An ache, not a pain. Jack still didn't have enough of a hold on reality to feel pain yet. He would feel it later though.

"Doc?" The voice was familiar. "Hey, what are you guys doin' with the Doc?"

Different. Not drunk, but Jack still knew that voice.

"You got the lady doc, too? Son of a bitch."

*Unmistakable*. Jack thought, *Martin Di Marini*.

"You let them go, you mutha fuckas, or I'll beat the shi…" Di Marini stopped talking.

Jack didn't know if they hit him, killed him or what. He opened his eyes again. Di Marini was still standing, but now he had his hands up in the air.

Brasil had drawn a gun. He was about the same size as Di Marini, 5'6" or so but a tough knot of a man.

Other voices invaded the night, "Hey, I know that white boy." The voice was uninvited, but familiar and also welcomed. Another frequent flier from Hamilton's ER, street name; Slick.

"Hey, Briggy, that's Doc! What the fuck is goin' on up in here?"

Jack was never so happy to hear Slick's voice in his three years at Hamilton. He was a regular at the clinic and was often brought in shackles down at the ER on busy Friday or Saturday nights. Usually because of some havoc he had rained on someone else.

When Jack disarmed Slick in the ER a couple of years ago, the deputies brought him up to the residents' desk and he threatened, "Next time Doc, next time." Nodding his head as the cops took him away.

The next time their paths had crossed, Jack was intubating him after relieving the pressure of a knife-punctured lung on the ramp to the ER. He would not have made it into the building had it not been for the medical intervention.

Jack hoped Slick remembered.

He did.

"Back off, big man." he said. "Now." Slick pointed to the thug near Jack then beckoned his gang to close in around them. Two of them had guns drawn. *An equalizer*. Jack prayed.

His cut buddy, Brigdon Lang, stepped up to the front. A light-skinned black man in a wife beater and dirty, oversized jeans. A shaved head brandished keloid scars on his scalp like medals of valor.

Briggy was bigger than the guy lording over Jack. *Jailhouse muscles, mean, hard, Jailhouse muscles.* Jack realized. *The result of having nothing to do all day, but press weights, punch the heavy bag, and masturbate. Makes them big, fast, and ornery.*

Briggy had just gotten out a week ago. He raised open hands up in challenge to the kidnapper standing in front of Jack. Still flat on the ground, Jack thought he saw the ex-con crack a little smile.

The man in black looked nervous. He threw a punch which was easily blocked then landed a kick to Briggy's side.

Briggy's smile widened. "That's it?" Baritone voice, like the rumble of an erupting volcano. "That all you brought?" Now that volcano was rumbling with laughter before erupting into violence.

Jack was behind the thug now. *The bad thug,* Jack reminded himself. *One that snatched us.* Jack drew up on his knees and elbows and thought: *Ralphie.*

Briggy hauled off and swung, first a feint then a left. The beauty of the blow for Jack was that Ralphie saw it coming and couldn't do a damn thing about it. There was a sickening crack, as Briggy connected with Ralphie's front teeth. The man in black tripped backward over Jack and landed on demolition debris.

Di Marini seized the opening and executed a modified Aikido move on Jason Brasil. Snapped the wrist of his gun hand and with a lupine grin, Di Marini disarmed the leader.

"That's right, bitch, I was Special Forces too, ya know!" Di Marini spat as the little man went down.

Di Marini picked up the gun, checked it then chambered a round like an expert. Side stepping the fallen Jason Brasil, he aimed it at the thug holding Anita.

Joe was unsure of the next move to make. He didn't know if this old drunk was invested enough in Anita to bargain for her welfare.

Anita slipped in to the chaos of the moment and kicked back against Joe's kneecap. It didn't really hurt him, but it made him flinch and she stepped out of reach. That was all Di Marini needed. He fired. Not a bad shot, considering the darkness, the adrenaline rush, and the un-reliable range of a short-barreled handgun.

Like riding a bike, even for a drunk, some things you never forget. He winged Joe in the arm opposite Anita.

Seeing that he failed to go down, Anita assumed that Di Marini had missed. She whipped out the unfurled wire that was once a hanger and flailed it with amazing accuracy and no remorse. She caught Joe in his right eye. He dropped to his knees. Blood tricked through fingers clutching at the socket as if to prevent the eyeball from falling out.

Approaching headlights changed the scene. Every-one froze. No blue lights flashing, the car was not a cop's.

A figure got out of the car and moved slowly through the mist. Sultry, feline strut, no fear. Everyone stopped until she was nearly in the midst of it all. Bathed in the headlights, a woman's lithe silhouette loomed over the gathered combatants.

"Okay, boys, everybody calm down, alright?" Lucy Velasquez announced. Jack was not sure what to make of this development, but he had a bad feeling about it.

He stayed low.

"Look, let's not make this harder than it has to be, okay, boys?"

*Lucy,* Jack thought, *Hope she brought help, these guys could hurt her even with that gun in hand.*

Having dispatched Ralphie-boy, Briggy must have been feeling invulnerable.

"Let's have that pop gun, babe." He walked toward her. "You might hurt yourself with it. And you're way too pretty to…"

Two quick whispers were nearly lost in the night wind. Jack heard them. Slick may have heard the second one. No doubt, Briggy heard neither one.

He took two more steps toward Lucy. They were clumsier than they were when he confronted Ralphie. Somehow, his feet couldn't seem to keep up with his thighs anymore, and his legs couldn't keep up with the rest of his body. As Briggy fell to his knees, his big arms looked unbearably heavy for him. He finally went down face first into the muddy street at Lucy's feet. The obituary a few days later, would read - Brigdon "Briggy" Lang had been a promising trained boxer until…

It took a second or two for Slick's gang to recognize what had just happened. They were accustomed to hearing the bang of gunshots, not the soft kiss of a silencer.

Lucy was unbelievable with a side arm. She took out the two armed men backing up Briggy flat footed while they were still thinking about what they saw. The others froze and raised their hands in surrender or ran off, scared into the darkness. Jack and Anita thought Lucy was their savior. Hoped to see her turn the gun on Brasil and his bullies next.

There were four gang members left. Slick was not among them. Jack was in no position to know if Slick went down or ran off into the night by then.

There was a bang.

Di Marini fired off another shot, this time at Lucy. If surviving combat teaches a man anything, it's when he is facing death. It's just a feeling, a little tickle at the back of the neck. It told him Lucy was the immediate threat in this theatre. She stood at least fifteen feet further away than Joe was from him. His aim was shaky. Too many years in the bottle and no matter the training, the reflexes just don't snap back like they used to.

Lucy smiled at him. Jack saw that much. Then, she sidestepped the Porsche's headlights. Di Marini raised his arms to block the suddenly blinding light. That might as well have been a lazar painting a target on the old guy. Lucy cut him down with a single shot.

"Okay, boys, see what happens when you don't listen to Mommy?" She gestured with her gun. "Hands over your pointy heads and lay them against the wall. You know the drill."

That's when Jack realized, *She's not on our side.*

She had changed since the party. *Form fitting black tee shirt and matching slacks, like the kidnappers.* Hair tied in a ponytail again. Apparently, this was how she dressed for her night job.

She changed the magazine out as the gang members complied with her request. She appraised Ralphie lending Brasil a hand up, then checked on Joe, still pampering his injured eye.

"Okay, fellas, sound off, left to right," she said. Lucy realized they thought she was a cop.

She executed them with one shot each as they said their names. The first two went down like dominoes. The third realized he didn't have a chance at her mercy so he decided to go down swinging. He bolted for a broken piece of wooden fence, but never made it. Lucy was ice cold and her aim was wicked with that gun. It was as if the weapon were an extension of her being.

The fourth man turned around to curse her, but the bullet speeding through his teeth reduced it to a grunt.

"*Killer* Joe." She jibed. "Get up and grow a pair. Didn't you ever see **_300_**? You have a spare." She laughed. "Stop whining."

Joe was still babying his ruined eye as he staggered toward the others. "Damn, it hurts." He stumbled a step or two. "Feel nauseated. Fuckin' bitch, I'm blind. Come on, Ms. V, you gotta get me to a hospital. Mr. Quirk has connections. He has a whole wing we could use. Best doctors in the…"

*Lucy said nothing, not a thing.* Jack watched in disbelief as what just happened sunk in, *She just raised her gun. One smooth motion, aimed and shot through his hand clutching the eye. Her own man. Dropped mid-sentence without another sound.*

Lucy knew what she was doing. One doesn't learn where to place kill shots like that by luck or trial and error. Trauma surgeons, snipers, and assassins have that kind of carnal knowledge of death. This was routine to her. Just business. Ice cold business.

*Maybe a little pleasure.* Jack thought.

"Get in the truck you two before you join the body count," Lucy said to Anita and Jack.

Lucy made Jack's skin crawl and he shuddered. Anita steadied him. They all got silently back into the SUV, victim and thug alike.

Brasil had a few words with Lucy through the driver's window, which he obediently opened at her behest.

"Just follow me and keep up." Jack heard her say. He was learning that the softer Lucy spoke, the more dangerous she was.

She casually walked back to her Porsche and drove off after flicking her lights at the other vehicle.

# Chapter 29: Lucy's Way

Jack followed the compass readings as the SUV drove through east Atlanta to Clifton Road. Their kidnappers weren't talking. Lucy had spooked them as badly as she had him and Anita. Jack had given up trying to guess what Lucy was up to.

*We're near The Hamilton Memorial Institute,* Jack realized. *The elite clinic where the old guard saw their private patients. Old money Atlantans. The best resources of the Hamilton Medical Center staff and research.*

The clinic maintained a treatment room for its partners, but not an ER opened to the general public. It was not, therefore, a true Emergency Department.

If true hospitalization were necessary, a patient might be transferred to the exclusive West Wing ICU of the Medical Center downtown for comprehensive care. The best of the best of the house staff got the privilege of covering these patients on call for less than half the usual fee for night call at other local community hospitals.

It occurred to Jack, *We're headed there for reasons to do with Helen Holcomb and Anita's experimental drug. That makes sense.*

Problem was, they *passed* Hamilton Memorial. Past Gerkes Primate Center on down to the dark end of the street. There was a long stretch that was poorly lit. The SUV finally slowed near the entrance to the CDC.

Jason Brasil stopped the car and donned a cap with a security insignia on it, as well as an orange striped vest over a blue jacket.

Brasil gave a hand signal to Ralphie and addressed Anita and Jack in the back seat.

"Follow along and you live," he said.

Jack looked at him attentively, given their recent history, he waited for the *or else*.

He shrugged. "That's all. Follow along and you live: Don't follow… you don't.

Ralphie adjusted a cap on his head similar to what Brasil wore. They saw Lucy in the rear view already sporting a security cap of her own as she drove up behind them.

The guard at the gate seemed to recognize all of them, but called them by names Jack didn't recognize. The look on Anita's face reflected the same confusion. Then her expression changed.

*Her throat looks like it's constricted and her eyes are watering.* Jack scanned her in the light filtering through tinted windows from the guard station. *Was she hurt back there and I didn't notice? She's watching Brasil. What's he writing?* Jack craned his neck to see what Anita saw. *Just signing-in on the guards clip board. Fancy signature. Looks like a celebrity autograph with that tail wrapping beneath it.*

Jack took five normal breaths before Anita took her next. He touched her hand to get her attention but she was transfixed on Jason Brasil.

Brasil told the final sentry "We're playing chaperone to out of town med students. From up north."

The young doctors remained silent until they passed the checkpoint.

*How did he sell that story in the wee hours of the morning?* Then Jack saw the first hint of dawn on the horizon. *It must be close to 6 am. Not unusual to change guard at that time. Not unusual for doctors to start rounds between 6 and 7 am either.*

The guards waved them all the way through the research facility to the main building. Anita and Jack were escorted out of the SUV to the second floor. A sleepy looking brunette with bleached highlights was at the information desk. She was short and plump, and nearly oblivious to the entourage.

Even their approach didn't spark any vigilance in that one.

"We're scheduled to see Dr. Butler." Lucy explained.

Anita and Jack were paraded past her to a suite of labs and offices. Lucy led the way.

Jack was familiar with the outer offices of the CDC. So was this marauding party. *This has got to be the slowest elevator I've ever rode.*

"Why are you doing this?" Anita asked quietly.

After a moment's hesitation, Lucy answered. "This is bigger than you and that little molecule you developed. The assay is worth more. International money."

Anita didn't respond.

"Do you even understand what that means?" Lucy asked, "That kind of money buys freedom."

Nothing verbal from Anita, just a penetrating stare at first, then, "Your man, Brasil. He killed Harry Mehta, didn't he?"

Brasil found his voice. "What makes you think that?"

"That signature," Anita growled. "It's very unusual, but I saw it once before. The graffiti, in the MIT lab. It was you!"

Lucy looked at Brasil. "Figures. I don't know why he puts up with your clumsiness, Jason." She turned to Anita. "You intellectuals think you're so damn valuable. Like the light of the freaking world would go out if you got snuffed. There's always another scientist." Lucy reflected a second or two and added, "And nurses are a dime a damn dozen." She patted her handbag.

"You were in Boston. The Annie Henderson case. Wait. Did you have anything to do with what happened to Harriett and Bobbi, Lucy?" Jack asked.

"Their lives sure weren't worth the price of these boots." Lucy laughed and kicked up a heel. They got off the elevator. Lucy gripped Anita by the shoulder. "Don't get smart again. I'll be glad to knock the two of you out, stuff you in the closet and pick you up on our way out, after we finish our business."

The two women held a staring contest that Lucy won in seconds, then laughed turning her back to them both. They were still flanked by her henchmen. It was only a couple of dozen steps to their destination.

Jack thought it odd to see Lucy knock at a closed door after the conversation they just had.

She waited patiently for a response, which seemed to take an inordinately long time. The woman who answered was Asian. Tall and slender but sort of plain at first blush. An oversized lab coat hung loosely on her frame.

The woman introduced herself as Chen. She used a proper Chinese name that Jack couldn't make out.

*English isn't her first language, but she doesn't really have an accent.*

Chen seemed tired, yet polite as she ushered them in to the offices. They were in the outer office where Ms. Chen was both the secretary and lab assistant it seemed. Her boss was more attentive. Dr. Serena Butler was a fair-skinned black woman that Jack guessed was in her fifties. She had streaks of gray mixed in with brown hair, which came just past her ears. She was a mature, statuesque woman. Dr. Butler had nice big eyes, with an arcus senilis that gave her eyes a captivating blue-gray appearance as if she were wearing contact lenses. She had a proud posture, elegant.

Jack hadn't read any of her work, but Anita's shoulders went back and he thought her attention level went up by a factor of two when she saw the name on her badge. Again, Anita said nothing.

By this time, Jack had learned that when Anita wasn't talking, he ought to think twice about opening his mouth, too.

Lucy greeted her for the group, "Dr. Butler, we've been patiently awaiting your position on fibromyalgia syndrome detection and treatment. We were pleased when you were selected to sit on the Advisory Committee to the Senate subcommittee on healthcare. I hope you are also going to recommend adoption of this amazing fibromyalgia remedy. This is really a hot button topic these days, Doctor."

Lucy spoke very knowledgably about the clinical ramifications of FMDS400. Jack thought it was odd. Not out of character and it was typical of Lucy's thoroughness in detailing a product. Problem was, it wasn't her drug.

*Didn't she work for Glazer Corp?* Then Jack noticed, *Lucy changed clothes again. Subtly. Light blouse over her tee shirt. Looks more like a slick black jersey material now in the morning light. She must have added a necklace and make-up to her look in the car on the way over. Ditched the hat somewhere along the way and ran a comb through her hair to give a little style to it.*

There was more. Lucy was not only talking about the FAME DAYS study, she was talking about disease detection. That was key to CDC involvement.

Anita's facial expression telegraphed her thoughts. Sure enough, she focused on the conversation intensely. Anita and Jack had talked about NIH and FDA involvement. That was regulatory. The CDC had a different impact on the potential approval. It was indirect, but in some ways even more important than the FDA.

The CDC could deem the treatment unnecessary. Fibromyalgia syndrome and chronic fatigue are not life threatening, they are lifestyle altering. The advisory board could recommend that the drug not be approved on the grounds that it was not medically needed at this time, given the economic climate. That would be the prudent position given the fiscally conservative atmosphere in Washington these days.

The thing that Jack had missed was the detection part. Anita never mentioned an assay for detection of the condition. Far as Jack knew, there wasn't any.

"Ms. Velasquez, I know you're eager to win approval for your test. I also appreciate your support for my research and my board appointment, but as I told you in the beginning, my appreciation has its limits. I will advise the Secretary of HHS as well as Congress in a responsible way. Now if that means your assay gets approved, but the drug doesn't then so be it. We're still crunching the numbers."

"May I see your data, Doctor?"

*Why is Lucy so persistent?* Jack wondered.

"Ms. Velasquez, you know good and well that that is not ethical," Dr. Butler told her. "I know you're anxious, but you'll have to wait."

"Of course, Doctor, I apologize. I am too close to this project I guess. It's been very stressful for me. I'd like to freshen up a bit." Lucy asked, "Do you have a restroom nearby?"

"Yes, there's one in the outer office. You don't even have to go out to the hall." She pointed to where Ms. Chen sat. A thick stainless steel bracelet tinkled at the wrist as Dr. Butler gestured.

*A medical alert bracelet.* Jack observed, *Lucy must have noticed, too.*

Lucy excused herself and took her purse with her.

*The same one she usually carried at the hospital.* Jack didn't notice accessories often, but this was an omen. *Bad things were about to happen.*

In the outer office, Ms. Chen had put on her face and done something interesting with her hair. Jack and

Anita watched Lucy walk out past her, confirming directions to the bathroom.

Ralphie went out of the inner office and Ms. Chen's face lit up like a Christmas tree.

*So the "War Paint" was for him,* Jack supposed. *Cute smile.* He didn't think of Ralphie as particularly handsome, but he never did quite know what women liked.

Ralphie wore a security uniform. Jack guessed he had probably been laying some kind of seductive groundwork for some time before today.

It must have occurred to Anita before it occurred to Jack, *We're alone with Dr. Butler,* Jack saw, *and Lucy's out of the room. Ralphie's pre-occupied with Ms. Chen in the outer office.*

"Dr. Butler," Anita began. "I'm Anita Thomas. I met you at The Nordstrom Clinic. I was on the FAME DAYS project. You spoke—"

"At the Crawford Center. Yes, I remember. As I recall, you were said to be a very promising researcher. What are you doing here, Dr. Thomas?"

Brasil came back into the office. Jack had nearly forgotten the little weasel had been there at all. *Obviously, he wasn't the one who got Ms. Chen churning.* Jack looked at Jason and suppressed a sneer. *No way would anyone describe him as anything, but gruesome. Like a stunted troll under a bridge.*

Brasil was carrying something in a small, vinyl case. He nodded as Lucy re-entered from her trip to the restroom.

Ralphie strode slowly toward the hall door still ajar behind Ms. Chen and closed it. Brasil followed Lucy back into the inner office with Dr. Butler. Ralphie and Ms. Chen had a little privacy.

*She expresses her feelings pretty obviously.* Jack thought watching her body language.

Anita and Jack had been hovering at the door between the two rooms, ready to exploit any conceivable
opening. Both men had been injured the night before.

At last glance, Brasil whispered something to
Ralphie as he passed him on the way into Butler's office.
Jack didn't like anything those two cooked up between
them.

Lucy re-engaged with Dr. Butler. "Look, Doctor,
even if you don't show me, could you please just check
the status for me?" Lucy pleaded. "I'll stand over here
while you do." She promised.

"Ms. Velasquez, it is Saturday morning. I seriously doubt there's been any activity on the report since
yesterday afternoon," Dr. Butler said.

She was losing her patience.

Brasil moved into position to keep Jack in check
in case he got any brave ideas. None had yet occurred to
him.

Lucy gave some kind of sign to Ralphie in the
outer office. He moved in behind Chen, hugged her amo-
rously around her waist, and caressed her cheek with his.
Chen responded with tacit, coy offense. She did not resist
though. Not yet.

Lucy turned around to face the desk where Dr.
Butler had accessed her computer. Ralphie had slid his
arms up to just below Ms. Chen's breasts. What happened
next wasn't very nice.

Ralphie began to hug Chen; first, affectionately,
then like a bear. No, a bear hug would have simply
crushed her mercifully. This was torturously slow. More
like a python. She couldn't call out for help. Couldn't
breathe.

From the door, they could see her struggle for a
while. Jack wanted to go charging in and knock him out.
He knew better after last night. He thought he might take
the little guy, but Jason Brasil had his hand in his pocket

directing something cylindrical through the fabric. There was no mystery as to what it represented.

He touched the index finger of his free hand vertically against closed, smiling lips. It upset Jack more than it did Anita. She understood whom she was dealing with while Jack was still learning.

It wasn't long before Ms. Chen went limp, but watching it felt like an eternity. Ralphie kept squeezing, though. The freshly applied lipstick hid the blue color change that usually showed in the lips first. She broke a cold sweat and then became that ashen hue over the next few minutes.

Lucy confirmed that Ralphie had Ms. Chen under control before digging into her purse. She had a wet wipe right on top. She was on Dr. Butler before Jack and Anita knew it. They could smell the ethanol and chloroform saturating the wipe cupped around the doctor's mouth and nose from across the room. There were only two, maybe three muffled grunts before Dr. Butler went silent.

*Okay, she's out. Let her go, you bitch!* Jack thought Lucy was just going to knock her out so she could gain access to Dr. Butler's data. Not the case at all. Lucy held the wipe tightly over Dr. Butler's face long after she had lost consciousness. Then, she too had turned that haunting, ashen color that made every physicians heart race.

Lucy was now laying Dr. Butler's body face up on the floor, the wipe yet over her mouth. Lucy pinched her nose shut.

"Bring the secretary in here, Ralphie," Lucy commanded. "Put her down on her knees next to Butler and prop her up."

*Meticulous,* Jack was disgusted with what he was compelled to watch. *With no more emotion than if she were arranging flowers in a vase.*

"Get her hands on doc's belly." Lucy said. "Tracks of tears." She touched Ms. Chen's face. "Hmh, that'll be a sentimental touch when the police investigate." Lucy smiled.

Lucy had torn open the Doctor's blouse down to the waist and cut the front of her bra through between the cups with a pair of scissors from the desk. She gave five deep compressions of CPR while holding Butler's nose and mouth shut. Digested food bubbled through the corners of Dr. Butler's lips as she regurgitated, then aspirated her own gastric content.

"Jason, get those leads on her chest."

She watched his confusion as he tried to comply with placement of the Automatic External Defibrillator he had retrieved from the hall.

"Look at the god damned pictures on the leads, Jason." She said with the most exasperation that she had shown in hours.

Jack wasn't sure that Lucy had ever shown remorse in his presence. He followed what she had in mind now. He knew the CPR protocols like the back of his hand. He had taught classes on it. Lucy and Brasil hooked the AED leads up to Dr. Butler's chest.

*Who would question a heart attack in a fifty something year old African American diabetic?* Jack knew. *Who would question her loyal assistant performing CPR on her? Furthermore, who would question that same loyal employee not getting her hands clear quickly enough to not get zapped by the AED jolt?*

Anyone would put it together that the thing stopped Ms. Chen's heart when it discharged. Obviously, she would have been emotionally impaired, especially with tears running down her face at the time of her own cardiac arrest. Not clearing the victim before delivering the shock would be a believable mistake even for one trained in CPR.

Once the setup was satisfactory, Lucy shoed Jack, Anita and Jason Brasil out of the office. Ralphie performed chest compressions on both Dr. Butler and Ms. Chen.

*No other witnesses.* Jack's thoughts came to him unbidden. *No second-guessing the scenario.*

Lucy pulled out a thumb drive and walked toward the desktop as they were leaving. They overheard her say, "911?" into the phone receiver. She sat down and crossed her legs while the download progressed. Jack and Anita were guided out by Brasil. The digital clock read 6:40 a.m.

The last thought Jack had was Lucy's beta-blocker pharmaceutical pitch, "Remember doctors, most heart attacks occur between 4 and 8 am."

# Chapter 30: Caipirinhas

David Rivers' Audi cruised down Peachtree at an easy 35 mph. A soft mist lingered long after the rain cooled off the brutal Atlanta heat. Khandi and Al enjoyed the vibe as David swooshed through puddles in the streets. They too, had gotten through the darkness and reached the cosmopolitan city lights of the downtown club district. Apparently, the area was untouched by the black out.

"Reminds me of NYC, David." Khandi said. "Smoother streets though." She leaned back against Al's chest.

"I love coming to Atlanta. Very cool." David agreed as he palmed the wheel of his ride around some pedestrians inching into the road at the corner of Peachtree and Harris. "Are you from Nuevo York, Khandi?"

She hesitated for a moment. "I am, but I'm not Latina, Davíd is it?" His complexion was too deep to be a swarthy Sicilian.

"You have a good ear, Khandi." David said. "So what is your background?"

"It's complicated." She said simply. She was coming down from her high. "I like to say 'I'm just me'."

"Real mixed up, huh?" David asked.

"You have no idea." Al answered for her with a laugh, then caught a playful elbow in the ribs.

"Know what you mean. I changed my name from Davíd Rivera to David Rivers when I went into the Rangers."

"Covert ops?" Khandi perked up. "What did you do?"

"Surveillance." David said shortly.

"Sniper you mean." Khandi said then clapped her hands loudly. "Bad-ass!"

David smiled as he had scored points with Khandi without telling her a thing.

Davíd Rivera spent a little too much time looking in the rearview mirror on such a strait road for Al's taste. He hugged Khandi tighter to him. David just smiled and looked out the driver's window shaking his head.

"So Al, what's your story?" David asked, still driving with a confident ease.

"What do you mean?"

"Where are you from, man?" David clarified patiently with the least threatening tone he had.

After a beat, "Chicago." Al answered. "Southside."

"Chi-town. Cool." David said. "You go to school there or here?"

"A little of both actually. University of Illinois for undergrad." He checked Khandi's eyes for the expected approval that he knew he'd get on mentioning his sports prowess. "Baseball scholarship. Then it was on to Ann Arbor for Med school."

Al didn't brag often, but he did like to see Khandi's pride beam at his accomplishments.

"Then Internship at Hamilton hey? Sweet!" David said, impressed. "I hear Hamilton takes one out of every twelve candidates who apply. What a coup."

Khandi didn't like his tone. She thought it condescending somehow. "Ann Arbor graduates get their first choice of training programs more than 90% of the time, you know." She said hugging Al's arm tighter.

David sized up the situation swiftly.

"Look, Khandi, I meant no offense. I'm a 'New Yorican' from Washington Heights," he looked at Al, "Spanish Harlem. I know what an accomplishment it is to get out of a bad situation. My only out was the service."

"David, I don't know what 'situation' you're talking about. My father is an assistant Principle and my mother was a paralegal at Goodyear and Karp until she re-tired." Al said emphasizing the disparity between his background and David's.

David said nothing. He drove the last couple of blocks to the nightclub in silence. He gripped the wheel more tensely than he had all night.

Khandi was happy it wasn't someone's neck. David was lean but bulky up top. She had second thoughts about Al's off the cuff comment about "situations."

*Earth Tones* fit the Peachtree beat: Trendy, chic and exclusive. David valet parked. He was all smiles again as he climbed the single step to the entrance.

The reflections of luxury cars, mostly black and silver, shone against the wet pavement mottled with pud-dles where the ground was less than perfectly even. The jet-black lot had recently been resurfaced and outlined with bright reflective white traffic paint.

Khandi hesitated at the step as Al led her into the den of hedonism ahead of David.

"I don't know, Al, it's been a crazy enough night as it is. Don't you think we've had plenty of excitement for one night?"

Al took her hand in both of his. "You want to go home, Khandi?" He asked.

"Kinda," she said, looking into his eyes.

"Hey guys, gimme a break." David realized that they were both begging off the club scene. "I've been traveling all day. I'm playing host to a company party for you folks that I didn't really want to go to and got my hand busted up on top of it all. At least let me get a decent drink and air it out a bit. If I host you two, the company will pay for it. I'm not made of money like Luciana Ve-lasquez. Don't let the suit fool you."

Al felt bad about the slight earlier. "Come on, Khandi, one drink and we'll head home, okay?"

Khandi knew Al so well. "Sure, babe, one drink."
They followed Davíd Rivera in.

The colors inside were comfortable, almost edible.
A different theme from anteroom to bar to dance floor.
Earth tones; Chocolates, caramels, peanut butter tans and
raspberry/grape pastels.

European style, ultra-modern furniture with a lot
of stainless steel and hardwoods in the tables and chairs.
Hardwood dance area dappled with sparkling lights from
a twirling disco ball added to the party atmosphere. So
many of the girls wore mini-skirts and form fitting party
dresses.

Khandi spoke loudly in Al's ear over the pounding
bass of the sound system, "I could handle a drink or two
in here." She indicated the attractive crowd and smiled.

Al squeezed her hand and led her to the bar. It was
going on 2 am. Khandi danced, trying to entice Al onto
the dance floor. He waved her off. Al was beat by then.

David offered to dance with Khandi. She took him
up on it. Al knew Khandi didn't go for his type. Had it
been Lucy offering, it might have been a different story.

Al didn't mind that Khandi liked girls. Pretty ones.
She was good at getting chummy with a chick, sneaking a
feel or two, then sharing the experience with Al. She had
no interest in David.

David tried to get a little too cozy with Khandi.
She usually sympathized with the raging storm of male
hormones. She was expert at diplomatically evading a
guy's advances. She ended the dance early and sat at the
bar. She took the last seat leaving David to the other chair
next to Al, the one nearest the door.

"Barkeep!" David shouted, not making eye contact with Al. "Drinks all around." He said pointing to Al
and Khandi, then gave an order in Portuguese.

"Try this, Khandi. I think you'll like it." He took the drink from the bartender and handed the glass past Al to her with a gentle shake. "It's called a Caipirinha. Taste it." He gently commanded them both. "It's prepared with a Brazilian liqueur called Cachaça. It's a favorite in Latin America."

Khandi and Al looked at each other after a sip and nodded vigorously. David ordered another for Al. Using practiced sleight of hand, he spiked it the same way he had just done to Khandi's drink. He hugged them both when they appreciated his choice. Deftly, he placed a micro camera device on Al, on his lapel. Discrete, subtle. He pretended to check messages on his cell and grinned. David could see Khandi and himself every time Al panned his jacket's lapel past them.

After an hour of cashews, Caipirinhas, sports and swimsuit model comparisons, David stood and stretched. The bartender announced last call. It was three o'clock on the dot.

"Looks like it's time for me to dispose of you two." David smiled. "You ready?"

Khandi smiled a closed-mouthed, sultry smile. "I'm ready to get disposed of." She gazed up into Al's eyes stretching those long arms around his neck. She kissed him.

The cars parked in the lot outside had thinned out. David flicked his fob after the valet brought it up front then disappeared. The passenger doors unlocked and the trunk flew open.

"Oops. So, who's getting in the trunk?" David asked.

He sounded like he was joking.

Khandi said. "Depends on who's the most drunk." Her eyes were glazed. She looked from Al to David. "I guess that'd be me." She hiccupped. She took a few steps toward the trunk playfully then did a clumsy about face.

Al put a hand on her shoulder to stop her.

"I agree, Al. Khandi is way too fine to throw in a trunk. How 'bout you get in the trunk? You can take a nap 'til we get you home and I can have Khandi all to myself." He laughed.

"Not funny, man." Al said.

Even after a few drinks, Al never lost sight of Khandi's honor.

"Look, I'm kidding. We're gonna put Khandi in the trunk, but I'll drive very carefully." He laughed absurdly now. "No speed bumps, though, okay?" He said to Khandi, draping a heavy arm around her neck and shoulder and stumbling as if drunk spinning her away from Al.

"If you think anybody here is getting into that luxuriously spacious trunk, you're one crazy asshole." Khandi said, trying to unwrap his arm from her neck. He stepped back toward the passenger side of the car and pulled her tighter to him. Khandi looked around the parking lot, now abandoned but for the three of them.

"Get in the fucking trunk, Al." He said with no inebriated affect. "I'll snap her neck without a second thought." David said as Al moved toward their side of the car.

Al stopped mid stride. He froze realizing Khandi's jeopardy. *This dude was crazy,* Al thought.

Khandi sobered quickly. She had seen some desperate situations in her short life. Harassment, attempted rape, assault for being the wrong color or ambiguous gender. She had learned a lot, too.

Khandi bit down on his arm mercilessly until it bled. He loosened his grip slightly. She raised her foot up high and kicked down hard on the outside point of his ankle with her heeled shoe.

She heard him say something about "Crazy bitch" as she reached for his injured left hand. She grabbed his fourth and fifth fingers with her fist and wrenched downward. Al must have heard the cracking sound from across the parking lot.

David came around with his fist toward Khandi. She thought he'd aim for her face. His target was a foot and a half lower.

He struck her in the gut. She caved over and down. Al looked like he was going to lose his mind.

He charged over the car like OJ Simpson and pounded at David. David had four inches and forty pounds on Al, but the attack was fierce. Al hit him with several quick jabs, too fast for David to block. From the looks of David's head going back, those punches more than stung, but they failed to score any more than a loss of balance. It was like beating on a tree stump with a hammer.

When David's turn came to trade blows, Al was dismally out classed. Still, David took Al seriously and that was all Khandi needed to recover and regroup.

She drew a 1960's steel nail file out of her purse, pulled David's right pant leg up above the ankle from where she lay behind him and drove the point straight through the Achilles tendon and twisted.

David went down. Al saw Khandi get up and run toward him. The parking lot was fenced in and the path around David too narrow. He waved her off and pointed down the block. He wanted her to give David a wide berth. Before she did, David managed to grasp Khandi's pant leg. His grip was fierce, but she fought until the seam ripped.

Al had retreated to the parking lot entry when he saw Khandi make her first break, but now he was easily fifty feet away from them. There, a pair of matching Crape Myrtles stood planted at the gate, their bases covered decoratively by fist-sized river rocks.

Al hefted one that felt right. He wound up and hurled the stone. He aimed at David's head, but it pelted him on the shoulder instead. Didn't knock him out but he had to release Khandi's pant leg now torn up to her thigh. She scrambled clear again and turned back to Al for guidance. David was down on his knees, but still between them in the narrow alley and the fence restricted her from getting safely past David even with the accumulated injuries.

Al moved his lips silently as he counted off streets the way he often did when thinking back through records or journal articles for details that he had seen.

Like many doctors, Al had an eidetic memory. He thought he had seen an all-night restaurant three blocks back.

"Park & Penny," he mouthed and threw another rock at David while he was down. He hoped Khandi had understood him. Al was a middleweight. He couldn't have wrestled the keys out of David's hands and he knew it.

Khandi ran one way out of the enclosed lot and Al ran in the opposite direction with David grabbing at them both from his knees.

David hobbled painfully back to his car. He got behind the wheel. He made a tourniquet out of his necktie, and bound his leg above the ankle, then started the car and took off after Al. He pulled out a PDA and scanned it for correlation with Al's camera point of view. He grunted when the camera image went dark. He figured Al must have taken off his jacket to avoid being spotted. David looked into his own reflection in the rear view mirror and cursed to himself.

He drove slowly, scanning signs of Al. The city lights were growing fewer and further between as the hour grew late.

He locked on the Park & Penny diner. There was a crowd of college kids leaving the restaurant. A beardless boy stood in the street in an effort to hail a taxi for his crew.

David had an uncanny talent for hostile site appraisal.

He couldn't see Al from his vantage. He also knew he couldn't chase him down when he found him. He had to draw him out.

David gunned the Audi. The kid in the street went down flat to the silent horror of his watching friends still on the curb. The Audi backed up a few feet, slowly, as if possessed by Satan, and idled.

Al came dashing out at the sight of the crowd gathering round the accident victim. He stretched into the sleeves of his jacket he'd been carrying under his arm. Al was never a soldier. He knew he was being stalked, but he didn't realize he was being baited.

Al waved the crowd out of the way to assess the patient. He looked up to rebuke the driver. Still shining headlights on the scene. They blinded the lapel camera David had planted on Al's coat but for the car's minicam, it was like a spotlight.

Al's eyes went wide in recognition and his jaw dropped open.

David limped out of the car, aimed his Browning at Al's chest, and fired point-blank.

David called out in a falsetto voice, "Someone shot the doctor! Call for help, someone please."

He scanned the crowd for Khandi. Nowhere to be seen. He searched Al's pockets and lifted his cell phone, wallet and any other identification he had, then hobbled back to the car.

With his Achilles tendon severely injured, he had to stomp the pedals with the force of his leg instead of the precision pressure he would have applied with his calf via the Achilles tendon. He peeled off, but his driving was shaky. David would have to dump the car and lie low for a while.

# Chapter 31: House of Brasil

Lucy and Brasil had made their way to the lobby with Jack and Anita in tow. Like the other handful of civilians present in the building at that hour, they pressed themselves to the walls as rescue workers began pouring into the halls.

The information clerk was fully awake this go-round, but she was focused on the wave of incoming personnel, not the by-standers. The coven of witnesses had to walk back through the metal detectors to get to the exit.

To Jack and Anita's surprise, no alarms went off.

*Whatever Brasil's carrying in his pocket isn't metal. Probably isn't a gun either. Game change. With big Ralphie staying behind to report to the authorities it's two against two... and Brasil hurt his little wrist.* Jack smirked.

Lucy guided them to the elevators, which went down one floor to the lower level parking lot. Jack touched Anita lightly on the fingertips to draw her attention. He looked at Brasil then at Lucy, hoping she would understand that this would be the order of attack. She mimicked his eye movements and subtly nodded.

When the elevator doors opened, Lucy entered first followed by Anita, then Jack. Jason Brasil brought up the rear vigilant as to what was going on in the lobby and who was watching. Jack maneuvered between them. The second the elevator doors closed, he shoved Brasil face first against a stainless steel wall, and threw an elbow at Lucy's nose.

Knocked the wind out of Brasil, but Lucy blocked his attack and countered so quickly that Jack found himself staring up at the ceiling of the elevator before the doors opened to the garage. Before he even knew what was happening, Lucy seized his arm in some kind of weird lock he'd never seen before.

"Good morning to you too, Jack." She pretended to yawn. "See, Anita, this is all Jack is good for, short, hard and to the point. Completely predictable every time. No imagination. No stamina."

She winked at Anita and whispered, "You haven't missed a thing!"

After Brasil recovered, he pointed the cylindrical item in his pocket first at Anita, then quickly at Jack, then back again. He rose to his feet, and secured Anita as Lucy forced Jack up to his feet. The doors opened to the lower level parking deck. It was abandoned.

Using hand signals only, Lucy directed Brasil toward the daylight and the parked SUV in the open lot. He marched Jack a few steps ahead with Anita sandwiched between himself and Lucy this time. He stopped to toss the pink highlighter in the trash.

*Damn.* Jack swore to himself. *He swiped it from Chen's desk to mimic a gun in his pocket.*

As their footsteps echoed through the empty deck, Jack couldn't help but think, *They weren't armed as we watched them murder Dr. Butler and Ms. Chen in cold blood.*

He also realized Lucy had just kicked his butt single handedly without even breathing hard and that in the doctor's office they also had big Ralphie for back up. Still, he and Anita might have tried at least.

They walked past CDC personnel and into the warm summer morning outside its doors. They reached the vehicles. The suburban and Lucy's Porsche were parked with an empty space strewn with pieces of a broken beer bottle between them in the sparsely occupied lot.

Lucy opened her car door, grabbed a backpack, and tossed it to Brasil. He caught it with both hands and unzipped the pocket. This time he withdrew a real gun, semi-automatic.

Lucy looked at Jack and shook her head sympathetically, then closed her door and drove off. It took him a while to recognize the sentiment. He had never seen it from her before.

The parking lot was across from CDC's front entrance. Jason Brasil, Jack, and Anita watched as Emergency Medical Service vehicles careened into the fire lane.

Ten minutes later, they finally saw EMS come out pushing two gurneys, both bodies covered head to toe in white sheets. Ralphie related a heartfelt account of the rescue attempt to the drivers and first responders by the time security guards were directing the vehicle bearing Brasil and company to exit the area.

Brasil pulled over under a tree on Clifton Road. He pulled a utility knife out of his back pack and cut through the driver's seat belt. He eyed Jack and drove the knife through the airbag in the steering wheel. Brasil invited Jack to take his place.

*If I get any heroic ideas and tried to pull some James Bond stunt, I won't have the safety restraint.*

Brasil crossed over to the passenger seat before turning over the keys, and buckled Anita's belt. When secure, he jammed the knife into the mechanism and twisted it. He looked at Jack and grinned.

*Little piss-ant,* Jack thought, *Anita can't make an easy break for it at a stop light or something.*

Brasil climbed into the back seat behind Anita and tried to buckled in. Jack saw him wince at the effort.

*Bad wrist.* Jack thought, suppressing a smile. *Di Marini did some real damage last night.*

Brasil shifted to the seat behind Jack where he could cross the seat belt into its sheath with his left hand and tossed Jack the keys.

They drove west on Ponce Deleon Avenue toward the Inman Park district. Jack gazed down North Highland

Avenue and thought of Maynard's. Hunger pangs hit him for the first time. After what they just saw, he didn't have much hope for Anita and himself getting a last meal.

*This little shit isn't the merciful type.*

Jack drove evenly towards Grant Park. It had already occurred to him that Brasil was the character he had spotted at the park last week while jogging and the week before seated at the bar in Maynard's and half a dozen times at Hamilton.

*He must live in the area.* Jack realized.

At Brasil's direction, he slowed in a residential section of two and three story houses, which looked like they dated from the 1930's. They were on a quiet, tree lined, old Atlanta street. About 40% of the lots in the neighborhood were vacant or recently demolished. Many of the remaining houses appeared to bear signage indicating protection by city ordinances for their historic value.

They must have been near his home, because Brasil tapped Jack on the shoulder with the barrel of his gun, no silencer. He didn't care if he was seen with it, nor that use of the weapon might draw attention. He had Jack steer into a driveway on the left, sandwiched between a vacant lot and an abandoned house. There was a separate garage with double wooden doors.

Sticking the gun in his pants, Jason Brasil cut the seatbelt, made Anita get out and help him open the doors. Mostly to keep Jack chilled out, he pulled then held the gun on Anita as he tossed her the keys. She opened the garage and he ushered them both in.

*This set-up has all the makings of a train wreck in slow motion.* Jack could already imagine Jason Brasil torturing Anita and him in tandem. *This won't end well.*

As he drove into the garage, Jack saw it for the dilapidated shack that it was, neglected for decades. Daylight poured through the spaces between weathered pine boards that failed at walling it in from the elements.

By this time, Jack's hands were shaking and his breath came shallow. Brasil waved him out of the van as Anita closed the garage doors behind him.

Jack stepped out of the vehicle and toward the beckoning gun. Now his breathing sped up and he broke into a sweat. His knees were shaky. Anita came up next to him and laid a hand on his forearm. Jack calmed a bit, but still had that fatal feeling of foreboding.

"Okay, you guys, out and cross the yard as fast as you can without running. Stop on the back porch and wait for me. Go!" Brasil ordered.

Anita and Jack hustled across the space in seconds. The grass was still slick with the morning dew. Funny how one notices the little things when thinking it will be for the last time. Jack was already thinking about all the things he wouldn't experience in his life: *marriage, children, grand kids.* His mind was calculating possibilities for escape while scenes from his past flashed before him. He still didn't see an opening in Brasil's defenses in the immediate future.

Jason maneuvered them to the rail while he found the key to the back door.

*He must have twenty keys on that ring.* Jack thought.

After a little fumbling, Brasil found the one that opened the door. He hesitated for a moment, looking from gun toting hand to the key holding hand. He put the key in, turned the lock then stepped back. Jack thought he saw Brasil grimace at the effort. He made them push the door open and precede him in.

The kitchen stank of decaying food. The sink contained a pile of dishes patrolled by sorties of fruit flies. The only light filtered weakly through yellowed shades pulled down over the windows, which looked like they were at least forty years old.

He waved them past a trash can filled to the brim with an assortment of crumpled paper bags mixed with cups of matching fast food restaurant logos. They found themselves in a sparsely furnished front room.

Brasil herded them up the narrow staircase to a back bedroom of the house. The door was an impressively solid oak with an external padlock hanging opened on its latch. As he opened the door, it occurred to Jack, *It's not original stock for the house. Brasil reinforced this room for a reason, and there aren't a lot of reasons for a design with the lock on the outside.*

Brasil was smiling now. Whatever was coming up, he looked forward to it with perverse anticipation. He crossed to the only piece of furniture in the room, a steel cabinet. It, too, had a padlock on it, but this one was locked though.

*Again that awkward hesitation when it comes to unlocking the door.* Jack saw that this time Brasil switched hands, holding the gun in his left hand and un-locked it with his right. *He definitely winced a little as he turned that key.*

Jack was reminded again of the injury Di Marini dealt him the night before. *Had he really broken Brasil's wrist or only sprained it badly.* Jack almost smiled. *It doesn't matter. One is just as bad as the other in the short run.* That was his opening.

Jack waited.

Brasil opened the door and fished out two pair of stainless steel handcuffs, tossed one of them to Anita. She caught it clumsily then dropped it to the floor with a clat-ter. She stooped to get it and Brasil pointed his gun to her for a second, then back to Jack.

"No funny business, huh? I'm in no mood for any shit, no matter what Velasquez says." He smiled again. "I'll plug the two of you."

Anita nodded, gaze locked on his. She was shaky. Jack knew she was scared. So did Brasil, but he enjoyed that. He touched her hands as she fumbled with the cuffs.

"Put these on your boyfriend's wrists over there, then I'll put the bracelets on yours, darlin'."

He showed her how they worked. Anita recoiled from him a little. He enjoyed her dread.

"Clap them on behind his back." He pointed with the gun in his left hand.

Anita brought her elbow down hard on his right wrist still holding the other end of the cuffs. The little guy actually screamed when she struck him.

She stepped into him as he began to bring the weapon around to strike her and keep Jack at bay. With all of her weight, Anita shoved him off balance and he stumbled toward the gun safe. Down, he went, firing a wild shot as he fell.

Brasil dropped the gun when he hit his head on the corner of the safe. Jack kicked the gun out of his reach, then bore his teeth in a slow predatory grin. He had been waiting to take this little worm down since that day in Grant Park. Jack stepped between him and Anita then crouched, bristling for a fight. Jack wasn't so confident when Brasil unsheathed that knife from his ankle scabbard and stood. Jack took a prudent step back toward Anita. She pressed the cuffs into his hands.

"Brass knuckles." she whispered.

The mismatched men danced slowly, cautiously for a moment as Brasil feinted with the knife. Jack was bigger than he was with a longer reach.

*Nice to have the size advantage for a change.* Jack thought, *Still this son of a bitch was Special Forces.*

He could fatally underestimate this mercenary easily. Jack was careful not to fall for anything obvious. He remembered what his brother Mark taught him: *Don't give away anything as you move.* He kept his eyes on Brasil's eyes. *I hope to God he has a tell.*

Brasil soon realized to get Jack he had to commit to an attack. The thug tried a roundhouse kick.

He caught Jack in the ribs and took his wind. *Lord, that was fast!*

Jack grabbed the foot and rolled against the direction of the kick. Brasil had to let the knife go to protect his head and cradle his wrist as they hit the floor together. Anita searched for an opening to help Jack. He scrambled after Brasil before she could intervene. Jason's right wrist had been beaten up pretty badly over the past twenty-four hours, but he groped for a choke hold on Jack's neck.

Jack rolled back and elbowed him as hard as he could just above the nape of the neck. He was dazed, but managed to answer with a backhand to Jack's face. Jack started out planning to fight this guy not wrestle him. Jack caught his left wrist, rotated and hyper-extended Brasil's arm at the shoulder. Jack knew he didn't dislocate it, as intended, but he was happy to see that he hurt him all the same. A checked kick by Jack landed below the knee and brought them both to the floor again. They fell together, but Jack came back up on his feet before Brasil did, just not soon enough to press the advantage.

Both men rose, each unarmed this time. Jack didn't even feel guilty about his injured wrist. Jack tried to catch him between alternating jabs then changing up with an inside elbow thrust when he got close in.

It was like he was reading Jack's mind. Brasil knew every set up and combo Jack threw at him. Jack was getting frustrated until he remembered something Mark's friend, Kip, said to him— "When you're fighting someone who has evenly matched or superior skills to your own, be patient. Wait him out. Block and engage, block and engage. Wear *him* down or wear his *patience* down. He'll want to put you away quickly. Eventually he'll make a mistake rushing the pace and overbalance his stance. That will be your chance.

*Jason Brasil is one patient son of a bitch!* was all Jack could think, *but he is getting pissed.*

It wouldn't have been long before Jack gained the advantage, but then he heard Brasil grunt between blows.

Anita had improvised a weapon out of her scarf and the stainless steel handcuffs. Realizing who had struck him, Brasil turned, red faced, to Anita. He charged her totally, ignoring Jack. He uttered something too guttural to understand. Probably a curse. Jack didn't know.

Brasil raised his right hand over head to strike her with a balled fist. Jack came close, grabbed it and wrung it like a dishrag. Jason Brasil howled.

Jack kicked the back of the man's knee and brought him low. He tried to recover and Jack dropkicked him through the door, which had been opened through the whole tussle. Brasil landed a couple of feet from the door, but the momentum carried him a ways farther.

Anita whirled that handcuff weapon and let it go like David must have gone after Goliath. Hit Brasil square in the nose.

Jack didn't realize there was part of a banister to the landing. He had focused on the destination door coming in to the room. Brasil went through a gap in the rail.

Still, it wasn't that easy to get rid of the little monkey. *He actually grabbed the ledge of the landing with his bad hand.* Jack was amazed.

Anita picked up the gun he had held on them, marched up to the edge and aimed it right at his face. She pulled at the trigger, but nothing happened.

Somehow, one of them had engaged the safety in the skirmish. It wouldn't fire. Anita screamed an obscenity that Jack didn't even think she knew and bashed Brasil's little fingers off the landing with the butt of the gun.

When he let go, Anita watched him from over the hand rail. He was writhing slowly over a broken wooden chair on the first floor. A look of pure satisfaction on her face, she turned and walked back into the room to check on Jack.

"Jack, are you okay?" She was already examining him for fractures, cuts or stab wounds.

"I'm fine." he said, then asked, "Brasil?"

"He's done. Let's get out of here, Jack. We've got to get the authorities in on this. That bitch, Lucy has got to be stopped."

She turned and walked toward the door. Jack noticed a backpack hanging on the back of the door. He pulled it off the hook and began to rummage through it.

It contained a pair of high-end, military grade binoculars, a wireless netbook and a satellite cell phone. There was an assortment of knives and an extra magazine for the gun she carried. Then, in a pocket separate from the rest, he found a packet of cash, $1,500.00, several passports with different names, but all with Jason Brasil's photo on them.

They checked the room for anything else that they might need, especially the keys to the van. They must have been in Brasil's pockets. Jack thought of something that he hadn't gotten a chance to tell Anita earlier.

"Anita, I got a call from Sam Reardon last night. Antony was assaulted." He barely got the sentence out before she reacted.

"Is he alright?" She demanded. "Why the hell didn't you tell me when it happened, Jack?"

"I heard from Sam when we were in the club last night. As you may recall, things started to happen quickly after that. I haven't had a chance to speak to you since then. Our phones were confiscated, so I haven't heard anything since the first call.

She stared at Jack for a long moment before cutting her eyes from him.

*Disappointment,* he guessed, then headed for the door.

They climbed down the stairs and passed Brasil, gurgling on the floor. His ribs were broken and his chest bleeding. He was sucking for air. Anita knelt and examined his chest wound.

"Pneumothorax. He won't last long without medical help." she said.

"Do you actually want to call E.M.S. for this douchebag?" Jack asked her.

"Are you crazy? Let him croak!" She gave Jason Brasil a lingering look that could have frozen even Lucy's blood. "Come on, Jack. Let's go."

# PART 3

# Chapter 32: On the Run

It was ten o'clock on Saturday morning on their "Golden Weekend" and Jack was escaping from Jason Brasil's lair with Anita Thomas on his arm. He had just beaten a special ops marine hand to hand.

*Wonder how the rest of this weekend will shape up?*

Anita couldn't find their confiscated cell phones in Brasil's van. Maybe Lucy had them, maybe they were at the bottom of some sewer, they didn't know.

"Jack, these weapons... this one's a Glock 18. There's two sided tape wrapped around the handle and trigger. Matted finish, deliberately made to obscure prints. Same for the knives."

"I don't think we can go home, at least not to your apartment," he said. "Lucy must have you under surveillance."

Anita objected, mostly out of sheer exhaustion and worry for Tony. "How do you know she's watching me, Jack? She's probably got bigger fish to fry. This is some serious hardware they're parking." As she replaced the pistols he added, "The serial numbers have even been filed completely off. This stuff doesn't come cheap."

"Anita, Lucy told me last night that she lives in the Lattimore Hotel. The apartment in your building was a convenience." he stopped at the corner of Edgewood and Euclid Avenue.

"No one leases two apartments of that quality in the same city. They're only five miles apart! She had to set the second one up for the sole purpose of keeping an eye on your every move. We can't go there." he said firmly.

She took in a deep breath and sighed.

*Anita already came to the same conclusion,* Jack thought, *but didn't want to accept it.*

"Jack, we're fighting in the dark. They know so much more than we do, we'll never beat them. They're five to ten steps ahead of us. Dr. Butler is… was internationally recognized as an experimental neuropsychologist. Her medical training was actually in rheumatology, though. She headed the Immunology department at the Falkner Academy for Neuroscience in New Orleans until Katrina washed it away. She had just set up an A.I.R. Division when the levies broke. Do you know how few combined Allergy, Immunology, Rheumatology programs there are? Dr. Garcia tried to recruit her, but the appointment was blocked by Dr. Hargrove."

"Yes, I heard him comment on that mistake many times in morning report. So do you want to go back to the CDC campus?" Jack asked.

"No they'll be watching it. Hamilton University Medical Sciences building too, so we can't use that either." she said.

"Then what?" he was out of ideas hours ago.

Anita snapped her fingers. "Georgia Tech! I can get into their network and access the CDC's common database. We'll do better working on campus than remotely. It'll raise fewer alarms." Anita smiled.

"So on to Ivan Allen Boulevard and step on it." Jack said. "Got it, Chief."

"Jack, can I call Sam on that sat phone in the pack?" Anita asked.

"Sure. Dial 404 555-3312 extension 50 to get the residents' desk in the ER. Sam's probably off duty by now, though."

Jack drove across town at the speed limit just enjoying the drive with Anita in the seat beside him. The morning was sunny. The rain the night before bestowed a cool freshness to the day that Jack hadn't felt since spring.

Anita dug around in the bag on the back seat until she found the satellite phone. She punched in the number Jack gave. He knew she was calling for an update on Tony Fusco. He knew what she'd hear was that he had a broken nose, maybe some bruised ribs and pulled muscles, nothing serious. The expression on her face told him he was wrong.

"Jack, you had better take this." She handed him the phone with a quivering hand.

"Wheaton." he said into the phone with the receiver to his ear. It was another resident.

"Hey, Jack, Sam is still here. He's been waiting for you to return his calls all night."

Jack Wheaton heard a shuffling of the phone and then Sam Reardon's voice dominated the chatter before he began talking into the mouthpiece.

"Jack, this is Reardon." Whenever Sam began a conversation like that, it was always a bad situation to follow. "Where the hell have you been? I've been calling you since 1:00 am!"

"Long story, Sam. What's so important?" he failed to remind Sam he was off duty. After a night like last, he respected Sam more than ever. If he wanted to talk to him, it would have to be important.

"Jack, Dasher Clay is dead." Sam Reardon waited a couple of beats to let that revelation sink in before dropping the next bombshell on him.

Jack listened as Sam described how Stormi Seales was being held for the murder. Not by the police, but by Psych.

"The chief resident argued that he knew Stormi personally and could not imagine how she could do such a thing while in her right mind. Tox screen and full psych work-up are in progress." Sam whispered. "Slow progress."

All Jack could manage to get out was, "Damn!" Then, "Where did this happen?" his voice was cold as ice. He knew Lucy had something to do with it. Jack listened for long minutes as Sam delivered the gruesome details blow by blow.

"Sam, I know you have to go home sometime, but if you're there at Hamilton, watch out for Lucy Velasquez. I can't give you any details, but don't tell her any more than you absolutely have to tell her. And don't let her get you alone either. In fact, don't turn your back on her under any circumstances. "Don't ask, Sam, just trust me on this." Jack was depending on Sam's military conditioning to follow orders in a tense situation.

"Okay, Jack, this is your call, man. Oh, you better call Dr. Hargrove ASAP. He's called at least twelve times since midnight."

"Sure, Sam. Thanks. Take care of Tony, too." he said.

Jack really meant it. He nearly forgot Anita was there. After hearing about Dasher, all that rivalry nonsense went out the window.

Jack didn't call Dr. Hargrove back until they reached the Georgia Tech Campus parking lot. If the big Honcho called Jack twelve times, whatever he had to say to him, he didn't need to deal with while he was driving. Jack didn't realize he was calling Dr. Hargrove's home number until the sound of an eastern European woman answered formally. "Hargrove residence."

"This is Dr. Jack Wheaton. I believe Dr. Hargrove is expecting my call."

"Of course, doctor. I'll get Dr. Hargrove immediately." She said with what Jack could only guess was extraordinary urgency because the switch off was as if Dr. Hargrove was right next to her as she answered the phone.

"Jack. Where are you?" Hargrove's voice said nearly in panic.

"Parking lot of Georgia Tech. I have Anita with me and she's safe for the moment. Seems like a lot has happened since we last spoke, sir." Jack tried to reassure him. Dr. Hargrove expressed some relief then asked for his charge.

"He wants to talk to you, Anita." he said, then handed her the sat phone.

"I'm fine, sir. Jeff is taking good care of me. You should have seen hi…" She listened to a question for a moment then, "Sorry, I mean Jack, Dr. Hargrove. You should have seen him in action–"

She nodded a couple of times. "Yes sir, a knight in shining armor." She smiled, then handed Jack the phone back and said, "He wants to talk to you again."

"Yes, Dr. Hargrove?" Jack said, taking the phone back.

He listened to the chairman of Medicine tell him about the trouble with Dasher Clay and Stormi Seales again. "I have a lot to tell you, sir." Jack said interrupting him to let him know he had already spoken to Sam Reardon in the ER that morning.

"Sir, you should be alone for this conversation, do you have some privacy there?"

Hargrove answered a cautious affirmative and questioned the security of Jack's phone.

He explained that they were using an acquired Satellite phone. Best security going. "Sir, Lucy Velasquez is a nasty bit of business. I witnessed her murder both Dr. Selena Butler and her assistant Ms. Chen." Jack listened to his response. Incredulous as expected.

"Anita was there to see it, too. Cold blooded murder, sir. Never seen anything like it."

Jack listened to a brief, grief stricken choke, then, "Jack, don't call the local authorities, I believe this bunch can manipulate local law enforcement with relative ease. I'll call Homeland Security in on this. I can have them down here by nightfall, first thing in the morning at the latest. Avoid your apartments, too. Do you two have any place you can lie low for a while?" He asked.

Jack didn't tell him about Di Marini and the gang members. He wouldn't have cared anyway.

"Dr. Hargrove, these guys are well trained in hand to hand combat techniques. One of them took out Anita's boyfriend in short order and this little guy, Jason Brasil, just about handed me my head."

Hargrove thought he was exaggerating the account of the fight and said how certain he was that Jack was well prepared with his black ops skills.

"Sir, he laughed at my martial arts technique. I'm not sure I can effectively protect Anita from these merce-naries."

His hesitation told Jack that he did indeed expect them to be as dangerous as described. "What do you need, Jack, APD Red Dogs?" Hargrove asked.

"No, sir. I wouldn't be able to tell the good guys from Lucy's thugs."

Hargrove made sounds of uncertainty on the other end of the line.

"They are that good." Jack said, "I have no inten-tion of letting them get that close to us again unless I'm ready for them."

"I have a gun, but I don't know how to use it well enough to effectively engage in a fire fight. It may come in handy if I have to bluff. I had something else in mind, though."

"Anything you need, Jack, name it." Hargrove said.

"Any way you can call in some of those military style morphine ampoules we use on the ambulances?" Jack asked.

"Yes. I know what you're talking about, but is that what you really need?" He asked skeptically.

"My name's not Bond or Bogy, sir, but we need a discrete weapon that we can use to our advantage in close quarter in-fighting. We'll need about ten apiece. We're near RiteRx Drugs on Spring Street. Oh, and Dr. Hargrove, they took our IDs and wallets, so you'll have to talk the pharmacist through this personally and describe us to him in detail."

"I know Bill Stewart personally. I'll see if he's on duty. If not, I'll have him get over there in a hurry." Dr. Hargrove said then added, "Good luck, Jack."

Jack thanked him and hung up. He turned and looked thoughtfully at Anita.

"What's next, Jack?" she asked.

"Anita, who's 'Jeff'?" he asked pointedly.

Anita said nothing for nearly a minute, but Jack could tell she wanted to while the tears welled deeply before leaking from her eyes.

"Jeff was my brother. You remind me of him, Jack." She laughed without humor. "Sound just like him. If I close my eyes, I can see his face every time you speak." She closed her eyes and shook her head.

"Did he look anything like that kid you pronounced on the ramp a couple of weeks ago?" he asked.

She nearly wept into hysterics. Jack didn't know what to do.

It really wasn't more than thirty or forty-five seconds, but it just seemed like forever before she pulled herself together.

"Jeff was my older brother. When I was nine, he was sixteen. We lived in Great Neck, Long Island NY, in a "safe" neighborhood. One night, there was a knock at the door. When I asked who was there a foot kicked the latch off and the door flew open. Three thugs burst in. I don't know if it was random or planned. They wanted electronics and cash.

It wasn't very late, maybe 9 or 9:30 pm. Jeff and I were down stairs. Dad and Mom were upstairs in bed. The robbers were armed, but unsure of themselves. Even I could tell they were scared. They were shouting at me to point out "the goods". Jeff heard and realized what was happening. My brother would never let any harm come to me under any circumstances.

What's the expression, 'He brought a knife to a gun fight'. The first guy shot him in the chest point blank. Blew a hole clean through his body.

I must have deafened them with the shrieking, because they tried to calm me down, not threaten me into silence. Looking back, I guess they couldn't have been more than a year or two older than Jeff. They were all crying before I knew what was happening. One of them fell over with his hat and part of his head flying past the other two and into the fireplace.

My dad was on the landing of the steps, sawed off shotgun blazing. He shot the second thug in the chest while he was coming down the last two stairs. The third guy had dropped his gun in the living room and couldn't find it. He was bawling like a baby on his knees searching for it to protect himself from my dad.

I watched Daddy bash in the back of his head, then when he fell over on his back, my father beat his nose back into his brains with the butt of the empty shotgun until well after that boy stopped moving and the crunching of bone changed to a nauseating mushy sound.

That kid on the ER ramp looked just like Jeff did that night, haircut, wound and everything. Maybe even the same shirt. I nearly held it together, Jack, I almost did.

When you opened your mouth, I heard Jeff speak again after seeing his face for the first time in sixteen years. I lost it, that's all. Sorry I didn't tell you." She sniffled. "Every time I hear your voice, I see Jeff's face and just know he's coming back to protect me."

Well, that was it. Nothing else mattered. In that moment, Jack knew that Anita was forever out of his reach romantically. He felt like the king of all fools.

It began to rain again. The drops splattered across the windshield until the campus in front of them blurred out of focus.

Jack started the van and followed Dr. Hargrove's directions to the drug store. Anita was staring out the passenger side window with an expression Jack couldn't begin to interpret. He pulled into the parking lot of the RiteRx on Spring Street and 17th.

Pharmacist Bill Stewart was behind the counter in the pharmacy. He looked like he had just arrived. Bedhead and still donning his white jacket, Stewart came to the window as they entered his store. They could even hear the shuffle of slippers moving on the tiled floor within the enclosure as they approached.

"I'm Jack Wheaton, Mr. Stewart. I believe you just got a call from my boss, Dr. Hargrove?" Anita joined him from behind. "This is Dr. Anita Thomas."

Stewart made a call on a personal cell phone rather than the store phone.

"Wes? Bill. Your young clinicians are here. Now, let me have that story again, they need *what?!*"

Pharmacists demand a lot of secure information from both doctor and patient to dispense controlled substances. The DEA will shut a pharmacy down in a minute for apparent impropriety. They didn't even have proper identification much less medical credentials and he was dispensing military grade class II narcotics to them on Hargrove's say so alone. It felt to Jack as if they were secret agents being fitted with the latest spy gadgetry.

Jack gave in the list that they needed. While he collected it, Jack and Anita browse the store. They packed up their supplies, which included a couple of toothbrushes, a comb for Jack, a brush for Anita and couple of large tee shirts with looped pink ribbon insignia in the left breast area. Jack grabbed a couple of bottles of water.

He picked up a disposable cell phone before leaving and activated it on Hargrove's personal account. He and Anita thanked Mr. Stewart. Even at this point, Jack didn't trust this sat phone from "the Devil's Workshop." For all he knew, Lucy might be tracking it even now.

Bark at the SUV, Jack's stomach groaned.

Anita laughed. "Was that yours or mine?"

"Sounds like a gastric concert to me. I know *I'm* famished." Jack thought about the most popular fast food restaurants clustered on the corner of Edgewood and Auburn Avenue. Sizing up the competing fair, Dr. Wesley Hargrove's words echoed in his mind. *"Don't contact the local authorities."*

He thought he might have become paranoid, but he said to Anita: "Let's get off the beaten path. I don't want to go anywhere where there might be security cameras networked into a central hub."

She nodded thoughtfully. "Okay, Jack. I agree with that logic. So where do we eat?"

"There's a great 'greasy spoon,' hole in the wall 'bout half a mile from here. They barely have electric lights, but they sling the best down-home grub in Atlanta." he said.

# Chapter 33: Librarian

By noon, the lunch crowd began filtering in to Abbey's Café. Jack was surprised to see how young Abbey was when she came to their table to deliver the check.

"Twelve bucks even," she said, figuring the bill in her head then she scribbled the final tally down on a receipt pad and patted it as she laid it down on the table.

"How was your meal, sweetie?" She looked back and forth at Anita, then Jack as she stuffed the pad back into an apron pocket.

"Great food, Ms. Abbey." he said. "Stick to your ribs good," he emphasized.

"Tell yo' friends!" she demanded cheerfully.

As she turned to attend to an incoming customer, Jack tugged at her apron. "Say, Ms. Abbey, do you know a general store that might sell some pants our sizes?"

She raised her hands to her hips and looked him right in the eye. "Don't know. Gordon's sell's some, but I'm not sure he'll have any to fit yo' bony butts. Most folks I send his way eat here more often than you two I suppose." She then smiled to take the edge of the quip.

"Thanks, ma'am." Jack said. He left her one of the twenties he pulled out of Jason Brasil's wad and hoped it wasn't counterfeit. She zipped a yellow marker across the bill, smiled and returned his thanks for the eight-dollar tip as they left.

They made their way back toward the downtown area after a little light shopping. They had dressed down since ditching the rest of their semi-formal wear from the Lattimore affair.

The tees they picked up at RiteRx Drugs and the khaki slacks and tennis shoes from Gordon's General Dollar store fit well for the college atmosphere. Less conspicuous, they headed back to Georgia Tech campus.

Once past security, Anita took the reins and navigated to the student center and research library. She flashed her smile and said something confidentially to the receptionist. The young man produced a bio-scanner and Anita rubbed her finger across it. Jack watched the blue-grey light from the computer screen dance across the young man's face and he looked up at Anita.

"Welcome to Georgia Tech, Professor Thomas. There will be a librarian at your disposal if you need one. Can I bring you a cup of coffee or refreshment, ma'am?" He asked her.

Jack was dumbfounded. He had never seen that kind of red carpet rolled out for faculty. He treated Anita like a visiting dignitary.

"That won't be necessary. Dr. Wheaton and I will need some privacy for about an hour and a half to two hours. Please see that we're not disturbed," Anita said in a rather official tone.

"Yes, ma'am." Was the simple, unsurprised answer from the receptionist.

Anita led Jack into the back room of the library as directed by the receptionist. She sat down, pulled her chair up to the computer on the only desk and turned on the lamp. The rest of the room was dim.

Jack surveyed the space from the door. Taking in the opulence of the décor, it occurred to him that this room was too comfortable for students and most of the faculty.

*How the hell does Anita rate this kind of courtesy?*

"Jack, why don't you catch a few Z's on the sofa? I'm tapping into the NIH data bank. It'll include the CDC network and I may be able to trace what Lucy downloaded this morning. I want to know what she's up to."

He startled her a bit when he appeared at her shoulder. "Not a chance, sister, I want to see what this is all about." Jack regretted using the term "sister" for a moment, but Anita didn't seem to mind.

"Suit yourself Jack, but it's been a long day. You must be sore and exhausted."

"I am, but I wouldn't miss this for all the sand on the beach."

She knew her way around the GA tech interface portal. Jack felt silly for a second thinking that she might have had a hard time learning the Hamilton medical records system.

"Anita, how do you have access to all of this?" He gestured to the whole room and beyond.

She sighed, missing maybe half a beat before navigating onto the NIH staff page. "Jack, I haven't been completely honest with you."

"No shit!"

"It's not something I really *could* have been honest about. That would have defeated the purpose." She turned to look at him.

"Defeat what purpose?" he asked.

"Well, it's not quite witness protection, but I'm sort of in hiding. I'm not really an intern."

"Go on." he said, listening intently now in spite of his fatigue.

"I'm an associate professor, Jack. M.D. PhD. I was tenured at Nordstrom before my disgrace. I have national security clearance from Homeland Security and full access to all confidential files at Hamilton and by extension to every educational institution in the state, courtesy of Dr. Hargrove.

"And all of this is over fibromyalgia syndrome? I can't believe it."

She shrugged. "Jack, do you remember what I said about why the mitochondrial suppression gene developed anyway?"

"Yeah," he answered slowly.

"I mentioned the idea of a *purposeful suppressor* gene to Gil and Harry. Well they were intrigued. So I ran with it as I always do when challenged or encourage or whatever." She shook her head. "I was so damn clever. You know what I realized?"

"What?"

"I realized that we could trace the gene against the NIH database. That's where Monty Hill came into the picture. Turns out, we were able to trace the gene mutation to the second migration out of east Africa thirty thousand years ago. When man fled the Ice Age drought, they were hunter-gatherers. The further north they migrated, the colder it got. Famine threatened their very survival.

The solution: Hibernation, mostly women, children and some men who were less virile, old or lame somehow tanked up on calories in the summer and fall then went into a reduced metabolic state. The younger women were often gravid by then."

Anita went into academic mode as she described her scientific findings. "During the winter months, the strongest men competed for game. Their libidos were suppressed and those testosterone-based energies redirected toward the hunt. They were detached from their female companions for months.

Note how nicely this correlates with the timing for championship games in the major sports: World Series, Super Bowl, College basketball championships, all staged from the harvest season to spring thaw. The timing of professional basketball playoffs in late spring is consistent with its fourth place popularity with descendants of the Northwest Eurasian region.

Similarly, for many women, seasonal affective disorder correlates with the greatest intensity of sports fanaticism. The frequency of bad hair days and mental health days also correlates well with the other phenomena."

Jack was highly impressed. "That actually makes sense, even to me."

"Well, get this: the gene would be useful for about twenty thousand years longer. It then became a liability. Do you know why, Jack?"

"The development of agriculture," he answered with authority. "Civilizations that developed agriculture along with the domestication of certain animals needed all hands on deck. In the hunter-gatherer scenario you described, more than half the populace was dormant for a large part of the year. By contrast, without a defined breeding season, an agricultural society could increase the birth rate by 25% or more, increasing the workforce for harvest, construction and administration of more complex government."

"Exactly. Historically, most advanced civilizations absorbed or supplanted these simple hunter/gatherer communities. The population explosion also supported standing armies. Here's the rub. Some of these hibernator clans were captured, enslaved, or otherwise married into the larger society. The hibernation gene was down regulated, not expunged from our genetic code. Nature doesn't have an eraser.

Given the variables we could actually verify, we surmised that about 10 to 15% of the populace still carries this hibernation gene to this day. During times of stress, the gene is more likely to be expressed, especially during the dark or cold seasons."

Jack nodded, following her logic. "This explains why mostly white people get fibromyalgia syndrome."

"Not exactly. There has been so much intermarriage before the establishment of so-called modern races that the gene is actually well distributed among all the races with the exception of the indigenous Australian people. They migrated from Africa earlier and remained isolated longer. You are really seeing an example of variable penetrance in the distribution of fibromyalgia.

The breakthrough was the connection between the mitochondrial down regulation and the hibernation process. Suppression of the Mitochondrial activity only makes sense if food is scarce and the level of activity is very low, too low to gather food, hunt or even defend oneself." Her eyes were red, her lower lids puffy. Still she gazed at Jack to make sure he was following.

"It's not even a life altering condition," he said and felt immediately stupid. Wished he could've taken it back.

Anita frowned, "Like it or not, fibromyalgia affects millions in this country. Hundreds of thousands of hours of lost 'life', not 'lives' are at stake. So many of these people just exist. The demand for relief is what drives this contention. Billions are up for grabs to the company that perfects a treatment for fibromyalgia syndrome or chronic fatigue. ...or prevent it from coming to market."

"Or can predict it with certainty." he added. "Lucy talked about a diagnostic assay. If Glazer really does have a bioassay for fibromyalgia syndrome, they may have a metric in the pipeline. If you can—one--diagnose Fibro, then--two measure it, you can, at least theoretically, determine when it's been remitted, even cured."

"You forgot to say 'three', Jack." Anita smirked. "Exactly what I was thinking. Lucy stands to profit like a Power Ball winner if she gets her hands on both pieces of the puzzle."

"And you are in her way," Jack said solemnly. "They all need to keep you very quiet."

She turned back to her work and added, "She's heavily invested with all of this equipment and these henchmen. Mercenaries don't come cheap I bet."

"I agree," Jack said. "I bet she's responsible for Dasher's death as well as the two scientists. Did you know Dr. Butler, Anita?"

"Mostly by reputation, but we did meet once. I'm surprised she remembered me at all. I was a new post doc at one of her lectures five years ago. I asked her a bunch of questions until she got bored with me I think." Anita chuckled. "Her loss is a major blow to the research community, you know?"

"Not to mention poor Ms. Chen," he said grimly. "Did you even know her first name, Dr. Thomas?"

Shamed, Anita hung her head for a moment, but said nothing. She resumed her work in a few seconds, but Jack knew his rebuke had hit home.

"I can see that Glazer supported Dr. Butler's work toward a theoretical basis for the bio-assay. She didn't have any direct involvement on FMDS400 until early this year. The files are encrypted, though. I can't open them."

She wrestled with a dilemma Jack wasn't privy to, then asked him: "Jack, do you have an e-mail account that you haven't used in a few months?"

"I have the Hamilton intranet account. We use it for intra hospital communication and medical record completion."

"No. That won't do. They'll be watching that one too. Anything else?" She asked.

"Wait a minute. There's one I used once a couple of years ago when I applied for a research grant to pay for an oncology project for a hematology fellow."

"Was she very pretty, Jack?" Anita asked.

Jack could hear the smile on her face as she spoke without seeing it in the dim light.

"Gum-shoe_Pete@HamiltonMedicalCenter.edu. Try that one, Anita." He said.

She did. The message went through and returned a confirmation. She dusted her hands together and said a satisfied, "Done. Now I just hope Monty doesn't relegate it to his spam collection." She looked back at him and giggled. "Gum-Shoe Pete? Seriously, Jack?"

He still loved the sound of her laughter, even at his expense.

"Hey, I love spy movies. James Bond, Sam Spade, Phil Marlow... all of them."

Anita nodded as she regarded him with admiration. I rarely admit it but I love Raymond Chandler and Dashiell Hammet. Their movies, too. At least the ones with Bogart in the lead." She grinned "As you told Dr. Hargrove, I wish I had a little more 'double 00' skill."

"Me too, and I've seen all the movies," Jack grumbled. "Thought I was pretty handy with my hands until today. Ate a tall order of crow, didn't I?"

"I thought you did okay against trained killers, Slugger." She glanced over at the couch. "Well, we have a couple of hours before dark. They won't bother us for hours."

"What?" he said.

For an entire second, Jack let himself think it was a come-on but by this time, he knew, *No freakin' way.*

"Do you want the couch? I can get comfortable by curling up in between the two plush chairs."

The 'other' idea didn't even occur to her. Jack got a little angry, but he refused to let her know that.

"Sure, I'll take the couch. I'll set my watch for ninety minutes." he frowned.

"Oh, now what?" Anita cringed at his expression.

"I just thought of something: Anti-Car Jack program. Betcha a nickel the van is equipped with one. I think we need to ditch it before nightfall."

"I have a better idea." She reached for the keys. "You did get all the important stuff out of the van, didn't you?"

He cocked his head quizzically and waited for her to elaborate on her notion.

She opened the door. "Excuse me." She, said beckoning to the young man at the desk. "I was wondering if you could get Security to do me a huge favor?"

He nodded.

"Can you have someone drop my vehicle off at the Brookwood station park and ride lot? I know it's a little far, but we borrowed it urgently and the owner doesn't have campus clearance, so he can't get in to get it and we won't be going back his way."

"No problem, ma'am. I'll have Roger and Gene drop your friend's vehicle off there. They carpool and go right by there on their way home. Their shift ends at 3 pm. Will that be satisfactory?" He asked.

"That will be just fine. Thanks, George," she said, finally reading the nametag on their surrogate benefactor's jacket.

"Problem solved," she said with more satisfaction than she'd shown in weeks.

They finally settled down for a quick nap and actually got the full time Jack allotted minus about ten minutes.

The Sat phone rang.

Anita and Jack were immediately alert and apprehensive. Jack opened the connection, but said nothing until he heard a familiar voice from the other end.

"Jack?" It was Sam Reardon's voice.

"Yeah, Sam. I'm here. What's up?"

The silence on the line chilled Jack to the bones. Anita stared without a single blink.

"We just identified a John Doe found on North Avenue near Peachtree. Gunshot victim. Jack, it's Al Williams!"

# Chapter 34: Styx

"To hell with this cat and mouse shit." Jack looked squarely at Anita. "I want to see my intern. I owe him at least that much."

He asked Sam Reardon to meet them at the entrance to the subbasement tunnels. It was off limits. Residents sometimes used them to sneak their girlfriends in to the campus, then back out again, especially if the partners were less than reputable. Reardon was there looking nervous as a cat in the rain.

He showed them through the doors and closed them hurriedly behind the two fugitives locking them back securely. He held Jack's gaze for a moment. He knew Sam wanted to know what was going on but Jack shook his head once. He still couldn't tell him.

Sam led them to the morgue checking to see that the way was clear first. Sam led them through rows of tables where he slowed to a stop. The body under the sheet was the only one in the room that had a toe exposed. A yellow tag had a sharpie inscribed label that read Jon Doe #9. Before the other end of the sheet could be raised, Anita turned away and drifted toward the door. Jack neither heard her tears nor her steps. He didn't hear anything, but his own heart pounding.

Sam lifted the sheet up off the head and chest. There was no mistake. It was Al Williams.

If solid ice could speak, it would have sounded like Jack at that moment. "Any details, Sam?"

"We don't know anything, Jack. Sorry. We didn't even know it was Al until a pathology resident recognized him from a Morbidity and Mortality session last year. One of the medicine interns came down and ID'd him, then called me at home." Sam made a grim gesture indicating why he was here again nineteen hours after the end of his shift.

"I got special permission from Hargrove himself to stay on call for anything out of the ordinary that comes in on any of us." He indicated them, wagging his thumb between himself and Jack.

"Thanks, Sam." he said and gave him a man-hug, fists clutched between their chests.

Jack turned to leave, then thought about that Satt phone again.

"Sam, if you need to get me again, call me on this phone." He indicated the new prepaid phone he picked up early that day and gave Sam the number. He programmed Jack's name to come up when he called.

Jack hoisted the duffle bag up upon his back. Anita shouldered into the backpack from the Grant Park house and preceded him to the morgue doors. She was still crying.

"You two look like crap. Why don't you stay in the Path resident's Call room for a few hours? Get some rest if not sleep."

*Anita is running on fumes, just like me.* Jack clapped Sam on the shoulder and headed down to the call rooms.

Jack woke up hours later. It was close to nine pm. He heard his intern breathing softly in the bed across the room through the darkness. Jack edged his way around the spare furnishings to her bed and shook Anita back to wakefulness.

He gave her a minute, then turned on the lamp. The bright fluorescent light was rude even with a warning. They organized themselves and looked at each other.

"Khandi!" Anita said it even as Jack's thought crystallized.

There was no report of a companion, dead or alive when they found Al. They had to find Khandi. If she were alive, someone had to tell her.

Jack went through a checklist of everything they needed to take with them and reached for the phone. He looked at Anita for a moment and dialed from memory.

The phone rang in his ear until the greeting engaged with a dead man's voice and went to voicemail. Jack hung up.

"Do you know where she works?" Anita asked.

"Yeah. I do."

They made their way back out through the catacombs to the street exit two blocks from the hospital. No outsider would know to look for any one exiting from there.

Jack and Anita walked down three blocks to Edgewood Avenue, then south towards Bigger Street. They crossed through Oakland Cemetery to Memorial Drive. The night was warm, but the walk was chilling given the events of the day so far. The neighborhood changed around them. They were near their destination.

# Chapter 35: Taking Khandi

The Magic Pony was on a dark, run down stretch between Loomis and Park avenues. The sign glowed in pink neon lights. Jack and Anita stood on the sidewalk across the street from the club. She looked at him in disbelief.

"Khandi works there?"

He shrugged, then crossed the street toward the front door. Two sentinels at the entry were checking IDs and patting down male patrons for contraband, weapons, etc. When his turn came, they didn't know what to make of Jack. They frisked him fruitlessly.

They got to his bag and demanded that he open it for them. Before Jack could come up with a plausible lie, one of the waitresses came running out of the bar waving the bouncers off him.

It took Jack a moment to figure out why this young woman was getting involved. Her make-up was heavily applied. Anita was the first to recognize their friend and she hugged her warmly. Khandi was dressed in leggings, a black skirt past her knees and a tapered long sleeve white cotton blouse.

"They're friends of mine, Derrick. Let them through, I'll vouch for them."

They hesitated.

"I said, I'll clear it with Fats, now let them through." She pushed the nearest guard out of the way and led Anita and Jack into the establishment.

It was the typical gentlemen's club. Walls, beams and ceiling painted flat black with accents of pink.

Khandi nearly pushed them down into seats at the bar. "What are you guys doing here?" she asked, clearly uneasy with their presence. She seemed out of place in the club. Her hair was pulled up and back primly, which she touched up into place nervously. It was more than just embarrassment. She was scared.

"Khandi, we have to talk--" Anita began.

"You bet your life, we have to talk. Not here, though. There's a lot I have to tell you two." She beckoned the bartender while she picked up a tray of drinks.

The urgency with which she did so told Jack that she had been in the middle of delivering an order when they showed up.

"Private party, Stan. I'll need a VIP room." She raised her eyebrows at him. "Red Velvet?"

He nodded and she thanked him with a head bobble.

She pulled Anita and Jack by their sleeves as she dropped off her order.

Jack thought he heard one of the men say "Thanks, Kara." And pulled out a five-dollar tip for her.

Khandi blew him a hurried kiss and shuffled Anita and Jack into a side room separated from the main hall by heavy red velvet curtains. The curtains didn't close completely no matter how she tried to arrange them.

"Damn," Khandi said, totally frazzled. "Stay put. Don't leave this area for anything."

*I've never seen her lose her cool before.* Jack noted.

"Where the hell are my glasses?" She patted her uniform down. "Jack, I'll be back. I'm going to have to perform tonight. Got any cash?"

He nodded and sat next to Anita on the vinyl sofa while Khandi dashed out of the draped alcove.

"Jack, what's going on? Why is Khandi working here and what does she mean 'perform'?"

Presently, they heard applause in the outer room. Music started again. They both recognized the beat. A DJ's voice projected, "And now for a rare treat, the luscious, Kara Mel!" More applause and sensuous music with heavy drum and bass rhythms followed.

Jack was tempted to peek, but he followed Khandi's instructions to the letter.

"At least Khandi's safe. We have to get her to stay with some friends for a night or two though," he said.

Anita started to nod, then froze. Her jaw dropped.

Whatever it was that frightened her, it was behind Jack. The bags with the weapons were out of his reach on the floor at Anita's feet. If it were a threat, he would have to deal with it hand to hand. He was NOT ready for what he saw when he whirled around.

Anita didn't know about Khandi or the work she did. Jack soon learned that he didn't either, and for that matter, it was likely that neither had Al.

If Jack's eyes had been cameras, he could have put the pictures on the Marquis outside the club.

Khandi had let her nearly waist length hair down. She lost all of her clothes while she was at it. All but an onyx choke collar, a white thong and black stilettos.

She strutted her way into the room, draped her arms around Jack's neck, and planted a kiss on his face close enough to his mouth to fool anyone behind her because the applause broke out again.

She smiled, pushed him down on the sofa, straddled his lap, arched her back and fluffed her hair.

"Pull the curtain closed, Jack." She ordered. "Anita, stay to Jack's left, back and out of sight."

"Khandi?" Jack asked, thunderstruck. He was looking up into her face before he realized she was wearing black rimmed glasses.

"Hey Jack." She turned to Anita and nodded humbly. "Sorry about all this."

Khandi was embarrassed and evidently, a little ashamed. She performed the lap dance like she had been doing it all of her life.

*She is really selling it too.* Jack thought. She stepped back and did a floor performance then came back to Jack's lap.

"Jack, he nearly killed me. David did. Al saved my life." She smiled. "You should have seen him. Fought like a demon. Man can he box. That monster, David's like a freakin' bull though. We just did get away, but Al told me to meet him here, I think. He just kind of mouthed it to me. I waited here for hours then I went to my apartment. I've been trying to reach him. He's not answering his cell or home phone."

"Khandi, we're in danger." Jack said.

"I know," Khandi said in an urgent low voice. "She's here."

With that, the hairs on the back of Jack's neck stood on end. He mouthed, "Who's here?"

She said, pulling his head into her bosom, then whispered, "Lucy."

Jack tried to pull away and she pulled his face back in to her chest.

"No, Jack. You can't react. She's in there with Fats and the door's open. Don't think she can see us, but it was closed ten minutes ago," she said. "Go ahead and put a ten in my thong."

"Huh?" Jack said.

"This is a strip joint, Jack. This ain't free!" She said intensely. "Put a ten in my thong. I'll give it back later."

Jack had to struggle to hear her over the music. He realized that that was why she kept pulling him close. Not that he minded so much, but she was Al's girl.

She stretched her legs straight around his neck and dipped her head down to the floor, then came back up to continue her conversation with Jack.

"If Lucy is in the back room with Fats, they're up to no good, I can tell you that!" Khandi said.

"What do you mean?" Anita asked.

"Fats is in into some dirty shit," Khandi said. "I don't know all the details, but I have more privilege than the other girls."

"So you have a relationship with this Fats, huh?" Anita concluded.

"Not a relationship, relation. But there are things he doesn't share, even with me. Anyway, this is not Lucy's first time in here though. I just recognized her twenty minutes ago. Knowing her connection to that bruiser, there was no good to come from her seeing me and I was ready to take off for the night," Khandi said. "Then you showed up.

"Lucy's been coming in here for the past month. I didn't recognize her because she's been showing up with a blonde wig and dressed like a skank."

"Lucy?" Jack said with disbelief at the description.

"Lucy! Tight daisy dukes, tee shirt tied below the boobs, bobby socks and sneakers. So with that blonde wig, I never put it together, until now. We get a dozen or so over the hill strippers or prostitutes looking for work every month. I don't pay attention anymore unless they've got real assets to offer." Khandi bowed her head in shame. "The only reason she registered in my mind is she kept getting past the goon squad directly to Fats. Those girls are usually screened out first or filtered to the bottom layer of the Flesh Trade.

"I don't know if she knows what her boyfriend is up to but I don't think she is what *you* think she is. Even if she is a high grade call girl, I would advise you to stay away from her." Khandi pulled Jack's head back by his curls and looked down into his eyes. "She's bad news, Jack."

*Khandi is worried about me?* This gorgeous woman was like a naked stranger. Bouncing hourglass figure and thighs a porn star would kill for was warning him about some "bad girl". All of that while giving him the lap dance of his life.

*Life's funny and cruel all at the same time.* Jack almost laughed to himself.

Somehow, he had yet to tell Khandi that her man was dead.

"What's this Kara Mel stuff?" Anita asked. Jack had the same question, but remained speechless.

"I'm a bookkeeper and sometimes a waitress when I'm needed." She waved her hands across her body. "Not a stripper. I'm doing this because Lucy knows who I am. I had to figure out how I was going to get you two out of here. I would have dragged the two of you out if I hadn't just taken a hundred dollar order. It was cash and I still had it in my apron. This chick is sharp. Doesn't miss a trick. Lucy would have checked out the commotion if we tried to dash." She stood and faced Anita. "She's never seen me like this."

She was wearing stilettos to accentuate her calves. They were more like costume props than what she had worn to the Ball the night before.

"Why 'Kara Mel'?" Anita asked slowly.

Khandi seemed to be pleading for understanding from Anita. "I go by Kara Mel because none of these sleaze bags need to know my real name!"

*That's a body forged for sin.* Jack thought as he watched her explain.

He took her hand and pulled her close. She didn't resist and straddled his lap again. He grasped her around the waist and found his courage. Jack was about to tell her the news. *She's going to freak.*

He pulled her ear close to his mouth and whispered, "Al is dead, Khandi, someone shot him."

She stopped moving to the music. For nearly five seconds, she didn't move, not even to breathe. Her skin turned a flushed tone of red, glistened then formed beads of sweat. She began to push away from him.

"No. No, Jack. No." The tears didn't well up behind her glasses until she spoke. It was as if it wasn't real to her until she said it aloud.

"I'll kill the fucker." Khandi was hyperventilating. "Then I'll find that—"

"No, Khandi, you can't—" Jack tried to reason with her.

Foolish.

"Fuck that shit, Jack. I'm going to blow that bastard to hell. I've got a thirty-eight behind the bar." She began to pound on his chest to break free. "Let me go, Jack."

"Khandi, people will think I'm molesting you. Stop it! You'll have the bouncers in here on me any minute," Jack pled.

She just fought with him all the harder to get free. Then, suddenly, she stopped. Her eyes glazed a little, Jack was still holding her tightly by the wrists but she was no longer struggling.

Khandi looked over at Anita, and then down at her own right butt cheek, so Jack looked, too.

Anita had jabbed her with a morphine hypo, full dose. Khandi swung a sleepy gaze back to Jack, nearly in slow motion. Her eyes rolled back in her head and she slumped forward onto him, limp as a kitten.

Jack cradled her head and rocked her in his lap for a few moments. He was close to tears himself.

"Sorry, Jack," Anita said. "I had to do something."

"Oh, yeah. This is better." Jack said, cradling Khandi like a baby. "All we have to do now is sneak an unconscious stripper out of a titty bar past two giant bouncers and hail a cab in this part of town. Piece of cake."

"We've got to get out of here and get her to safety. But where?"

Jack peered through the curtain to be sure no one was coming for them. No change in the mood out there. Just a lot of jeering and crass promises. Then he stopped for a second and listened closer. He wasn't sure at first, but then he heard the unmistakable voice of Slick in the outer room.

There he was at the stage stuffing singles into a pole dancer's G-string. Survivors of last night's shootout flanked him. They occupied the first row at the stage.

Jack looked around the alcove Khandi called the Red Velvet room. Ruby curtains on all four walls. They probably dampened the yelling from Khandi's outburst. Along the floor, though there was a break in the molding to form what he hoped was a doorframe.

Salvation. There was also a fire exit. He and Anita crossed to it. Above the door as he swept the curtain aside with Khandi's feet was a sign that read, "Emergency Exit. Alarm will sound if opened". Jack and Anita looked at each other, assessing the risk.

"What the hell, you gotta die sometime." Jack decided. "Grab our stuff." He faced the door, shifted Khandi from the cradled position to a fireman's carry to free up an arm and pushed the door opened with his foot.

No alarm. They both exhaled, grateful for the fire code violation.

Before they knew it, they were in the parking lot behind the club and out of sight of the bouncers, David Rivers and Luciana Velasquez. Jack thought they were free and clear.

*Luck might be a lady,* Jack's focus went to a lone figure in the dark. *but she ain't easy, not tonight.*

Another dancer was leaving. She must have forgotten something because she stopped in the middle of the lot, turned and headed back to the dressing room door when she saw them.

"What are you guys doing with Kara?" she asked.

She wasn't scared. The tone was rather of matter of fact under the circumstances, but she reached into her bag and held her hand there as she awaited the answer.

Jack and Anita thought they knew what she held in her bag.

Jack resorted to a fuzzy version of the truth. "I'm Jack Wheaton, a friend of Al's. Al's pretty sick. It was too much for Khandi tonight. She fainted." He waited for her response.

"You're Jack?" She smiled, a wide gap shone between her front teeth. "Kara's been talking about you a lot this month." She cocked her head with pleasure. "Is that Anita?" she asked.

"Yup." Anita answered for herself and waved.

"Kara's a pretty tough chick," the woman said. "How sick is her doctor friend?"

"He's in the hospital and I don't mean seeing patients." Jack said. Again, fuzzy truth.

She pulled her empty hand out of the bag. "Okay, get her into my car. That '93 caddy in the corner." She led them through the parking lot to her car.

In the streetlight Jack saw her figure under an over-sized cardigan sweater, which she quickly wrapped around herself. *Yes, she's working in the right place.*

She was a pale white girl, about 23 years old he guessed. This kind of life was hard on a woman. In any other setting, Jack would have guessed her age to be 28 or 30.

She had purple hair cropped short with a bleached white bang. Black eyeliner applied a little too thick matched her false eyelashes.

"You were going to work? Miss…" Jack asked.

"Candy, Candy Caine." she said.

Jack and Anita almost laughed. "Okay. Candy. You were on your way in, right?"

"I just forgot my schedule for next week is all. I hate having to call in and catch all kinds of grief from the manager for asking at the last minute." She had apparently stopped chewing the gum in her mouth when she confronted them. She made up for lost time during the conversation.

"Well, if you have to go back in, can you get my friend's attention?"

"Depends. Who's your friend?" She asked.

Candy came off as very casual, but she was wary.

Jack smiled. "First row, left. Leader of the pack. Name's Slick. Tell him Doc needs a word at the door." He winked at her. "Tell him it's about a tip."

"I don't know, Doc. Seems like a lot of trouble. I just want to go home. Been on my feet for hours."

She was staring him deliberately in the eyes as she spoke.

Jack pulled a twenty out and added, "Please?"

"Well…" She took the bill.

*Not enough.* Jack stuffed a fifty into the fist still gripping the crumpled twenty. She looked down at the cash in hand.

"I'll be outside the Velvet Room door," he said, assuming that seventy dollars was enough to secure her help.

She turned smiling, and trotted to the back door and disappeared through it.

Jack put Khandi on the back seat and positioned her as comfortably as possible. For Khandi, the space was long enough for her to stretch out full length, heels and all. Nineteen Ninety three Caddies were boats. Anita cradled Khandi's head in her lap. Jack knew her main concern was protection of Khandi's airway while she was sedated.

"I'll be right back."

As he turned to leave, she said, "Where are you going?"

"I've got to do something about Lucy. She got the drop on us last time. I think I can turn the tables on her this time around. Slick's in there with his boys." He smiled and winked at her, too. "Keep your eyes opened."

Jack went back through the fire exit to the Velvet Room and waited for Slick behind the curtain. He watched "Candy" whisper in Slick's ear as he enjoyed the stage show.

Jack imagined the message had been delivered when he saw the gang leader's expression change to the look he had given Dr. Wheaton last year in the ER. He got up, straightened his pants legs with authority and strode to the curtain concealing Jack from the audience.

"Whatchu doin' up in here, Doc? Thought you'd be gone from this world by now after they took you away in that SUV last night."

There was no joy in his voice at seeing Jack in one piece.

"It was close, Slick." he said. "Real close!"

Slick had lost several members of his gang last night. He lost respect too, leading them into a situation with no defined up side or down side. Jack had to give him both now.

"Look, Slick, she and her boys killed two of my people, too. You remember Dr. Williams who used to run the floors with me. Helped me put in the chest tube when your lung collapsed. He and another doctor got hit to-night." he told him.

"So, what's it to me? I ain't messin' with that bitch again!" He started to leave.

Jack grabbed his arm. Dangerous move.

He looked down at Jack's hand, then slowly up to his face and smiled a carnivorous smile.

"Now you and I have an uneven score, Doc. We could settle it right now if you want?" He said.

Jack knew he meant it. He wanted to get back at someone. Didn't much matter to Slick who it was.

"I don't have a lot, but I got two hundred if you think you can put her in a hospital somewhere. I'm not picky as to inside the building or just to the ramp." Jack said.

Slick knew the meaning of a "Ramp consult" even if not by that name.

While he was considering the proposal, Jack added, "There's a loaded thirty-eight behind the bar under the cash register. Could give you a leg up on her."

As they spoke, Jack saw David Rivers walk into the club. To Slick, David's limp looked like that swagger that was usually associated with black guys with *juice*. That little dip that said, *That's right, and I'll kick your ass too.*

"That guy's with her by the way." He nodded to David. "Word on the street is he's from the Bronx and don't take no shit off anybody." Jack watched Slick regard him. He thought he could peel the resentment off Slick like an orange by that point. "'Specially no country boys." he said in Slick's vernacular.

Slick squeezed the four fifties in a fist brandishing a gold, four-finger ring. "See what I can do, Doc." He pushed the ball of cash down into his pocket as he made his way back to his seat with his posse.

The whole walk there, Slick never took his eyes off David until the man disappeared into the manager's office where Jack assumed Lucy was carrying on some dealings with Fats.

Jack watched for a while before leaving. He wasn't sure that Slick had the backbone to stand up to Lucy and her mercs again. Then he smiled as three of them including Slick conferred between dances. They got up and strolled to the bar. Slick and a big guy engaged the bartender. Seemed like there was an issue with the service.

Jack grinned when he saw the little guy roll over the other end of the bar and disappear only to roll back over, toting a handgun while Slick and the other thug settled the drink issue amicably with the distracted bartender.

The little man tucked the weapon away before anyone could notice. The three of them went from the bar to the restroom together with the big guy standing sentry. Jack knew how the rest of the story would play out.

*Poor Lucy and David,* he sneered as he left his vantage in the Velvet Room via the fire exit. He met Candy at the car. The motor was running and Khandi was still asleep with her head on Anita's lap.

*She must be having pleasant dreams,* Jack mused.

He jumped in next to Candy and she drove off. He watched The Magic Pony disappear in the side view. If it were a movie finale, Jack would have thrown Lucy and David a one-finger salute shouting to them that *Al Williams sends his regards* while driving away in a Cadillac full of women.

# Chapter 36: Safe House

"So, you a real doctor?" Candy looked askance at Jack as they drove east on Memorial Drive.

"Yep." he said without looking at her either.

They were heading toward her apartment. It became a monotone word game: Who could communicate in the fewest words.

"Not a student?" She twisted toward him a little at the second question.

"Nope."

She half started the next question twice before she got it out. "How much do you make a month?"

"Not enough!"

She laughed. "Amen to that."

"So your real name Candy?" Jack asked after thirty seconds of silence.

"Hell no! Only crazy girls use their real names in dives like that." She declared.

"So what's your name?" he asked.

"You a stalker?" She looked at Jack sidelong, but more exaggerated this time.

Jack thought he saw a corner of a smile. It was less flirting than getting to know him.

"Haven't got the time, babe," he laughed.

"Too bad." She sucked her teeth.

Candy slowed at the Indian Creek MARTA station and turned up the hill to an apartment complex. It was an older building, but seemed neat and well kept.

Jack noticed a police station was on the same block. *Must have been a selling point for a single girl in her profession.*

She pulled into a perpendicular parking space in front of the breezeway. Jack woke Anita and then picked the naked girl up to carry her wherever the dancer directed. Anita had slipped a large tee shirt from the duffle bag over Khandi while she slept. They followed Candy into the complex.

The Dancer led the way up the stairs to her second floor apartment and opened the door. She waved them in as she keyed the pad to deactivate the alarm. The owner surveyed the one bedroom apartment from the door before turning on the light or advancing any further into the room herself.

"Put Khandi on the bed in there, Dr. Jack." She pointed to the bedroom door. "The light switch is to your left."

He found his way into the room. Neatly kept. The switch was where she said it'd be. He laid Khandi on the bed, checked her carotid pulse. Jack patted her on the cheek, which triggered a brief grimace. He turned back to the door to confirm that Anita was okay. She had the bags in tow.

"So who drugged her?" Candy asked.

Anita and Jack looked at each other. Anita raised her hand.

"How'd you know?" Jack asked.

"That," she said, pointing at Khandi on the bed. "--is no fainting spell. When a girl is out cold like that, she either got slugged or drugged. She doesn't look beat up and you doctors are more… sophisticated than that." Candy had folded her arms across her chest and leaned against the doorframe behind them.

"Must have been strong," she said. "Khandi doesn't go down easy. She going to be okay?"

"Yes, she's going to be fine." Jack said as he covered her half bare body with the bed sheet. She needs to sleep it off, though. She'll come around in an hour or so."

"Any chance we could get a pot of coffee going, Candy?" Anita asked.

She followed Candy and Jack out of the bedroom only after changing her own tee shirt.

"So… we were talking about real names?" Jack prompted.

Their host nodded, "My friends call me Eleanor."

She opened a cab.net door and pulled out a bag of ground coffee with one hand and a stack of filters with the other.

"Not a stripper name is it?" Jack said.

"Thank god! Poor Khandi." Eleanor said. "Funny thing is, when she arrived at the *Pony* a year ago, there were two girls other than me using the name Candy—Candi Appell, Candy Cain and Kandie Shoppe." Eleanor shook her head in reverie, "I remember I said, 'If you're applying for one of the waitress positions, you don't need a stage moniker.' It was just us girls after Fats made his decision. 'And if you're not sure, try to pick something more original. She looked at all us with this little sideways grin and pulled out her wallet. She was the only one dressed. We took turns looking at her license and laughing so hard we had a regular fart fest." Eleanor's smile faded.

"We really like Khandi. We'd all be pretty pissed if any harm came her way, Jack."

She didn't smile at all when she said that. "I used to call her 'Caramel drop'. That's where she got the idea for the name, Kara Mel." Eleanor seemed to have a bit more affection for Khandi than just a co-worker.

"Eleanor, do you mind if we check our e-mail?" Anita spied the computer in the corner.

"Knock yourselves out." She said then they all laughed at the pun.

While Anita booted up the computer, Jack enjoyed the aroma of fresh coffee steaming from the machine on the counter.

"You kind of like Khandi, don't you?" Jack asked.

"She's a real good friend." Eleanor said, then went silent. She looked down at a plush pet pallet while the brew percolated through the gourmet grind.

"You got a pet, Eleanor?" he asked, following her gaze.

"No. Lollipop sleeps there sometimes." She said and held his stare for a few seconds to allow him to get the drift of the implication. "Khandi is a special girl, Dr. Jack. One in a million. I want her to be happy, even if it takes more than one person to do it."

Eleanor wasn't the most educated woman he'd ever met, but she was nearly poetic in her expression of emotions. Jack reflected on how she, and Al, and Khandi might have mingled in the off hours. *Wondered how Lollipop figured into their exploits.*

"I guess I don't have to worry about her getting some clothes on when she wakes," he said, indicating the difference in their heights with his hand. Eleanor stood at least 5'10" in bare feet.

"I've got a few things that she can fit into around here." That confirmed Jack's conclusions that Khandi had spent more than a few nights here.

"Excuse me, Eleanor, I need to check my voice messages." he stepped into the living area just outside the kitchen and parked his butt on a stool. Jack took out the Sat phone and dialed his own number. When the four rings cycled through, the answering machine picked up. He keyed in the code to play back his messages. Five from Sam earlier in the day and last night, three hang-ups and one from Christie. He listened to it all the way through then gestured wildly to get Anita's attention while he rewound it remotely. He played it again on speaker mode.

"Hey Jack. Give me a call when you get this. I've been in Sub clinic all day today. I got pulled to run the infusion center by Dr. Lee, you know, that number two in

Rheumatology? Creepy guy by the way. Stares through you, not at you. Can't ever tell what he's thinking. Asian men that tall just seem weird to me, I can't help it. We had three patients. He was working with that PA, what's her name... Walker? That nice drug rep guy was there, too. The top one with the funny movie director's name, visiting with his sister he said. Did you know she has some autoimmune disease? Anyway, I'd love to go out for drinks or a movie or something to salvage this 'F'd-up Saturday. Call me Jack."

He put up a finger to Anita's lips for silence as he heard a random shuffling noise in the background followed by footsteps that Jack didn't hear the first time he played the recording. Then there was the echo of his apartment door slamming shut and gently latching as Christie's message played out—"Oh, by the way, I didn't know there was a new infusible drug for fibromyalgia, did you?"

# Chapter 37: Eagle Eye

Anita placed a hand on Jack's shoulder. She hadn't seen him like this before, not even in the midst of a fight for his life. He was visibly rattled and she could relate to that. They were *in* his apartment, listening to his private messages. Who knew what else? She realized he wasn't so much scared as he was pissed off. He was determined to find out who was behind the scenes manipulating what seemed to be everyone.

"We've got to go, Eleanor," Jack said. "Can you take care of her?" nodding toward the bedroom.

"Yeah, I got this."

At that, Anita followed Jack to the door and waved a silent goodbye. They left Eleanor's apartment and bolted straight to the MARTA station. Jack put the Sat phone on an empty seat of an eastbound train while they waited across the platform for a westbound train.

"I don't know if they bugged my home phone or the Sat phone but by now they must know Brasil is dead. They'll be watching for us. We've got to stay one or two steps ahead of them somehow."

"If they got into your apartment, they must have gotten past your friend Slick and his gang," Anita said thoughtfully. "It couldn't have been peaceful. Want to call the ER to see if there have been any casualties?"

"Good idea." \He looked back at Eleanor's apartment. "Hope she can keep Khandi calm and away from Al's apartment for a while."

He peered eastward down the tracks as the rumbling of a train engine percolated up through his feet to his hips. "We can't chance another visit to Hamilton. Maybe we can draw them to a logical target and slip by them somehow." His words were lost in the roar of the motors and air brakes.

The train was almost empty. Anita and Jack settled into a couple of adjacent seats at the back of the car. Jack was getting accustomed to sitting with his back against the wall.

When they came to the next stop, the train waited in silence for three minutes. MARTA conductors tended to do that after midnight. Jack checked the cheap watch on his wrist. 11:45.

"I've got an idea. If I can talk Sam into cutting off that damn ponytail and shaving his beard and mustache, he could pass for me in the dark. What's that night administrator's name, Lynette something?"

"You mean the one with the Four Star social life?" Anita chuckled. "You think she looks like me? Thanks Jack. But do you want to put them in danger?"

It was a legitimate question. He thought about having Sam recruit a couple of hospital security guards to escort them, but he didn't really think they'd be a match for Lucy and her thugs. He had to think through his improvisation a bit more.

"What about this? We have our very good looking decoy couple pull up to my apartment, escorted by four or five armed guards, make a fuss about getting out and checking the block before going into my building. Two guards will stay in the car, two will remain stationed at the elevator entrance and one will ostensibly accompany 'us' up to my apartment.

What they'll really do is get on the elevator, press the button for my floor and get right back off. They can bolt for the alley and get a waiting ride back to the hospital. Once in the car, the guard returns to the others and makes like he just secured the two of us in the apartment then left.

Lucy will either stakeout the place or try to steal in quietly. Either way, she's where we want her to be and she's disappointed." Jack grinned at his own brilliance.

"Did you just make up that whole elaborate scheme off the top of your head?" Anita asked.

"Yep," he said proudly.

"Well, okay. I guess it could work, but I live by your old philosophy." She said.

"What old philosophy?" he asked suspiciously.

"KISS; Keep It Simple, Stupid!" She grinned. "We figured that they have the Sat phone bugged, right?"

He nodded.

"So, we call the phone and wait for some passenger or vagrant to answer it then keep the poor schlep on the line for the minute or two necessary to trace the call, assuming someone hasn't already started calling from it, in which case, they'll have done our job for us," Now she was beaming with pride. "and Sam doesn't have to cut off his pony tail."

"Okay, but mine is still a good back-up plan. We've been trying to get Sam to cut his hair for years." Jack thought for another few seconds. "Speaking of satellites, we can get the guards to use the satellite surveillance to focus on my building for covert activity."

"Hamilton has satellite surveillance?"

"When the gangs moved into the area a few years ago, the hospital took a few hits for stolen equipment and drugs. We got a grant for infrared satellite coverage in conjunction with the APD. That's Atlanta Police depar--"

"I know what APD is, Jack." She laughed. "I've been here a month, you know."

"Sorry. Anyway, we can check on what's happening at my place right now. We still have that secure line we set up with Sam. He can direct security. He has special authority from Dr. Hargrove."

He dialed Sam from his disposable phone.

"Reardon." Sam's voice resounded from the phone. Jack turned down the volume to a comfortable level.

"Sam, this is Jack." he thought for a moment.

He had to know if he was answering under duress. "Where are you?" he asked.

"Where the hell do you think I am? I'm spending my Saturday night off in the damn hospital. What's up?"

Sam sounded normal enough to Jack. He had given him ample openings to express some atypical chatter.

"Has Lucy or her boyfriend, David, been into the ER, hopefully for treatment of some broken bones or bullet holes?"

"No, not Lucy, but our old buddy, Slick and his boys were here an hour ago. One had a grazing gunshot wound to the arm. The rest just needed observation for tear gas exposure."

*Shit,* Jack thought to himself. *Lucy is still breathing, on the loose and as dangerous as ever. Where the hell are they getting these weapons?*

"Sam, I need you to get security to spy on my apartment building. You know, with that infrared thingy." he said, trying to hide his glee at playing master spy.

"Come again?" Sam asked. "You want me to do what?"

"We think someone is watching our homes. We just want to know where they are and when they're on the move." he explained.

"Sssooo, just what are we to look for, Jack? There's likely to be a lot of traffic down your street on a Saturday night."

Sam's question was logical. *A real spymaster would have concise instructions right about here.* "Start the clock now. I'll call you back in about half an hour. Get the Hamilton neighborhood watch going and hit me back at this number after about thirty minutes of observation." Jack waited to confirm that Sam followed all that and hung up.

"What now, James?" Anita said in a sultry voice and a passable British accent.

"Now, Moneypenny, we wait." Jack did his best Sean Connery.

"Ah, the original." Anita said. "I do love a classic."

The train rolled on until they reached Five Points station. They got off the train and jogged toward the nearest exit.

Locked.

They doubled back, and found a more popular exit, and then took their leave of MARTA. It had served them well.

It was a good three blocks to Anita's apartment building and the street was dark. That worked to their advantage. Jack made the call to the Satt phone.

Finally, some good luck: The person who answered sounded inebriated. Jack talked to him for a while then told him to meet him at the first Baptist church in Clarkson. There would be a reward for the return of the phone.

Jack checked his watch. *Eighty two seconds, Traceable.*

Anita and Jack made their way down the darkest alley and onto a dumpster between her building and the Chinese restaurant next door. They climbed up and over to the courtyard, then slinked through the shrubbery to the stairs. Anita lived on the eighth floor. They avoided the elevator as Anita told him there were monitored cameras mounted through the courtyard. She stopped him before they got to her floor.

She reached over a span of the stairs between floors and searched for something in the girders. Anita got a eureka look when she found what she was looking for: A spare key.

"Why wasn't it under a rug or potted plant near your door?"

"Tony taught me that," she said proudly. Then, "Jack, is Tony still in the hospital? If he's home he may be in danger or worse!"

*Home,* Jack thought, *not **her** apartment.*

She looked at him with those puppy dog eyes and he said, "Hold on a minute." He dialed Reardon again.

"Sam,- Jack. Is Tony Fusco still in the hospital?"

"Yeah, we're observing him for concussion. Why, you want to talk to him?" He asked.

"No, just wanted to confirm his whereabouts. Wouldn't want to shoot him by accident," he said, looking sarcastically at Anita as he did.

She gave him an *"Oh, Jack"* look.

Jack motioned for her to hand him the semi-automatic pistol from the bag and her smile faded.

"Any activity at my place?" Jack asked Sam.

"As a matter of fact there was a beehive of activity about five minutes ago. Before that, there were two cars idling across the street. How did you know?" Sam asked bewildered.

"A hunch." Jack turned back to Anita. She handed him the gun.

"Who says hunch these days? What the hell is going on with you two?"

"I'll be in touch later, Sam." He said.


Silently, he and Anita made their way down the hall to her apartment. Jack crept up to the door and listened for long moments for any sounds within.

Total silence.

He motioned for her to unlock the door while he covered her with the semi-automatic. He was surprised to see her with a revolver in hand.

"Where the hell did that come from?" Jack found himself tiring of surprises every five minutes.

"Apparently, Brasil didn't take any chances either." She whispered. "My hand bumped into this in a hidden holster in the pack."

They went in single file. Jack motioned Anita to look around for any sign of disturbance.

Anita would have been a great sleuth. She acknowledged with a single nod then listened.

Nothing.

Room by room, she went as he snapped the gun into firm readiness with every move. Each time she beckoned him on when satisfied with the integrity of the space.

They wove their way to the back rooms with windows on the courtyards, her bedroom, and the dining room. The master bathroom had no windows so they entered, closed the door and laid down a bath towel along base, then turned on lights for the first time since their arrival.

They both sighed in relief and laughed at the rush. Anita set the backpack on the counter and Jack set the duffle bag on the floor and took inventory. There were the passports with Brasil's aliases on them, a tee shirt, too small for Jack, but might have fit Anita loosely, two magazines for the automatic he carried, and a box for the Smith and Wesson. A tripod with telescoping legs, a pair of heavy binoculars and digital camera with a fire wire attachment remained in the bag. Anita noticed a 'female' fire wire connection to the high-end binoculars. She pointed it out to him. All Jack could say was 'Damn'. The last item in the pack was a portable 500 gigabyte hard drive.

"I have to say, Jack, this has been the most bizarre day I have ever been through." Anita wrapped her arm around his. "If we don't both make it out of this, I want you to know that this has been the most interesting date I've ever had, too." Then she kissed his cheek.

Before he could get mushy, she declared: "It's Sunday morning! Got to check e-mail." She made for the door to the bedroom.

Jack grabbed her by the arm as she reached for the doorknob.

"Your computer is almost certainly compromised. They were monitoring the satellite phone and my phone. Why would they not count on you trying to access the internet from your own home?" he asked.

Her shoulders slumped.

The weight of the moment returned as Jack regarded her. "Do you really know how to use that?" he asked, pointing to the pistol.

"This one?" she said, hefting the revolver, "Enough to take the safety off. I fired one once with my dad at a gun range."

"How'd you do?"

Anita sighed.

Before she could answer, Jack said, "Let's call Eleanor. Khandi must be up and around by now. If I know her, she'll be pacing a hole in the carpet. Get her to go through the recent history and have her read the in-coming e-mail. There's only the one you're interested in isn't there?"

"Make the call." Anita said and sat down on the toilet lid.

Khandi's voice greeted Jack at Eleanor's number when he dialed it.

"Khandi, how are you feeling?" he asked, glad to hear her voice.

"Sleepy and itchy as hell." she said solemnly.

"It's the morphine. It will wear off soon. Try a little Benadryl if she has any in the house."

"The oil and lotion are the only things keeping me from clawing my skin off." Khandi complained. "I was waiting for your call before I took a shower." There was silence for an awkward moment. "Is he really dead, Jack?"

"Sorry, Khandi. I wish that was a bad dream, too."

"Tell Anita I said thanks." Khandi sniffed, then with a little levity. "Morphine, huh. Good stuff. Best rest I've had in weeks."

"Yeah, you were pretty animated back at the Pony…"

"Don't remind me. That was the most humiliating thing I have ever done. Can't imagine what Dr. Thomas must think of me. She must think I'm a nutty slut. Last thing I remember was you saying something that made the room close in on me then waking up with Eleanor looking down at me pinning my hands to the bed. Apparently, I started scratching in my sleep."

Jack guessed Eleanor was by her side because she added, "Not a bad way to wake up."

"Khandi, a lot has happened that we couldn't tell you in the club." Jack prepared her again.

After a second or two, "I'm listening."

"Dasher Clay's dead and Stormi is in custody. Before you ask, no, she didn't do it. Lucy Velasquez is an assassin and David works for her. We put Slick and his gang on to them armed with your thirty-eight, but they both got away and put some of those guys in the ER Lucy and company staked out my apartment, but we drew them off. I think we're finally a step ahead of them."

"Speaking of steps, that David Rivers should be walking with a pretty good limp." Khandi bragged.

"What do you mean?"

Jack had noticed the limp in the club and assumed he affected that for the ethnic ambiance of the room.

"I hacked through his Achilles with a nail file," she declared.

"Khandi, it's me." Anita said taking the phone from Jack. "I need for you to go into Eleanor's browser and find the last access to the Georgia Tech thread."

She gave Khandi a moment to follow her instructions.

"There's an e-mail from LAMHillPHD@NIH/genetics.gov from less than an hour ago."

Anita pumped her fist in the air just after putting the phone on speaker mode.

"That's great, Khandi. Read it to me." Anita commanded her.

"It reads, 'Glad you're safe. Sorry to hear about Dr. Butler and her assistant. According to the coroner and APD, the woman officially had a heart attack and her assistant took a lethal shock during resuscitation. The security guard got a commendation for his efforts to rescue two people at the same time."

Jack and Anita looked at each other. *Ralphie!*

"Researched your Luciana Velasquez and David Rivers. They do work for Glazer Corp but they entered the company's ranks through the security division not pharmaceutical sales. Dossiers are attached.

"They're PDFs, Anita. Want me to open them?" Khandi asked.

"Later. Go on with the text of the e-mail, please," Anita instructed tersely.

Khandi resumed her recital of the message. "Lucy and David have been in Pharmaceutical sales for 18 and 7 months respectively. They both have military records. Lucy Velasquez, born July 4th, 1980 Chicago, Il, was a marine. Highly decorated and honorably discharged at the rank of second lieutenant. Worked her way up the ranks at Glazer Corp under the tutelage of Orson Quirk. Listed as one of their top reps nationally. Seems she's afforded a lot of latitude for her accomplishments.

David, listed as Davíd Rivera, born NYC, NY September 12, 1986 army ranger, special ops. Qualified as an expert with several classes of firearms. Good with a knife and lethal hand to hand. Apprenticed in NYC with Lucy until he was deemed ready to run his own territory.

There's nothing on your "Jason Brasil", "Joey" or "Ralphie". Dad said the "cleanliness" of those files means they're either aliases or their names have been expunged from the records by high-level intelligence personnel. As it stands, they are "non-entities".

Orson Quirk is a regional manager for Glazer Corp as he claims to be. His "story points" check out except one funny thing. No listing of siblings but there is an O. Tyler Quirk listed as a junior VP with Dekker, Nordstrom and Andersen Pharmaceuticals. Peculiar thing is their SS#s differ by transposition of the sixth and seventh numbers only so they don't

```
show sequentially in a database
search.
     There is a bid with the FTC for
DNA to acquire Glazer next year. Don't
know if this connects.
     A Mertz mechanic found surveil-
lance equipment in the rental car
after we used it. Reported it to Home-
land. Dad got reamed pretty bad by the
Under Secretary when it came out that
I had rented the car.
     They were unsuccessful tracing
the bug's operators. It could just as
easily been a bomb if they wanted ei-
ther of us dead and no one would know
who did it. It's now a credible case
on its own merits. Dad's en route with
help. Should be in ATL by morning. Be
careful. Whoever they are, they know
what we talked about two weeks ago.
     Lamonte'
```

"Then these attachments referenced above." Khandi said as she ended the narrative.

"So who's 'Dad'?" Khandi asked, drawing attention to the reference.

"Major General Douglas Hill, Homeland security. This case now involves murder and armed mercenaries so it is federal and a security threat by definition." Anita answered.

"Jack, Anita, I want these animals as bad as you do. Worse! But you're no match for them. You wouldn't believe the physical strength of that Rivera. He's superhuman." Khandi pleaded with Jack and Anita. "You two should get into a closet somewhere and hide 'til the cavalry arrives in the morning; it's only a few hours."

"Maybe we'll do just that, Khandi, but I can't promise you anything. We have to stay ahead of them or we're dead. As for you-don't go home. See if you and Eleanor can go away for a day or two. If you two are as close as I think, they may come looking for her to tie up loose ends, too."

"Lollipop! She's at Al's."

"Khandi, don't go after your dog! It's a trap. Promise me you'll let Eleanor get you out of there for a while." Jack waited for no more than the ten seconds it took for her to realize he was right.

"Will do, Jack, but if anything happens to Lollipop, it's on." She hung up after a last "good luck."

"Jack, Khandi and I were talking Friday night. I know that you and Lucy... got together," Anita said. "I saw you."

Jack hung his head, but said nothing. What could he say to this woman for whom he had the utmost respect?

"Jack, you can't let those feelings for her get in our way. When the time comes for her to be taken down, you have got to let it happen."

Jack turned out the bathroom light before leading Anita into the dining room where they set up in silence. He screwed the binoculars onto its tripod and focused them on Lucy's apartment. Anita connected the camera and made ready to record at a second's notice. Now they waited for Lucy to make the next move.

Jack thought to himself, *She has to come home sometime.*

# Chapter 38: Mommie and Poppie

After the waiting became unbearable, Jack begged Anita to tell him more about the Fibromyalgia drug she developed.

She sighed deeply. "Jack, you should really get some sleep. What you did in the call room and the library wasn't sleep." She rubbed her eyes. "I don't know what you'd call that *fit* you went through."

"Can't sleep now. Might as well keep me focused."

"Okay, do you remember reading about when ibuprofen, indomethacin, and naproxen hit the market in the '70s? More potent, less toxic, easier dosing schedules than aspirin? They said that plain old Bayer was dead.

Then we discovered that the anti-platelet effects of aspirin were greater than those of the derivative Non-steroidal anti-inflammatory drugs. Made it a life-saving first measure for heart attacks, strokes, blood clots. It heralded the rebirth of aspirin."

"Come on, Anita."

"Jack. It's old, simple and obvious. Controlled hibernation is all we have to do for the millions afflicted with some of these functional disorders. Let them sleep. We've been scratching at the surface for years with the use of sedative hypnotics and narcotics. Too short. We need to induce them for 6 to 12 weeks of sleep.

Warm, damp, safe place to let them burn off their excess fat while they slept. Gluconeogenesis and Lipolysis supported nutritional needs and fueled modest heat for the inert body. Dehydration protein synthesis of myofibrils and collagen took care of most of the body's free water needs.

It could be done in their own homes with a sleeping bag, a nasal gastric feeding tube for minimal water with a little dextrose and a foley catheter.

We isolated a small, molecule we called HIT, Hibernation Inducing Trigger. I created the molecular model for it. Just a matter of matching it up. Not so easy. It was evanescent, floating in a lactic acid and acetone milieu. It's unstable, that's why it was so elusive. Once the Lactate cleared, HIT broke down.

We found a cheap way to stabilize it using a one to one ratio of ethanol to HIT to create Hibernation Inducing Trigger Molecule. Turns out it's a really small molecule. Simple once you know it's structure. HIT Moll is stable and can be produced at an infinitesimal fraction of the cost of FMDS400."

"We can already make them drunk. There's no Nordstrom trickery to that," Jack said, still not fully grasping Anita's proposition.

"Jack, you only need a couple of drops--0.8 ml of the concoction subcutaneously to put a susceptible person into hibernation stupor for six to twelve weeks." She rubbed her eyes again, "Oh, they can wake up if the house is on fire for example, but as soon as the adrenalin rush is over, they can go right back to sleep. Almost like Narcolepsy."

Then Jack came up with something. "Why do you have to inject it? If it's conjugated with ethanol, can't you just drink it? Alcohol passes through the stomach pretty quick."

Anita was stunned. "Why didn't we catch that? Of course, it would be easily absorbed through the gastrointestinal mucosa. That might require a slightly higher dose, maybe 5 milliliters, a teaspoon, but still negligible volume and ethanol toxicity. That's brilliant."

I've been working out the formula since March. Monty and I nearly had it." She pounded Jack lightly on the chest, "That's why I had to go up to Maryland week before last."

Jack gestured his curiosity. "So?"

"Monty and I made it in an NIH lab over the weekend while everyone was off. Didn't work but I figured out what we did wrong. Dumb mistake. We didn't have time to run it again and I couldn't record the production procedure for him before I returned to Atlanta."

The hours were catching up to him. "Bet you can't wait to get back to a lab, huh." He slumped to the floor and yawned.

Anita kicked at his foot. Their preparation and patience were rewarded. Jack got to his feet in time to see David enter Lucy's apartment right behind her. The doctors watched from their makeshift blinds at Anita's apartment.

Usually, when cops stake out a suspect, they have a plan. Jack and Anita had none. Just the binoculars in the backpack and two guns they didn't know how to use.

Anita's place was a floor lower and directly across from Lucy's flat.

As they watched, someone wedged down the Venetian blinds to survey the courtyard and Anita's apartment. Anita thought she and Jack might have been seen because the blinds spread and eyes stared down at her window for ten seconds from Lucy's living room before letting the blind re-align. She left them open, maybe to keep an eye out for Anita's return.

David and Lucy were naked within three minutes of closing the door behind them.

"It seems Lucy has an accomplice…with benefits." Anita announced. "That Puerto Rican guy from New York City. Davíd, wasn't just a henchman."

Jack looked through the binoculars at Anita's commented. *Dude is really punchin' her ticket.* Jack knew by then that Lucy had been pumping him for information as well as bodily fluids, but it was only when he saw her with Davíd that he realized what she wanted. When he described the encounter, the abridged version, to Anita, she surmised that Lucy collected Jack's semen and blood for reverse bioengineering or something for Glazer Corp. Maybe they wanted to have an independent version of something like FMDS400. They probably strove to eliminate the seizure side effects.

Jack had his fun with Lucy, but what she was doing with this David was a whole different distraction. They went through every position Jack knew and then some.

Unfortunately, Anita was watching the peep show with him.

Jack could feel the pity gushing from Anita as the scene went on. She knew Lucy had played him. Jack just stared through the binoculars. He couldn't bear to look at Anita.

He continued to watch. Anita didn't want a turn at the binoculars. She asked Jack what he was seeing every so often, but never for details.

Lucy left all of her blinds slightly opened. You couldn't see in to her apartment from any angle except from Anita's floor. She probably left it that way in case Anita survived and returned to her apartment. She'd know the moment Anita turned on her lights. In the darkness of Anita's apartment, the setup worked exactly opposite to Lucy's intensions.

They watched Davíd work her around that place from the dining room to the living room, to the dresser to the bed. Jack learned some new positions from the play that night. They were going at it for at least forty minutes straight.

After fifteen minutes of Jack's silent observation, Anita asked, "What do you see?"

"Viagra at work," he said without looking.

She took the binoculars from Jack for a quick look for herself then down at his watch again. "More like Cialis," She corrected.

"Why is the light so dim and flickering?" Anita swiftly answered her own question, "Candles." and handed the binoculars back to him.

Finally, there was no movement in the apartment for five minutes or more.

"Maybe they're asleep," Anita suggested.

Jack waved her down silently and kept watching through the binoculars. He knew Lucy. She wasn't done yet.

The lights came on. Lucy stood up, breathing heavy and shiny with sweat. Jack reminisced the feel of that nude body framed against the contrast of her walls. He remembered the color as Dragon Red. Lucy pranced to the end of the bed. Once there she shook her hair out, stretched and smiled in the direction of the headboard where David was out of their line of site. Jack remembered that it was tasteful wrought iron with teak wood posts, down pillows and satin sheets. The whole motif was traditional Chinese.

"We'll never be able to catch both of them unaware. They're too well trained. This David must be the guy who laid out your boyfriend." He said to Anita still not taking his eyes from the binoculars. "We won't survive a shootout with those two. Slick and his band didn't. We'll need a weapon we can really depend on against him. Maybe her, too." Jack whispered to Anita in the dark. "We'll have to separate them."

He watched Lucy turn her back to the bed. David sat up, his thick back and right shoulder visible in the window. "Then we'll need some luck." he added.

Jack could see Lucy talking to David from the bathroom door. She went in and turned on the shower. Didn't close the door or turn off the lights. Through the magic eye of the binoculars, Jack could see her silhouette through the translucent shower door. It was a long shower, too.

Anita looked puzzled. "Why are you watching so intently, Jack?"

"Something's up. I can't quite put my finger on it though. This shower is running too long for her. What is she waiting for?" he murmured.

Then David got up, peered into the bathroom and rummaged through her drawers. He stopped his efforts, relaxed then went back to the bed. Jack noticed a purple patch on his left shoulder and the bandage on his left hand.

Lucy came out of the shower and posed at the door for a moment with one hand out stretched toward the top of the doorframe. She had taken the time to comb and fluff her hair but somehow didn't dry off. She still glistened.

David crouched and ran his face up the side of her body and she laughed.

*Scented oil from head to toe, no doubt.* Jack thought.

Again, a little too much. He knew Lucy.

She crawled along the bed. Jack could see her facial expression clearly.

"Again?" he said aloud.

Lucy was on him again. Somehow, she worked her way to the side of the bed. In the reflection in the mirror, Jack could see her taking it from the back for a while.

Through the acuity of the binoculars, he could see her expression. *She's faking it! Why is she faking it with him? Why?*

Change of positions. The next thing Jack knew, she had David's arm in a Greco-Roman lock, her leg wrapped around the arm twisted behind his back which she sat on now.

"She must weigh in at a buck twenty-five or so." Jack mused. "Legs mostly, like a dancer's."

He dialed the binocular to maximum.

Lucy had David's wrist and it looked like she was bending back his ring finger and pinky.

"This isn't rough sex. She is really trying to hurt him." he said absently to Anita. Jack continued in voyeur role. Lucy braced David's hand against her neck as she wrenched it.

*If only I could see a little lower into the room.* Jack thought.

David was in shadows now. Lucy turned toward the night table a bit, switched on the lamp, started to reach for something there then stopped and returned her free hand to grip David's. He now had his thumb and index finger on her neck.

*He couldn't have any leverage.* Jack knew that move now. She had him cold. In the added light, Jack saw the full jeopardy for David in the mirror across from the bed. It hung on a hook at a little tilt toward the floor.

*His chest is poised above that damn newspaper skewer.* Jack remembered how Lucy had a habit of shoving her newspapers down on it when she had finished reading them. When he first saw it, his thought was that would be pretty nasty to stumble over in the dark. When he suggested that she get rid of it. She just shrugged it off at the time. He saw why.

"What are they doing?" Anita asked now with more urgency.

"Lucy is talking to him now." he whispered. "She's winding her neck to the side, away from his hand. What's he doing, scratching her?" Jack asked more to himself than to Anita. "Now she's smiling and bouncing up and down on his back. Whup, she just stopped. She's releasing his arm now." Jack said. "Maybe it is just really rough sex."

He watched some more. "Yep, he just tossed her across the bed. Now he's on top." Jack didn't bother to mention her hands caressing first up then down the length of David's arms. "There go her legs in the air and now wrapping around his waist." He passed the binoculars to Anita.

"Jesus! Give it a rest why don't they! It can't be fun anymore!" she commented but could not seem to look away.

Anita watched for a few seconds longer. "Well, I think she's finally done for the night. She's relaxing from the coitus position." She looked at Jack for a second, "Her arms and legs just dropped down and out of sight." She passed the binoculars back to him. "Show's over."

Jack knew Anita was disgusted with the whole affair.

"David's checking messages on his phone now. Not happy about that one." he observed. "He's packing up his stuff. Huh, whatever that last message was he's pissed about it. He's looking around the room now. He's saying good-bye or something to her. Goodbye kiss, lights out and he's done." Jack concluded.

"Anita, if we go straight over there, we can get the drop on her. She'll think he forgot something." Jack said. "This could get rough."

Somehow, Jack expected Anita to object to letting him subdue or force information violently out of a woman. She didn't.

All she said was, "Let's go."

When David left the courtyard below them, they skirted around the walkway, and sprinted up the stairs to Lucy's apartment. Jack was sure she hadn't gotten up to put the chain on the door. She had to be exhausted.

With some of the stuff from Brasil's bag, Jack thought he could pick the lock quietly enough. Once inside they would have to move fast. He didn't want to admit it, but he thought Lucy might be better than him at hand-to-hand combat. He thought twice about using the gun. If he pulled it on Lucy, he'd have to use it. If he did, there'd be no forthcoming information. If he didn't, there was a good chance she'd take it away from him. And she certainly knew how to use it. He left the Glock in the bag. For all his sixty-pound weight advantage, he might not be able to take her even with surprise on his side.

When they arrived at her place, the door was ajar. They eased the door open wide enough to enter and stole their way through the living room and dining room in the dark. Jack still remembered the layout of the apartment. He picked up the Venus de Milo statue as a club to gain an added advantage to surprise.

Lucy's bedroom door was wide open. There was a little light streaming in from the bathroom. They hadn't disturbed her with their entry. Lucy was still sprawled across the bed, glistening with sweat, just a corner of the satin sheets draped across her naked midsection. The ceiling fan spun a lazy breeze to stir her thick, ginger hair. The white forelock waved independently. Her head was facing away from the door, and she was spread eagle on her back, one leg hanging off the near side of the bed like the last time Jack saw her there.

She hadn't moved yet. She was still. Very still.

Jack only realized that he had hesitated when he felt Anita's nudge from behind.

Jack abruptly abandoned stealth, marched into the bedroom, put the statue down and turned on the light by the bed.

He heard Anita begin the whisper, "What?" then stop. Suddenly, she knew what Jack knew: Luciana Velasquez was dead.

He moved closer to examine her body. Her eyes were closed. Her mouth, too. There was a peaceful expression on her face, as if she were sleeping. Not a care in the world.

Jack removed the corner of satin sheet partially covering her nude body. He approached the examination like a ramp consult but for his personal involvement. Her skin was slick and shiny. No pulse. No movement in that magnificent chest anymore. Her throat was badly bruised on the left.

"Guess it wasn't rough sex after all." Anita said with no remorse.

Might have been Jack's imagination, but he thought he detected a mocking tone buried in that comment. He looked around the room for clues to the exploits, which just cost Lucy her life.

How did it relate to her attempt on David's life or her own murder? How did the Magic Pony or her boss, Orson Quirk fit in? Was he even really involved in her criminal activities? He might have been innocent, but that one still gave Jack the creeps. So quiet, so inappropriately peculiar. He was still out there.

That's when Jack noticed the cell phone on the bed next to her body. He checked that last message that disturbed David so much. *It was her phone he was checking, not his.*

"What does it say?" Anita asked as Jack brought up the text files.

"It says 'X Poppy: 30K'" Jack was puzzled. "What the hell does that mean?"

Anita was feeling around the mirror on the dresser.

Nothing made sense to Jack at that point. He collapsed onto the stool by the dresser across from where Lucy lay. The moment was a little much for him with a recent lover dead on the bed in front of him. All the evil she was into had come home to roost. There was an unimaginable mix of emotions. Anita wasn't paying attention to Jack and his ambivalence.

"Anita, what are you doing?" he asked.

"I saw something red flashing back here before you turned the lights on. I'm trying to reach it." She stretched her arm as far as she could then, "Got it."

"Got what?" he asked.

"Cell phone." She answered looking at the device.

"That his?" Jack asked completely lost.

Anita didn't answer immediately, but after a few seconds, she shook her head and said, "I think this one is hers too." Her brow furrowed. "Looks like an iPhone but more it's more complex." Anita said, then plopped down on the bed next to Lucy's body making it bounce up and down a couple of beats like a coed passed out at a slumber party. Anita sniffed twice then turned and ran a finger along Lucy's abdomen.

"Baby oil." Anita rubbed the substance between her thumb and index fingertips. "I wondered why she was still sweaty after forty minutes out of the shower. Greased up to limit his grip. Probably why she lost her grip on his hand, though. She really does think of everything.--or she did."

"Why two phones?" Jack asked.

Anita thought for a moment again. "She set the Smart Phone behind the one-way mirror to spy on her partner. Her phone had an app for some kind of motion sensor so that whenever he moved, she could track him and catch whatever secrets he was keeping from her."

"It must have been hard keeping secrets from her for long," Jack said absently, then realized who he was talking to again.

"Anyway, it's out of power. That was why it was flashing…"

They rummaged around the dresser and found the charger and played back the past couple of hours. Anita sped up the sections of playback that were uncomfortable for her and Jack to watch together. Then she caught up to when she jumped in the shower. Lucy had received a text

message from someone named "Fats". They had been assigned their next marks." Anita stopped.

"Fats?" Jack asked.

"Yeah, that was Khandi's boss's nick name, too."
Anita snapped her fingers softly, " In the club- I'll bet
they were getting untraceable weapons from Fats too."

"Hard to travel on airplanes with unregistered
weapons."

"Uh-oh." static filtered into the audio. "It's not
charged enough to support the speaker yet." They
watched the rest of the recording while Anita narrated
play by play.

"Luciana, long shower. Davíd, rifled through her
drawers. Didn't notice him sniff her underwear there."

*After that night?* Jack mused, *Why?*

"There was some kind of Personal Digital Assistant device, apparently encrypted." Anita paused the
playback. "David had the missing password to the item
that Lucy stole."

"That must have been what David had in his
breast pocket at the ball." Jack said.

"The password I'm guessing was *his* secret,"
Anita said. "He slipped it into his backpack and then returned to the bed. I'd give my right arm to know what's
on that hard drive.

They went at it again, with a lot of "Poppy" and
"Mommy" talk back and forth. Very intimate stuff. Lots
of clanging and banging." Anita brushed the wind chimes
with her fingertips, her soft laugh lost in the gentle tones.
"No pun intended. I guess the bed shaking rings these."

"She never said much when we were together,."
Jack observed.

"You should count yourself lucky, Jack. Towards
the end, she had him in the arm lock. Hear that little click
on the recording as his arm reached its limit. She

maneuvered him over the newspaper skewer and then sat on his back as we saw from my place."

The recording played, volume up for a few seconds before fading again: "Poppy, just let it go. It'll be over before you know it." Lucy urged him. "Your heart will just stop. No pain, no suffering. Believe me. I've done this before. It is much better this way."

"That's the first time, I heard a trace of a Spanish accent from her," Jack said.

They listened as Lucy went on to tell David how much she truly cared for him and that she would miss being with him much more than she'd miss working with him.

"Boy, he would not give up." Anita said. "A few grunts once in a while, but he held on for dear life. He supported his weight and hers on one arm braced against the floor over certain death." She pointed to the deadly device. "See the droplets of his sweat on the newspapers at the skewer's base."

"At this point, she gets frustrated with him." Jack observes on the screen. "He just won't fall on the skewer. Thinking back to what I witnessed from the window, I couldn't understand why she was winding her neck like that. At first, I thought he was clawing at her out of desperation. She was so sweaty, and covered in all that oil, he couldn't get a grip. Then I realized, this son of a bitch was smart and cool."

"He was applying steady pressure to her carotid artery. Lucy was getting dizzy. It was clear she had expended a great deal of energy in her sexual escapades all night. She was a bit dehydrated from all that sweat."

"Then too, she had just come out of a hot shower so she was all flushed. In spite of her training, it would not have taken much to make her feel faint by that point."

"She was trying to reach something on the night table, but I couldn't tell what?" Jack said, looking where

Lucy had reached during the struggle, but there was nothing.

Then Anita found the antique Korean letter opener on the floor next to the night table. "Stabbing him in any meaningful way would have been awkward from her position on his back."

Then Jack found the box of soft wipes Lucy always carried. Anita opened the lid and immediately closed it back, fanning the fumes away from her face.

"Chloroform and ethanol," she said. "Used to use this stuff to subdue rats in my graduate experiments. The ethanol reduces the volatility of the chloroform so you can work with it extensively without being overwhelmed yourself in confined spaces." Anita just shook her head. "She wasn't trying to stab him, Jack." She looked at him. "You're lucky you didn't end up dead messing around with her."

Jack acknowledged with a grimace. "While Lucy was fiddling around in the dim light looking for the weapon to end him, she loosened her grip just enough for him to grip her carotid body firmly between his thumb and forefinger."

"Probably the basis for the *Alien* neck pinch thingy legend. The carotid body contains a nerve plexus, which regulates the Vagus nerve. When compressed, it slows the heart down."

"And he had already been applying pressure to the Carotid artery, reducing blood flow to her brain for the past several minutes." Jack said, "She's been up as long as we have at least. Probably hadn't eaten or slept all day either. She was quickly running out of time, and she knew it. She started bouncing on his back to try to drive his torso down against the point." Jack touched the point of the spike. "She had some success, too. Check this out." With the back of his fingernail, he scratched at a trickle of blood already dried on the tip.

"Her speech starts to slur a bit as the recording plays on." Anita had reduced the volume so she had to hold it to her ear to hear. The device wasn't an iPhone. It hadn't powered enough to run speaker mode. "She was bargaining with him to kill this "Fats" guy instead of each other, then that it was a bad business decision.

Her last word was a question: 'Poppy?' She said before losing her grip on his arm and passing out." Anita shook her head.

"That's when he threw her limp ass on the bed, stretched his arm some and massaged the shoulder vigorously." Jack noted. "That bruise must have been dealt by Al with that rock he pitched down at the club. So both Al and Khandi had gotten in their licks."

Anita tapped the screen to get Jack's attention. "Seemed that Lucy started to come around again. When he spread her legs for the last time, we assumed it was sexual. He was eliminating her leverage against his body." Anita said.

"When she caressed his arms, she was still dazed. It was a semiconscious attempt at fending off his strangle hold."

"He must have been pissed." Jack said. "He didn't choke the crap out of her, he crushed her windpipe."

"I don't think 'Mommy' ever completely woke up from the first struggle before he finished her off on the bed. From the angle of her head, he may have broken her neck for good measure."

"She was lucky, he could have spiked her on the newspaper skewer and let her squirm for the last minutes of her life." Jack said. "If her orders were to get rid of David, she'd do it. Just business after all and she'd have Ralphie clean up the mess while she went down the corner diner for breakfast."

"No, Jack, this was the ultimate betrayal," Anita argued. "David couldn't believe she would try to kill *him*.

Not until he read that text message. Look at his face there." She pointed to the image on the little screen, "No, stabbing someone is cold and impersonal. Strangling a lover's last breath out of her body is intimate… passionate. Like that kiss he blew her when he left. It was from the heart, I think."

A curl of smoke issued from the bedside candle as it contacted the wax. Anita licked her thumb and forefinger and extinguished the little flame with a pinch.

Jack shook his head, took a last look at the cold body on the bed and closed his eyes, *Wish I could feel sorry for her.*

# Chapter 39: Chill

"We have to call the police," Jack said, reaching for the phone. Anita blocked him.

"We can't do that," she said. "This is federal now, remember? Let General Hill and his people handle it. They'll clean up the body and the rest of the evidence in a few hours. Local law enforcement will only muck things up at best. At worst, some of them may be in on this. Remember what Dr. Hargrove warned us about?" She advised him with calm, logical reasoning. "They had to get this weapons cache from someone. Might have been a bent cop."

"Okay, but we better get them in here in a few hours before she and this whole place start to reek." His shoulders slumped. "I can't sit here and watch somebody I slept with rot."

Anita frowned at him.

"I know, I sound conflicted again." Jack shrugged. "What do you want from me? I'm just a man."

Anita cut him a cold look and dialed information on her cell phone. "Office of Homeland Security, please?" She shook her head at the phone as if the person on the line could see her. "No, local offices, thank you." She waited.

"This is Professor Anita Thomas calling for General Douglas Hill. I believe he may be expecting my call."

There was conversation on the other end then Anita covered the speaker. "General Hill is on his way in from the airport. They expect him within fifteen minutes."

Anita gave them Lucy's address and informed them that there was a young woman's body in the master bedroom.

"She was murdered and we have the whole thing recorded,"

Jack didn't feel very comfortable sitting in an apartment with a dead body for another hour or two just waiting to answer more questions about the past forty-eight hours. Following conventional wisdom meant just that—wait.

It made perfect sense and led Jack to the worst decision he had made all month.

"Let's bolt. We have to get to Dr. Hargrove and debrief him first. The General can catch up. I have a feeling we don't have all the answers yet." Jack was walking toward the door already.

"Don't you think we should stay put?" Anita said. "I mean, they are the cavalry."

Jack could tell Anita was drained. This was not what an academic personality was used to. She had held up incredibly well until now. Game for anything.

"What's that smell?" Anita asked, wrinkling her nose. She followed the scent to the kitchen. An unopened bag of carry out rested on the table. Receipt stapled to it said three pounds of oysters, and long grain rice. Next to it a bottle of Chardonnay. Anita examined the ticket on the bag, threw her hands in the air. "You have got to be kidding me."

"I know we should stay until the authorities arrive, but I have this nagging feeling that we don't have all the players accounted for. I don't even know that we've got the big dog pegged. Looks like Fats is pulling the strings here, but something about that Orson Quirk. How does he have a sister with fibromyalgia syndrome here in Atlanta if he's from Mississippi? Why did Christie ask about an intravenous treatment for fibro? Something here is just wrong. We have to put it right. We owe it to Al, and Dasher, and Stormi and everyone else who didn't have to get killed." He implored her with hands spread wide. "We can't do that babysitting Lucy back there. She's not going anywhere."

"Alright, Jack, I guess you have a point. When those oysters go bad, they'll smell worse than she will." Anita dialed the thermostat down as far as it would go. "I'll lock the door behind us. It's going to get chilly in here." She pulled the door until it clicked softly in the latch.

Jack stopped in the hall half way to the elevator and asked, "Anita, did you hear Christie mention that there was some kind of testing going on in the Infusion Clinic?"

"Yes, she said they were drawing blood every four hours."

"You remember Lucy talking to Dr. Butler about a detection assay?" Jack asked. "What if it wasn't just theoretical?"

"Yes. As far as I know, there's no such animal as a 'Fibro test'." Anita nodded thoughtfully. "Consolidation. That was what Lucy was alluding to in the hall at the CDC. I thought she was just ranting. She was talking about freedom." She crinkled her brow. "If Glazer has developed an effective test for Fibro, it'd be worth a fortune to anyone with an infusion clinic, if approved."

"Do you have Lucy's phone?"

Anita dug around in the backpack to retrieve the phone. Jack handed her the automatic, safety on, to stow in the bag in exchange for the cellular. He flicked through the contacts list on the phone. No names, just the numbers.

They took the elevator down to the ground floor. Jack pulled out his phone and checked the number he dialed for the Sat phone, matched it up against Lucy's contact list. He found it two entries down from the last outbound call.

"Looks like she may have reported to someone."

"Maybe she received instructions." Anita leaned back against the wall and rested her eyelids. "The next call may have been her giving directives based on her own new orders."

Jack hoped that they were close to a conclusion. They couldn't have kept up that pace forever. His back and shoulders ached like hell.

Anita snapped to attention. "Jack, call the last two numbers. Don't answer, just listen to who picks up. See if we recognize the voices."

Jack put the phone on speaker mode and pulled out his cheap phone. It was simple, but it did have a digital memo function for dictating To Do Lists and messages.

"Take this number down," he said as he read it out to Anita and dialed it at the same time.

"Tell me you have Dr. Thomas and Dr. Wheaton." A man's voice said with intensity.

*No niceties, straight to the point. This was one used to command. The Big Dog.*

Familiar, but neither Jack nor Anita could place the voice. Jack hung up without saying a word.

"Next." Jack commanded to Anita as he dialed the last number in the list. A male answered.

Neither of them could forget Ralphie's voice in a million years.

"I'm en route." Then he asked, "Need anything?"

Jack hung up.

"Looks like she's down to just Ralphie in terms of her squad." Anita said. "Wish he were a smaller man." She palmed a morphine ampoule.

Anita had been holding the elevator door closed for a few minutes while Jack placed the calls to minimize the sounds of the outdoors for the sake of a better quality recording. The door alarm began to sound. She released the door and they exited the elevator.

"Where he's headed is what I'd like to know." Jack mulled over Ralphie's likely whereabouts.

They wound their way through the courtyard. The sun was rising.

Jack dialed Khandi on his phone. He assumed she was still at Eleanor's. He was wrong, again.

He covered the receiver. "Eleanor says that she dropped Khandi at her apartment." Jack pounded his fist on a fence post. "Damn. I told her to stay put." He said into the phone, "They may be waiting for her."

"Oh no, not Al's apartment," Eleanor explained *"Her* apartment."

She gave him Khandi's number. Jack was dialing it before they reached the corner. The phone rang twice.

"Khandi, where the hell are you?" Jack demanded.

"Well, good morning to you too, Jack."

"Khandi, Lucy is dead."

Silence for a moment, then, "Shit." Khandi whispered. "You actually killed her?"

"No, David did." Jack said.

"We need to move. Do you have wheels?"

Khandi met them a block south of Anita's apartment in a shiny, midnight blue convertible Beemer. She cruised up to them, top down and her hair draped across the headrest.

"Need a lift, guys?" She asked, unlocking the passenger door as she broke to a stop.

"Sweet ride." Jack said, forgetting about the danger of Khandi going off on her own. "Yours?"

Khandi answered with no more than a curl of the lips. He and Anita hopped in and they took off.

"Where to, Jack?" Khandi asked.

He seemed to have most of the answers. Even Anita deferred to him for direction. What the women didn't know was that this was a case of the blind leading the blind.

"Hamilton Clinic, East wing. You know where the entry is?"

Khandi nodded and swung the car around at the next stop sign.

"Khandi, where are your glasses?" Anita asked, her voice tinged with concern as Khandi wheeled the car at faster than posted speeds.

"What glasses?" she asked Anita, confused.

"Last night at the club, you were wearing eyeglasses."

*And not much of anything else.* Jack thought smiling, but awaiting her answer himself.

"Oh, those. Window pane glasses. My vision's better than twenty-twenty. I use them as a disguise. Works for Clark Kent. After seventy years, no one's recognized that he's Superman yet. Makes Sarah Palin sexy as hell, too. So why are these guys chasing you two anyway? Seems to me that they already have the formula for this great treatment and the test to find the disease, what do they need you for?"

Anita and Jack looked foolishly at each other. They had been running for their lives for the past two days, barely escaping false imprisonment and certain death.

*Why hadn't Brasil just shot us?* Jack wondered. *Why didn't Lucy just execute us like she did those gangsters in the alley or Dr. Butler and Ms. Chen Saturday morning?*

They had something the mercs wanted or they were otherwise somehow still of value to them. The question Jack and Anita hadn't asked each other was *What?*

"Anita, can you think of anything that you've done or that you know that they don't have access to by now?" Jack turned to ask Anita who rode in the back seat.

"Wait, Khandi, did you print out that e-mail you read?" Anita asked.

339

"Wondered when you big brains were gonna ask for the transcript." She chuckled, and handed the two sheets of paper back to Anita.

Anita scanned them. "That must be it! Here's where Monty says there was advanced listening equipment in our car. It had to be Lucy and her bunch. They heard what we talked about that day."

"And just what did you talk about that day, Anita?" Jack asked.

"What I told you about, HITMol." Then she hung her head. "HITMol, the cheap alternative to FMDS400 that could make the millions of dollars spent in research worthless. How could I have been *so* stupid? They want *that* formula, of course. I didn't think Monty and I talked about it in the car, but I guess we did. That's where they found out about it."

"I have to call Christie. She may know who was running the show at the Infusion Center. Whoever that was is our mystery man, the Alpha Dog."

Jack punched Christie's number into his phone. The voice on the other end was familiar, but it wasn't Christie's.

"Hello Jack," the male voice said. "You're getting to be a real pain in the ass, you know that?"

It was at that moment that it all came together for him. The voice was that of Orson Quirk. No affectation of self-effacing, country humility. This was a cinema level mastermind.

"You and Dr. Thomas are very important to me. Let's talk." Orson ordered, but with the return of that disarming country tone. "What's the harm in talking?"

"Where is Christie?" Jack demanded.

"Oh, she's safe." Orson Quirk said, "She lent me her phone. So helpful in the Center yesterday, too. She's hanging out with Ralphie right now. You remember Ralphie don't you, Jack?"

Orson was threatening Christie and he wanted it to be clear.

"What do you want?" Jack asked, motioning for the semi-automatic from the bag.

"Meet me at the West gate to Hamilton Medical Center in an hour. I know you are on foot so it'll be a brisk walk. See you then. Don't be late."

He added more ominously, "Don't call the police, Jack. It wouldn't be good for you."

The line went dead.

"Why is he so sure you're on foot, Jack?" Khandi asked still driving at her lead-foot pace. "Just because the buses aren't running and taxis don't prowl downtown on Sunday mornings?"

"No, because he had us on surveillance from my apartment elevator. We were on to that as a possibility when we were running from Lucy and David. We let our guard down when she was taken out of the equation. He must have tapped into the security cameras."

"Bet he has been watching Lucy as well as watching us," Jack said. "He probably has her place wired. Her bedroom. Pervert."

Anita couldn't suppress a little smirk, which Jack caught in the right visor's vanity mirror.

They came up on the north end of Hamilton Medical.

"Drop me at the entrance coming up. If he doesn't expect me for another half hour, maybe I can surprise him. I got a thing or two to do first though." He began gathering his supplies in his lap. "Khandi, get Anita to Homeland Security office."

"Washington, D.C.?" Khandi asked.

"No, the local office is in the federal building on Spring Street. I want the two of you to stay there."

"Since when did you start giving orders, Kemo Sahbee?" Khandi asked, frowning.

341

They pulled up to the north entrance of Hamilton Medical Center.

"I'm no hero, Khandi, but this guy is going to disappear like a puff of smoke if we don't pin him down. He may beat Homeland to Lucy's place. Evidence may be altered-or burned. Please get Anita to safety and stay out of trouble."

"I'll do it because I agree with you on this one."
"I'm an Indian American not an American Indian."

"Native American," Anita corrected. "Get it right."

"Just so you know, they never went in for that Sidekick shit either." The smile Khandi added didn't hide her apprehension of him going it alone against these thugs.

"Okay, so we're all politically correct. Can I go now? I'm going to hold Quirk while you send in this General and his guys to round up this wild bunch."

"Well, do I at least have permission to sedate Anita if she resists orders?" Khandi grinned and looked back at Anita in the rearview. "I'm dying to use one of those Morphine thingies."

"Jack, we'll be back in fifteen minutes, twenty tops. Don't take any chances."

Then she pulled his head close to hers and planted a firm kiss right on his lips. Not a sensuous, romantic kiss, but it felt great all the same.

*Definitely worth waiting for.*

Anita moved up to the front passenger seat as Jack jumped out and got his bearings. He pulled all the communication devices out of the backpack and slipped them in his pockets.

# Chapter 40: Mouse Trap

Jack entered the hospital via the house staff entry. The night administrator who served as the Anita decoy last night was back at work after her little adventure. A couple of orderlies were flirting with her.

"Hey, Dr. Wheaton, what's up?" Lynette knew she had been involved in some kind of prank but figured the punch line would become public on Monday. She was prepared to wait until she saw Jack.

"Thanks, Lynette." Jack shook off her waiting stare with a gesture that said, *Not yet, sorry*.

She frowned and dropped her head back into her deskwork.

Jack had Lucy's phones, Brasil's phone, and the disposable phone from RiteRx. A treasure trove of data. Incriminating data. He was not going to take the chance of big Ralphie just taking it all away from him. That's when he had the idea to download the data into his old PS2. A diversion for slow nights better than TV. It stopped working right over a year ago. Just the joystick, though.

Jack closed the door to the 5A office and searched his desk there. Had to scavenge some batteries from the Welch Allyn oto-ophthalmoscope but he got the Play Station to power up. He plugged in the USB cord and downloaded everything from all the devices. It took about 15 minutes. While he waited, Jack took a chance and input Al's PIN to access medical records.

*Let's see; Quirk, Quirk, Quirk. There can't be more than one or two Quirks in the system. What was his sister's name?*

There was Helen Holcomb, whom Jack knew all too well, then Olivia Tyler and Campbell Brookes were the only new names in the Infusion Center yesterday. *Which of those was Quirk's sister? Probably neither. Bet it was a story he fed to Christie to get her to cooperate with minimal questions.*

Jack was wrong about that, too.

He waited for his download to finish. When it was done, he replaced the PS2 in the back of the drawer and covered it with the old requisition forms, half-finished task lists and discarded journal articles that had piled up in the desk over the past five or six years.

A separate device in each pocket of his pants, Jack left the office and took the back stairs to avoid attention. Great idea. Problem was Jack came out of the stairwell right at the security desk.

He recognized William, the day supervisor for Hamilton Security, standing at the desk. He gave a friendly nod. Jack nearly soiled his pants when he saw Ralphie sitting behind the desk in a Hamilton security uniform. He had his feet on the desk, and his fingers laced casually around the back of his head.

Jack was glad for Ralphie's slow wit, it gave him a chance to turn without panicking but when the goon stood up next to William and pointed at Jack, he remembered how big he was. When Ralphie sounded the alarm, William was confused.

Jack and William had known each other for years, he didn't expect William to take him as a threat.

Sam Reardon had done his job too well. He put security on high alert because of what had happened to all the medical staff victims racked up in the ER over the weekend. William followed Ralphie's lead and gave chase.

Jack hauled it toward the next nearest exit but found that more security officers had joining the pursuit.

He found himself weaving and bobbing to avoid guards like an Atlanta Falcon's receiver. Jack set off the sprinkler system on the Surgical floor by pulling a fire alarm.

Nurses scrambled to move patient per fire protocol. He leapt over desks, threw chairs down and dashed half a gallon of liquid soap on slick, waxed floors as the sprinklers sprayed, successfully sending big men in pursuit sprawling like ten pins. Familiar faces saw Dr. Jack Wheaton running from the cops and didn't know what to make of him. They neither helped nor hindered.

Jack could have used a hand from Sam Reardon. He knew there was no way a resident, even a dedicated one, would stay on riding shotgun for more than forty-eight hours. Jack would have to deal with the situation on his own.

It looked like a clear sprint to the west exit until he saw Ralphie's sneering face as he blocked Jack's egress dead center.

Ralphie fiddled with the nobs before speaking into the two-way radio at his shoulder. Then he just stood there. It was like they had just switched games from American football to Soccer. Ralphie was now playing goalie. Jack could hear the posse of security guards gathering around the corner behind him. He knew there was no way past Ralphie and he counted at least five separate voices coming down the hall. There was only one out.

Jack ran for the staircase by the exit and pounded the door opened with his shoulder. Ralphie bared his teeth although he didn't move but to talk into his two-way. As Jack took the steps three at a time, he heard Ralphie misdirecting the search party.

Sensing something wrong, Jack stopped on the third landing. He realized where he was. They were renovating the west wing of the hospital. The fourth and fifth floors had been finished first for visiting family access via bridge. It connected to the Hamilton Medical Inn across Peachtree from the hospital.

The second floor door was locked with a chain and padlock. Jack caught his breath and pulled out the disposable cell phone. Two bars for reception and a red battery icon blinking. Jack looked up the stairwell and prayed before he dialed Khandi's cell.

"Jack." Khandi's voice was like music from heaven.

He looked down at the time on the phone, then put the receiver to his ear again. "They're all over me here, Khandi. Meet me in front of the McKee D's across from the hospital in ten minutes. And Khandi? Be ready 'cause I'll be running."

Jack hung up to the sound of Anita demanding answers from Khandi in the background. He was actually glad he didn't bring the gun when he snuck into the building. Would have made the consequences much worse when he got caught, and Jack had no doubt that he would.

Janice Walker appeared, silent as a cat, at the fourth floor landing above him. She was looking down right at him, something silver flashing in her hand. At the same time, Jack heard the door at the base of the stairs open and Ralphie's gloating whistle echoing up the stairs in no particular hurry. There's a difference between getting caught and getting screwed. Jack was screwed.

He went up against Ralphie two nights ago. *Hand to hand, that gorilla was no joke.* Jack looked up at Walker and began to climb the stairs hoping that was only a knife clenched in her hand when he nearly tripped over the fire extinguisher. One of the workers must have carelessly left it in the middle of the landing. From their respective vantages, neither Walker nor Ralphie could see him there.

The renovation of the private West Wing of Hamilton Medical included marble faced, enclosed stairwell to be decorated later. Jack tracked Ralphie's approach by that annoying whistle. He could still see Walker's hand on the rail above him. She was waiting for Ralphie to herd him to her. He had been herding Jack in this direction since the security desk.

Jack didn't think Ralphie was that bright.

He held his breath and lay in wait. As Ralphie hit the corner of the landing, Jack discharged the fire extinguisher in what he had hoped was Ralphie's face. He misjudged his height and caught his upper chest in the burst.

Ralphie had his baton drawn and swung blindly in surprise. Jack only startled him; his vision was not affected by the carbon dioxide fog.

"Sneaky little bastard, aren't yah?" Ralphie growled.

Jack had a three-step running head start on him, which he expanded to a full flight by throwing the empty tank at him. When he reached the fourth floor, Walker was waiting. Jack froze. The silver object was not a blade: It was a gun.

"Hey, Doctor Wheaton. You really are something." She aimed with both hands as she spoke. "Well, we've had just about enough of this crap now."

Before she pulled the trigger, there was this shrill war cry like a marine or a Navy Seal. Walker raised an arm in a defensive block of an airborne ashtray while firing the weapon. The projectile hit the wall next to Jack. Not even a chip in the marble at the impact point.

Jack was already charging at Walker when Anita tackled her from the same side as the ashtray she had just thrown. Jack grabbed Ms. Walker's wrist just below where she gripped the tranquilizer gun before she could get off a second shot.

Jack overpowered her and turned the gun in toward Walker's abdomen. She was stronger than she looked. She might have shot him or Anita before Ralphie reached her with his brawn and baton if not for Anita's quick action.

She had a morphine ampoule in her palm. She drilled it right into Walker's jugular vein. Walker went down the way Khandi did Friday night. The narcotic dose designed to suppress the agony and adrenaline of a two hundred pound soldier with traumatic injury wiped Walker out.

Jack grabbed the gun and fired the final dart as Ralphie came within baton range. It hit home in his arm, but he was over 250 lbs. Ralphie had a little fight left in him, but Jack was more of a match for him in this state. He flipped Ralphie to the floor and disarmed him. Then, with great pleasure, Jack placed a Super Bowl quality kick to his chin.

*Game over.*

# Chapter 41: Orson's Bid

Anita led him back the way she came, up through the Inn. Khandi was waiting with the car idling at the curb. Jack opened the door for Anita and grabbed the bag from the back seat. "Please get Anita to safety this time Khandi." he said. "At least until the General arrives."

Khandi shrugged as he added an insistent, "Please?"

He dug the automatic out of the backpack, stuffed it into the back of his pants, then pulled his shirt down over it. Jack patted the car and Khandi pulled off toward Spring Street.

As Jack walked up to the west gate after his little detour, Dr. Robert Lee was strolling out of the building with one hand around Christie's arm. Dressed in a golf shirt, beige slacks draped in a long white coat, Lee was too preoccupied with her to see Jack.

Christie looked disheveled as if she had been in a scuffle. Jack thought she might have made a few fruitless attempts at escape from Ralphie's clutches. She simply looked tired now that she was in Dr. Lee's custody.

Lee held an ornate handled letter opener in his hand. An etching of a snow Tiger decorated the handle. The weapon was identical to the blade they found at Lucy's bedside. Lee was tossing bits of breadcrumbs from a brown paper bag over the patio as they walked. He still hadn't seen Jack yet.

*Time for a bluff,* he thought.

When Lee finally saw Jack, he dropped the bag and began to grip the letter opener as a dagger, but Jack had already pulled his Glock and removed the safety.

The notion of having a knife at a gunfight must have crossed Dr. Lee's mind.

Jack smiled and beckoned him to take his hand off the girl and come closer to the gate.

"Christie, take three steps away from the good doctor here," Jack commanded, aiming the weapon's barrel at Lee's left eye. Jack was selling the marksman thing as best he could. The nerd bought it, though.

"You all right, Christie?"

She sidestepped the tall man and glared at him as she approached the gate.

"I'm okay."

Jack guided Christie through the gate, then closed it. It had one of those old skeleton key locks. Frozen by rust and layers of paint, the tumblers no longer moved evenly when turned.

*Lazy maintenance men.* Jack thought.

He found a little screwdriver from the lock-pick set in his pocket. Jack jammed it into the key hole sideways until it passed into the fence half of the latch. He took his belt buckle and bent the tip so it couldn't be easily removed. Jack kept his gun trained on Dr. Lee. Christie hugged his left arm desperately.

Jack felt like a 'double O' doc for a time. Didn't last long, though.

Black birds descended on the courtyard. First, a few, then by the dozen. It was spooky. A feeding frenzy for the bread crumbs spread by Dr. Lee. A living black satin blanket covered the patio. No sooner did the sea of darkness settle down than it began to boil once again.

Orson Quirk appeared at the door of the West Wing and walked through the courtyard to where Lee stood. As he did so, each crow took wing. The Murder taking flight was like a curtain parting as Orson crossed a threshold from hell. The inky wings peeled up into the sky like a wisp of black smoke.

"You're early, Dr. Wheaton. Either you're faster on your feet than I've been led to believe or you have resources I haven't identified yet." Orson smiled. "You never seem to be where I expect to find you. That gets to be very annoying." His smile faded.

He was flanked by Janice Walker, still shaking off the effects of the morphine to stand next to Dr. Robert Lee.

*How the hell did she recover from all that morphine?* Jack wondered.

Quirk assessed her briefly, nodded and disposed of an exhausted epi-pen in the nearest waste can.

Jack nearly dropped the gun when he saw Dr. Wesley Hargrove, Chairman of the department of Medicine amongst those gangsters.

"Why don't you come to this side of the fence, Jack? There's more money over here." Orson coaxed. "Do you realize what we've achieved here?" he asked. "A 95% specific and 98% sensitive method of identifying fibromyalgia syndrome."

Dr. Robert Lee found his voice. "The "F" Factor, developed by Glazer Pharmaceuticals, multiplied by the ratio between Malic acid and P protein as an index of Mitochondrial efficiency then normalizes it with a constant we derived. It can actually separate fibromyalgia syndrome from depression and malingering. The first reliable biomarker for fibromyalgia in history. As long as we treat the patients identified with…"

Quirk waved him to silence.

"Think of all those cases of self-reported disability that can now be refuted." Quirk rubbed his hands together. "The insurance industry will go gaga over this. The best thing, it doesn't *cost* a lot to manufacture."

"But I bet it won't come *cheap*!" Jack asked. "How much is enough?"

Quirk squinted. "Do you see what Dr. Thomas represents? She threatens both DNA Laboratories and Glazer Corp. If a cheap, low risk treatment comes to market too soon, FMDS400 becomes a worthless vat of goop. The magnificent bioassay Glazer has becomes useless too. Who will spend $500 on a test for a disease that can be treated for $50?"

"So you're going to raid what's left of our medico-economic reserves?" Jack wavered momentarily.

Quirk took a step closer. "How are you doing, Jack?" He asked.

"Better then you are." Jack said, mostly out of anger, but then it struck him that this is not the kind of man that asked idle questions. He also had access to information that's hard to come by via ordinary mortal means. Jack rubbed the wound healing on the back of his left hand.

"The Fibro serum. You've been watching me to see how I responded." Jack thought for another beat. "Seizures. You've been observing me for seizure activity. That's why you kept me alive through all of this. Always kept me in sight. Kept Anita around to analyze the "case" if I became sick. What better motivation would she have than to have her protector fall ill to her creation? Lucy, Brasil, even Ralphie--" he nodded toward the oaf beside Quirk. "--could have killed me at almost any time this weekend."

"The two patients who officially had these *Fibro fits* began showing signs within the first forty eight hours." Orson said, "We didn't have many male subjects among the adverse event group. When we checked them with the F-factor assay, they were negative. You, Dr. Wheaton, were not. You're special now Jack. You're on the inside track."

Recounting the events of the past few days, Jack wondered, *When did they test me for the F-factor? They're describing a blood test. That would require a specimen and a assay.*

Orson searched Jack's eyes for understanding. "Son, you'll find that swimming upstream can be invigorating for a time, but it's a young man's game." Orson grew somber. "No one's young forever. You get tired of playing by the rules all your life."

"Sell my soul to make a buck? I don't think so."

"You can make much more money in a day dancing with the devil than you can make in a lifetime with a pen and stethoscope. Come on, be smart, Jack. Change the game. Help us convince Dr. Thomas. She can be rich too. There's enough for all of us." He stepped closer to the gate. Orson Quirk was now within five feet.

"What about Lucy?" Jack asked softly. He still couldn't believe he harbored any sympathy for her by that point.

"Lucy became... ambitious." Orson's face reddened. "She tried to go into business for herself. She even tried to turn Ralphie here." Patting the big man on the back close as he was to him now. Only two feet from the fence.

"Brilliant woman. Did you know she was trained as a pharmacist?" Quirk asked. "Basophilia. That's what lit up around the seizure foci in Holcomb. We found it in the old housekeeper who wrecked her car in Boston too. No one else thought to look for those cells in brain tissue. They're never in there. The few cells they find are never important.

Nurse Christie and Dr. Lee discovered the aberration. Your Helen Holcomb revealed to Christie that she and Annie Henderson had gotten away with some interesting shenanigans. They switched bags. On their way back from the rest room." He laughed. "Imagine that? Annie was in the placebo arm. She and Helen figured that out. Well, Helen decided that she could give Annie the experience of relief." Orson shook his head in amazement. "The interruption was the key! To suffer a *Fibrofit*,

one had to have a treatment break long enough for the immune system to 'remember' a previous antigen as foreign.
When we looked back at the only other known seizure
case it was a woman for whom we had withheld an infusion for 2 months for treatment of pneumonia. We were
stuck trying to figure out if the fever/infection caused the
seizure. Then came Annie Henderson and we knew we
had a problem.  When Helen Holcomb became sympto-
matic, I saw a golden opportunity."

"It was our first chance to see the interaction between FMDS and the F-factor outside of—"

"I'll do the talking if you don't mind, doctor."
Quirk glared at Lee before returning to his good natured
demeanor with Jack. "Lucy didn't know about the old
switcheroo. She did learn something interesting when I
reviewed her private reports on you, though.  Latex, even
in non-allergic subjects, stimulated a histamine release.

Seems Lucy found basophils covered with the F-
factor and FMDS400 degradation products. You demonstrated basophilia, but only in your urine and seminal
fluid. Didn't ask her how she got it. She never left any
loose ends when she investigated did she? She loved the
camera."

Quirk lowered his voice. "It loved her too. She
never did understand loyalty, Jack. Terror, intimidation,
accommodation, not the same thing. That doesn't get men
behind you.

Reward works. Especially money." Orson's voice
became a rasp, again. "So much money," he said, rubbing
his thumbs against his first two fingers as he raised his
hands toward his face.

Orson cocked his head, listening. "Not much time
left, Jack. They're coming."

"What's that got to do with me?" Jack said, then
heard the sirens in the distance. They seemed to soothe
Quirk's angst.

"A dead woman in a man's bed tends to motivate law enforcement."

"David?" Jack asked.

"Picked the wrong team." Was Orson's answer. "A man's got to use the bigger head for thinking. Give her up, Jack. Anita's not giving it up to you. Where's your loyalty to her coming from--frustration? You think if you play hero long enough she'll fall into your arms and part her legs?"

*Okay, so Orson is going to play that card.* Jack thought.

"Think about it, Jack." Christie whispered in his ear. "That's a shit load of money."

Jack looked down into her deep blue eyes. She wasn't *with* them, but she was wavering. He noticed her clothing for the first time, she wore a tight smiley face tee shirt, skinny jeans and sandals. Jack was disgusted, but he had to admit to himself, it was a lot of money to blow off.

Jack considered the possibilities. Bankrolling a large multi-specialty practice in some rural town like Bakersville, GA was appealing. So was cleaning up. Jack could name his own price with all insurance companies and hospitals. He could *own* a for-profit hospital.

*Must have been the real estate deal that upset him at the club the other night.* Jack realized. *Lucy was buying medical properties for infusion business. That's not me.* Not after witnessing first-hand what went into the making of that kind of money. He firmed up his grip on the gun.

"Why do they want me, Quirk?"

"Orson, Jack, call me Orson." He drawled as the sirens came closer.

"Orson, why do they think I killed Lucy?" Jack asked.

"I believe the police received a tip that screams were heard coming from your apartment in the wee hours." Orson told him. "Neighbors smelled the scent of decay emanating from your door this morning. What can I say, Jack? Habeas corpus."

"We watched her die in her own apartment," Jack nodded to Orson. "So, that dog won't hunt."

Orson Quirk shrugged. "You seem to be a very violent and perverse man, Dr. Wheaton. Killing girls during sex," He shook his head subtly. "They were going to find Nurse Christie's body in your apartment, but Lucy was already conveniently dead, so…"

Christie snapped her attention to Quirk at that, and clutched Jack's arm tighter.

"We have proof, Orson."

"You're referring to the camera equipment that was in Dr. Thomas' apartment?" Orson smiled. "Wasn't yours to begin with, Jack.

Funny, I really thought Lucy would have gotten the better of David. Well life's full of surprises isn't it?" Quirk thrust his wrist up to clear his sleeve and looked at his watch. "Well, the police are closing in.

"I can still get you off, Jack." Then Orson looked him in the eyes. "Hartsfield-Jackson. I have a jet on the tarmac, flight plan ready and cleared for Frankfurt. Beyond the reach of any authority with the beautiful and willing Christie and more money than God. All you have to do is ask, -then" he hesitated for emphasis, "cooperate."

Orson Quirk was the quintessential chess master. Like all great chest players, he understood one thing clearly: You only have one piece on the board of intrinsic value, the rest are just… useful.

*If Orson eliminated the recording of Lucy and David's antics and alerted Atlanta police, he probably set me up good.* Jack's only consolation was that he had gotten the drop on him and still held a loaded gun. That was until he heard his name over a bullhorn from behind.

"Atlanta Police!" the amplified voice announced. "We know you are on the premises, Dr. Wheaton. You are a person of interest in a capital crime. Please step out into the street unarmed. No one has to get hurt."

Both the sound of running boots behind him and Orson's widening smile told Jack that he had better drop the gun instantly. That of course let the cop behind him skip to the part where he said, "Place your hands on your head."

Jack thought the latter sentence was actually much cheerier than the click of a revolver followed by, 'Drop the gun, NOW sir!'

Jack felt his heart beating in his throat. Strong hands guided his forearms together behind his back. The handcuffs were colder than Jason Brasil's. Maybe because Jack was so flush. He could smell the machine oil as they rattled around his wrists.

A female officer led Christie away to safety. Two cops in blue uniforms led Jack from the gate. As he made the one hundred eighty degree turn as instructed, Jack felt a smile curl at the corners of his mouth.

There was a tall, clean-shaven man in a hunter green trench coat wet at the shoulders. *Must have rained at Hartsfield-Jackson airport.* Jack mused. The newcomer was expected, but not by Quirk.

"Who's the ranking officer here, gentlemen?"

Jack didn't have to wait for General Hill to identify himself. He was flanked by an army captain and lieutenant as he parted the sea of blue uniforms aggregated at the street entrance to Hamilton's west wing.

His arrival was cause enough for Jack to smile, but as an added bonus, he watched as armed men and women in dark suits flashing federal badges and guns entered the courtyard on the other side of the wall. They offered Orson and his gang the same hospitality, with which APD treated Jack.

Jack half turned toward Orson and mouthed, "Check." He couldn't see Quirk, but Jack knew he read his lips.

A slender gray haired man in blue bore a single gold cluster on each shoulder. He looked at Jack then at General Hill with piercing eagle eyes.

"Major Scott Jennings, APD SWAT Unit." He didn't physically salute the general, but he conveyed the same respect by his bearing.

"Major, I represent the Department of Homeland Security. We've been investigating the folks on the other side of this gate for the past 18months." General Hill said. "Thanks to Drs. Wheaton and Thomas, we have a well-documented, detailed chronology, and physical evidence to merit the apprehension, arrest and detention of that bunch without bail."

The general removed his hat, revealing a bald-head.

"With all due respect, General," Jennings spoke with an unexpected Great Lakes accent. "We have the dead body of a known acquaintance of Dr. Wheaton at his place of residence. We had a legal warrant to search the premises and documented probable cause to support issu-ance of said warrant."

Jack thought that Jennings gave more explanation than the situation called for at that point. Of course, he thought he might have been biased by his knowledge of the events of the day.

"Regardless what evidence you have on the other party, I am obligated to take Dr. Wheaton into custody if for no other reason than to question him on the circum-stances surrounding this young woman's death, sir." Jennings said.

General Hill frowned.

*I'm no lawyer but the reasoning seems sound to me.* Jack thought upon hearing the explanation.

"I understand, Major. However, the Government insists on a representative of Homeland being present during the questioning whether Dr. Wheaton has an attorney present or not."

He squared his shoulders toward Major Jennings. "Does APD have any concerns about jurisdiction on Mr. Quirk and his associates, Major?" The General waited for the answer.

"No sir." Jennings, like many top cops, was surely ex-military.

General Hill turned to one of the SWAT specialists. "Son, can you get this gate opened for me?"

Hill deferred to Major Jennings for permission mostly out of courtesy. He had already established jurisdiction and by rank, had the power to enlist local authorities under the remnants of the Patriot Act among other laws.

With a nod from Jennings, the specialist swung his carryall from his shoulder to the ground as he knelt by the gate. He whipped out three pieces of hardware that made short work of the ruined lock. He stood and proudly ushered the General into the courtyard.

"Well, Mr. Quirk, you've been a busy man!" The general rocked once or twice on his heels. Hands happily in his pockets, he raised an eyebrow in anticipation of Quirk's response.

Quirk was silent while the Homeland agent zipped the plastic cord around his wrists.

*Bet they're tighter than my handcuffs.* Jack reflected.

Finally, Quirk scowled and asked, "What are the charges, General?"

"Domestic Terrorism, false imprisonment, attempted murder, accessory to murder... Pick one or all. There are more charges to come from what I can see."

The General beckoned for an agent to release Dr. Hargrove.

"Oh, sorry, General, he's with me." Orson smirked. "I have tapes to confirm that."

"Sorry, Quirk, we have records of Dr. Hargrove acting on behalf of Homeland Security for the past six months. You rolled snake eyes on that one."

Jack thought he sensed the General's confidence fade a little, which worried him. *Hill's getting to the bottom of his bag of tricks.*

The General ordered Quirk and his accomplices taken into custody. Quirk had nothing to say and after a single warning glare, neither did his henchmen. This time Orson Quirk and Jack left the party in two separate cars.

# Chapter 42: Shell Game

Sid "Fats" Applebaum was found dead in the comfortable executive chair behind his desk in the business office at the Magic Pony. He had been pithed with a slim blade between the base of the skull and the first cervical vertebra.

Post mortem, the killer had positioned him to appear to be eating a sandwich with a bite stuffed in his mouth and his elbows propped on the arms of the chair.

A bullet had pierced through the left lung, ripping the apex of the heart. Had he still been alive when the shot was fired, he would have likely not lived long enough to feel the pain from the wound.

David had apparently come in from the door behind Fats and fired a single, well-placed bullet from there. The most logical scenario was that he circled the desk to inspect the effectiveness of the shot. He would have checked for a pulse in the victim staring into the darkest corner of the room seeing nothing. The question that remained was who shot David?

David was on his knees, head in Fats' lap with a gaping bullet hole in the back of his own head. Ballistics reconstructed the shot. It had to come from directly above. Someone might have been standing right above him when he knelt to check Fats' pulse. Such a close range gunshot would have left blood spatter all over the assassin.

More likely, the shooter fired from the darkness of the second floor. There was renovation in progress and several ceiling tiles were missing in the office including one directly above Fats' chair. The hole reached to the attic above. There was a remnant of carpet draped over the hole in the attic floor. The absence of powder residue on David's head favored the latter explanation.

Fortunately, the bullet didn't match the gun Jack carried at the time of his arrest and neither his nor Anita's prints were on the casing eventually found in the attic.

*Bet any money there's a smart phone somewhere with all the specifics of that shooting in crisp detail.* Jack thought. *The authorities will never find it, though.*

Before his head was pressed down into the squad car, General Hill signaled his captain to accompany Jack in the back seat and escort him to the police station. He patted the officer on the shoulder.

"Keep your eye on this man, Bill. He's important to us," General Hill stooped down to peer inside the vehicle. "He's a genuine hero."

General Hill arrived right behind Jack's escort. In fact, he beat the cop riding shotgun to the door to get Jack out of the back seat.

Still handcuffed, Jack looked up and asked, "Anita?"

"She's safe, Jack." General Hill said, "She and that funny little Khandi Barr of yours were at Khandi's place practicing yoga together when my agents arrived. We escorted them to the downtown station in the back of an unmarked car to take their respective statements."

With a laugh, the General added, "By the way, they both send hugs and kisses. You're a lucky man, Dr. Wheaton."

"Can I see them, General?"

The expression on his face terrified Jack. General Hill had the look of a man trying to find a way to deliver disappointing news.

"They're here," Hill finally said. "I'll see if I can have them brought around for a few minutes, Jack."

The Atlanta cop guided Jack threw the squad room to a holding area closely followed by the general's aid. When Anita rounded the corner, Khandi was on her heels with the infamous Lollipop in her arms. Anita nearly tack-led him.

He looked into Anita's eyes and said, "Wait for me. I shouldn't be long." From there, he was taken back into the bowels of the building for questioning.

It would be the last time he saw Anita Thomas.

Antony Fusco sat on a bench outside a detective's office without cuffs or other restraints. Obviously, he was not under arrest. His raccoon eyes, nearly swollen shut, peeked out above a bandaged nose. He gave Jack a double nod of approval as he passed by. Jack smiled at the trib-ute.

Dr. Wesley Hargrove was waiting in the holding cell when Jack arrived. He filled him in on some of the other events of the weekend before he was moved to an interrogation room. Jack heard that Tony confirmed Da-vid Rivers as the assailant at the Lattimore. The medical examiner described David's condition at the time of his death. "Good-looking guy having a really bad day."

She recounted the bruises to the face and left shoulder, courtesy of Dr. Al Williams, not to mention the partially severed Achilles tendon, complements of "Khandi the Knife." The left shoulder, badly sprained, with at least an incomplete rotator cuff tear delivered by the late Luciana Velasquez with love. David had gotten last licks there, though. His final labor, the murder of Fats Applebaum resulted in a gunshot to the back of the head. Not even Hercules could have survived.

Jack was glad to see General Hill himself already waiting for him in the interrogation room when he was brought in by APD under the watchful eyes of Lieutenant Bill White. The General saw to it that APD didn't even ask Jack his name until he had legal representation.

With guidance from Dr. Hargrove, Jack had pro-cured the services of one of the finest defense lawyers in

Georgia. Ted Garrison was thoroughly familiar with the case by the time the first detective arrived.

The dead girl in Jack's apartment was the first hurdle to cross. Federal crime scene investigators arrived an hour and a half later than the Atlanta city personnel did, but the two agencies cooperated better than their corresponding enforcement counter-parts.

Investigators confirmed that Lucy's body had indeed been moved. They sampled Jack's cheeks for tissue and genetic matching. Further sampling of the victim revealed that fluids from every one of her orifices contained DNA from another male. Jack suggested that they might want to try matching it to David. Ted Garrison said the tests were already in progress.

Jack's account of the deaths of Dr. Butler and Ms. Chen were also corroborated by the autopsy. They found traces of chemicals not related to resuscitation in Dr. Butler's lungs. She was not in Diabetic Ketoacidosis when she died. Although the ethanol in the mixture had evaporated by post mortem examination, the presence of Chloroform pegged the crime as a murder.

Chen's rib injuries were more consistent with circumferential compression than CPR trauma. Jack learned that Ms. Myuong Chen went by Mindy among her friends. She was a shy, hard worker and well-liked by her peers.

Lucy had a second set of recordings that incriminated Quirk and his other cronies. Whenever she planned a caper, she considered almost every contingency. Whoever scrubbed her apartment for Quirk missed that stash. Remembering the last time he saw Lucy, eyes closed, spread out limp on her back, Jack imagined her feigning that final sleep with a smirk on her face. *Yeah, someone on Quirk's payroll was in trouble.*

"The irony is everyone involved had a fighting chance to survive this ordeal except Quirk's henchmen,"

Ted Garrison said. "Mercenaries are like members of crime families, they never can get out. Not really."

Jack pondered his words. "Sold their souls to the devil. Poor Lucy. She almost got out of the game. Such a pity. So much anger."

Ted Garrison prepped Jack like a master. He covered every angle even the painful ones. They dissected every shred of evidence and anticipated how the opposing side would spin it.

# Chapter 43: Pass the Bar

Enter Harlan Sprayberry, U.S. special prosecutor in the case of the people v. DNA Laboratories, Glazer Corp and Dr. Jack Wheaton. Most of the time Jack resented lawyers. A popular position among doctors until they needed one. As the case progressed, Jack recognized his own attorney as out gunned. Like Sprayberry, he was up against heavy legal hitters.

Ted Garrison was managing partner at his firm. They pulled out all the stops, Hargrove saw to it. Expense seemed to be no object either. The firm called some special political favors in for Jack. All resources were fully engaged.

Wesley Hargrove came from old money. Still, in this age of austerity, he nearly succumbed to the temptation of the riches Quirk offered. He heard Quirk out, like Christie did, only further.

Jack got the sense that Hargrove nearly shook hands with Satan. What changed his mind was when Hill and Anita told him that his son's death was probably connected to this DNA plot. That turned him back to the light. He was going to see to it that they paid for Gil's death, whoever *they* were.

Somehow, Jack thought his defense was payment for some kind of personal debt between Hargrove and Garrison. Never did come out in the open why they spent so many billable hours defending a medical resident who couldn't pay them if they garnished his wages for the next fifty years. Jack wondered if some of that money might have been funneled from some Homeland Security slush fund to assure equal representation somehow.

Lawrence, Cohen, Sheffield and Sprigg. Jack hadn't heard of them before. Few people had. Garrison had heard of them by reputation only. He even had to do some research to get their profile. Took two independent investigators a week to get that.

The head partner, Asa Lawrence, Jr. was a few years under fifty and full of vitality. Fit and slim with an athletic physique brushed from head to toe with what must have been a two-week Caribbean tan. Second-generation attorney. Garrison scrambled to sort out which 'Lawrence' he was up against. The private eyes' reports apparently combined data on both father and son. Same name, but the son was the real shark.

This firm was so exclusive, they bore a light public footprint. They rarely went to trial. Usually settled issues out of court in favor of their clients. They defended Glazer Corp.

Garrison counted only twelve cases argued before the bench over the past thirty years, each a win.

Johnson, Wendicott and Griffin, also a top shelf firm, defended The Nordstrom Clinic and Dekker, Nordstrom and Andersen was championed by Etienne, Provost and Tate, a Swedish/French international outfit not for criminal participation, but to protect their 'proprietary interest' in FMDS400.

The discovery phase would have had any other defense team angling for a plea deal. These two just dug in deeper. They requested all of Garrison's and Sprayberry's recordings, notes, anything Jack and Anita acquired from Lucy or her henchmen.

"We could allege any of these thugs as being associated with Quirk, but without the Lucy connection, the case against Quirk is fragile to say the least, Jack." As Ted Garrison described it, "It had a few cracks the opposition might work on with that battering ram of resources they called their fleet of associates. A loose group of independent lawyers and small firms Lawrence recruited, vetted, and contracted then sic'd on us."

In spite of all the support from Garrison's group, Jack felt as if he were on his own in the way of resources. Between those two corporations, they brought about ten million dollars of legal muscle to the opposing table. Asa Lawrence painted Jack as leader and Lucy as one of *his* accomplices… or hostage.

Neighbors placed Jack Wheaton as the man going into Lucy's downtown apartment the night before the Lattimore party and not leaving until the next morning. Strategic surveillance footage caught him with Lucy and her crew unbound and apparently under no duress. The fire at Crescent Point and the assault at the CDC when Butler was killed were also a matter of video record. The subtle editing spoke to extensive influence over the police and traffic security. Spoke volumes.

They didn't make a big deal about Al's murder. A black man gunned down on the streets of Atlanta on a Friday night. Either he was on the wrong side of the law or it might have been a case of mistaken identity. The dismissal of Al's death by the DA, U.S. Attorney, and the defense teams made Jack sick.

When Jack voiced his sentiment to Garrison, Ted whispered to his client, "We're struggling to defend *you* here, Jack. These guys are good. We try to tie Al's death in with no evidence to support it and they'll make laughing stocks of us and our defense."

\"What about Khandi? She was there. David Rivers nearly killed her, too." Jack squared his shoulders ready to go to battle with his own lawyer.

"Jack, I interviewed Ms. Barr. She didn't see the actual shooting. Per her own testimony, she was on her way back to a strip club where she was employed."

Jack pouted a protest.

Garrison pressed him. "Seriously, Jack, how much weight will a conservative, Atlanta jury give to the statement of a 'pole dancer' by her own admission under the influence of an unknown substance at the time?"

"So what you're saying is they'll just dismiss her testimony? She was in love with the guy. Put her on the stand. Use that passion, Ted."

"Jack, Jack. I did listen to her. Where was she when you told her about Dr. Williams' death?"

"At work." Jack conceded. "But she's a bookkeeper there, not an exotic dancer."

Clearly, Garrison wanted to end this line of defense for good and he showed his legal savvy while doing that. "No, Jack, where was she *exactly* when you told her?" Garrison didn't wait for him to answer. "Wasn't she on your lap, completely naked, performing a lap dance under the stage name of 'Kara Mel'? A stage name for Ms. *Khandi Barr* who is actually a transgender? Who in their right mind is going to believe her?" He held Jack's head with both hands and caught his gaze.

"Jack, they'll rip her and you and our defense to shreds before we can present your case to the judge or jury."

Jack was alone in the cell with Ted Garrison, guards on the outside gave them the privacy they needed to plan.

"There are a lot of levels to this case, Jack. The city is arguing with the feds about jurisdiction. The murder of Gil Hargrove and Harry Mehta crossed state lines so Massachusetts has yielded to federal authorities without any guff."

Garrison paced the floor. "Problem is it's an election year, so everyone running is posturing to show how tough he is on crime. The Fulton County DA won't yield to the evidence that Lucy's body was moved *after* she was killed. He's drawing a rosy picture of a beautiful, respected pharmaceutical representative seduced by a violent, sadistic medical resident who deals cocaine and travels back and forth to the middle east and South America."

*My Transitional internship.* Jack remembered.

"We have to get those charges commuted to the level of terrorism." Garrison stopped pacing to face his client. "It's risky, I know. It adds fuel to your federal trial."

"Thank God we have the feds behind us."

So naïve.

"Not necessarily. The Department of Justice, the FBI and Homeland Security are in-fighting over this one, Jack." Garrison hung his head. "As I said, it's an election year."

"So they'll watch me go over the cliff rather than see the other team take credit for the win?"

Garrison nodded. "I can't even get an audience with his majesty, Harlan Sprayberry. The U.S. Attorney's office assigned him to the case. All three enforcement organizations are courting him for their prosecutor agendas to take precedence. Actually, word in legal circles is that he gave his left testicle to get this case. He's focused like a laser site on Quirk and DNA. There is some evidence pointing to identity theft or false identity concerning Quirk."

"What do you mean?" Jack asked.

"Well, from what I hear, there is a second Quirk on payroll. Not Glazer Corp's, Dekker, Nordstrom and Andersen's. One 'Tyler Quirk'. Now how many Quirks do you imagine there could be in big Pharma? Sprayberry's betting that our Orson was fashioning a golden parachute identity to live large in Europe on his earnings. This Tyler Quirk is a German Citizen. Some kind of obscure VP of foreign marketing. We have no record of him visiting the US. There is a conspicuous absence of photographs of this guy on the company website. If we can get Sprayberry to work with us to group your charges with the international infractions, we may beat this as an all or nothing verdict. If the Fulton county D.A. cooperates with the U.S. Attorney in this he can't try you again in the City of Atlanta because of the double jeopardy rules."

Garrison rubbed his chin a moment and said, "If we can implicate any of the ranking officers as complicit with the conspirators, we can get the D.A.to back off to save face for the Atlanta Police department." He smiled. "We don't have to prove it, we just have to *imply* it hard enough."

"So what's next?" Jack asked.

"We see what the other guys have." Garrison said with a wink. His face was etched with fatigue.

Ted Garrison had requested all of Asa Lawrence's records under the rules of discovery. Lawrence enthusiastically replied in the most helpful way possible.

Garrison's firm received 894 crates of transcriptions of all recorded evidence translated into in English, Swedish, Norwegian and German. The pages were collated, but occasionally out of order. Not often, but just enough so Garrison couldn't automate separation of the English version.

Rarely, phrases were omitted from one or more translation. The claim was that as Justice had "rushed" the trial along at eleven months instead of the customary two years, there were bound to be occasional editorial and "typographical" mistakes.

The copies were sent to the Fulton County District Attorney, the Department of Justice, the DEA, Homeland Security and the FBI. The law demanded that all copies, in all languages, were true duplicates to confirm that each party had the same evidence. Of course, they were, but again, just a few sheets out of order every few hundred pages slammed the brakes on any headway made by ambitious associates or paralegals.

"Discovery. Yeah." Garrison said. "We showed them ours, then they showed us theirs. Theirs was bigger."

The judge had to review the evidence, too. Trial didn't begin for three more months.

# Chapter 44: The Sharper Edge

"Do you remember much about those four weeks?" Mark asked.

Jack's brother's usually robust, journalistic voice was a tinny whisper from the partially assembled speaker.

"About Anita?" Jack raised confounded hands palms up in the air. "–everything."

"Sounds more like romance than news, Jack." Mark said. "Maybe this isn't a story for–"

"I'll admit," Jack said, "this woman was amazing. Felt like my heart ran a hundred eighty beats a minute and every breath I drew was pure oxygen, but it wasn't just hormones. For many reasons, *all* parties were heavily invested in her.

Fibromyalgia relief? Sheer genius."

"Same as Fibrositis?" Mark asked, showing his lack of knowledge. "Isn't that a rare disease or something?"

"Fibromyalgia. There's no inflammation, no 'it is.' Just pain, never ending pain. No cure and few prospects for relief.

"Anita discovered a way back. An 'On' switch to a gene buried in our DNA for ages that could provide relief to millions and an obscene fortune to the chosen few with a patent. Hell, that was lost in the media circus that followed, but she was really the linchpin to all of this mayhem!

"After our testimony, the Feds sequestered Professor Anita Thomas. No one could see or talk to her, not even Homeland. After all we had been through, he tore us apart from the moment they collected the bodies 'til the trial.

"That's when I was indicted on multiple counts of murder, accessory to murder, domestic terrorism,... well, you know the deal. Everybody with a TV does. That U.S.

Attorney, Harlan Sprayberry, was an ambitious son of a bitch."

Jack's apartment was typical of the cookie cutter, mid quality, two-bedroom apartments of the ATL. It had become infamous over the past fourteen months. Gawkers assembling in the parking lot for a gander at the Medical Mogul Murderer next door. He was packing to move at week's end.

"But you played a pivotal role in the discovery of evidence, arrest, and conviction of felony insider traders, domestic terrorists, and murderers." His brother posed the obvious question. "Why would they sacrifice you? You turned state's evidence."

"People were dead, Mark. Someone had to fry. Sprayberry wanted bigger fish though. I was just the pole. He didn't care if he broke me pulling them out of the muck."

"Reading about that, I thought it was just a threat on the Government's part." Jack's brother Mark laid the groundwork for the interview set to begin the moment the young doctor put together the A/V equipment he sent.

Mark wanted network quality cinematography. Skype had too much stop motion streaming artifact and only the one camera angle. This was big. Mark had to do better than that. The compact device he shipped to his brother had studio quality recording capability with four tentacled, high quality mini cameras, each remotely operable once assembled.

"Sprayberry didn't want to jeopardize his damn case. **DNA** and Glazer Corp. Harlan had a jones for that conviction so bad, he would have gutted his own mother with a nail file to win. He threw me under the bus without a look back, Mark. Didn't ask the surviving witnesses squat in court. No wonder he got a split decision on the verdicts. He tried to connect me with one of the Quirks.

We later found out that Olivia was not his sister, but his wife. Tilly Olivia Quirk institutionalized and zonked on psych medications for over a decade. We tracked her birthplace down to the Adirondacks in New York. She was born in 1951. Tyler Orson Quirk was using her social security number. That's why Tyler and Orson had such different socials. Quirk legally, dropped the "Tyler" from his name in the Mississippi archives more than twenty years ago. There was no standard record of the change anymore. In the south, men often go by their middle names anyway. I mentioned that on the stand and Sprayberry dismissed my testimony without follow up. Quirk walked. That was my affirmation."

"So I'm not clear on why they might play it that way, but just go ahead and tell me the whole story from the beginning." Mark advised. "I'm recording this so just go,–in your own words."

"Do you think your readers would be interested in the medical house staff structure?"

"I don't think that's, germane to this account, do you Jack?"

"Figures–"

"What do you mean 'figures'?"

"You wouldn't mind if we were lawyers."

"Why do you think that?"

"Because, Mark, Lawyers come off as 'deliciously slimy', which translates to 'interesting' on screen or in print. Your average, bored American will spend his bottom dollar to share a juicy piece of a lawyer's life. Flip through a TV Guide or scan the books on the best sellers list.

A doctor, on the other hand, unless he's a hotshot surgeon, is like a crust of day old bread; a hungry man will devour every crumb to keep body and soul together, but he'll never spend a red penny for it if he has a few bucks in his pocket."

"Look, Jack, no offense, but I don't think the daily goings on of a class of residents or interns really compares with international intrigue. Just try to minimize it, huh?" The advice came across as a garbled request wheezing from the electronic gismo. The device was hyped to be a state of the art webcam array and invulnerable to wiretapping or internet phishing. A Television studio in a box.

"What?" Jack asked.

"STEP BACK," Came the tinny shout.

"Oh, sure. I can step back from the lens…"

"Can't you dial up the volume?" Mark asked.

"The dial is on maximum now." Jack fidgeted around the mechanism under construction on his desk not knowing what to do with it next.

"Man, for a guy with a medical license you're helpless with technology." Mark's comment was nearly lost in static. "How'd you score all that CIA spyware anyway?"

"Well, I never worked with one of these video phones before, Mark. I'm sorry. It's new technology to me. I can't even get a picture of you or get you on speaker mode. Are you receiving me okay?"-

"Great. Some 'double-aught' doctor you are."

"Look, I didn't invent all of the techno-crap they seized, I just used it." Jack countered defensively. "Simple point and shoot stuff. It had a USB port so I thought, 'What the hell! Stick it in and download.' Right into my broken PS2 then I yanked the batteries back out. The feds didn't check. Couldn't check, apparently. The old desk was hospital property with potentially confidential info in its drawers. HIPPA and all."

"What's that again?" Mark asked.

"Oh, Health Insurance Portability and Accountability Act. It means 'off limits' unless you were a doctor or healthcare professional addressing a patient's needs.

The Feds couldn't touch it without a warrant or official waver." Jack took a self-congratulatory bow. "What can I say?"

"This is ridiculous." Mark objected to continuously screaming into the phone to be heard. "You're standing too close, Jack. Just respect its 'personal space'. Pretend it's me or Nancy Grace or someone."

"Okay. That helps, just talk to it like it's a person? Is that how TV anchors do it?"

"Man, you are so far from an anchorman, it's not funny." Mark chuckled.

"Oh, so you got jokes huh? Well may be *The Sharper Edge* isn't ready for this news piece. Maybe I'll peddle the story to *Time Magazine* instead.

"I'll tell them the whole tale of how Decker, Nordstrom, Andersen Laboratories tried to stifle this brilliant woman's life's work and even her life itself. How the FDA should have done its job, and stepped in earlier. How even in the face of a lethal, blockbuster drug, silence can be bought for a price. A portrait of innovation, intrigue, murder and sex... sometimes in that order.

"How 'bout that? Not bad, huh?"

"I can see we'll need a ghost writer on this one."

"Ghost writer, my ass! Never read a byline with that kind of gravitas in your column."

"Jack, this is no joke. It's my job at stake here. Quit playing around."

"Alright, I'll get serious. Guess a disaster like this is a career making scoop... or do they still use that term in journalism?"

"Yeah, we get them from all the coppers, dames and mugs on the lam, Jack."

"Funny. Now where was I?"

"The Players. Who came first?" The sound of Mark's voice was getting weaker by the minute drowning in static.

Jack plugged his MP3 earphones into to the faulty video phone, then stuffed the soft ends into his ears. He could hear his brother better.

*"The Fulton County DA really pushed to see to it that I got to spend time behind bars for something done in Georgia. Finding David and matching his semen and epithelial tissue to Lucy's secretions, basically, torpedoed that case, no thanks to Harlan Sprayberry's legal genius. It was the only time in the last year that the letters "**D**", "**N**" and "**A**" worked in my favor.*

*When it came to the Government's case against Orson Quirk, Harlan focused mostly on fraud and insider trading. He made the case that Quirk was employed simultaneously by Dekker, Nordstrom and Andersen as well as Glazer Corp. The name of Tyler O. Quirk with that northeast Social security number went nowhere. Because Tyler Quirk was technically a German citizen working on German soil, the US Attorney could not subpoena him or his records without cooperation from Berlin.*

*Any criminal charges against **DNA** were dropped in the first round of hearings. Since no law enforcement agency could prove Orson Quirk's connection in any way with **DNA**, their collective hands were clean. They did, however, file suit against me and Anita–"*

Jack listened to the voice through his earphones and answered. "You heard me right. Dekker, Nordstrom and Andersen Laboratories alleged that since Anita worked on the Fame Days Project she, herself, had insider information and per her contract, she could not engage in any competing research or technology for seventeen years. Dekker, Nordstrom, Andersen claimed that whether it was effective or not, Anita's HITMol formula was derivative of the original project and hence, subject to patent protection.

Seemed like no matter what I described, Quirk's team made credible counter arguments that painted me in cahoots with Lucy until I eventually 'turned' David and betrayed her. Lawrence even sketched a scenario where I lent David my apartment to screw Lucy then, by my order, kill her when she was of no further use to me.

Not like Lucy could deny anything or defend herself. They even planted cocaine in my apartment to tie me to Lucy's murders. Dead women could tell tales no better than dead men could.

Their case against me related to steeling FMDS400 by inoculating myself with the drug for the purposes of reverse engineering the structure. I was portrayed as a sophisticated *mule* intent on transporting the Fame Days formula to the international market for recombinant reconstruction in foreign laboratories."

Jack scratched his head. "I had to admit, it was an interesting angle, since that was exactly what Lucy and Quirk planned to do with me in the first place. I thought that a better approach to breaking Glazer Corp's case was its recruitment and development of Lucy and David by Glazer Corp.

Their special ops military background tainted them in spite of Lucy's exemplary marine record. Turns out Lucy had a variant of PTSD. She hated being under Quirk's thumb but couldn't escape him. Lucy used sex and shopping as analgesia for emotional or physical pain. Garrison used that leverage effectively and broke some ice in my favor with the judge. He tried to expand the mercenary ring to include Lucy's whole crew but again, you need suspects, witnesses, persons of interest. The list was mighty thin.

Dr. Lee claimed that he and Janet Walker were simply coming out to the courtyard to counsel Quirk about the treatment his sister received the day before."-

"Right. It really wasn't his sister, Olivia was his wife, but we didn't know that yet. Olivia didn't know if she was coming or going, but she had a documented history of chronic pain and serially normal examinations. No one could argue that she didn't have fibromyalgia. Quirk had her institutionalized in a Swiss Pain clinic since his divorce 15 years ago.

None of us caught the connection to Quirk's sister, Olivia Tyler of Switzerland, and Tyler O. Quirk, German citizen. Quirk ordered the hit on Lucy when he caught wind of her real-estate investment."

"What does real-estate have to do with any of this?"

"Oh, yeah. Sorry. He discovered that Lucy was buying up infusion clinics all over the US and Europe. She would have cleaned up and bought her freedom from him. Quirk couldn't have that. He couldn't trust any of her henchmen either.

They found Ralphie Dunne in his home squatting on the crapper with a half-eaten hamburger and French fry wrapper in a fast food bag dripping with grease at his feet. The autopsy revealed three ruptured diverticuli of the colon and frank peritonitis. A bloated belly full of gas, poop and pus. He was three days alone, locked in his apartment. No sign of forced entry.

Walker had a swimming accident two months into the trial. The detectives surmised that she had been trying to fight off a chest cold and had a coughing fit in the deep end of the pool. No sign of foul play. She too was alone at the time of her demise and she too had already given her testimony under oath and had been cross-examined by both Harlan Sprayberry and Ted Garrison.

Without witnesses, the Government's case against Orson Quirk fell apart like a house of cards in a hurricane.

They never did find Jason Brasil. His passport collection disappeared from the Atlanta police evidence room. The names registered in the desk sergeant's log-book included everyone but the one I reported as my assailant under oath.

We never even learned one-eyed Joe's last name. It was like he never existed. Nobody matching our description of that brute was found anywhere in the state.

The casualties from Slick's crew were chalked up to gang related violence. They never took any testimony from Slick in spite of the fact that they actually had him in custody for another infraction at the time. No one cared about people from *that* part of town.

No one even knew Martin Di Marini was dead," Jack said.

"They took a five-minute statement from Khandi. She offered more, but Fulton county, the City of Atlanta and the Feds dismissed her, promising to recall her if they had any additional questions.

She never got to tell them that she could shed light on the activities of Sid "Fats" Applebaum. They never learned that he was her third cousin, nor anything about the illegal activities in which he engaged including gun-running, racketeering, extortion, etc. After the Feds took the place apart, the title to the heavily leveraged property passed to the childless proprietor's only acknowledged heir."

"–and that would be Khandi Barr." Mark said.

"Fortunately, the new owner had an intimate working relationship with the Pony's employees, especially Eleanor, and a knack for accounting." Jack said.

"David Barr's second cousin had gotten Khandi out of the 'escort' business to take self-serving advantage of those bookkeeping skills of hers. She had learned them at the knee of a father who was ashamed of a son who grew into something he couldn't abide." Jack concluded his preliminary summary of the case everyone wanted to hear about.

"So after a year-long combination of detention, a polite term for jail; protective custody, a euphemism for house arrest with hospital privileges; and negative PR, translate: Slander, I got my day in court. Thank god for my lawyer. He was on it from day one.

So, how much of this thesis can I tell in my own words, Mark? I mean after your writers get to it?"

# Chapter 45: Tech Support

The doorbell interrupted the preliminary interview. "Hold on, Mark, there's someone at the door."–

"No, I'll see who it is and tell them I'm occupied. Stop worrying, the trial's over, remember? No more cloaks or daggers." Jack pulled the earphones out of his ears, and stepped away from the phone on the desk to check the peephole.

"Hah, speak of the devil!" He opened the door to admit two small visitors. "Come on in."

He bent down to pet Lollipop who was barking and hopping enthusiastically for attention. Khandi came in and made herself at home on the couch.

"Hey, Mark, may I introduce the infamous Ms. Khandi Barr?" He finished the flourish before he remembered that neither the speaker nor the camera was working. Khandi shrugged in confusion as she looked around the apartment, empty except for Jack, Lollipop and herself.

As she sat down to cool off from the midday walk, Jack began fiddling with the tangle of wires in the box again. Khandi popped up off the sofa to lend a hand. "What's all this?"

"Studio in a Box" Jack said, hands on his hips. "Supposed to be ready to use, no assembly required." He shook his head. "Not!"

"Don't hurt yourself, Doc." She elbowed Jack out of the way. "Now let's see... This goes here and that one goes there. Pull that out of that hole– How'd you ever fit that in there, Jack?" She asked then turned a knob Jack had dialed a dozen times in the failed attempts at set up.

Mark's face appeared on the screen and his voice boomed, full of electronic feedback, out of four small, powerful speakers. Jack and Khandi rushed to dial the volume down.

"So you're Khandi Barr, huh? I've been hearing some unbelievable things about you the last couple of days."

"Don't believe half of it." she said, shaking her hair out, then plopping back down on the sofa. "Seriously."

She wore snug, royal blue shorts and a form fitting red and white horizontally striped shirt down to her midriff soaked in perspiration.

"Mind if we cool out here for a while, Jack? It's hotter than hell outside. Must have lost a pound in sweat. Got started too late in the day for this time of year."

"Sure. No problem." Jack sat back down and began the conversation with Mark where he left off.

"So what happened to FMDS400 and the what… HIT Molecule that Dr. Thomas developed?" Mark asked.

"Bullshit." Khandi declared in the background. "She was robbed."

"Well, as I was saying, **DNA** made the case that they would be irreparably harmed if the formula became public knowledge or the HITMol formula was submitted before FAME DAYS study was assessed by the FDA. They lobbied to get it delayed for seven years after FDA approval of FMDS400, whenever that might be."

"Like I said, bullshit" Khandi repeated.

"Khandi, Mark is recording this interview." Jack made a bug-eyed face at Khandi before turning back to the camera.

"Since Anita was not officially represented, there was no one to object on her behalf. HITMol got buried for an undetermined period. We're not going to see a cheap remedy for Fibro anytime soon."

"Or an expensive one for that matter." Khandi shivered.

Both brothers had already noticed the twin protrusions the chill had grown through the stripes in her top.

"Jack, you got a shirt I can borrow?" she asked. "I'll freeze in this wet tee shirt the way this air conditioning's blasting in here." The sneeze shook her whole body.

"Thought you were so hot?" he asked.

She had already dropped her shorts to the floor and was pulling her shirt over her head, back to the video phone and what she thought was off camera.

"I was, fifteen minutes ago." Khandi said. "Wet clothes can get cold in just a few."

She wore something purple and risqué from Victoria's Secrets on her bottom. She bounced to the bedroom as immodestly as if she lived there.

"What the hell? Did you see that, Jack?" Mark asked, when she disappeared. "That's not a guy!"

"I guess words failed me then." Jack just nodded and smiled. "Khandi hates wearing bras, but she usually does only to contain her big breasts. Not today I guess, too hot."

"That chick is a knock out. You can't tell me that's a man, Jack."

"I never did."

"How do you rate–" Mark cut himself off as Khandi re-entered in a fresh dry button down Oxford three sizes bigger than the shirt left on the floor. There was a towel draped over one shoulder. After drying her sweat soaked hair, she tossed the used towel on the sofa and pre-occupied herself rolling the sleeves up from well past her fingertips to forearm length. Khandi picked up her wet clothes and hung them out on the balcony to dry in the late August heat. As the sliding door opened, Jack's head turned expectantly to the sound of wind chimes.

"Yeah, Mark. Anita got royally screwed!" Khandi had already grabbed the TV remote and propped her legs on the back of the couch as she chimed into the interview uninvited.

She lay upside down on the sofa, smooth caramel legs slung over the back and head hanging off the edge of the seat cushion as she got comfortable again.

"Khandi, do you mind? I'm in the middle of something important." Jack said as the volume came up on the television.

"Sorry." Khandi rolled up right, turned the TV off and began to play with Lollipop again.

"So what about the Test for Fibro from Glazer Corp?" Mark asked. "The "F" Factor, wasn't it?"

"That's the only thing that may actually come out of this. It's awaiting FDA approval." Jack said. "There was something that Lee started to say in the courtyard, It's our first chance to study the interaction between the F-factor and FMDS400 outside of… something when Quirk cut him off. I think they're connected somehow. Maybe Quirk spiked the damn staff with Glazer's magic reagent. If so, does FMDS yield Fame Days without the F-factor? No one knows."

"What's the stock going for these days?" Mark asked.

"Sixty bucks a share." Khandi broke in one more time. "Up from twenty six dollars a share. I got myself twenty thousand dollars' worth eight months ago. More than doubled my money!"

"What she said," Jack answered, hiking his thumb over his shoulder at Khandi.

"Tried to get you to invest, Jack. It was still rising two months after the end of the trial. No conflict of interest." Khandi rocked up off the couch, turned on the stereo and danced to *Mambo Number Five* in the background.

She stopped, embarrassed about the noise she caused, pulled the MP3 player out of the dock and picked up the ear buds from the desk where Jack was trying to finish his interview with his brother. Lifting her hair to insert the tips into her ear canals compelled Mark to stop talking for a moment, as most men did when Khandi raised her long arms and hair overhead. She mouthed the lyrics while she danced in silence.

"Jack, if all of these plot lines can be corroborated, I think we have a bestselling expose´ here." Mark said.

Apparently, the song ended because Khandi settled down on the sofa again and played with Lollipop, tugging one end of the towel as she grabbed it.

Jack smacked Khandi gently on the leg to get her attention.

"Hey, will you please…" He waited until she pulled the earphones out and motioned for her to pull up a chair. "Mark thinks this story may make a great book."

"Cool!" Khandi said. "That's great for you. Now can he make you a regular with–Hey what station do you report for, Mark?" She had already fished the business card out of the equipment box beside the desk.

"Mark's with The Sharper Edge Magazine."

"Oh." Khandi murmured.

"Now what's that supposed to mean?" Mark asked.

"Well, no offense, but that's kind of a small venue for a story like this. I'm thinking more like CNN or Headline news." She shrugged. "Fox News, MSNBC, OWN maybe?"

"Jack, if she isn't already, hire this one as your agent."

That drew a big grin out of Khandi. "If I'm only getting fifteen percent you better make it worth my while. I was involved in this. I'd better get some real money out of it. Jack needs seven figures, maybe eight.Jack could be as big as Sanjay Gupta."

"I don't know about Dr. Gupta's contract, but we are launching a cable magazine this fall. We could have Jack on the interview circuit by the end of October and fast tract a hardcover based on ratings before Christmas."

"Wow… wait a minute, this November? I couldn't write this up that fast if I typed 24/7 between now and then."

"Don't worry about that, you did fine. We'll get the book written for you. How do you think all these celebrities churn books out? Think they really write them?"

Jack popped Khandi on the arm again. She had engaged Lollipop with the towel she dried off with pulling at the end of it.

"Will you quit that?" he chided. "Do I come to your house and tear up your stuff?"

"Chill out, Jack. She doesn't have any teeth. What's she going to do, gum it apart?" Khandi was nonchalant. "Besides, with this deal I just got you, you can afford a whole new set of towels." Then under her breath, "Good ones next time.

"I'm going to start looking for a real apartment for you. Maybe Buckhead. One floor or two, what do you think, Jack?"

"I think I have to take a leak, guys." Jack excused himself and disappeared through the bathroom door near the kitchen.

"So where hoe you broadcasting from?" she asked, through the receiver when Jack shut the bathroom door.

"I'm in Brussels." Mark answered. "It's where one of the main investors lives, we also have offices in New Your, and we're renovating space in L.A."

She looked skeptically into the camera. "Really?"

"Well, it's an old TV recording studio here. The Newark office is real, but really small. It's true we have an L.A. site, with a Beverly Hills address but it's just a business office park on the outskirts of town. Since we're being honest. So what's the real deal with Jack?"

"He really misses Anita." Khandi confided. "I think she got under his skin. I haven't been able to pull him out of this funk. He's your brother, Mark. Have any suggestions?"

"He's never been serious about a woman as far as I remember. Purely adolescent sex-capades. You should have heard his account of the HITMol Affair." Mark's voice dropped to a whisper. "What ever happened to Anita? Jack never really said."

"Broke the poor dude's heart, man. He waited for her after they read the verdict. General Hill told him she'd meet him in front of the West entrance to Underground Atlanta; it's an entertainment mall here less than a block from the Federal building. He stood there for hours in the rain like a blind fool.

Wrong girl, wrong street, wrong time." Khandi frowned. "The Justice Department held jurisdiction by then. They made her disappear. Her and Antony Fusco.

She never would have been safe as long as she had that HIT thing in her brain. Glazer would never have stopped trying to get it and DNA would have stopped at nothing to squelch it. They packed her up and shipped her off in some kind of Federal Protection program. Jack was the decoy in case there was a hit out on her. They were watching Jack, waiting for him and Anita to come together.

Thing is, we think she's still with Fusco to boot." Khandi shook her head. "That's eating him alive. He could have chewed nails. Didn't sleep for a week either."

"How do you know, Khandi?" Mark asked.

"Cause I stayed wit—Hey!" she caught the innuendo in a second. "I slept on the couch and checked frequently."

Mark, now visible in the video phone, just smiled. A smile that reminded Khandi of Jack's Cheshire grin.

"Look, you know a lot about me, so get this; I don't like to sleep in a lot of clothes so even if a guy is in the doldrums, I can't take any chances of accidental and unauthorized entries in the night, okay?" She placed her hands on her hips. "And especially not with a guy that horny."

The toilet flushed and water began to run.

"That was blind, crazy love. The real deal." She finished, realizing Jack would be out of the rest room any second. "Anita was fine as hell, though."

The bathroom door opened. Jack exited and resumed his seat at the desk.

"So as I was saying, Mark." Khandi said, changing the subject for Jack's sake. "I think the *HITMol Affair* is weak as water for a book title. This was really, something special. Why not give it a more literary title. One that Fibro suffers can sink their teeth into."

In unison, Mark and Jack asked, "Do you have something in mind, Khandi?"

"Well… Now that you asked, how *The Painkillers*? Catchy? See Jack told me this story about Aspirin being a dead drug until they discovered it thins-"

"We got it Khandi, thanks," Mark said. "Jack, I'm only half kidding about making her your agent."

"He couldn't afford me, Mark." She laughed and stood. She disappeared to the balcony to check on her clothes.

"What ever happened to Helen Holcomb, Jack?" Mark asked, drawing his attention.

"Oh, she's fine. No seizures and only mild pain. She and the other two patients did just fine. Pain free for nearly a year." Jack rocked back and forth a bit on his chair at the thought. "Olivia Tyler flew back to Europe last I heard." He smiled. "Ms. Holcomb blogs about government conspiracies to withhold the cure for Fibro from the public." Then he whispered, "I think Khandi secretly eggs her on."

"How can you tell?" Mark asked.

"It's the kind of thing she would revel in, Mark. That and she has a theme that runs through all her aliases and titles."

"She doesn't strike me as a woman who spends a lot of time searching the Blogosphere about the down and depressed."

Khandi returned to the desk dressed in her original clothes. At a hundred degrees, it didn't take long to dry damp cotton clothes in direct sunlight.

"All dry?" Mark asked.

Pinching the fabric, Khandi looked at Jack. "Good enough for government work. All the same, I'm calling a taxi from here, one with good air conditioning that accepts pets. One hundred degrees is crazy."

Jack felt the material and chuckled.

"Nice chimes out there, Jack, where'd you get them?" Khandi regretted the question before the last word left her mouth.

A faraway look consumed him. Khandi clapped him gently on the shoulder a couple of times, caught Mark's questions gaze on the screen and solemnly shook her head. She whipped out her cell and pecked a short message. "Well I'm off guys." She announced after confirming that her taxi service got the text.

"Where to, Khandi?" Mark asked.

"Eleanor's. DragonCon's next weekend. She wants a final fitting of her costume, but she can't make up her mind."

"Who is she going as this year?" Jack asked.

"Who cares? I just like seeing her change costumes. They're all made out of skin-tight latex." She shook her hand loosely at the wrist. "Yeow!"

"Hey Khandi, let me get your e-mail." Mark asked before she left.

"Sure, it's Sweet_Tooth@MineSprung.net." She flipped her phone closed.

"Sweet tooth, huh? Not Kara Mel?" Mark raised an eyebrow a couple of times.

"You know way too much about me, Mr. Mark." Then she grabbed Jack by the collar. "Jack, give me a holler the next time your brother's in town. We'll hang out and do something fun. I know a few places. May be I can get his Magazine some real office space in Atlanta. I've got some property down off 10$^{th}$ and Peachtree that may do nicely. Yeah." She nodded. "That could work."

Something by *Hiroshima* began playing on the sound system and she turned it up as she danced toward the door happy as a lark. "This is my *mellow*." She leashed Lollipop and led her back out, still bobbing her head doing a two-step to the jazzy tune.

"Wow. I never saw that coming." Mark said when she closed the door.

"Calm down, Mark. I don't think she's interested in you in that way."

"No, I don't mean that. I mean she seems like a real friend, someone who cares about you."

"She's good people." Jack agreed.

"How's she doing?" Mark asked. "After all, she lost Al didn't she? Stormi too. There was some real trauma. I gather Khandi was closer to Al than Stormi was to Dasher, though."

"Yeah, Stormi never did recover completely. Lots of emotional scars. She's on track to take a position with the Hamilton Medical Associates in the radiology department. She toyed with taking a job up in Bangor, Maine, but she felt a closeness with the rest of us survivors."

"You, Jack?" Mark asked.

"Not me, bud, Sam Reardon. They seem to be spending some time together these days.

Khandi was more deeply involved with Al, but she grieved then moved on. She has very complicated relationships. Of course, financially, she does very well. She owns several buildings; apartment complexes, mixed use strip malls and she still has a piece of the Magic Pony."

"Sounds like a great resource, for an investigative journalist."

"Mark, sounds like you have a new assignment in mind."

"Well, my young apprentice, as luck would have it…"

# TROA_File_1
# closed

# Afterword:

I hope you have enjoyed reading *The Painkillers*. This has been a fantasy about the potential for a more effective, naturopathic remedy for fibromyalgia.

If one day, we are so blessed as to brandish a trusted marker and wield a block buster remedy, physicians will be lining up to take a crack at this beast called fibromyalgia, too.

I hope that one day soon, there really will be a miraculous cure for conditions like chronic fatigue and fibromyalgia. Fiction like this story aside, you may rest assured that the pharmaceutical industry, at least in this writer's opinion, is striving to better the world's health and in partnership with the medical community, is investing time, money and the best human resources in the world on this and many other ailments that plague our communities.

While we do that, I would be delighted to entertain you with the misadventures of Dr. Jack Wheaton, Khandi Barr, Mark Wheaton and a host of new and old friends and foes in years to come.

ABOUT THE AUTHOR

Glenn Parris writes in the genres of sci-fi, fantasy, and medical mystery. Considered by some an expert in Afrofuturism, he is a self-described lifelong sci-fi nerd. His interest in the topic began as a tween before the term Afrofuturism was even coined. As a graduate of The Bronx High School of Science, as were Samuel R. Delany, and Neil de Grasse Tyson, he was in good company to have his interests cultivated.

He enjoys writing cross-genre in medical mystery, science fiction, fantasy, and historical fiction. His debut novel,

The Painkillers, is the first in The Jack Wheaton Mystery series. He was part of the all-star cast of authors for Marvel's *Black Panther: Tales of Wakanda* with the short story "The Underside of Darkness". His latest full length work was released in May 2022 titled *Dragon's Heir: The Efilu Legacy.*

www.ingramcontent.com/pod-product-compliance
Lightning Source LLC
Chambersburg PA
CBHW050916030726
47503CB00007BB/2328